Praise for The Huntress

"Carroll strikes a balance between froth and craftsmanship."

—*Publishers Weekly*

"Fast-paced historical fiction with a supernatural twist."

—*Booklist*

Praise for Susan Carroll's other books in the Dark Queen series

"An intoxicating brew of poignant romance, turbulent history, and mesmerizing magic."

—KAREN HARPER, author of *The Fyre Mirror*

"With a pinch of both the otherworldly and romance to spice up the deep look at the Medici era . . . Susan Carroll writes a wonderful historical thriller that will have the audience eagerly awaiting [the next] story."

—*The Midwest Book Review*

"[A] riveting tale of witchcraft, treachery, and court intrigue."

—*Library Journal,* Starred Review

"Utterly perfect—rich, compelling, and full of surprises. A fabulous, feminist fantasy from a masterful storyteller that's bound to be one of the best books of the year!"

—ELIZABETH GRAYSON, author of *Moon in the Water*

"Enthralling historical detail, dark and intense emotions and the perfect touches of the paranormal. [Carroll] leaves readers to savor every word of this superbly crafted breathtaking romance."

—*Romantic Times,* Top Pick!

"Ms. Carroll sets the stage well for intrigue and magic spells and draws the reader into her web."

—*The Historical Novels Review*

"Readers in the mood for a marriage plot spiced with magic should find that this one does the trick[!]"

—*Publishers Weekly*

"A definite suspense thriller and a page-turning read."

—Bookreviewcafé.com

"Delightful . . . Susan Carroll writes a wonderful historical thriller."

—*Affaire de Coeur*

Twilight of a Queen

ALSO BY SUSAN CARROLL

Winterbourne

The Painted Veil

The Bride Finder

The Night Drifter

Midnight Bride

The Dark Queen

The Courtesan

The Silver Rose

The Huntress

Twilight of a Queen

A NOVEL

SUSAN CARROLL

BALLANTINE BOOKS TRADE PAPERBACKS • NEW YORK

Twilight of a Queen is a work of fiction. Names, characters, places, and incidents are the products of the author's imagination or are used fictitiously. Any resemblance to actual events, locales, or persons, living or dead, is entirely coincidental.

A Ballantine Books Trade Paperback Original

Published in the United States by Ballantine Books, an imprint of The Random House Publishing Group, a division of Random House, Inc., New York.

Library of Congress Cataloging-in-Publication Data

Carroll, Susan.
Twilight of a queen : a novel / Susan Carroll.
p. cm.
ISBN 978-0-449-22109-9 (pbk.)
1. Catherine de Médici, Queen, consort of Henry II, King of France, 1519–1589—Fiction. 2. France—History—Henry II, 1547–1559—Fiction.
I. Title.
PS3553.A7654T86 2009
813'.54—dc22
2009021024

Printed in the United States of America

www.ballantinebooks.com

2 4 6 8 9 7 5 3 1

Twilight of a
Queen

Chapter One

Paris, Autumn, 1587

THE FOG ROLLED THROUGH THE STREETS OF THE CITY, turning day into twilight. Even by mid-afternoon, the haze remained so thick that two companions strolling side by side could have lost each other in the mist.

Shops closed up early, citizens retreating behind locked shutters and doors. Nerves were stretched taut in a city that already seemed on the brink of revolution. The more superstitious declared that the fog was an omen of an impending disaster, the herald of some great approaching storm.

Others far bolder muttered that the fog was a sign of only one thing, that the witch they had tolerated in their midst for too long was practicing her foul sorcery again.

That Italian sorceress, that devil's daughter, that Dark Queen . . .

Catherine de Medici, Dowager Queen of France, peered down from the heights of her astrological tower affixed to her private residence, the Hôtel de la Reine. The cold damp weather had settled deep into her aching muscles and joints, making her feel every one of her sixty-eight years. She dabbed her handkerchief, wiping a drop of moisture from her rheumy eyes. For once the obscurity of her vision could not be set down to her fading eyesight.

The fog blanketed everything. She could not see even into her own courtyard let alone the streets beyond her gates. But she found the heavy fog a mercy, a brief respite protecting her from all those sullen faces, those hate-filled eyes that followed her every time she left the Hôtel de La Reine to travel through the city to the Louvre.

It should not have bothered her, she thought. She ought to be accustomed to being hated and reviled. She had certainly experienced enough of loathing during her lifetime. She had only been eight years old the first time a mob had cried out for her blood, an orphaned heiress in Florence, a city seething with rebellion.

Catherine closed her eyes, and felt her mind slipping back across the years, as the old vision resurfaced, part memory, part nightmare.

Caterina's small hands clutched at the rough stones of the palazzo walls. Her heart thudded with fear as she peeked down into the courtyard, the angry mob painted in hellish hues of fire and shadow in the flickering torchlight.

"Give us the girl," coarse voices roared. "Surrender the

young witch. We want no more Medicis lording over us. We'll hang her from the city walls."

Past and present merged in Catherine's mind, her imagination transposing Florentines with Parisians. If Paris ever rose against her, she had no difficulty picturing who the leader would be.

Her longtime enemy, the duc de Guise, handsome, arrogant, a warrior's scar bisecting his cheek. François de Guise was the darling of Paris, their great Catholic hero. Catherine could envision so clearly how his aristocratic features would look etched in the firelight of the mob's torches. A thick rope of a noose coiled in his elegant hands, she could see his smile, almost hear his silken threat.

"Soon, Your Grace. Soon . . ."

Catherine clutched at her throat and opened her eyes. She was behaving more and more like some foolish old woman, she thought. Brooding over the past or worrying about a future that might never come to pass.

De Guise and his army were camped far from Paris. Even the ambitious duke would not dare invade the city and strike openly against the king, no matter how weak and ineffectual her son Henry had become. No, de Guise certainly would not dare, Catherine assured herself.

At least, not yet . . .

She turned away from the tower window. The folds of her mantle and her dark skirts brushed against the rough stonework. She had long ago eschewed the brilliant silks and jewels that had delighted her in her youth. Since the death of her husband almost thirty years ago, she had worn nothing but black, her thin silver hair scraped beneath a bon grace cap, her only adornments a white ruff encircling her plump throat and a jeweled cross.

Today she had not even donned a farthingale, the tower chamber too small to allow for wide skirts. The room seemed crowded enough just with herself and the two other occupants. Perhaps because one of those occupants was such an alarming specimen, a tall dark-skinned man, his fierce countenance tattooed with strange symbols, colorful feathers adorning the thick braids of his hair.

One by one, he lit the candles placed at the points of a pentagram drawn on the floor. He moved silently. Catherine had never heard the native speak beyond a grunt. But the white man who knelt half-naked within the circle of candles struck Catherine as being more the savage.

The candlelight played over the cords of Xavier's throat and sinewy shoulders, the dark dusting of hair on his bared chest. His long black hair fell forward, partly concealing the scar from a wound where someone must have come close to slitting his throat. His face was lean and weather-beaten, thick black brows jutting over deepset eyes, the blue-gray hue of an icy winter sea.

Catherine had consulted many astrologers and seers over the course of her lifetime, the clever and learned Ruggeri brothers, the venerable and ancient doctor, Nostradamus.

There was nothing venerable about Xavier. He was a virile animal. A powerful wind blown in from distant lands few civilized Frenchmen would ever set eyes upon. He flexed his shoulders more like a man readying himself for battle than one preparing to sink into a trance. Then he nodded at his dark-skinned . . . Amanuensis? Guardian? Companion? Although Catherine had received the two men at her palace several times before, she had yet to determine the exact nature of their relationship.

Xavier's nod sufficed to make the native retreat from the circle of candles and take up a small primitive-looking drum. He began to tap out a low beat. Xavier stretched out his arms and commenced a rhythmic chanting in some guttural native tongue.

Catherine was far too old and wise to be taken in by some exotic performance, by a mere display of masculine pulchritude. Yet she devoured Xavier with her gaze. The insistent beat of the drum, his deep chanting echoed through her, causing her heart to speed up, her sluggish blood to course through her veins.

Despite the chill of the day, she felt flushed and warm. She experienced a fluttering the like of which she had not known for years. Perhaps not since she had been a bride of fourteen, presented for the first time to the stalwart young prince who was to be her husband.

The drum and Xavier's chant throbbed harder, faster, until Catherine felt as though her heart must burst from her chest. He flung back his head and emitted a savage cry, his eyes rolling white in their sockets.

Abruptly both the drum and Xavier fell silent. His arms dropped to his sides and he stared straight ahead, his eyes glazed, as sightless as though he had been struck blind.

The only sound in the tower was an indrawn breath and Catherine was startled to realize it was hers. She pressed her hand to her thudding heart. Xavier had told her when he plunged into the deepest part of his trance, she could pose her questions. Questions that would help her determine whether this man was the sorcerer he claimed to be or one of the cleverest frauds she had ever encountered.

Catherine cleared her throat, endeavoring at the same time to clear her wits.

"Tell me what you see, monsieur," she commanded. "What lies ahead in the coming year?"

"A time of great change and upheaval," Xavier replied in a deep monotone. "There will be a mighty battle, a war costly in bloodshed."

"Bah!" Catherine snorted. "The civil war between the Catholics and those blasted Huguenots has been raging on forever and shows no promise of ending soon. Any fool could offer me such a vague prediction."

"If you want better answers, ask better questions."

Catherine thought for a moment and then said, "Can you see anything regarding the duc de Guise? Will he ever march on Paris? Will he wrest control of the throne from my son?"

"King Henry is safe for now and will be as long as he never seeks to harm the duke. If His Majesty sheds so much as a drop of de Guise's blood, Paris will rise up in revolt."

"A clever answer, monsieur, but again, no great revelation. I have been warning my son about that very thing these past two years and more. Tell me something specific. Tell me . . ."

How much longer do I have? Will I be dead soon?

Catherine moistened her lips, but could not bring herself to ask. Did she really want to know the hour of her own death? It was her greatest dread, facing the emptiness of the grave, being forgotten, her life and power reduced to nothing but dust.

Instead she framed the one question that would be the true test of Xavier's abilities.

"There is an object that I have long been searching for. Will I ever find it?"

Long moments passed without Xavier answering, beads of sweat gathering on his brow as he stared intently at something veiled from her gaze. Or feigned to do so.

"Aha," Catherine thought cynically. "So, my clever rogue. I have stumped even your ability to come up with a glib answer."

She was on the verge of bringing this farce to a halt when Xavier replied, "No, you will never find the *Book of Shadows.* It was destroyed in London."

Catherine stiffened in shock. Few besides daughters of the earth like herself even knew of the existence of the *Book of Shadows,* a compendium of ancient knowledge and dark secrets long lost to the present-day world. And fewer people still knew that Catherine's desperate search for the book had stretched across the channel to England.

"How?" she demanded. "How was the book destroyed?"

"By fire. An Irishwoman named Catriona O'Hanlon, an emissary of the Lady of Faire Isle, battled with your agent, Ambroise Gautier. The O'Hanlon woman triumphed and set the book ablaze."

Catherine emitted a soft cry. How could Xavier know about these things unless the man did indeed possess the sight? Not since the late Nostradamus had Catherine encountered anyone possessed of such great ability. But any elation she felt at acquiring such a powerful seer was dimmed by what Xavier was telling her.

It had been over a year since she had sent her spy Ambroise Gautier to England in quest of the book. As the weeks had stretched into months, Catherine had been nigh feverish in her impatience, but she had had more pressing matters to occupy her, the constant civil war that threatened to bankrupt the royal treasury, the rising power of the ambitious duc de Guise, her son Henry's increasing instability, and her own failing health.

She had fretted, wondering if Gautier had acquired the *Book of Shadows* and decided to keep it for himself. But the book would be useless to him. The grimoire was written in code, a language so ancient, most wise women would not be able to decipher it.

Catherine had continued to hope that Gautier would return to her with the book, eager to claim the generous reward she had offered him. Xavier's words had extinguished that hope at last.

Catherine wrapped her arms across her bosom to stem the tremors of emotion that coursed through her; bitter disappointment warred with red-hot fury, her rage directed at Ariane Cheney Deauville.

As the Lady of Faire Isle, Ariane was acclaimed as a leader among the daughters of the earth. Especially among those wise women who believed as Ariane did, that a daughter of the earth's sole purpose was to be a healer, a beacon of light in an ignorant world.

As much as Catherine had been determined to acquire all that dark knowledge contained in the *Book of Shadows,*

Ariane had been just as bent upon seeing it destroyed. It appeared that Ariane had won.

Damn the woman for her ignorant naïveté and short-sightedness. Catherine's very soul sickened when she thought of how she could have used that *Book.* The grimoire was believed to have described weapons so fearsome, Catherine could easily have crushed the duc de Guise and any other enemy that threatened her. Spells so potent her youth and vigor could have been restored. Some said the *Book of Shadows* even contained the answer to the riddle of life itself, the secret to immortality. Now all those powerful secrets were lost forever. Gone, all gone, taking all hope with them.

Catherine closed her eyes, fighting off the black tide of despair that threatened to engulf her. When she had regained command over herself, she turned back to where Xavier knelt before her.

"There was a girl who had possession of the *Book of Shadows,"* Catherine said in a hollow voice. "Although quite young, she was reputed to be such a gifted sorceress, she could translate the book. Her name was Megaera, although many called her the Silver Rose and claimed that one day she would destroy me. What has happened to her? Is she still a threat?"

Once again Xavier paused over his answer, a furrow between his brows. "The girl has vanished from England. But without the *Book of Shadows,* she poses no threat to Your Grace."

Vanished? Yes, and Catherine had no doubt where. After destroying the *Book of Shadows,* the O'Hanlon woman would have whisked Megaera off to Faire Isle.

Never mind how dangerous the Silver Rose was, the idol of a cult of demented witches. Ariane would only have seen the girl as a child needing her protection.

If Megaera had indeed taken refuge on Faire Isle, that might explain certain things, one event in particular. Despite all of her healing knowledge, the Lady of Faire Isle had remained barren for years. Then last Christmas, Ariane had given birth to a son.

Catherine had been bitterly envious. The Lady was delivered of a healthy son while the royal cradle remained empty. Catherine's mewling daughter-in-law, Louise, had tried everything to conceive a child, purgatives, herbal baths, and pilgrimages to shrines. All to no avail. Scornful Parisians gossiped that it was the fault of the king. If the foppish Henry spent more time with his wife and less with his painted mignons, France might have its desperately needed heir.

The birth of a lusty boy would do much to shore up her son's tottering throne, win for Henry, if not the love, at least the respect of his people. Catherine had swallowed her pride and written Ariane a letter beginning with honeyed congratulations and ending with a demand to know how Ariane had done it. Catherine still chafed when she recalled Ariane's dry reply.

"Considering that Your Grace has borne ten children, I would hardly think it necessary to explain to you how babes are conceived."

Ariane had concluded by describing her son's birth as "a blessed miracle."

But was it? Or was it more likely that the saintly Ariane had been desperate enough to consult some darker source, that child sorceress, that Silver Rose.

Lost in her own musings, Catherine started at the sound of Xavier's voice. He was speaking although she had asked him no further questions.

"If Your Grace seeks power, you must look to the New World, not the old. Deep in the forests of the Amazon, there are secrets to be discovered, magic undreamed . . ."

Catherine ignored him, the New World of no interest to her. All the magic she desired was much closer to home. If it was true that Megaera had been able to translate the *Book of Shadows,* then the girl was likely clever enough to remember much of what she had learned. Rather than a threat to Catherine, might not the Silver Rose prove to be an incredible asset?

Catherine's pulse quickened with a glimmer of hope. She was scarcely aware of Xavier coming out of his trance until he attempted to rise. He staggered and might have fallen, but he was steadied by his giant companion. Shaking his head to clear it, Xavier stepped past the ring of candles to join her by the window.

The cold seeping through the aperture made Catherine draw her mantle closer, but Xavier seemed impervious to the chill air upon his bare skin. He braced one hand along the stonework and drew in a deep breath that caused his chest to expand.

Staring at his physique, Catherine noticed a detail that had escaped her before. His broad back was latticed with long white scars. Someone had made a vigorous attempt to break him beneath the lash. Studying the hard angle of

Xavier's jaw, the hint of arrogance that played about his mouth, Catherine doubted that they had succeeded.

He rubbed his eyes with his fingertips. "Forgive me, Your Grace. The trance is very taxing. I cannot maintain it for long."

"That is quite all right. This session proved most productive."

"Truly? I cannot always remember all that takes place when in my hypnotic state. My head feels as fogged as the city."

He gestured toward the clouded world below. "The blasted mist still has not dissipated. Everyone is saying this thick a fog is most unnatural."

"No doubt they all accuse me of conjuring it."

"Did you?"

Catherine arched her brow. Many whispered about her suspected knowledge of the dark arts, but few ever dared to tax her with it. Xavier's boldness surprised a bark of laughter from Catherine. She gave his arm a playful slap.

"You overestimate my powers, Captain Xavier. I am pleased to discover that I have not overestimated yours."

"And I am pleased that Your Majesty found me of use."

"I hope to put you to greater use still," she murmured, her hand lingering on his firm warm skin.

He smiled, but moved away from her, retrieving his discarded shirt. As he shrugged into it, Catherine's fingers twitched with an urge to help him smooth the linen folds over that powerful body. She curled her fingers at her side to stay the strange impulse, wondering what the devil had come over her.

As Xavier did up the laces on his shirt, he apologized, "I am glad you find me useful, but I could not attempt another of these sessions that soon."

"It is not only your second sight that interests me, but your skills as a sea captain. I want you to undertake a voyage for me."

His face lit up. "Above all things it is what I wish to do. Give me a small fleet of ships. Three or two, even one stalwart vessel would do. I would sail to the far corners of the earth, bring back such riches—"

She checked his eager outburst. "I have a much closer destination in mind. Are you familiar with the Faire Isle?"

The light in his face dimmed. He replied warily, "I have heard of the place. Just off the coast of Brittany, isn't it? The island of the witches."

"Only the ignorant call it so. True, the island is inhabited mostly by women. It is governed by one in particular. Ariane Deauville, known as the Lady of Faire Isle. She is extremely gifted in the arts of healing."

"If you are interested in healing arts, you could learn far more from the shamans in Brazil. You have already experienced a sample of that. The chacruna bark elixir I gave you appears to have done you much good."

The brew had done much to ease her pain, invigorated her enough to make the difficult climb to the top of the tower. But Catherine's joints had already begun to throb, making her dread the trek back down.

"Sadly, the effects of your elixir are only temporary. I am looking for something more permanent."

"Like a Fountain of Youth? The Arawak tribe claims

that there is such a thing in the land the Spanish call *La Florida.* A miraculous spring that could restore anyone who bathes in the waters to the full bloom of youth. I could—"

"—waste years hunting for such a thing," Catherine interrupted. Years she did not have. "I have no wish to send you in search of a myth."

"Then exactly what does Your Grace want?"

"The girl who calls herself Megaera. Despite her youth, she is reputed to be a powerful sorceress, possessing ancient knowledge, perhaps of the mystery of life itself."

"And this girl strikes you as being less of a myth than the Fountain of Youth?" Xavier scoffed.

"I have already seen evidence of her power. She knows how to grow deadly roses, how to fashion a knife with a blade so needle-thin, it can deliver poison direct into a man's veins."

"This girl sounds more like the bringer of death than life."

"Nonetheless, I want to see her, test the extent of her knowledge for myself. From what you said in your trance, I believe she now dwells on Faire Isle."

"Then invite her to come to your court."

"She is unlikely to accept such an invitation," Catherine said. "In the past, there has been some . . . unpleasantness between us."

Such as when I sent an assassin to kill her.

Catherine swept such thoughts beneath a bland smile. "That is why I want you to go to Faire Isle to fetch her. The women of the island are wary of strangers, but ships frequently dock there to trade. The presence of a sea captain such as yourself would not be considered remarkable.

"You could find Megaera and persuade her to come to Paris. If any man is capable of exerting enough charm, I am sure it would be you."

"And if the girl won't be charmed?"

"Then I am confident you are clever enough to find some other way to bring the girl to me."

"What if I am disinclined to employ my cleverness upon such a mission?" Xavier asked.

"You have entertained me greatly with your visits, all the stirring tales of your voyages. I am also greatly impressed with your abilities as a seer." Catherine sighed. "But alas, there are those in Paris who do not hold you in such high esteem, one in particular.

"The Spanish ambassador has waited upon me. He has been regaling me with stories about a certain French corsair known as the Jaguar. Perhaps you might have heard of him."

Xavier's lips twitched with the hint of a smile, but he replied blandly, "No, I cannot say that I have."

"Apparently, this corsair has gained rather a sinister reputation for preying upon Spanish and Portuguese merchants. He possesses such uncanny foresight, he always seems to know just where and when to strike. The Spanish are convinced he must be employing sorcery."

Catherine studied Xavier carefully for any sign of tension or alarm. He merely looked amused.

"And the Spanish ambassador suspects me of being this Jaguar? His Eminence struck me as such a drab dour man. Who would ever have imagined he had such a colorful imagination?" Xavier grinned. "So do the Spanish want this Jaguar hanged for piracy or burned at the stake?"

"Preferably both. That is why I should be extremely reluctant to allow you to be questioned by His Eminence, but you may leave me no other choice." Catherine spread her hands in a deprecating gesture.

Xavier's smile fled. "In other words, if I don't go to Faire Isle and abduct this girl for you, you are threatening to hand me over to the Inquisition."

Catherine frowned. If Xavier had one fault, it was that he lacked the finesse of a courtier. He could at times be disconcertingly blunt.

"I would not express myself quite so crudely, but yes. That is the proposal before you."

Something dark and dangerous flashed over his features. Catherine took an involuntary step back, recalling the vulnerability of her position, alone here with Xavier and his savage companion, her guards at the base of the tower not even within shouting distance.

The native appeared to understand little French, but the tension in Xavier's stance must have alerted him that something was wrong. The dark-skinned man drew himself up to his full height, his tattoos rendering him even more menacing. One word from Xavier . . .

But Catherine remained calm. Even if she had angered Xavier with her threat, he would not be foolish enough to harm the Dowager Queen of France. Knowing Xavier, the man would always be aware of his own best interests and act accordingly.

Ah, but then how well did she truly know Xavier? How far could she trust him? He folded his arms across his chest, his countenance inscrutable.

Catherine had once been adept at the ancient wise

woman's art of reading eyes. She had been able to penetrate beneath the masks that men wore, perusing their thoughts and sifting through their memories as easily as she would have read a book.

That ability had become lost to her as her eyesight had dimmed. But even if she was still possessed of her skill, it would not have helped her with Xavier. She suspected the man was as good at guarding his secrets as she was hers.

She adopted a more conciliatory tone. "I have no wish to see you hanged for a common pirate, monsieur. I believe you are destined for far greater things. Just find Megaera. Bring her to me and then I will outfit you with as many ships as you could desire."

He said nothing for a long moment, and then he smiled, and took her hand.

"I am as ever Your Grace's obedient servant." He kissed her hand, the gesture courtly for such a rough, unpolished man. In that moment, he reminded her of someone. But who?

The memory tugged at Catherine before drifting away, as frustratingly elusive as the mist.

Chapter Two

THE FOG HAD FINALLY DISPERSED, BUT XAVIER DID NOT consider it an improvement. He stared out at refuse-filled streets and narrow, close-packed buildings. Not for the first time these past months, he longed for the tang of salt air filling his lungs and the vast swells of the open sea.

His cabin aboard the *Miribelle* was much smaller than this inn chamber, yet he had never felt as confined as he did here with dingy gray walls closing in on him. The room felt heavier this afternoon, burdened with the weight of his companion's disapproval.

Pietro hunched his tall frame over the washstand, scrubbing the painted tattoos from a face that reflected both the proud bloodline of African warriors and the Indians of Panama. He plucked the last of the feathers from his braids and scowled at Xavier. He spoke in a deep cultivated voice, his command of the French language as flawless as his Spanish.

"You are playing a dangerous game, Captain."

"Am I? Well, it does not appear as though I am winning." Xavier glanced dourly at the object he had tossed upon the bed, the small purse he had received from the queen.

"Besides, you are in no position to lecture me," he added. "You have been gambling right along with me."

"Only to make sure that devil woman does not put a curse on you."

Pietro toweled off his face, his broad forehead knit into worried lines. "Unless you succeed in cursing yourself. The *macumbu* is powerful magic, meant for healing and enlightenment. Not this sort of trickery and deceit. The gods will frown upon this misuse of your powers."

Xavier plunked down upon a wooden stool and stretched his feet closer to the fire that crackled on the hearth. "Ah, but we both know I have no powers, although my trance was almost a magical performance. I thought the rolling of the eyes was a particularly nice touch."

"I hope you will not attempt it again. You cannot keep fooling this queen. She may be an old woman, but her mind is keen. She is a witch, that one."

"So my mother always told me," Xavier murmured. He stared into the fire, the flames blurring into a red-gold haze, his mind conjuring half-formed recollections from his childhood. The queen coming to visit their house in Paris and Xavier's mother forcing him to hide in . . . the aumbry? Her wardrobe chest? Someplace narrow and dark.

"Don't make a sound, petit, or the Dark Queen will get you."

"But what about you, Maman?" Xavier had clapped his hand to the hilt of the wooden sword his father had given him. "Let me stay with you. I can protect you even if she is a witch."

"No, no you can't," his mother had replied frantically. "She must never see you, never know that you exist. Bad enough the use that evil woman makes of me. Do you want her to turn you into a pawn as well?"

That threat had served to quiet him. At the age of five, he had taken his mother's words quite literally. He had shivered and imagined the sorceress finding him. Casting a spell to make his arms melt into his sides, his legs shrivel and disappear, until he became no bigger than a carved wooden pawn trapped forever on the witch's chessboard.

He'd often wondered since then if it had been his imagination spinning out of control or his mother's. Had the Dark Queen really posed any danger or had his mother merely been desperate to find some way to induce a wild hellion of a boy to behave?

His mother's fear of the queen had seemed genuine and yet there were times when Maman demonstrated a tendency to become a bit . . . overwrought.

Overwrought? Don't you mean a bit mad?

Xavier's fingers strayed to the scar at his throat. He was roused from his thoughts by a rap at the chamber door.

Xavier leaped to his feet, springing for his sword. Pietro did likewise, the queen's warning about the Spanish ambassador still fresh in both their minds.

"Captain?" a gruff voice called out.

Pietro released a long breath and Xavier felt the taut set of his own shoulders relax. He sheathed his sword before unlatching the door to admit his first mate.

The little man waiting on the threshold could not have presented a more disreputable appearance, his beard grizzled, his skin leathered from salt and sun, his eyes cast in a permanent squint beneath thick gray brows.

Tough and sinewy, his movements were little hampered by the wooden leg that had earned him the sobriquet of Jambe du Bois. The motley assemblage of his garb was complimented by a colorful parrot that perched on his shoulder.

The bird emitted a loud squawk as Jambe stumped into the room and Xavier bolted the door behind him. As Pietro put up his own sword, he frowned and shook his head.

"Never say you have been marching all about the city with that thing on your shoulder. Are you mad, mon ami? You know how valuable those birds are over here. Do you want to end up bashed over the head and the creature stolen?"

Jambe snorted. "I'd just like to see any varlet try to take the Sea Beggar."

"So would I. We would be well rid of the cursed nuisance." Xavier swore and ducked as the parrot flapped past his head and settled on the window ledge.

Beggar cocked his head. Eyeing Xavier with his usual malevolence, he screeched at him, *"Merde! Merde!"*

Jambe beamed. "Just listen to the brilliant boy. I have been teaching him to swear in French. I plan to work on Spanish next."

As if the blasted bird wasn't obnoxious enough, without being tutored by Jambe's awkward accent. The old man's flat vowels betrayed his English origins every time he opened his mouth.

Pietro, more tolerant of Sea Beggar than Xavier, coaxed the parrot onto his arm while Jambe faced Xavier with a bright hopeful expression.

"So how'd it go today? Was the information I gave you useful?"

Despite his disappointment over his session with the queen, Xavier could not repress a slight smile. Jambe was like a magpie, gathering up gems of gossip in every port. Over tankards of ale in Plymouth, Jambe had encountered a seaman who had recently been imprisoned in the Marshalsea. One of his cellmates had been a man badly burned from a fire, feverish, ranting about dark queens and silver roses. From this source had come the extraordinary story of Queen Catherine's search for the grimoire and the girl with the strange name.

When Jambe had related the tale to Xavier, he had been inclined to dismiss it as nonsense but had stowed the story away in his memory nonetheless. One never knew when even the ravings of a madman might prove useful.

"The information you gleaned helped convince the queen of my prophetic abilities," Xavier said. "The story worked powerfully upon her, but not the way we had hoped. It blew up in my face like a badly loaded cannon."

"What do you mean? Didn't it convince the old witch to open her purse strings?"

Xavier gestured toward the bed. Spying the silken purse, Jambe rubbed his hands and pounced upon it gleefully. But as he shook the small cache of coins onto the mattress, his gap-toothed grin changed to a scowl.

"What the devil is this? There is barely enough coin here to patch up the *Miribelle* and purchase enough supplies to sail the channel."

"Unfortunately that is all that the queen wishes us to do." Tersely, Xavier related what had happened in the tower that afternoon.

"So the old witch wants you to go to Faire Isle in search of this girl." Jambe let out a low whistle and glanced toward Pietro.

The tall black man stroked the parrot's feathered head, ignoring Beggar's playful nips at his finger. The two sailors exchanged a significant look that irritated Xavier although neither man spoke a word.

That was the trouble with men one had voyaged with for so long. They ended up knowing far too much of one's past. Both Jambe and Pietro were well aware that the Faire Isle was the last place on earth Xavier wished to go.

Jambe cleared his throat and asked, "Er—so will you carry out the queen's request?"

"No, I'll be damned first!"

"The witch will not be happy if you defy her. She threatened to hand us over to the Spanish," Pietro said. Despite the sailor's imperturbable expression, Xavier saw the shade of fear in his eyes.

"That is never going to happen, my friend."

"I know," Pietro said quietly. "Because I will die before I ever allow the Spaniards to take me alive again."

Xavier nodded. He felt exactly the same way, but Jambe grumbled, "There would not have to be all this noble talk of dying and we wouldn't have had to come a-begging of any queen if we had not wasted that last cargo we took. A hold full of African slaves worth their weight in gold and you insisted upon putting them all ashore, just letting them go."

"I had thought I had made myself clear on that score," Xavier said. "I won't make my fortune by trading in human lives."

"But why not? The entire world does so. The Turks, the English, the Portuguese, the Spanish. Even the Africans themselves." Jambe drew himself up into a self-righteous stance. "Slavery is even sanctioned in the Bible."

Under other circumstances, Xavier might have been amused at an old reprobate like Jambe citing holy scripture.

But he sneered, "I wouldn't know about that, not being a religious man."

"If you had ever been a slave yourself, Jambe, you would understand," Pietro put in quietly.

"Whether Monsieur du Bois understands is nothing to the point." Xavier subjected his first mate to an icy stare. "As long as I captain the *Miribelle,* there will be no trafficking in slavery."

"All right. All right." Jambe flung his hands in a gesture of defeat. "So then exactly what the devil are we going to do, Captain?"

A good question, Xavier thought as he gathered up the money Jambe had scattered across the bed. He frowned, cradling the handful of coin in the palm of his hand. Not much to show for all his efforts to charm that old witch, his weeks of being walled up in this crowded, noisy city.

He wondered what mad impulse had ever driven him to return to Paris in the first place. Curiosity to see the city of his birth after all these years, to finally put to rest the ghosts of his youth? Some wild notion that he might make an effort to turn respectable, find legitimate financing for the kind of voyage he'd always dreamed of, sailing uncharted seas, discovering lands no European had ever clapped eyes upon. Just like his former captain, Sir Francis Drake.

But Drake had the good fortune to serve a queen foresighted enough to appreciate all the promise, excitement, and opportunity of the New World. He also had the backing of prosperous London citizens.

There was little prosperity to be found in France these days, a country decayed by civil war and famine, ruled by a half-mad king and an aging sorceress.

Pietro was right. Xavier had been taking a mad risk by playing out his tricks upon Catherine de Medici, not the least of which was she might have recognized him. Xavier had been told he bore an uncanny resemblance to his late father, a fact Xavier hated. He had no desire to resemble the noble chevalier in any particular manner.

Was that really what this had been all about? Xavier wondered. He could not pay back his father for all the misery the chevalier had wrought in his and his mother's lives, so perhaps he had sought vengeance against the Dark Queen instead.

Xavier shrugged off the notion. Revenge required entirely too much hatred and Xavier considered himself a cold, logical man. Although he had to admit he had enjoyed the thought of making a fool out of the queen.

It turned out he was the one who had been played for a fool, Xavier thought ruefully. He dropped the coins back into the purse and turned to find his men regarding him expectantly.

"I reckon we must cut our losses and head for Calais, back to the *Miribelle.*" He held up the purse. "With some sharp bartering, this should at least get us enough provisions to set sail."

Pietro looked relieved and Jambe nodded in grim satisfaction.

"About time," he growled. "But then what?"

"Then we return to plying our trade." Xavier produced a small flask of brandy. Flourishing it aloft, he said, "Gentlemen, here's to piracy."

Uncorking it, he took a swig before handing it off to Jambe, who grinned and said, "To the *Miribelle* and to some fat Spanish vessel laden with gold, straying into her path."

After taking a gulp, Jambe wiped his lips on his sleeve and passed the flask to Pietro. The Cimmarone drank and added after his own quiet fashion, "And here's to a smooth sea and a strong wind."

Yes, Xavier thought as he took another drink himself, the brandy burning his throat. A strong wind to take him back to Brazil, to the Caribbean islands, to the ends of the earth.

Anywhere, as long as it blew him far away from France and the Faire Isle.

Chapter Three

"THE GIRL IS THE BOOK."

Meg whimpered in her sleep, her soft brown hair tumbled across the pillow as she thrashed from side to side, desperate to stop the boy from betraying her to the Dark Queen.

Meg clutched at Alexander Naismith's sleeve. "Sander, why are you doing this to me? I thought you were my friend. I loved you."

Sander stared at her coldly. "I was prepared to worship you, my Silver Rose. With your magic, we could have been rich, powerful, but you would have none of it. My devotion to you has been the death of me."

Shaking her off, Sander turned back to the Dark

Queen. "Megaera memorized the contents of the Book of Shadows. *She recalls every word, every page."*

"No, I don't. I remember nothing," Meg cried. "No matter what Sander is telling you, my name is not Megaera. It is Margaret Elizabeth Wolfe."

The queen smiled. "Ah, my dear, I know this boy speaks truth on one point. You are Megaera, the Silver Rose."

"The rest is true as well," Sander insisted. "That book is stored inside of her."

"I have nothing inside me. Nothing."

"I fear there is only one way to be sure of that, child." The Dark Queen stalked closer, her voluminous black skirts engulfing Meg. She reached for the golden scissors attached to the fob at her waist. "We shall just have to cut you open and see."

"NO!"

Meg sat bolt upright in bed, panting, her nightgown soaked in sweat. Moonlight filtered through the branches of the tree outside her window and raked dark claws of shadow across the wall as though Catherine de Medici's grasp stretched all the way to Faire Isle.

Meg shivered, fighting the urge to pull the covers over her head. It was only a dream, she reassured herself, another of her stupid nightmares. She hoped she had not cried out in her sleep, rousing anyone else in the household at Belle Haven.

She peered over the side of the bed toward the figure stretched out on the pallet before the hearth. Agatha Butterydoor did not stir. The elderly servant was half-deaf, her deep slumber punctuated by soft snores.

Meg listened for any sounds coming from beyond her

room. As the seconds ticked by and she heard nothing, she tried to relax.

She had disturbed no one with her cries. That meant that no one would rush to comfort her either. But she should no longer need that, Meg told herself fiercely. Having just turned thirteen, she was a woman grown.

She curled on her side, cuddling her pillow, seeking to reason the dream away. Alexander Naismith was dead. The treacherous young actor could betray her to no one. He had perished in the same fire that had destroyed the *Book of Shadows.*

The book was gone forever or so everyone else believed. Meg wished she did not know better. The retentive memory that had once been her pride had become her curse. She rubbed her temples.

The *Book of Shadows* was now lodged in Meg's head. It was as if she could feel those ancient brittle pages pressing against the inside of her skull. If the Dark Queen ever found out—

But there was no way the woman ever could. The queen was old. She was ill. She no longer had much power or influence over anyone, not even her own son, the king.

Ariane Deauville assured Meg that the Dark Queen was no longer a threat to her. Meg so desperately wanted to believe Ariane. The Lady of Faire Isle was exceedingly wise, but she had not experienced what Meg had, seen the things that Meg had seen. Those frightening visions that insisted a confrontation between Meg and the Dark Queen was inevitable.

Meg trembled and groped beneath the coverlet for the object she kept hidden there. She stole another nervous glance in Aggie's direction to make sure the woman was still asleep before Meg drew the small glass orb out from beneath the covers.

Even in the night-shadowed darkness of the bedchamber, the crystal sparkled with its dark temptation. So many times Meg had resolved to rid herself of the scrying glass, consult its strange power no more.

But if she had been able to light a candle without wakening Aggie, Meg would have succumbed to the crystal, delving deep into the glass's depths even though the images she found there could only result in more nightmares.

Meg tucked the scrying glass back within the folds of her blankets. She wanted to close her eyes, drift back to sleep, but she was too fearful of her nightmare rising up to claim her again.

After tossing and turning for several minutes, Meg swung out of bed and stumbled, stubbing her toe against a wooden stool. Wincing at the pain, she suppressed her outcry.

It was disconcerting how clumsy she seemed to have become this past year, her body changing so much, sometimes it no longer felt like her own. Her arms and legs had become awkward, alien things, her budding breasts a source of both wonder and embarrassment.

Meg limped to the window and eased open the casement, welcoming the fan of crisp autumn air against her flushed cheeks. Below her, the moonlight sketched a scene of bucolic serenity, the frost-struck gardens, the solid comforting shapes of the stables and barn, the distant outline of the apple orchard.

Belle Haven was a snug manor nestled in the heart of

an island. What could be more secure than that? Meg was supposed to be safe here.

She sighed and rested her head against the casement. The initial waft of cool air that had felt so soothing penetrated her thin nightgown, raising gooseflesh on her arms. Meg started to close the window when she caught a glimpse of movement below.

Someone else was obviously having a bad night. A woman clad in a gray cloak wandered the garden, moonlight limning her pale skin and light blond hair.

No, not a woman, only a ghost of one. Lady Jane Danvers was so quiet, so self-effacing, and there was a sorrow in her eyes that haunted Meg.

Meg tensed as she watched Jane vanish down the garden path. Suddenly the night shadows no longer seemed quite so peaceful or the rustling of the trees so friendly. Jane shouldn't be out there, wandering alone. But then Jane did not know what Meg had seen in her last vision, because Meg had never warned her.

With a wary glance at Aggie, Meg tiptoed about the bedchamber, scrambling into her boots and fumbling for her cloak.

JANE DANVERS DRIFTED DOWN THE GARDEN PATH, TWIGS AND dead leaves crunching beneath her feet. She could almost hear the echoes of her old nurse's voice scolding her.

"Mind your shoes, Mistress Jane. Don't stray from the path."

Despite how exhausted she was, Jane's lips tipped in a

sad smile. Sarah's advice had always been sound, full of a simple wisdom. Don't stray from the path . . . perhaps if she had heeded Sarah's warning, she would not be in her present predicament.

Exiled. Penniless. Alone.

The chill of the autumn morning penetrated beneath her cloak, causing Jane to shiver. The bed she had recently quitted had been warm, but it still held no inducement for her to return to the house. She was unable to sleep, her head far too full of unwanted thoughts, as crowded as an overstuffed wardrobe chest. What a pity that troubling reflections and memories could not be as easily discarded as worn-out garments.

If she had experienced such an uneasy night in her house in London, she would have lit a fire in her antechamber and tried to lose herself in a book. Or retreated down to the great kitchen and allowed the old cook to fuss over her, prepare her a soothing cup of mulled wine.

But Belle Haven was not Jane's home no matter how often Ariane Deauville begged her to consider it so. Not wishing to be any more of a burden to Ariane's household than she already was, Jane preferred to keep her restlessness to herself.

She roved farther down the path until she found the bench tucked behind the massive oak tree, well out of view of the house. Brushing aside a scattering of damp leaves, Jane settled upon the bench, wincing at the feel of cold, hard stone beneath her.

She wrapped her cloak tightly around her, consoling herself that it could only be another hour before dawn, the beginning of a new day in which to arrive at some sensible plan for her future.

Her future . . . Not that she expected much from that. By the age of thirty-two, most women were settled in life, with a hearth, husband, and family. She was childless, twice-widowed, and what family she had remaining were most reluctant to claim her.

As Jane shifted on the bench, seeking a more comfortable position, she heard the crackle of the letter she had thrust into her cloak pocket. She wondered why she had not just tossed the missive into the fire. It had been humiliating enough to write to her cousin Abigail begging to be allowed to join the Benton household in Paris without the sting of Abigail's repeated refusals.

At least this time, Abigail had been honest enough to offer an explanation.

My dearest Jane, as much as I feel for you in your present difficulties, there is little I can do to aid you. It is not convenient to receive you at this time. Our house here in Paris is overflowing with other English Catholic émigrés and frankly, cousin, you have acquired a most unfortunate reputation.

No one minds that you were imprisoned in the Tower and accused of conspiring to assassinate Elizabeth. Indeed, you would have been acclaimed a heroine if you had succeeded in ridding England of its heretic queen.

It is the fact that you were accused of sorcery that many, my own dear husband in particular, find so disturbing. You were fortunate not to have been burned at the stake, but George feels you cannot be all that repentant. Else you would not have spent this past year dwelling on Faire Isle, which everyone knows is an island inhabited mostly by witches.

Jane experienced a rare spark of anger as she thought of the contents of the letter, Abigail's last remark particularly rankling. Jane would never have spent the last year on Faire Isle if she had had anywhere else to go.

She ought to write back to Abigail, protesting her innocence. She had never plotted to assassinate the queen, and as for the charge of witchcraft, Jane would have been the last woman in the world to dabble in sorcery. Not after an obsession with alchemy was what had destroyed her younger brother.

As for Abigail's beloved George, the man had not found Jane inconvenient in the past when he had needed to borrow money from her to settle his gaming debts.

But that was a bitter thought and Jane did her best to suppress it. She could not entirely blame her cousins for shrinking from her. Only a year ago, Jane herself would have been leery of anyone coming from this island of witches.

Not witches, Jane reminded herself. Daughters of the earth, that is what Ariane and the other women who inhabited Faire Isle preferred to be called. After dwelling among them, Jane had discovered much to admire, especially in Ariane. The Lady of Faire Isle was learned and astonishingly skilled in the healing arts.

But Jane was wary of the Lady's pagan beliefs and her

ability to penetrate one's thoughts was far from natural. No matter how kind Ariane was to her, Jane feared she would never be comfortable remaining on Faire Isle.

Life as a Catholic in England had its own perils and uncertainties, but at least there, Jane's role had been clearly defined. Widow of a prominent London merchant, mistress of a great household, devoted sister. Now that all that had been torn away from her, she was no longer certain who she was meant to be, where her duties lay.

"I am a stranger in a strange land," she thought, recalling the passage Ariane's niece had read aloud from her Huguenot Bible yesterday eve.

Young Seraphine Remy had a fine voice, passionate in its intensity, but as a Catholic, Jane knew she should not even have been listening.

Guiltily, she fingered the gold cross suspended about her neck, starting a little at the sound of snapping twigs. Peering round the oak tree, she caught the flash of a lantern in the distance. Someone had entered the gardens from the direction of the house. Coming in search of her? One of Belle Haven's servants, perhaps, or even worse—the Lady herself.

Jane's cheeks heated as she thought of trying to explain why she was creeping about Belle Haven's grounds at this hour like some kind of thief.

"Your ladyship?" Someone called in a low tone as the lantern bobbed closer. Jane breathed out a sigh of relief as she recognized the voice of Margaret Wolfe.

Faire Isle's other exile. Although Jane supposed it odd that she should think of Meg that way. The girl was French-born and had strong ties to the daughters of the earth that should have made her better suited to life on this island than Jane was. And yet Jane sensed that Meg felt as lost as herself.

"Jane!" Meg called again, louder and more urgently. She held the lantern aloft and glanced about so frantically, she was in danger of darting past where Jane sat concealed beneath the tree.

Jane stood up and replied, "Meg, I am over here."

Meg spun about, the light from her lantern illuminating her face that appeared ice-white amidst her tangle of cinnamon-dark hair. She vented a tremulous breath, the depth of her relief astonishing to Jane.

The girl hurled herself at Jane, wrapping one arm around Jane's neck. Jane blinked in amazement. Meg tended to be reserved, rarely given to such displays of emotion.

Although surprised, Jane returned the embrace, murmuring, "Bless me, child. What is all this?"

She cradled her close and felt Meg's thin shoulders shake. "What's wrong, Margaret?"

"N-nothing. I saw you disappearing into the garden and I thought . . . I feared something might—"

Meg sank down upon the bench Jane had vacated, setting down her lantern. "The air is very raw. I—I was worried you might take a chill."

Jane regarded Meg quizzically. She had a feeling that was not at all what Meg had meant to say, but Jane let that pass as she observed how Meg shivered.

Jane had sensibly taken the time to dress before pursuing her nocturnal ramble, donning her warmest gown. Meg had merely flung a cloak over her nightgown and thrust her bare feet into a pair of boots.

"You are far more likely to take a chill than am I," Jane said. Bending down, she tucked the hem of Meg's cloak snugly about her legs. "What are you doing awake at such an hour?"

"I might well ask your ladyship the same thing."

"Jane. Merely Jane. There is no more ladyship," Jane reminded her. She ventured to touch the girl's cheek. Her skin was so cold.

"Were you alarmed by another of your bad dreams?"

Meg shook her head in quick denial. "Nothing so childish. I—I just couldn't sleep. You know how it is when one reads just before bedtime. Your head becomes stuffed full of words, too many ideas."

Jane settled beside Meg on the bench. "There is nothing childish about being distressed by nightmares, Meg. I still suffer them, too."

Meg angled a wary glance up at her. "What do you dream about?"

That I am still locked in my cell in the Tower, shaking with cold, listening to the rats rustling through the straw. That Ned breaks down the door to rescue me, my brother clad in a bright crimson doublet. It is only as Ned draws nearer that I realize, it is his own blood that dyes the fabric, streaming from the gash in his throat.

But it was unthinkable that Jane should relate such horrors to a child who suffered enough from her own.

Jane pasted on a brittle smile. "Oh, sometimes I dream that I am back at court and have forgotten to dress myself. I make my curtsy to the queen clad only in my shift."

"No, you don't." Meg stared, holding Jane's gaze captive with a look that was far from childlike.

The lantern at Meg's feet cast an eerie glow over the angular blade of the girl's cheekbones and white skin. Her eyes were wide, black in their intensity, and Jane could feel Meg pushing at the locked corridors of her mind.

"You dream you are still a prisoner. You dream about your brother's murder."

Jane opened her mouth to reply, but no sound came. In that moment she understood why even here on this island, some of the women feared this girl and called her Megaera, the dreaded Silver Rose.

Jane averted her gaze, edging away from her.

"Jane, I—I am sorry." Meg faltered. The deep ringing tones of her accusation dwindled to a voice that was small and contrite. "I didn't mean to read your eyes. I try to keep out of other people's heads, but sometimes I cannot seem to help myself."

Meg seemed to shrink, no trace of the formidable Megaera remaining, only a troubled young girl. She buried her face in her hands. "Oh, how you must hate me."

"Sweetheart, why ever would you think such a thing?"

"*You know.* For what happened to you. Your arrest, your imprisonment in the Tower. It was all my fault—"

"Oh, hush, Meg. We have been through this many times before. When I sought out Father Ballard, I had no idea he was part of a conspiracy to assassinate Queen Elizabeth, but I knew I was breaking the law by smuggling a priest into my household to celebrate the mass. My arrest was entirely my own fault."

"You weren't just charged with treason. You were accused of witchcraft because of *me*. The queen thought you were the Silver Rose."

"That was the doing of Sir Francis Walsingham, spinning his tissue of lies," Jane reminded her, although she could scarce speak the name of Elizabeth's spymaster without loathing. But honesty compelled her to admit, "It was also partly owing to my brother's reckless meddling with alchemy. When Sir Francis discovered the secret workshop that Ned kept in our home, he had enough proof to condemn me to the stake seven times over."

Jane placed her hand over Meg's. "Which is exactly what would have happened but for you. You came forward and told Elizabeth the truth. I owe you my life."

"No, you owe it to *her.* It was Her Majesty that pardoned you in all her wisdom and graciousness."

Jane had her own opinion of the queen's graciousness, but she kept it to herself. Meg had developed an attitude of heroic worship for England's queen and could see none of Elizabeth's flaws.

"My release was still the result of your courage. It was astonishingly brave of you to confront Elizabeth. Things could have gone very differently for both of us if the queen had been in one of her less forgiving moods. You have no idea, Margaret, what a truly extraordinary, amazing girl you—"

"Please don't say that." Meg tugged her hand away, the girl's eyes filling with distress. "It is the kind of thing the witches in the coven of the Silver Rose were wont to say about me. My mother obliged them all to worship me as though I was some kind of idol. I fear Maman was quite insane."

Jane had heard things about the late Cassandra Lascelles that gave her cause to shudder and be glad she had never crossed paths with the woman. But she replied tactfully, "I never met your mother, so I cannot presume to pass judgment upon her."

"You would not because you are always so kind, but you may take my word for it. My mother was an evil, demented woman. She was obsessed with this prophecy that she would give birth to a powerful sorceress who would conquer the world with her dark magic. I was a great disappointment to her because the mere thought of becoming such a creature gave me nightmares."

What a dreadful legacy to have left this poor child, Jane thought, as Meg wrapped her arms about herself, her face so pale that her freckles stood out stark against her skin, making her appear so young.

If my daughter had lived, she would not have been much older than Meg is now.

The thought caught Jane by surprise. She seldom allowed herself to reflect upon the babe she had lost many years ago. She had been so young herself and unwed, the loss had seemed a blessing, a relief.

Only of late had she begun to recall that stillborn girl with an ache of grief and unbearable yearning that now caused her to fold Meg into her arms. The girl stiffened for a moment before melting against Jane.

Jane rested her chin atop Meg's head, murmuring into the girl's hair, "So is that what you were dreaming about tonight? Your mother and her prophecy?"

"No."

Meg was quiet for so long that Jane feared that was all she would say. But at last the girl confided, "I—I dreamed Sander was alive and betraying me to the Dark Queen, telling her that I retain the *Book of Shadows.* Like any nightmare, it was all nonsense. I would be quite foolish to allow it to distress me."

Meg tried to sound dismissive, but Jane heard the quaver in her voice.

"Not foolish, my dear." Jane smoothed her hand through Meg's hair. "Alexander Naismith did abuse your trust and friendship most cruelly. But both he and that terrible book were destroyed in the fire."

"I know."

"As for the Dark Queen," Jane continued. "You need have no more fear of her. You are well protected here on Faire Isle. The Lady is being most vigilant. Her brother-in-law Simon Aristide regularly steals into Paris to gather reports. The queen's health is failing. She is barely able to retain power over her own son, the king—"

"*I know.* In my head, I know all that. But here—" Meg drew away from Jane and struck her fist over the region of her heart. "I am still so afraid. You think me brave, Jane, but I am not. I am such a coward that I wish my papa were still here, although it is quite wrong of me."

"It is not wrong at all. It is perfectly natural you should long for your father's protection."

"But Papa would never have left if he had thought I was in any danger and it is not as if I am a little girl anymore." Despite her stout words, a wistful expression stole over Meg's face. "I knew when we first came to this island, that Faire Isle was too tame a place to long hold a spirit as adventurous and bold as that of Martin le Loup."

"But surely your stepmother might have remained—"

Meg shook her head. "Catriona O'Hanlon is a warrior

too. Besides, my papa tends to be rash and impulsive at times. It relieves my mind to think that Cat is there to keep him out of trouble."

Perhaps that was true, but Jane still could not help reflecting that Meg's welfare should have been of first importance to both Martin Wolfe and his new bride.

Meg drew farther away from Jane. Whether she read Jane's thoughts or merely guessed at them, Jane could not tell. She was aware that at times her face could be far too transparent.

"Neither my father nor Cat would have gone to Nerac if it had not been a matter of the greatest importance," Meg said. "The duc de Guise and his army are bent on destroying all of Navarre, killing every last Huguenot, including the Remys. Not only is Gabrielle Remy Ariane's sister, but her husband is my father's oldest and closest friend. Of course Papa would wish to go and fight by Nicolas Remy's side, help him to defend his home.

"As a Catholic, I cannot expect you to understand." Meg bit down upon her lip and cast Jane a pleading look. "But surely you would not wish any harm to come to the Remys even if they are not of your faith?"

"Of course not, child. Not to Gabrielle and Nicolas Remy or anyone." Jane said. "I detest the very thought of war, all this senseless destruction masked under a cloak of piety, so much innocent blood spilled. It—it is like a wound to the earth itself."

A slow smile spread across Meg's face, the impish expression transforming the girl's somber features.

"Why, Jane, you are starting to sound more like a daughter of the earth every day."

"Am I?" The notion rendered Jane uneasy, but she laughed. "I think I sound more like a foolish woman who has kept you out here talking too long."

Meg's lantern had burned itself out during their conversation, but it scarce mattered for the sky had lightened to a pearly shade of gray.

Jane rose, flexing her stiff shoulders. "It is nearly dawn and the housemaids will be stirring, but perhaps you will still be able to get a little sleep."

She extended her hand and tugged Meg to her feet. "Otherwise you will be too drowsy to absorb Ariane's lessons in distilling herbs, knowledge that will be important to you if you are to become the next Lady of Faire Isle."

"That is by no means certain," Meg said, falling into step beside Jane as they retraced their steps along the path.

"But as I understand it, it is tradition for the Lady to name and train her own successor. And Ariane has no daughter."

"Yes, but she has her niece, Seraphine. There is also Carole Moreau, who has been learning much from Ariane."

"Seraphine is too headstrong and Carole not nearly as clever."

"But she is *of* the island. She has grown up here, but as for me—" Meg hung her head. "While everyone in Faire Isle has been kind enough, I sense them studying me, watching for any sign that I might become Megaera, my mother's evil daughter."

Jane wished she could have offered Meg some kind of reassurance, but even she was aware that was true.

"Sometimes I wish I could have stayed hidden in England," Meg continued. "Life was so much simpler when I was able to be plain Margaret Wolfe, no one fearing or expecting anything of me. I—I miss my English days, although I am sure not as much as you do."

She halted, glancing almost shyly up at Jane. "It is very selfish of me, but I have been glad of your company. Although I realize I must lose you. You had a letter from Paris today. I—I suppose you will be going soon?"

"No, my cousin finds herself entirely unable to receive me."

"Oh!"

Meg's expression of delight appeared to escape her involuntarily. She colored, looking chagrined. "That is—I mean, oh, that is too bad. I am sorry if you are disappointed.

"But I do so value your friendship. Next spring, Ariane intends to hold a council of the daughters of the earth. It is then that she will announce who the next Lady will be. I—I will be so nervous. It would be such a comfort if you were still here with me."

Jane stared at the girl, both surprised and touched. She had felt so lost, so discarded, so useless this past year. To discover that there was someone who needed her made her cousin's rejection seem of less importance.

"I'll be here, Meg," she said with a tremulous smile. "I believe I can safely promise you that."

Meg beamed and gave Jane a swift hug. But as she pulled back, the lines of the girl's face set into Meg's familiar somber expression.

"Can you promise me something else? That you will never ever wander off alone again as you did tonight?"

"I don't make a habit of it, but Belle Haven is such a

peaceful place and even the paths through the woods are well worn and safe—"

"For others, maybe, but I don't think they are for you."

When Jane regarded her in puzzlement, Meg shifted her feet, looking uncomfortable. "I have been consulting my scrying ball again."

Jane's breath hitched. "Oh, Meg, you shouldn't have. Even Ariane does not approve of you meddling with such disturbing magic. I thought you were going to get rid of your crystal."

"I have been meaning to. I use it very infrequently because some of my visions—" Meg broke off, that unsettling expression passing through her eyes again. She appeared to give herself a mental shake. "But the last time I consulted my glass, my vision was all about you."

"Me?" Jane took an uneasy step back from her.

"The vision was not as clear as some others I have had, but you were lost in a jungle and being preyed upon by a large ferocious black cat."

Jane found Meg's conjuring with her crystal every bit as alarming as the girl's ability to force her way into Jane's mind. But Meg looked so worried, Jane attempted to smile and make light of it.

"There is no jungle on Faire Isle and the only black cat I have seen is the kitten in the barn, although it is rather a feisty little thing. When I attempted to pick it up, it hissed and scratched. But I thought we had made our peace when I offered it a saucer of milk."

Her words evoked no answering smile from Meg. "My visions don't always make a great deal of sense. Just tell me you will be careful. *Promise me!*"

"Very well, I—I promise."

Meg appeared relieved, the tense set of her shoulders relaxing as she headed toward the house. As Jane followed her, her own mind was far less quiet. She could not help noting that Meg had avoided any pledge to dispose of her scrying ball.

But even more disturbing was the thought: No matter how inexplicable Meg's visions, they had a strange way of coming true.

Chapter Four

Spring, 1588

THE SHIP CUT THROUGH THE MORNING MIST, APPEARING AS suddenly as though it had sprung from the depths of the sea itself. The sails billowed ghostlike against the pearly gray sky as the *Miribelle* bore down upon the Spanish merchant vessel.

No alarm was raised upon the *San Felipe* at first sight of the *Miribelle.* The holy cross of Spain fluttered from the mast. Only when the pennant disappeared and the *Miribelle* sailed under no flag at all, did fear spread through the Spaniards.

One seaman, more sharp-eyed than the rest, spied the carved figure adorning the prow, a snarling jungle cat ready to pounce.

"Aiee! Corsairs! The Jaguar!" the seaman shrieked.

Fear escalated into panic, the crew of the *San Felipe* diving for weapons and scrambling to load the cannons.

Aboard the *Miribelle,* Xavier swore at the freckle-faced lad who in his eagerness had lowered the pennant too soon. The *Miribelle* was not yet in range to discharge the culverins to any effect.

Dominique shrank from the captain's fierce bellow, but there was more exasperation than anger in Xavier's voice. Despite the frantic activity aboard the *San Felipe,* there was no way the vessel would escape. The *Miribelle* might be older and less seaworthy, but she was lighter and faster than the Spanish ship, which rode low in the water, pregnant with the promise of a rich cargo.

Fists planted on his hips, Xavier regarded the narrowing distance with grim satisfaction. All around him, the *Miribelle* was a hive of activity. His crew might be a collection of strays gathered from the gaols, alehouses, and wharves of a dozen different ports, but Xavier knew he could count on his men to pull together with the precision of the best trained naval ship.

Sea dogs readied grappling hooks, loaded muskets, and prepared the cannons, grizzled faces flushed with anticipation of the fight to come. Only Xavier did not stir, waiting . . . waiting for just the right moment to open fire. He was annoyed when his concentration was broken by a tug at his sleeve.

Scowling, he glanced down at the fresh-faced young man at his side. Another of his strays, but one Xavier could have done without, especially at a moment like this. Father Bernard was one of those missionaries who had ventured to Brazil with grand notions of saving the souls of the natives.

Xavier had been obliged to rescue the priest from a tribe of Indians who were less than enthusiastic about being baptized into the Catholic faith. But the earnest priest had proved such a nuisance, there were times Xavier wished he had let the Tupi have him.

"Captain, I must protest," Father Bernard said. "I thought you meant to forsake these—these military engagements and pursue a different course, one of exploration and enlightenment."

"So I did until the French queen *enlightened* me by the paltry size of her purse. Besides, I don't consider this a military engagement, merely a commercial transaction."

"It is an act of war, my son, and France is at peace with Spain."

"Perhaps back in the civilized courts of Europe. But you have sailed with me long enough to know that beyond the latitude that marks the borders of the New World, there is only one law. *No peace beyond the line.* Now you will oblige me by returning below."

Xavier added in an irritated afterthought, "And I am not your son."

He strode away, roaring out the command to fire. The *Miribelle* shook as the cannons discharged the first salvo. The *San Felipe* issued a thunderous response, neither ship causing any damage, all smoke and noise. Cannons were not as effective on the open sea as they would have been if Xavier had been able to corner the Spanish vessel in a cove.

Clapping his hands over his ears, Father Bernard trailed after Xavier. "Your men are such fierce fighters and you outnumber those Spanish merchants. This will be murder."

"Not if they can be persuaded to be reasonable."

"And will all your crew remain likewise?"

The priest gestured anxiously in the direction of Pietro. Stripped to the waist, his dark cheeks streaked with paint, the tall Cimmarone armed himself with both a pistol and a cutlass. The fierce expression on Pietro's usually gentle face gave even Xavier pause.

He stalked closer, placing a cautioning hand on Pietro's arm. "Just remember, we are not out to settle old scores. If these men surrender, I don't intend for this to be a bloodbath. So keep your temper in check, my friend. We don't want to horrify the good father here by behaving like—"

"Pirates?" Pietro cut in.

"I was going to say Spaniards."

Pietro bared his teeth in a grin. "I will answer for my temper, Captain. You just look to your own."

Something whistled through the air, a pistol ball splintering the wood of the mizzen mast. The *San Felipe* must possess at least one marksman or else someone had got off a lucky shot, coming close to putting a bullet through Father Bernard. The fool blinked, slow to comprehend his narrow escape.

Xavier gave the priest a rough shove. "Damn it! Get below. Now."

The two ships were close enough for the grappling hooks to find purchase. The shouts, smoke, and chaos of battle intensified as Xavier drew his sword and led his men in a charge, scrambling over the side of the *San Felipe.*

The Spanish crew was easily overwhelmed between their terror of Xavier's reputation and the ferocity of his men. Even young Dominique gave a good account of himself. The boy held his own against a much larger opponent when the captain of the Spanish ship came up behind him. Before Xavier could roar out a warning, the captain discharged his weapon straight into the boy's back. Dominique's eyes flew wide, crimson blossoming on his white shirt as the boy crumpled to the deck.

Bellowing with rage, Xavier cut down Dominique's opponent and then rounded upon the Spanish captain. Their swords came together in a clatter and spark of steel. The Spaniard was a small dapper man, deft with his weapon, but Xavier beat him back with the sheer fury of his rage.

The sounds of battle, the scent of blood, the Spanish accents triggered in Xavier hot flashes of memory. The smoking ruins of the French settlement, the charred remains of the bodies, men, women, and children. The chains chafing Xavier's wrists raw. Arms aching from being bound to the bench of the galley, the stifling sense of being buried alive, the sting of the lash against his skin.

He barely noticed the Spanish captain's sword flying from his hand and sliding across the deck. The man's bearded features were a blur as he sank to his knees. Xavier raised his sword to deliver the death blow, but was prevented by strong rough hands seizing his arm.

Snarling, Xavier fought to shrug free of the grip. Pietro's face swam before him, the Cimmarone's cool accents penetrating the haze of his anger.

"Captain! The ship is ours and that man has surrendered."

Blinking, Xavier saw the Spanish captain cowering at his feet, his trembling hand upraised in a gesture that was part protective, part plea. Xavier flushed, feeling suddenly sick and ashamed, but he saw nothing but understanding in Pietro's dark eyes.

Catching his breath, Xavier staggered to the deck rail until he managed to regain control.

Gazing around, he saw the truth of Pietro's words. The ship was indeed theirs. The Spanish crew had tossed down their weapons, their posture as abject as their captain's.

As Xavier regained his icy control, he took stock of his own men. He had lost but two. One was already dead and the life was swiftly ebbing from Dominique.

That idiot priest had disobeyed Xavier's orders and come over to the Spanish ship. Father Bernard knelt over Dominique, attempting to take the boy's final confession and administer the last rites. But the boy had nothing to confess except those sins he had been led into by sailing with Xavier.

Hunkering down, Xavier thrust the priest aside. Dominique clutched at Xavier's hand, the boy's pale face contorted with pain.

"S-sorry about the flag, Captain."

"No matter, lad. We won. Your share of the cargo will make you a wealthy man."

"Gold? There—there was gold?"

Xavier had no idea what was in the hold of the ship, but he nodded.

Dominique tried to smile, ended up coughing blood. His grip on Xavier's hand slackened, but he sought Xavier's eyes with anxious desperation.

"M-mother . . . sister."

The boy could scarce get out the words, but Xavier understood the reassurance Dominique sought. He pressed the boy's hand.

"You need not worry. I shall travel to St. Malo myself and see that they are looked after. I swear they shall not want for anything while I—"

Xavier faltered, doubting that Dominique had heard his promise. The boy's hand went limp, his eyes empty. Xavier felt for a pulse and realized Dominique was gone.

Xavier knelt by him for a moment. How old had the boy been? Twelve? Thirteen? Xavier was hard-pressed to recall that he had been even younger than that when he had first followed his father to sea.

As Dominique's captain, Xavier supposed he ought to murmur some words over the boy. If he had been a praying man, he would have done so, but it had been a long time since he had any faith in a god. So long he couldn't even remember.

Releasing Dominique's hand, he stood up, leaving Father Bernard to close the boy's eyes and make the sign of the cross over him.

As Xavier stalked toward the Spanish captain, the defeated man had regained his feet and was trying to recover his dignity. He flinched as Xavier bore down upon him, but managed to announce in a shaky voice, "I am Capitan Miguel Antonio Sebastian de Lopez."

Xavier sneered. "What a great deal of name for such a *little* man."

"I must protest your unwarranted attack upon my ship, señor. This is an outrage."

"Yes, it is." Xavier gestured toward Dominique. "Is this your notion of honor, to shoot a boy in the back?"

"No honor is required when dealing with pirates."

"How convenient. I am always astonished at how many codicils there are to the Spanish code of honor."

The little man bristled. "Am I to be criticized by a French brigand with no honor at all? I suppose besides robbing me, you mean to slaughter all of my crew."

"You and your men are my prisoners. Everyone shall be treated well enough. Except you, perhaps; I ought to hang you from the yardarm for murder."

Captain Lopez blanched at the threat. Overhearing it, Father Bernard emitted a faint cry of protest. Ignoring them both, Xavier strode away, snapping out orders for the transferral of the prisoners and the cargo to the *Miribelle.*

The cargo proved to be a modest cache of silver and a load of brazilwood, not the treasure trove of gold that his crew always hoped for, but the wood would fetch a decent price back in the markets of Europe. Xavier ransacked the captain's cabin for the kind of treasure that mattered most to him.

With so much vast unknown territory opening up, maps were frequently inadequate. Xavier had an unquenchable thirst for knowledge of seas he had never sailed, lands he had never seen. As he gathered up what charts, journals and letters he could find, he heard the stump of Jambe's wooden leg as his first mate came to report.

"Last of the cargo's nearly moved, Captain."

"Good. As soon as everything is secure aboard the *Miribelle,* set the *San Felipe* adrift."

"Seems a great waste."

"No doubt it is, but we don't have enough crew to man her."

Perhaps he might have had, if he could have persuaded that French witch to have properly funded his voyage instead of— But Xavier checked the thought. There was little profit in continuing to fume over that.

Jambe scratched his scraggly beard and frowned. "Beg pardon, Captain, but perhaps instead of foundering this ship, we ought to set the *Miribelle* adrift. This here is a sound vessel, more seaworthy than ours."

Xavier hesitated, knowing the old sea dog was right. The *Miribelle* had seen years of hard wear, the last of the small fleet his father had sailed out of France. Xavier himself questioned how well the ship would survive another violent storm. But the thought of scuttling the *Miribelle* tightened a queer knot in his chest.

He shook his head. "The *San Felipe* is like too many Spanish vessels, designed on heavy, awkward lines. I agree we need to replace the *Miribelle,* but I won't be abandoning our lady for a lumbering hulk like this."

"And what of all these Spaniards you've taken prisoner?" Jambe demanded. "What's to be done with them if we sink their ship?"

"I am sure I will think of something," Xavier replied with a thin smile.

XAVIER KEPT THE SPANISH IN SUSPENSE AS TO THEIR FATE FOR the next two days and had to admit he took a shameful pleasure in doing so. Perhaps he was becoming too much like the jungle cat he'd been named for, toying with his prey. He quieted his conscience with the thought that his was a mild form of cruelty compared to what the Spanish captain would have done to Xavier and his men if the situation had been reversed.

The limited amount of stores aboard his ship did not allow him to continue the torment for long. By the third morning, he arranged to have the prisoners set ashore on a secluded cove of the peninsula La Florida.

Xavier went with the landing party himself and pointed Captain Lopez in the right direction. "A day or two's march that way will bring you to a Spanish settlement. You'll find enough water and forage to sustain you en route."

As Lopez opened his lips to speak, Xavier cut him off. "There is not the slightest need to thank me for my generosity, captain."

"G-generosity!"

The little man choked on his indignation. Since realizing he was to be spared, the Spanish captain had recovered much of his bravado.

He glared at Xavier. "You have made a great enemy on behalf of your country."

"You are mistaken, señor," Xavier replied smoothly. "I have no country."

"Pah! Don't think to fool me. You are a Frenchman, as lawless and arrogant a corsair as any of these English pirates who have also been preying upon Spanish shipping. Well, the English shall be the first to pay for their insolence. They and their heretic queen, Elizabeth. Philip, his most noble Catholic majesty of Spain will—"

Lopez broke off abruptly, looking so comical in his dismay over what he'd let slip, that Xavier laughed.

"Don't distress yourself, señor. You have not spilled any great secret. Even here at the ends of the earth, we have heard the rumors of Spain's great enterprise, the vast armada being assembled in Madrid, your king's hope of invading England."

"Not a hope, señor. It will soon be a reality. And when King Philip has dealt with the English dogs, he will turn his attention to punishing insolent Frenchmen like yourself."

"I shall await His Majesty's coming all atremble. From palsy belike. I shall be an old man by then."

"You will never live to be old, señor," Lopez snarled.

"I daresay you are right. But this conversation waxes tedious, and you have a long walk ahead of you." Xavier sketched a mocking bow, then turned and headed back toward the waiting boats.

Lopez bristled, but rounded up his men. As they marched up the beach, Xavier could still hear the Spanish captain grousing. "His most Catholic Majesty shall hear of this iniquity. I vow he will."

As he clambered into the pinnace, Xavier could not resist getting in the last word. He called out, "I shall send a message to King Philip on your behalf. I will likely be in a better position to do so than you. I expect to be anchored off St. Malo six weeks hence."

Chapter Five

XAVIER'S PREDICTION PROVED OPTIMISTIC. THE CROSSING of the Atlantic was smooth and uneventful but the *Miribelle* was yet some twenty leagues from the French coast when the ship was beset by something seamen dreaded worse than a storm. A dead calm, not a breath of air stirring. The *Miribelle*'s sails hung limp for days, the ship as motionless as if she had been riding at anchor.

Xavier chafed with frustration, finding it maddening to be stayed this close to the end of his journey. But he knew it could be worse. He'd once been stranded at sea so long, he and his crew had been reduced to eating boiled leather. At least their stores were likely to hold out, although there was much grumbling among the men when Xavier reduced the rum ration.

Idle sea dogs were rife for mischief, but Xavier trusted to his redoubtable first mate to keep the crew busy enough they did not end up at each other's throats.

Struggling to curb his own restlessness, Xavier retreated to his cabin, a narrow berth that scarce allowed him headroom to stand upright. The furnishings were sparse, his bunk, a small desk, his sea chest, and the wooden cage he had battened to the wall to accommodate that infernal parrot. Beyond the bars, Sea Beggar gave him the beady eye and set up a loud squawk.

"Damn your eyes! Damn your eyes!"

"The feeling's mutual," Xavier muttered. When Sea Beggar continued to shrill at him, Xavier flung his cloak over the parrot's cage to silence the creature. Settling behind his desk, he updated his ship's journal and then pored over the charts he had taken from the *San Felipe.*

The maps proved mighty disappointing. Xavier had hoped for some detailed etching of the straits of Panama and what lay beyond, perhaps even a hint of a route to that fabled land Marco Polo had once written of, a place that the explorer referred to only as *Beach.*

But the voyages of the *San Felipe* had been unremarkable, the Spanish vessel charting no land that Xavier had not seen for himself. The letters that Xavier had taken from Captain Lopez's cabin proved of greater interest. One of these was written in code that intrigued Xavier enough to attempt to crack it, if for no other reason than that it afforded him entertainment during these days of enforced idleness.

Much to his satisfaction, he finally succeeded in unraveling the cipher. The missive was from one of the recently appointed governors of La Florida to the Duke of Medina Sidonia.

The governor began by congratulating his old friend, Medina Sidonia, on his appointment as admiral of the armada. The letter went on to explain how the cargo being transported by the *San Felipe* was destined to line the purse of a powerful French nobleman, François, the duke of Guise.

> *. . . Monsieur le duc is a devout Catholic and most eager to help His Majesty in his quest to crush the heretic English and their queen. If only we could likewise count upon the support of the French king, but Henry Valois is a most erratic man. Indeed many say he is mad. In the past he has been far too lenient with Protestants in his own country. It is feared that Henry might take the notion to come to the aid of Elizabeth, something that must be prevented.*
>
> *His mother, the Dowager Queen Catherine, professes friendship to Spain, but we all know the Italian witch is not to be trusted. I have heard that her health is failing and she no longer possesses the power and influence she once did. Myself, I cannot believe it. I fear we shall have no peace from the intrigues of that Machiavellian woman until she is in her grave.*
>
> *Spain's only hope for alliance in France lies with the duke of Guise. The duke has pledged himself to create a diversion that will prevent the French king from sending military aid to England even should he wish to do so.*

A diversion? Xavier frowned. What the devil did that mean? Guise's actions struck him as outrageous. It was surely treason to do the bidding of the king of Spain, taking bribes from a country that was France's most ancient enemy.

But Xavier did not see what he could do to prevent it, even if he was inclined to bestir himself. During his sojourn in Paris, he had had a brief glimpse into the political intrigue and religious strife poisoning the court of Catherine de Medici and her half-mad son. Xavier had been glad enough to sail away and leave it all behind him.

The letter made it sound as though the launch of the armada was imminent, perhaps as early as this spring. Xavier supposed he might make some effort to see that this letter fell into English hands, perhaps those of Sir Francis Drake.

He had once sailed with Drake for the span of a year. Indeed he owed both his life and his freedom to Sir Francis and Xavier hated to be in anyone's debt. But the letter was so vague, Xavier did not see what use it could be to Drake or anyone else.

While he debated the matter, he was annoyed by the appearance of Father Bernard. The young priest peered into the cabin, regarding Xavier with a wistful expression.

Father Bernard usually busied himself attempting to provide spiritual succor to the men and many actually welcomed it, the only reason Xavier allowed the man to remain on board.

But he had developed an irritating habit of hovering near Xavier, as though he hoped to become his father confessor as well. Xavier had no use for a confessor and even less for anyone attempting to enact a fatherly role, especially a man younger than he by several years in age and a lifetime in experience.

When Xavier ignored him, Father Bernard cleared his throat. "I—I hope I do not disturb you, Captain."

"Yes, you do," Xavier said, without looking up from the papers sprawled across his desk.

His curtness did not discourage the man. It never did. Father Bernard shuffled his feet and tried again.

"I just thought you might want to know the wind has not yet picked up."

"Truly? You astonish me."

"Do you think it likely to do so soon?"

"I have no idea. Second sight is not one of the gifts I acquired when I sold my soul to the devil. However, I do possess enough knowledge of the dark arts—I might attempt to conjure up a modest breeze for you."

Father Bernard gave an uneasy laugh as though he thought Xavier was jesting. Or he hoped he was.

"I prefer to rely upon my prayers, Captain. I have earnestly beseeched the good Lord to send us a wind and I have every confidence he will do so soon."

"Far more likely he'll send us a typhoon. In my experience, your god seems possessed of a devilish sense of humor."

If Father Bernard was shocked by Xavier's blasphemy, he gave no sign of it. He said, "It occurs to me that our voyage will be over soon and we have never really had a chance to talk."

"No? Well, I am a man of few words, Father."

And most of those were curses. Xavier bit back the urge to swear as Father Bernard perched unbidden upon the edge of the bunk, looking like a man settling in for a long prose.

"Do you still intend to make berth at St. Malo?"

"Yes, that is my course."

"It is a fine and noble thing you are doing keeping your promise to young Dominique—"

"There is nothing noble about my decision," Xavier interrupted, "I never do anything that inconveniences me. I just happen to find St. Malo as good a port as any other to transact my business."

Father Bernard smiled, giving Xavier one of those wise looks that suggested he knew better and which made Xavier long to stuff the priest out the nearest porthole.

"I believe an English port might serve your purpose as well and be a deal safer. You may find yourself less than welcome back in France. Monsieur du Bois told me all that transpired in Paris. Queen Catherine does not seem like the sort of woman to forgive one for ignoring her commands."

Xavier grimaced, mentally cursing his chattering first mate. Jambe was worse than an old woman.

"I have slipped in and out of Spanish ports all along the coast of the Americas. I think I can manage to steal safely into St. Malo with the queen none the wiser. Trust me, the woman is not as formidable a witch as everyone fears that she is."

Father Bernard fell silent for a long moment before saying, "Faire Isle is not that far of a sail from St. Malo."

Xavier swiveled to regard the priest with frowning surprise. "Surely you are not suggesting that I carry out the queen's command and abduct that young girl for her?"

"No! No, of course not." Father Bernard hesitated, subjecting Xavier to one of his earnest soul-searching looks. "I just wanted to remind you that the queen was not the only one who desired you to sail to Faire Isle."

Xavier tensed, his fingers clamping down upon his quill so hard he crushed the feathers.

"Upon his deathbed, your father—" the priest began.

"My father was raving with the yellow fever, completely out of his head."

"He seemed lucid enough to me when I gave him the last rites. He grew so peaceful. He died with your mother's portrait clasped to his heart. The last word he whispered was her name. *Evangeline.*"

The priest clearly expected Xavier to be moved by that. There was only one problem, Xavier reflected bitterly. *His* mother had been named Marguerite.

"I thought I had made it clear to you. I have no wish to discuss any of this." Turning his back on the man, Xavier hunched over his desk again. "Now if you don't mind, I have some letters to write."

Father Bernard rose reluctantly to his feet. "I just thought this might be a good time for you to carry out your father's dying wish for you to take his journals, his last bequest, to Faire Isle."

Xavier gritted his teeth. "My father was delirious. He didn't even know who the devil I was or he would never have entrusted me with such an errand."

"No, I am sure he was—"

"Delirious," Xavier repeated with an edge to his voice. He glanced down and was annoyed to see he had mindlessly poked holes in one of the charts with the tip of his quill. *He,* who was never given to fidgeting, who never moved so much as a finger without some clear purpose.

He flung down the quill in disgust. "You want the journals delivered to Faire Isle, you take them."

"Your father hoped that you would do it."

"He's dead. He can't hope for much of anything now, can he?"

"That is true. Your father is at rest. I worry more about you, my son. I do not think you will ever know peace yourself until you fulfill your father's request."

"I have all the peace I desire. At least I would have, if you would leave me alone. And I am no man's son."

Father Bernard heaved a deep sigh, leaving the cabin with slumped shoulders and that sad look Xavier had come to think of as the young man's wounded puppy expression.

Xavier expelled his breath in a savage oath. He could greatly sympathize with those Indians who had attacked the priest in the jungle. Damned fool, blundering in where he was not wanted, meddling in matters he didn't understand.

For five years, Xavier had been separated, torn apart from his father after the Spanish attack on the French settlement. And for five long years, Xavier had searched, only to find his father dying in some remote mission in Brazil.

It had been his great misfortune that he had done so with that wretched priest at his side. Xavier would have preferred there had been no witness to those last hours with his father, the painful culmination to what had been an often bitter and stormy relationship.

He had hovered over his father's deathbed, searching for the words to prayers he couldn't remember, hoping for he scarce knew what. A final blessing from the old man, that he would at long last truly acknowledge Xavier as his son?

Instead his father had attempted to load one more burden upon Xavier's shoulders with his impossible dying request.

Whatever had possessed his father to request that Xavier carry his legacy to Faire Isle? No matter what that fool priest insisted, the old man had to have been out of his wits. For as long as Xavier could remember, his father had striven to keep his two worlds far apart, his life in Paris, his home on Faire Isle.

Why would his father have changed his mind and wanted Xavier to go to Faire Isle? The answer was simple. He wouldn't have, any more than the old man had ever wanted to admit that Xavier was his son.

Xavier stared down at his desk and drew forth a blank sheet of parchment. He dipped his quill in the ink and after a hesitation, scrawled out his signature. The words glared against the whiteness of the page, like some guilty secret not meant to be revealed. His full name, the one he never used because he was not entitled to it. His father had made that more than clear to him.

Xavier scratched his quill through the signature several times, so hard he tore the parchment. He crumpled up the page and flung it across the cabin.

Then he leaned back in his chair and locked his arms

across his chest as though he could wall out the emotions that threatened to breach the hull of his indifference, a dark floodtide of bitterness, hurt, and regret.

His gaze traveled to his sea chest. He stared at it for a long time before rising to his feet. Drawn almost against his will, he knelt beside the battered oak chest and threw back the lid.

He delved beneath charts and articles of clothing until he found the journals stacked on the bottom, a sum total of six leather-bound volumes. His father had kept records of their voyages ever since they had sailed from France, his writings interspersed with sketches of jungle plants, exotic birds, painted natives, animals unknown to Europe.

Xavier ran his fingertips over the cover of the most recent journal, wondering why he resisted the temptation to flip it open, devour the book's contents. His father was no longer here to say him nay.

Perhaps he was restrained by the knowledge that these journals had never been intended for him. But he had never had qualms about plundering another man's treasure before. Or in this case, a woman's . . .

No. He could not deceive himself. What kept him from delving through the journals was nothing but cowardice. Not the fear that he might stumble across an unflattering reference to himself, but the fear that there would be no mention of him at all in his father's journals.

As though Xavier had never even existed . . .

Perhaps the blasted priest was right about one thing. Those journals weighting down his sea chest were like a spike imbedded in his flesh. He never would have any peace until he got rid of them. He had buried the chevalier with his beloved Evangeline's portrait clutched in his hands. Xavier didn't know why he hadn't tossed the books into the grave as well.

He picked up the topmost journal. Such an insignificant thing really, a bit of cow's hide stretched around a collection of old parchment and ink strokes. Then why did it feel so cursed heavy?

Xavier hefted it in his palm for a moment before heaving a disgruntled sigh and dropping the book back atop the stack. Just like he always did.

Then he groped for the other object he kept buried in the bottom of the trunk. His fingers closed around a leathern jack, the flask filled with the amber liquid that had steered Xavier through more than one endless dark night or dreary idle afternoon.

He had learned how to distill the potion from an Indian shaman in Peru, a careful blending of certain kinds of jungle liana. The devil's brew, the Spanish priests called it.

But the natives had another name for the liquid, the vine of the spirits, a portal to another world, a place where the mind could expand to embrace the mysteries of the universe, visions that were not always clear or perfectly remembered, but elusive with promise. Not the kind of chicanery Xavier had practiced upon the Dark Queen in Paris, but true magic.

Xavier uncorked the flask. He'd been a trifle reckless last time and drank too much. This time he'd be more judicious. Xavier moistened his lips and took a long swallow.

The liquid coated his tongue and palate, the taste a strange mingling of bitter and sickly sweet. It oozed down his throat like a live eel, making him want to retch. He gulped, breathing carefully until the nausea passed.

He corked the flask and returned it to the trunk, closing the lid. Kneeling, he waited for the brew to take effect, just as the shaman had taught him, arms outstretched, eyes closed. He commenced a rhythmic chanting, the drone of his own voice mesmerizing him deeper into the trance.

His senses become more acute, the tang of his sweat sharp in his nostrils, the sound of his own heartbeat thundering like jungle drums in his ears.

He swayed in time to the beat, his breathing coming quicker. The first wave of pain in his gut caused him to double over. He chanted faster, clenching his hands into fists, as his head reeled. Lights exploded behind his eyelids, a maelstrom of fire and color.

His body lurched as though he had been hurled through some invisible barrier. A place where his breath stilled, his heart slowed, and his mind broke free of the crude barriers that bound him to earth.

He soared through the sky in a dizzying rush, past cities, over rivers and woods, seas and mountains until he touched down in the lush tropics of a rain forest. Violent tremors coursed through him as he felt his body changing, his limbs stretching, becoming fluid sinew and powerful muscle, his skin dissolving into a sleek pelt of dark fur.

As his four paws connected solidly with the ground, he no longer felt like a thing apart from the earth, but at one with it, a black jungle cat prowling through the thick foliage of the forest.

A snake rose up in his path, unfurling her diamond

coils with a menacing hiss. He drove her back with a savage snarl, continuing on his way, in search of his true prey.

She awaited him where she always did, near the river where it spilled over a cliffside into the roaring falls. A woman with long blond hair, wet and tangled about her shoulders like a mermaid's, but her eyes were more that of a sorceress, glowing with a pale blue light.

Sunlight poured through the gauzy veil of her gown, her body all ripe curves and lush with promise, as fecund as the earth itself.

He crept closer, and although he saw her eyes widen and her breath hitch, she did not flee. Not even when he prowled around her, brushing up against her thighs. She buried her fingers in his hair, caressing him with long slow strokes.

Only when he emitted a growl, full-throated with desire, did she back away. Mixed in with the tang of her fear was the delicious scent of her arousal, even as she turned to run.

Some part of Xavier was aware this was not the first time he had encountered this creature in his visions. He still had no idea who or what she was; witch, mermaid, or mere woman. He only knew he had to have her.

He plunged recklessly after her, not hesitating even when she dove into the falls. Crouching he leapt, soaring into the air . . .

Xavier sprawled on the floor of his cabin, bracing himself to strike the water. It came in a cold splash, striking him full force in the face.

He spluttered, trying to twist away from the rough hand that was shaking his shoulder.

"Captain, wake up."

Xavier forced his eyes open a slit. The rich green foliage of the jungle had disappeared, replaced by the close timber walls of his cabin. Gone was the powerful black cat. He was reduced to a mere mortal again, his limbs heavy and awkward, his head splitting.

He closed his eyes, trying to tumble back into the world of forest and falls, his veil-clad temptress. But rude insistent hands continued to tug at him.

"Captain! Damn it, man. Heave to!"

Xavier opened his eyes and this time managed to focus on the tall dark shadow hovering over him. Pietro thrust his arm beneath Xavier's shoulders and dragged him to a sitting position. The walls pitched up and down, causing his senses to swim.

"On your feet, sir."

"Give me a minute, blast you," Xavier muttered. "My head—"

The words caught in Xavier's throat as he realized it was not his head causing the cabin to pitch and roll. The *Miribelle* creaked and groaned as her timbers ground against each other, the sounds of his lady in deep distress, caught in the throes of a violent storm.

Leaning heavily on the support of Pietro's arm, Xavier struggled to his feet. "Damnation! Why did you not rouse me sooner?"

"I should like you to tell me how that's to be done when you've been messing about with that devil's brew." Pietro glowered at him. The Cimmarone's eyes burned with reproach, but it was nothing to the coals Xavier would heap upon his own head. But there would be time enough for that later. He hoped . . .

Steadying himself as best he could, Xavier lurched from the cabin. Peering down into the murky depths of the hold, he could hear the dark lap of water, the grunts and shouts of sea dogs manning the pump.

"How bad?" Xavier demanded tersely of Pietro.

"Bad enough. Jambe's above, fighting to keep us from steering onto the rocks."

"Rocks? We are near land? St. Malo?"

"Don't think so. We've been driven off course."

Which might prove a good thing, Xavier thought. The port of St. Malo was protected by a barrier reef that was difficult to navigate even in the fairest weather.

Xavier shook his head to clear it of the potion's effect, still feeling as though he were swimming through a fog.

The ladder leading above deck pitched with the ship. Xavier cursed his own clumsiness as he struggled upward, only saved from falling by the support of Pietro's strong arm.

He emerged into a world far removed from the morning's stifling calm. The deck heaved and shuddered beneath a roiling dark sky, angry waves spraying over the side. Flares of lightning illuminated the looming shoreline, harsh and unwelcoming. Granite rocks and a towering cliff that—

Xavier's heart stopped, his memory stirring with one of his father's rare tales.

"A high cliff guarded by a ring of menhirs, Louis. They are said to be giants, turned to stone by Mother Earth, given the task of forever protecting the island."

"And shall I ever see these giants, sir?"

The piping ring of his eager child's voice echoed through

Xavier's head. His unfortunate question had caused his father's face to freeze as though he suddenly recalled who he was talking to.

Xavier blinked as another burst of lightning lit the cliffside again. Faire Isle. Whether Xavier willed it or no, his father's two worlds were about to collide.

He had to suppress a hysterical urge to burst into laughter. Was this some monumental jest of fate or his father's hand reaching from beyond the grave? Either way, it didn't matter. Xavier wasn't having it.

Bracing himself, he launched across the storm-battered deck, heading for the helm. The rain beat against his face, half blinding him. Thunder boomed in his ears as though the *Miribelle* was besieged by the entire Spanish armada.

His beleaguered lady shuddered, heaving violently to one side, and shook him off his feet. He slid across the rain-slick deck, making a frantic grab for the rail. His wits, still dulled by the potion, rendered his fingers thick and clumsy. His hand closed on nothing but air.

The *Miribelle* pitched again. Xavier roared out as the unthinkable happened. His lady flung him overboard. For a moment time seemed to stop as he hurled into nothingness.

Then he was embraced by the cold arms of the sea.

Chapter Six

SUNLIGHT BATHED THE SEA, THE GOLDEN WAVES CARESSING the shore like a lover mending a quarrel, the rage of last night's storm all forgotten. Jane picked her way along the rocky outcropping.

Here on the far side of Faire Isle, the vista was harsh, jagged fingers of rock stretching out into the sea, the vegetation sparse, only the hardiest of marsh grass and shrubs able to find purchase on a granite shore.

Jane had always preferred a tidy expanse of meadow or the gentle green of a hillside. Never had she expected to feel this rush of breath, her heart swelling with each break of the waves over the rocks.

She cast a half-nervous glance over her shoulder, reassuring herself that she was still within view of the cottages that passed for a village on the wilder part of the island, a scattering of rough stone huts that seemed carved into the face of the cliffs.

Other women were stirring, venturing out to enjoy the soft morning. Young Carole Moreau twirled her small son in a joyous circle while nearby Madame Alain and Madame Greves shared baskets of bread and gossip. Madame Partierre trotted about, industriously gathering up driftwood to dry out for her fire.

A tough wizened old lady, she was one of the few who actually lived on this rugged coast. Most had traveled here from the tamer side of the island, the harbor town of Port Corsair. But there were a few who had journeyed farther, from Brittany, the Loire Valley, even from as far away as Poitou, all in anticipation of the council meeting that would take place atop the cliffs a week hence.

A strange and independent lot, these women who called themselves the daughters of the earth. Jane could only marvel at their boldness. She had never traveled anywhere without the escort of a kinsman or the chaperonage of a maid and at least two stout male servants.

The women of Faire Isle enjoyed a great deal more freedom than Jane had ever known, a freedom that she found both enticing and a little alarming.

She lifted her face into the breeze, the wind strong enough to tug at her carefully pinned chignon. For once she had not been prudent enough to don either a cloak or a cap.

As she struggled to replace a dislodged hairpin, Jane was seized by the sort of mad impulse she had not known since she had been a very young girl. She yanked out the rest of the pins and shook out her hair until it tumbled free in a wild tangle.

Smoothing it back from her face, she drank in the salt air and shielded her eyes with one hand. The sea seemed to roll on forever in a glorious expanse of sun-kissed blue, except that she knew it didn't.

It was little more than twenty miles across that channel to England, the realization causing Jane a familiar pang. How many years would it be until her regrets softened and her memories dimmed, until she would stop being struck by the thought: If I were still at home on such a day, at such an hour, I would be doing this . . .

As she gazed out across the sea, her eyes misted with an image of her London manor, with its stout stone walls and tidy knot gardens leading down to the riverside quay, the Thames teeming with wherries and barges.

Like everything else, her London manor had been forfeited to the Crown. Jane wondered which of her favorites Elizabeth had bestowed the property upon and if the new owner had been kind to her household of servants or if they had been obliged to seek situations elsewhere.

Had this person been careful of her garden or neglectful? Had they perhaps torn up the rose arbor she had so tenderly cultivated in favor of extending the dock?

Most of all she wondered who, if anyone, would ever pause by the remote corner of the London churchyard to pray over the unassuming stone that marked her brother's grave.

Edward Lambert, the last Baron of Oxbridge. It disturbed Jane that she could scarce call up an image of the reckless young man who had given her so many sleepless nights. But she recalled quite clearly the little brother who had clung so fiercely to her hand that summer they had become orphaned.

"What are we to do, Jane?" Ned had asked, turning his woebegone face up to hers. "Our papa fell off his horse and now he is all broken. We have no papa anymore. Who will look out for me?"

"I will, Neddie," she said, her hand caressing the silky strands of his blond hair, a paler version of her own. "I will protect and take care of you always."

A promise she had been unable to keep . . .

"Forgive me, Neddie," she prayed. Her eyes blurred with tears. She rubbed fingertips against her lids to stem the flow. When her vision cleared, she was struck by the sight of two cloaked figures making their way up the beach.

There was no mistaking the taller of the two young women. Seraphine Remy, the Lady of Faire Isle's eldest niece, was a beauty of statuesque proportions, her unbound hair falling over her shoulders like a shower of gold. She provided a dramatic contrast to her shorter companion, Meg's thin face framed by her dark brown hair.

Jane frowned. Ariane Deauville had given strict instructions that no one was to stray that far from the encampment. Jane glanced back toward the cluster of cottages and saw that everyone else had retreated inside, no doubt to get on with daily chores.

There was no one to notice the two girls wandering off but her. Jane fretted her lip, realizing that neither girl would be likely to welcome her interference, especially not Seraphine.

The lady's niece was headstrong to a fault. Meg had a

strong mind of her own, but she seemed almost mesmerized by Seraphine Remy, the older girl often able to override Meg's caution and persuade her into some imprudent action Meg would not usually undertake.

All the more reason she ought to go after them, Jane thought. Hesitating only a moment longer, she plucked up her skirts and headed off in pursuit.

Jane had never been a swift walker and the uneven ground made for rough going. Fortunately the two girls were not proceeding at a fast pace and as Jane closed the distance between them, she realized why.

From Seraphine's fierce gestures and Meg's repeated shakes of her head, it was obvious that Seraphine was attempting to persuade Meg into doing something against the younger girl's wishes.

As Jane overtook them, Seraphine held something out of Meg's reach. The two girls tussled for possession of the object, but they froze at the sight of Jane. Meg managed to snatch the thing back and hide it beneath her cloak. The girls sidled close to each other like soldiers closing ranks, Meg looking guilty, Seraphine defiant.

Jane smiled, greeting them as though she had noticed nothing amiss. "Good morrow, ladies."

Meg's curtsy was stiff and awkward, Seraphine's as smooth and haughty as any duchess.

"Lady Danvers. What an agreeable surprise." The girl bared her pearl-like teeth in a smile. At the age of sixteen, Seraphine had already mastered the art of saying one thing while her tone conveyed quite another.

"I confess I am surprised to see you both abroad so early as well. Where are you going?" Jane asked.

"Up there." Seraphine jerked her head in the direction of the distant cliffs, the ring of monoliths just visible atop the highest one. "Neither Meg nor I have ever seen the standing giants and we are perishing to do so."

"I am sure you will see them soon enough. The council meeting is barely a week away. In the meantime, I cannot think it wise for either of you girls to wander about unescorted."

"Oh, pooh. This is Faire Isle, not London or Paris. I am sure the notion of an unchaperoned girl is appalling to a lady of your—er, venerable years. But women have more freedom here."

"I was not thinking of propriety, so much as safety." Jane focused her gaze gravely on Meg. "You know that Ariane has asked that none of us stray too far. Apparently there are some rough fisherfolk on this side of the island, the women in particular a trifle wild and superstitious."

Meg started to speak, but once again Seraphine cut in before she could reply. "*My* mother told me those idiotic women were driven off Faire Isle years ago when the witch-hunters and the king's soldiers made their great raid. Besides, I am well able to defend both of us."

Seraphine drew back her cloak to reveal a short sword.

"Merciful heavens, child!" Jane gasped.

"Don't worry. I know how to use it." Seraphine patted the hilt lovingly. "My father taught me. Captain Nicolas Remy is a brave Huguenot hero, so fearsome he is called the Scourge. I don't know if I have ever told you that."

"Only a dozen times," Meg muttered.

"My father feels that every Huguenot must know how

to defend him- or herself. One never knows when we may be set upon by some papist fanatics."

"Seraphine!" Meg reproved with a significant look at Jane.

The girl merely shrugged. "I meant no offense to Lady Danvers."

"None taken," Jane said. "There is no civil war being waged on this island, which is why your parents sent you and your sisters here out of harm's way. There is a more tolerant spirit on Faire Isle."

"I hope so. Did your ladyship read the tract by Martin Luther I sent you?"

"No, I did not. I believe that faith should be a matter of personal choice. I have my own beliefs, but enough respect not to foist my creed onto others."

"Oh, so do I. Although it is very difficult to restrain myself when I know that I am right." Seraphine heaved a dramatic sigh. "Well, you are obviously here to recapture us. Considering what an obedient little girl Meg is, there is no point in us trudging all the way up to the stone circle anyway."

She exchanged a pointed look with Meg as though there was some added edge to Seraphine's barb that Jane did not understand, but Meg flushed.

"I shall just have to seek my amusement elsewhere." Seraphine crinkled her nose at Jane, her blue eyes sparkling with impish defiance.

Before Jane could protest, Seraphine strode off, nimbly clambering down the rocks to the shore's edge. The tide was coming in and a wave caught her off guard, lapping over her boots and wetting the hem of her gown.

Seraphine shook back her golden hair and laughed. Bending down, she slapped her hand through the water, wetting her gown even more.

Jane sighed, realizing it was useless to remonstrate further with the girl, trying to convince her to return to the safety of the cottages. Seraphine would remain right where she was merely to demonstrate that she could. There was little Jane could do other than seek reinforcements in the person of the girl's aunt.

Meg watched Seraphine's retreat down the beach with an expression torn between wistfulness and admiration.

"She really is magnificent, isn't she?" Meg murmured.

"That is not quite the word I would have chosen, although I grant you she certainly is an unusual girl."

Meg cast Jane a rueful look. "I am sorry for what Seraphine said about Catholic fanatics. I am sure she did not mean to be offensive. She can be rather passionate about her views."

Jane smiled. "It is all right, Meg. When I was a young girl, I thought I knew everything as well."

"What happened?"

I was seduced by my guardian's master of horse and gave birth to a stillborn child.

Jane lowered her lashes to conceal the thought.

"I grew older and more *venerable,*" she said dryly, eliciting a rare laugh from Meg.

As they headed back to the village, Meg continued to defend her friend. "Seraphine truly does have a kinder, gentler side, although she rarely shows it to anyone except her little sisters. And to me."

"The pair of you appear to have become fast friends."

More so than Jane thought was good for Meg. "I was astonished to see you quarreling."

"Oh, we weren't," Meg said, almost too quickly. "It was merely a—a small disagreement. Even the best of friends have those from time to time."

"Truly? It looked to me as though Seraphine had taken something of yours and was refusing to give it back. The same thing that you are now hiding under your cloak."

Meg stiffened. The girl could have told Jane to mind her own affairs. Jane had no real authority over her. But after a moment, Meg drew out her hand, the small crystal orb winking in the sunlight.

Jane had already guessed that the gazing globe might prove to be the disputed object. She was not surprised, merely saddened. But she asked no questions or made any criticism. Her silence finally goaded Meg into an explanation.

"We have not had any word from Navarre for a long time. Seraphine and I are both very worried about our fathers. Seraphine thought I could summon up a vision so that we might know if they are safe. I tried to explain to her that it does not work that way, that I have no control over what I see. The visions just come as they will.

"Seraphine thought that I could do it if I just concentrated harder. And maybe it would help if I made the attempt among the standing stones. The menhirs are supposed to have a mystic power of their own."

Meg shivered. "The idea frightened me. The last thing I want is for my visions to become stronger, more potent. I refused, but Seraphine snatched the crystal and headed for the stones herself. I only followed to get it back from her.

"But I was on the verge of relenting when you overtook us. Seraphine can be so persuasive. I—I know that both you and Ariane wish I would leave the crystal alone." Meg directed a plaintive glance up at Jane. "Are you very disappointed in me?"

"No, child, only very worried for you."

Meg nodded glumly. "I realize my visions are considered strange, even here on Faire Isle. Carole Moreau is afraid for me, too. She says if I keep meddling with the crystal, the other women will start to believe I am evil as my mother was."

"No one could possibly think that." Jane brushed her knuckles down the back of Meg's cheek. Meg had never been a robust girl and it struck her that Meg was looking paler and thinner, even more than she had been last autumn.

"I am more worried by what these visions are doing to you. It is as though they are putting shadows into your mind."

"The shadows are already there." Meg rubbed her temple hard, grinding her fingers into her skin. "No matter what I do, I can't seem to get them out."

Jane closed her hand over Meg's fingers to still the rough gesture before Meg actually hurt herself. Ariane would be so much better able to guide and council Meg. But for some reason, the one Meg always chose to confide in was Jane. The girl's trust both moved and overwhelmed Jane.

"Have you been having the vision about that dark cat again?" Jane asked.

"Dark cats, dark storms, dark queens, dark everything.

And none of it clear. All I am sure of is that there is some trouble coming, some darkness that will stain even the peace of Faire—"

A piercing cry cut off what Meg had been about to say. Jane ducked, thinking they were about to be swooped by one of the strident gulls who inhabited this side of the island. Then she realized the cry had come from behind them.

Seraphine raced after them, half-tripping over the sodden hem of her gown. Her usual confidence appeared shaken, a spot of color high on each cheek. The girl drew up beside them, clutching her side and gasping for breath.

"Seraphine, what is it?" Meg asked.

"Are you hurt?" Jane placed one hand on the girl's shoulder, but Seraphine shook it off.

"No, not me. *Him.*" The girl panted. "I—I found a dead man back there in the cove."

Jane and Meg exchanged a stunned glance. Jane was the first to recover.

"Show me," she said.

Seraphine gave a jerky nod. She turned and raced back down the beach. Despite being winded, the girl's long strides propelled her forward. Jane had difficulty keeping pace, Meg lagging even farther behind.

Seraphine leapt down the rocks with a recklessness that caused Jane to call out a warning. Seraphine ignored her, disappearing from view. Jane slowed enough to scramble down the rough ledge more cautiously. A twisted ankle would render her of service to no one.

When she reached the shore, she found Seraphine standing over a black-clad figure sprawled in the sand, the dark clothing stark against the white glare of the sun upon the rocks.

Hastening to Seraphine's side, Jane saw that the recumbent figure was indeed a man. Where he had come from, how he came to be washed up in this isolated cove, Jane could not begin to imagine. One of his arms was stretched out as though he had struggled to find purchase among the rocks from the battering of the sea. The same sea that now crept higher up the shore, the hungry tide threatening to return and drag him back into the ocean's maw.

"Is he still breathing?"

"I don't know. I didn't think to check. I—I—"

Jane knelt down. The man was sprawled on his stomach, his head turned to one side. She brushed aside a tangle of dark wet hair, feeling for a pulse at the base of his throat.

His skin felt so cold. But as she pressed her fingertips deeper, she detected a faint throb.

"He's still alive." Jane glanced up and was relieved to see Meg had caught up with them, the younger girl hovering just behind Seraphine.

"Help me to turn him over," Jane urged the girls. Seraphine sprang into action, but Meg simply stood there and stared.

He was not a large man, but his inert weight made him heavy and awkward. With Seraphine's help, Jane managed to shift him over onto his back. His right arm flopped at an impossible angle, a shard of bone piercing through the fabric of his sleeve.

Seraphine gasped and drew back, clapping her hand to her mouth, looking as though she was going to be sick.

"What—what should we do?"

It was rare that Jane ever heard Seraphine Remy at a loss, but before she could reply, she realized that the girl was not asking her.

Seraphine appealed to Meg. "What do we need to do, Meg? You have learned the most from Ariane about the setting of bones."

Meg didn't reply. The girl remained frozen in a way that was most unlike her. Usually when anyone was ill or injured, Meg was the first to leap in and offer help, so competent for one so young.

And help of some sort was desperately needed. The next surge of tide crept in closer, lapping at the heels of the stranger's worn leather boots.

"His broken arm is the least of this poor man's problems," Jane told Seraphine. "If we don't get him up out of this cove, he is going to drown. One of us is going to have to race back to the others for help. And it had best be you. You are by far the fastest."

Seraphine nodded, looking relieved to find some action she could take. Plucking up the hem of her skirts, she tore off running.

Jane bent over the man, brushing sand from his cheek, caressing his hair back from his brow. She found a lump just above his temple and realized he had sustained a head injury. When her fingertips grazed the swelling, Jane thought she heard the stranger issue a low groan.

"Sir? Sir, can you hear me?" She regarded the man hopefully. But there was no response.

"We must leave him alone, Jane." Meg spoke up at last. "Let the sea take him back again."

Jane shot a startled glance up at the girl, astonished by her words. Meg clutched her crystal orb with both hands, her face white, her eyes glazed, her breeze-tossed hair appearing like a dark halo.

"He's dangerous. He'll only bring trouble."

"Meg, how could you possibly know that?"

"He is a stranger. That's what strangers do," Meg intoned in such an odd voice, Jane shrank involuntarily from the man she had been hovering over.

Was this another of Meg's unnerving predictions or merely the fears of a young girl who had known too much turmoil in her brief life, pursued by witch-hunters, assassins, and the malice of a powerful queen? Small wonder that the girl would be wary of strangers, and this one had a rather alarming aspect.

Jane had no idea who this man might be, but she would have wagered what little she owned that he was no local fisherman tossed from his skiff during yesterday's storm.

He had the hard face of a man who had lived a hard life, the wind, rain, and blazing sun beaten into his very bones. His shirt, open at the neck, revealed the crease of a white scar as though his throat had been slit during the course of some fierce battle. Not the sign of a peaceful man.

But even if he proved to be the spawn of the devil, Jane could not simply abandon him to his fate. She had to try to help him. It was the right thing to do. And despite his harsh appearance, there was something gentler, more sensitive about the curve of his mouth.

His mouth.

Jane's breath caught as she recalled some healing

magic she had watched the Lady of Faire Isle perform upon a nearly drowned girl. Ariane had fastened her lips over that of the girl and breathed her own essence into the child, reviving her. The Kiss of Life, she had called it.

If the man could be roused, supported to his feet, it would make his rescue so much easier. Had Meg learned how to perform this magic?

But one look in Meg's direction told Jane she could expect no help from that quarter even if she could soothe the girl's fears or snap Meg out of her strange trance. Having issued her warning, Meg had backed farther away.

Another wave broke closer, this time splashing over the man's ankles. Oh, where was Seraphine? Had she even made it back to the village by now?

Jane had little choice but to attempt the Kiss of Life herself. She regarded the man doubtfully for a moment, then tried to copy what Ariane had done. She inserted her fingers into his mouth, prying his lips apart, seeking to clear away any obstruction. All she felt was the rough warmth of his tongue, the contact intrusive and disturbingly intimate.

Her cheeks burned. Before she could question the wisdom of what she was about to do, Jane drew in a deep breath. She bent closer and sealed his mouth with her own. She had barely exhaled her first breath when the man startled her, his eyes flying wide open. She stared straight into depths the color of an angry, storm-ridden sea.

Jane reared back, her heart thudding. But she could not be half so shaken as he, poor man. He groaned, peering groggily up at her. Recovering herself, Jane sought to reassure him.

"Everything is all right, sir. I am here to help you and more aid is coming." At least, she hoped it was.

It didn't occur to Jane that she was addressing him in English, until he blinked and muttered something in French. Even then his words made no sense.

"Witch or . . . mermaid."

"I beg your pardon, monsieur?" Jane replied in his own language, uncertain if she had misheard him or the poor man was delirious with pain.

He moistened his lips and repeated again. "Witch or mermaid . . . are you a witch or a . . . mermaid?"

"Neither," Jane stammered. "I am an Englishwoman."

He responded with a choked laugh before lapsing back into unconsciousness.

Chapter Seven

XAVIER SANK DEEPER INTO THE DEPTHS OF THE SEA. Some part of his mind urged him to fight, thrust his head above the waves before he drowned. But he could sense the pain nudging at him like the snout of a hungry shark, waiting to devour him should he strike for the surface. Far better that he remain where he was, drifting through the soothing darkness of the ocean.

If only she would let him. But his mermaid bathed his face and chafed his wrists, her siren voice calling to him. "*Monsieur? Monsieur, please come back to me. You must try.*"

Xavier forced his eyes open to narrow slits and focused on the person hovering over him, a woman with sun-kissed blond hair tumbled about her face, her eyes gentle, her mouth tender. The mermaid that had coaxed him back to life. As he felt the first throb of pain, he wasn't sure if he wanted to kiss her or kill her.

He groaned and tried to turn away, retreat back into the darkness, but she braced her hand beneath his head and raised him, pressing a cup to his lips.

"Please, monsieur. You must try. Drink this."

His tongue felt so thick and parched, he obeyed, taking a greedy swallow, only to sputter and choke. Whatever poison she fed him, it tasted viler than his shaman's brew. But unlike the magical elixir that guided him into a seductive trance, this evil potion revived his senses, made him acutely aware of the throbbing hulk that was his body.

Xavier groaned and swore. Christ, what the hell had happened to him? He felt as if he had single-handedly taken on a press-gang of burly ruffians armed with cudgels and lost. Pain . . . pain that stemmed mostly from his right arm, a hot burning pain that throbbed up into his shoulder and across his chest, seeming to radiate into every pore of his being.

But there was worse. As his vision cleared, he was horrified to realize that his ship had been invaded by . . . *women.* He was lost in a sea of skirts, some like his mermaid gathered close to his bed, still others crowding in the doorway of his cabin, or gawking at him through the window.

The women came in all range of sizes and ages from the little towhead who stared at him while sucking her thumb to the wizened beldame squinting and clicking her gums. They spoke amongst themselves, their voices sounding to him as shrill as a flock of seagulls circling his pounding head.

"Look. He's coming round at last."

"Give him another swig of that restorative tea, m'dear."

"Who is he? Where did he come from?"

"I don't know. He just appears to have been tossed up from the sea."

"The sea never left anything that prime at my door. Only dead fish and seaweed."

"All right, enough!" A tall, haughty-looking blonde elbowed her way through the press, regarding her companions scornfully. "Anyone would think you'd never seen a man before. Clear off and give the wretch room to breathe."

"Who died and made you queen, Seraphine Remy?" the toothless old woman huffed.

Her indignation was echoed by the others, the clatter making Xavier want to clap his hands to his ears. Except that he seemed unable to move his right arm.

His mermaid leapt into the fray, holding up her hands for silence. "Ladies, Seraphine is right. This poor man needs his wounds attended to, quiet and rest. Please, I beg you, retire. There will be time enough for your questions later."

Her low reasonable voice achieved what the haughty girl's commands could not. The women retreated, even the tall blonde leading away the thumb-sucking child. Xavier was left in blessed silence, alone with his mermaid.

He would have breathed a sigh of relief as his rescuer stole back to his side. But even that threatened to hurt like hell. And as his gaze darted about the room, he no longer felt relieved at all.

He was not, as he had supposed, ensconced in his cabin

aboard the *Miribelle.* He lay on a cot, surrounded by unfamiliar whitewashed stone walls, the furnishings sparse but decidedly feminine, a spinning wheel, a workbasket, the hint of a petticoat peeking out from a wardrobe chest.

Memories burst behind his eyes, like painful flashes of lightning. The storm, the *Miribelle* hurling him from her decks. The cold dash of the sea. Fighting to keep his head above the angry waves, gain his bearings in the darkness. Swimming toward shore, so tired, muscles aching. Resisting the longing to give in, sink below the surface. The tide tumbling him, driving him toward the rocks. Clawing desperately for purchase, almost gaining his feet, hit hard by another wave. Pain . . . incredible pain. On his feet again, staggering, falling. More pain. And then . . . nothing.

His mermaid returned to his side and tried to get more of her vile brew down his throat. With his left hand, he managed to dash the cup from her hand.

"No more of that damned stuff. Where am I?" he roared at her. At least he meant to roar, his voice came out more like a croak.

"On Faire Isle."

"No! Not possible."

"I assure you that it is." She bobbed her head, looking so solemn, he had to suppress a mad urge to laugh. She was a most earnest mermaid, nothing like the seductress of his potion-induced trance.

She pressed his left hand. "Don't worry. You are safe now."

Safe? On the island of witches, the last place this side of hell he'd ever wanted to be. He grated his teeth as he absorbed this information.

When his rescuer started to draw away, he clutched at her hand. "Where are you going?"

"Only to see if I can find the Lady. Someone should have fetched her by now. I cannot imagine what is keeping her."

"No," he said harshly. "I don't want—" He was mortified to realize he was clinging to her like a child, but in this nightmare world, she was the only thing that seemed real, besides his unrelenting pain.

"Just stay."

"I will." She smiled, a sweet solemn smile. With her free hand, she caressed his cheek, the only place he didn't seem to hurt. "Everything is going to be all right."

Damned if she almost didn't make him believe it, until she added, "I am sure the Lady will be here soon."

What lady? he almost demanded. But as his mind cleared, he knew his mermaid had to be speaking of only one woman. The Lady of Faire Isle. The thought of *her* tightened the knot in his gut. He had to get the devil out of here.

He grated his teeth against the pain as he tried to rise, a feeble effort at best. The mermaid easily restrained him by pressing her hand on his left shoulder.

"No. Please, monsieur. You must lie still lest—" Her warning was cut off when someone else burst into the room in a flurry of faded gray skirts and flapping apron. An elderly woman with a cloud of white hair and vague blue eyes clapped her hand to her mouth at the sight of him.

Xavier regarded her blearily. The old woman burst into tears and cried. "Oh, my dear master, is that really you?"

Master? Now what the devil? Xavier thought. Island of

witches, hell. He'd fetched up on an isle peopled by madwomen.

"Is it really you after all these years?" The woman beamed through her tears. "The sea took you away and now brought you back to us."

With another mighty sob, she flung herself upon his chest, jarring his right arm. She might as well have stabbed him. Xavier choked off a cry at the fresh spasm of pain that spiked through him.

"Mistress please!" His mermaid dragged the sobbing woman away from him. "I fear you are distressing our guest."

"Distressing me?" Xavier grated, letting fly a volley of oaths that would have blistered their ears if either woman had been paying any attention to him.

The old lady was clinging to his mermaid, half weeping, half laughing. "Oh, you don't understand. You don't know who he is. This is a great day for Faire Isle, Jane."

Jane? Xavier thought as he blew out a succession of quick breaths in an effort to gain some mastery over his pain. That was a ridiculously staid name for a mermaid or even a witch.

Jane struggled to calm the mad old woman, keep her from flinging herself at Xavier again. As she eased her toward the door, Xavier became aware of another presence, another pair of hands gripping the old lady's arms, reinforcing Jane's efforts.

"Agnes, my dear. What is all this?"

Xavier could not see who spoke, but the voice penetrated his haze of pain, cool, calm, and authoritative.

The old woman turned from Jane to embrace the newcomer. "Oh, milady. The joyous day we have prayed for is here. The chevalier has returned to us."

Xavier froze, even his pain forgotten as he realized for whom he had been mistaken. It should have come as no surprise to him. Closing his eyes, he could hear the echo of his mother's voice.

"You are the very image of your father, Louis."

Even now Xavier was not sure if his mother had been proud of that resemblance or hated him for it.

The old woman's cries faded into the distance and silence descended over the room. Xavier became aware of someone returning to his side. Somehow he sensed it wasn't Jane.

He kept his eyes closed as though he could avoid the confrontation he'd dreaded most of his life and yet had been unable to stop from imagining as well. But he had never pictured it like this, with him flat on his back, wounded and helpless before her.

No matter how he had resisted this moment, a part of him had regarded it as inevitable. He expelled a deep breath. Feeling strangely resigned, he opened his eyes and gazed up at the Lady of Faire Isle.

Tall, slender, she possessed a stately grace despite the simple brown frock she wore. Her chestnut-colored hair crowned her head in a circle of tightly woven braids, the strands threaded with hints of silver. Her countenance was more striking than beautiful. He fancied that it was usually serene, but she paled at the sight of him, her brown eyes wide.

So this was his father's beloved Evangeline. She was very like her portrait. But even as the thought occurred to

Xavier, he frowned, knowing that was wrong. Evangeline was long dead and buried like his own mother. In any case, this woman was far too young to be Evangeline. This could only be Ariane, the eldest daughter.

At least that was the word Xavier meant to form. But the whisper that escaped his lips startled even him.

"Sister."

"M-my God! Who are you?"

"Nobody that you want to know."

"Avoiding your acquaintance may prove difficult, monsieur, since the fates have chosen to cast you up on my island."

"The fates had nothing to do with it. It was the *Miribelle* when she listed during last night's storm."

"The—the *Miribelle*?" she faltered. "You can't possibly mean . . . my father's ship."

"No, *my* father's ship." Which Xavier prayed had somehow managed to ride out the storm and avoid breaking up on the rocks.

The lady bit her lip. He noted that she chose to avoid challenging him on the issue of fathers. Instead she asked, "What about the chevalier? Do you know—"

"Dead." He stabbed the word at her, effectively killing the flicker of hope in her eyes. Xavier felt a fleeting regret for his cruelty, but he was in too damned much pain to soften the blow.

She lowered her lashes, sorrow and resignation softening her features. But the steel was back in her gaze when she regarded him again.

"And you are claiming to be . . . ?"

"I am not claiming anything. If you are as good at reading men's minds as I have been told, I am sure you can figure out who I am for yourself." Despite the pain throbbing behind his eyes, Xavier looked defiantly up at her.

She frowned, her gaze narrowing as her eyes locked on his. Xavier returned her stare, refusing to blink, but damned if it didn't feel like the witch had cracked open his skull as deftly as he flung open the lid of his sea chest, his thoughts threatening to spill like treasures into her lap.

He gritted his teeth and slammed his mind closed, though the effort to resist cost him in pain and sweat, beads of perspiration gathering on his brow. Still, he refused to surrender, their eyes clashing in a merciless duel until Jane rushed forward to intervene.

"Ariane, please."

His mermaid had been so quiet, Xavier hadn't even noticed she was still there. Her puzzled gaze flickered between him and Ariane. Jane rested her fingers on Ariane's sleeve.

"I don't know what is going on or who this man is. But surely the important thing is that he needs your help. His arm must be set to rights."

The lady pinched the bridge of her nose and drew herself up more erect. "Of course, you are right, Jane." She forced a tight-lipped smile. "Very well, monsieur. Let us have a look at this injured arm."

"There is nothing wrong with my damned arm," Xavier denied despite the pain radiating up his right side. He shifted, half raising his head. "I only need—"

He choked off a cry of horror as he realized himself the full extent of his injury, the dried blood crusting around the rent in his sleeve, the hint of bone protruding. Ariane bent closer to examine the wound, but even her gentlest touch drove spikes of fire into his flesh.

"Leave it alone," Xavier snarled. Bracing himself with his left hand, he struggled to a sitting position. Over the protests of both women, he drew his injured arm protectively close to his chest, although the effort caused black dots of pain to dance before his eyes.

"Oh, monsieur, pray don't. You are only going to make it worse," Jane said.

Worse? How could this possibly get any worse, Xavier thought as his vision cleared and he stared at the wreckage of his once powerful right arm. He'd witnessed the kind of accidents that could happen too easily upon a ship, sea dogs injured in brawls or falls from the rigging, wounded during fiercely fought battles. He'd realized how fragile a man could be, hale and strong one moment, shattered beyond repair the next.

He'd helped to treat fractures this bad, knew what the inevitable outcome must be, although his mind recoiled from it.

"Oh, God." He sagged back against the pillows.

"Don't worry." Jane soothed. "Ariane will take care of you."

"The devil she will. Fetch me a doctor. Are there no men on this bloody island?"

Ariane folded her arms across her bosom. "None that will be of any use to you. Most of them are like my son, still in tailclouts."

"Please, monsieur." Jane tried to ease his fingers away

from his injured arm. "The lady is very skilled. She will have that bone set in a trice."

Xavier shrank away from her, snarling. "Set? Do you take me for a blasted fool? I have seen this kind of break before. I know that my arm is going to have to be . . . to be . . . *amputated."* There. He'd managed to say the dread word, acknowledged it aloud.

Ariane's brows shot upward. "You seem in quite a hurry to part company with your arm, monsieur."

"Because I have no other choice."

"I admit it may come to that. But I have had great success setting even worse fractures than yours. If you would just allow me to try—"

"No. Keep your damned witchery to yourself."

"That's enough," Jane cried. She eyed Xavier sternly. "The lady wants to help, so stop behaving like—like a recalcitrant child."

Color rose high in Jane's cheeks. So his calm mermaid did possess a bit of a temper. Under other circumstances, Xavier might have found it amusing, even rather adorable. But he focused on Ariane's stony countenance.

"Somehow I doubt that the lady is all that eager to render me her aid."

Ariane lifted her chin proudly. "I am the daughter of Evangeline Cheney. My mother was a gifted healer and she taught me all her skills, all her wisdom, to help those in need, whoever they might be."

"Well, I am the son of Marguerite de Maitland, a most accomplished courtesan and she taught me to be wary of witches."

Xavier tried to sneer, but his lips twisted into a pained grimace. "Of course you have no need to ask who my father was because you have already worked that out. In fact, my mother had me christened for him. Louis Xavier Cheney."

He tossed out the name as if he were flinging down a gauntlet and it had the desired effect.

Angry color flared in Ariane's cheeks. "That—that woman dared give you my father's name. You are a bastard. You have no right!"

"So I have been told. Perhaps now that you know all that, you are not quite so eager to lay your healing hands upon me, *sister.*"

Ariane compressed her lips together and for a moment he thought she would storm out of the room. Then she issued a deep sigh.

"Your mother Marguerite brought a great deal of misery to my family, robbed my mother's final days of all happiness and contentment. But it matters not to me what your name is or if you are the spawn of Satan. I am a healer and I believe I can help you."

Jane captured his left hand between hers, adding her own plea. "Monsieur, you strike me as a man used to being his own master, issuing commands. I realize how hard it must be for you to consign yourself to the care of a woman. But I have seen Ariane perform so many miracles. You can trust her, I promise you."

Xavier's gaze shifted belligerently from Ariane's stern face to Jane's softer one. He didn't know how far he trusted the Lady of Faire Isle, but he was surprised to feel himself yielding to Jane's calm persuasion. Perhaps because he had never seen a woman's face so entirely without guile. Perhaps it was because her eyes swam with genuine concern. But perhaps it was simply because he had no other damned choice.

"Oh, bloody hell," he growled at Ariane. "Go fetch your saw or blade or whatever you are planning to hack me apart with and get some of your own back."

"Fine. Jane, will you please cut away his shirt, while I go retrieve my weapon of choice." Ariane bared her teeth at him in a grim smile before striding from the room.

Jane dug out a pair of scissors from the workbasket and returned to the bedside. "I am sorry that your shirt must be destroyed."

"No problem, m'dear. It's always been my favorite fantasy, a beautiful woman ripping my clothes off."

His quip brought a becoming flush of color to her cheeks, a reaction he might have enjoyed if he had not been half dizzy with pain and apprehension of what was to come. He gritted his teeth and relaxed his injured arm so that she could begin.

For several moments the room was silent except for the snick of the scissors and his sharp quick breaths.

"I will try not to hurt you," she said. "But I fear your shirt is matted to your wound where—where—"

"My bone is attempting to exit my body?" He grated. "Don't worry about it. I won't be feeling much pain in that region once Ariane finishes with me. And I daresay my dear sister will enjoy it."

Jane paused to frown at him. "I don't fully understand your history with the Lady of Faire Isle, but Ariane is not the sort of woman to seek revenge or make you pay for the sins of your mother. She is an amazing healer. She will save your arm, Monsieur Cheney."

"Don't call me that. I am known as Captain Xavier or just plain Xavier will do. I never use my father's name. I—" He swore, nearly coming up off the bed as Jane peeled the last of the fabric away from his injured arm.

He sank back, panting, "I only mentioned that to—to—"

"To annoy Ariane? It might be less than wise to goad the woman who is about to set your broken arm."

"True, but as you may have surmised, mistress, wisdom is not one of my more shining attributes."

She smiled at that and he might have been tempted to smile back if he hadn't felt so exhausted and engulfed in a world of pain and bleak prospects.

Jane walked over to the washstand where she splashed some water from a pitcher onto a cloth. She returned to him and proceeded to bathe his face.

"It really is going to be all right," she murmured. "Although I know you don't believe that."

"I don't, but thank you for lying. You do it so sweetly."

He was grateful when she said nothing more. Another woman would have been tempted to continue jawing at him, either scolding or chirping brightly to distract him.

Jane quietly bathed his brow, the cloth cool and as soothing as her touch. He was startled to realize he was soaked in sweat. At least one good might come of Ariane Deauville mangling him in an effort to save his arm. An infection would be bound to set in and likely carry him off. That could only be a blessing. He was so tired. He felt like he had been fighting for so long, most of his life.

He closed his eyes, an odd memory coming back to him of his father, both of them standing on the deck of the *Miribelle,* one of their rare quiet moments together.

The chevalier had given him an odd bemused look.

"You know you are not like me, mon petit Louis. You are a deal tougher, a fighter. You will never back down from anything or run away. You are a survivor."

It was the closest his father had ever come to exhibiting anything like pride in him or praising him.

But as Ariane returned, bearing with her a small but ominous looking chest, Xavier did not feel so tough. She was followed by a sturdy-looking girl with sandy hair and a smattering of freckles across her nose.

"This is Carole Moreau," Ariane said. "She is going to assist me."

"A mere chit of a girl? The devil she is," Xavier said, gathering his injured arm against his bared chest.

"I am older than I appear, monsieur." Carole smiled shyly at him. "I was one of the women who helped get you on the litter and carry you up from the beach."

"What would you like me to do? Melt down my silver and cast you a medal?"

The girl's smile faded and she hastily retreated to where Ariane was opening up her chest. Jane sighed and shook her head at Xavier reprovingly. He subsided, too wearied to launch any further protest.

He knew he was behaving like a wounded dog, snapping and snarling at everyone who came near him, but he could not seem to help himself.

Ariane approached, holding up a small vial. "This draught will ease your pain, help you to sleep—"

"No! Just give me a belt of whiskey."

"I don't have any whiskey."

"What the bloody hell kind of healer are you?"

"This draught is better. It can—"

"I said no, God damn it."

"Then I need to get more women in here to help hold you down."

"No one needs to hold me down. Just stop nattering at me and get on with it."

Ariane muttered something under her breath. Xavier scowled. Had he heard amiss or had the dignified Lady of Faire just ground out a curse that would make some of his crew blush?

Belatedly Xavier remembered Jane's comment about his lack of wisdom. Grating his jaw, he said, "What I mean is, I don't need the God-cursed draught. But thank you all the same."

Ariane shot him a dark look, then gave a reluctant laugh. "Ah, male heroics. Very well, monsieur. Let us begin."

"Captain Xavier," Jane spoke up softly. "He calls himself Xavier."

"Xavier," Ariane repeated as though testing the sound of it. She stared at him expectantly and he realized that he still was shielding his injured arm with his left hand.

No matter what Ariane averred, Xavier was certain she could not save his arm. If he became infected, he doubted she would just let him die either. Somehow he sensed this woman who shared half his blood could be just as stubborn as he. The arm would have to come off.

His good strong right arm, his sword arm. Why couldn't it have been his left? He could have spared his left. But images filled his mind of himself climbing the rigging, tossing a grappling hook, steadying the tiller in a violent storm. Actions that required the strength of both arms.

But what did it matter, because he likely no longer had a ship anyway. The *Miribelle* was probably gone, his lady sunk to the bottom of the channel, his crew with her, Jambe du Bois, Pietro, Father Bernard. Everything he owned, everything he cared about, lost. And he was quibbling over a mere arm?

Xavier was horrified to feel his eyes sting with tears. He blinked fiercely and slowly uncurled his fingers, surrendering his arm to Ariane.

As she eased it away from his body, he cried out before he could stop himself. When she offered him a piece of leather to bite down upon, he didn't refuse. He had done the same thing for his first mate, the day Jambe's leg had been crushed by the cannon careening loose across the deck.

"Buck up, man. You can survive this, you tough old scoundrel. You'll be a more ferocious fighter on one leg than most men are on two."

Jambe had ground the leather between his teeth, glaring at Xavier like he wanted to murder him. A look Xavier now fully understood. Easy to be so bluff and reassuring when the limb in question was not your own.

Carole Moreau handed Ariane a cloth soaked in some substance that stung as she cleaned his puncture wound. No matter how careful she tried to be, each little movement jarred, sending out fresh waves of agony. By the time Ariane began to manipulate his bone back into place,

Xavier bit down so hard, he felt his jaw would shatter. Unmanly tears streamed from his eyes and there was not a damn thing he could do to check them.

He crushed Jane's hand in his own, trying to lose himself in her quiet eyes, trying not to scream.

Chapter Eight

JANE FLEXED HER FINGERS, WINCING AS THE BLOOD RUSHED back into a hand that had gone numb from Xavier's crushing grip. She'd scarce noticed, all of her attention focused on his pain-wracked features as Ariane reset the broken bone.

Mercifully it was over and Jane had managed to coax him to swallow the sleeping draught. Perhaps he had become too exhausted to resist or he was finally satisfied they were not going to hack off his arm. His lashes rested against his cheek, his face pale beneath its day-old shadow of beard.

Jane massaged her bruised hand as she studied Xavier, marveling at all he had endured. Flung from the deck of his ship in the midst of that violent storm, battling the waves only to be flung up on a hostile shore, half-drowned, his arm broken, his body battered.

Ever since her exile from England, her hold on the world felt so tenuous. Feeling so purposeless and set adrift, there were days she could scarce bring herself to rise from her bed, moments when she entertained the wicked thought of how much better it would be if some obliging illness would simply carry her off.

She could not help being fascinated by a man so stubborn, strong, and determined to survive. Even now Xavier slept with his uninjured arm flung above his head, his hand fisted as though he was still fighting.

Ariane moved deftly, immobilizing the broken arm between two slats, teaching Carole to secure the wooden splint with leather straps. Every lady should have some knowledge of how to treat illnesses and minor injuries in her household, but Ariane's knowledge went far beyond what Jane had been taught to consider proper and becoming in a woman.

All the same, she found herself listening hungrily as Ariane instructed Carole in the application of a dressing to the punctured flesh where the bone had pierced.

"With this kind of wound, it is better to use a poultice rather than stitches, far less chance of infection. You must apply the bandage snugly but not so tight it cuts off the blood flow."

Carole nodded, attempting to follow Ariane's directions. But she kept darting nervous glances at Xavier as though fearing he would awaken and roar at her. The girl was so clumsy that Jane itched to take over. She was relieved when Ariane did so.

"S-sorry," Carole said, her face nearly as pale as Xavier's. "It is just that—that we were obliged to hurt him so badly, Ariane."

"Often that is what is necessary to effect a cure."

"I know. But it is hard for me to watch anyone suffer so. I'll never be as good at this as you are."

"Yes, you will." Ariane glanced up from the bandage to offer her a reassuring smile. "Detachment is a skill that can be acquired like anything else. In any case, you no longer have to fret over Captain Xavier. He won't be feeling anything for quite a while."

Ariane gazed down at the sleeping man, Carole and Jane doing likewise. Xavier's fist had finally relaxed, his fingers slowly uncurling, his breath coming deep and even. He looked so peaceful while the three of them stood over him, wearied, their gowns sporting damp patches of sweat.

Ariane sighed and turned to Carole. "You had best get back to that rambunctious young son of yours. Jane and I can finish up here."

"Well, if you are sure . . ." Carole mopped her hand across her brow, making a show of reluctance. But as the girl hastened from the cottage, Jane thought she looked considerably relieved.

While Ariane packed vials and strips of linen back into her medicinal chest, Jane lingered by the bedside. Her fingers itched to smooth the damp tangles of hair from Xavier's brow. She buried her hand in the folds of her skirt to still the inexplicable urge.

"Do you think he will be all right now?" she asked.

"As long as infection does not set in. The poultice I applied should prevent that, but one never knows. However, if he takes no fever within the next forty-eight hours, I believe he may do well enough. He is young, strong. It will be a matter of keeping him still long enough to allow the bone to heal."

"After all he has been through, you don't think he would be rash enough to leap up and go haring off?"

"You have spent more time in the man's company than I have. What do you think?"

Jane studied the set of Xavier's jaw, truculent even in repose. "I think we had better tie him to the bed."

Ariane gave a dry laugh. "The draught will keep him quiet for a while, but someone will have to remain with him, keep checking for fever."

"I can do that. It would be good to feel useful for a change."

Jane became uncomfortably aware of Ariane's steady regard. A soft note crept into the woman's voice as she said, "You are of great use, Jane. I could never have managed today without you. Whether Captain Xavier knows it or not, he is greatly in your debt."

"Me? What did I do that was of such importance?"

"You soothed him, steadied him. I don't think he would have allowed me to touch his arm but for your persuasion. You won his trust. But I have observed that you have a gift for that."

"Likely because I seem so dull and meek."

"No, because you possess a quiet strength that radiates from your eyes. You are like the calm at the center of a storm."

Although Jane flushed at the compliment, she shook her head deprecatingly. "That is truer of you, especially when you work your healing magic."

"Usually mayhap, but in this instance my calm detachment was greatly tested. I am ashamed to admit how badly I wanted to march out of here and abandon this man to whatever devil was malevolent enough to cast him up on my island."

Ariane stared at the man on the bed as though he were a ghost risen up from her past and one she would be only too eager to exorcise.

Jane had borne quiet witness to the exchange between Ariane and Xavier, the undercurrents that she had only half-understood. She hated to ever intrude on another person's privacy. But Ariane looked so troubled, Jane could not refrain from asking, "Do you think Xavier really is your brother?"

"Half brother," Ariane corrected sharply. "I don't know. I don't want to believe it, but he is the image of my father. The likeness is rather unnerving. I see very little of that Maitland witch in him."

Ariane's mouth thinned. "You overheard enough, I am sure you must be wondering—"

"Oh, no, I am sorry. I should not have asked you anything. It is only that you looked so distressed, but I have no wish to pry into your family secrets."

"Unfortunately, it is not such a great secret. Everyone on this island is well aware of how my father betrayed my mother. This man's arrival will be sure to stir up all the old gossip. Far better you hear the truth from me."

Even as she said this, Ariane fell silent, looking reluctant to begin. She strode over to the window, the shutters flung wide open.

Jane had always thought that any illness, any injury, was best treated in a closed chamber, all noxious airs kept at bay. That was the established practice among London physicians.

But the Lady of Faire Isle was a firm believer in the benefit of fresh air. Considering the healing miracles Jane had observed the lady perform, Jane had come to believe that Ariane was right and all those learned English doctors wrong.

As though the Lady sought healing for her own troubled spirit, she lifted her face, the salty breeze stirring the tendrils of her hair.

"I suppose most of the world would consider infidelity no great matter," she said. "Many noblemen take mistresses, sire illegitimate children. It is the common way of things more often than not, a man's prerogative. After all, marriage is reckoned as nothing more than a matter of convenience, a way of aggrandizing estates or continuing bloodlines.

"But to those of us who consider ourselves daughters of the earth, marriage is supposed to be something more, a sacred rite, a profound union. Not for profit or position or even security. A man and woman should wed only for the truest love."

Ariane's gaze dropped to the ring encircling her finger, a plain metal band, very old and engraved with strange markings. Her face softened and it was obvious she was thinking of her husband.

Anyone who saw Ariane and Justice Deauville together could not doubt the depth of their love, passion tempered by the stronger more enduring steel of friendship.

Jane rubbed the spot on her left hand where her own wedding ring had once been, a costly golden circle of rubies and diamonds. She had seldom worn it, and put the ring away altogether after her second husband had died. A wealthy wine merchant, Sir William Danvers had been a kindly man but thirty-five years her senior. She'd learned to esteem him, but there was no denying that the prime reason for her marriage had been to salvage her family's waning fortunes.

Her first husband, Richard Arkwright, had not been as pleasant as Sir William. Dickon was a sickly, peevish boy, but as her guardian had acidly informed her, a young woman who was despoiled could not afford to be selective. A boy as young and inexperienced as Dickon could easily be fooled, unlikely to notice on his wedding night that his bride was not all that she should be.

Two marriages, one to cover her sins and one for wealth and security. Most of the world would not fault her for either reason. But as Jane observed the glow on Ariane's face, she experienced a stab of shame and envy.

But the light in Ariane's eyes dimmed as she folded her hands together and resumed her tale.

"My mother adored my father as he did her. Or so we all believed. Their love story was the stuff of legends; Evangeline, the beautiful and learned Lady of Faire Isle, and the Chevalier Louis Xavier Cheney, one of the boldest and bravest knights in all of France. Their wedding was a splendid event, their marriage much celebrated. A *conte de fée* come true."

"But like any fairy tale, there must always be a villain, an ogre or a bad fairy or a wicked witch. And my mother had hers close at hand. When she was young, my mother was intimate friends with Catherine de Medici."

Jane gaped at her. "The Dowager Queen of France? The woman that Meg refers to as the Dark Queen?"

"That is one of our politer terms for the woman, but yes," Ariane replied with a taut smile. "Well may you be surprised and perhaps wonder at my mother's lapse of judgment."

Jane tried to demur but feared her shock must be all too evident.

"I don't blame you for being astonished," Ariane said. "But believe it or not, Catherine and my mother had much in common. Neither of them was comfortable at the French court, Maman simply because she hated all the falsity of court life. Catherine because she was despised by the French people, scorned and mistrusted for her Italian lineage.

"And my mother and Catherine shared a strong interest in all the ancient lore and knowledge. It was natural they be drawn to each other. But my mother was a true daughter of the earth, studying the old ways in order to promote peace and healing. Whereas Catherine had a darkness in her, an insatiable craving for power and a ruthlessness to match. Their falling out was as inevitable as their friendship had been.

"Whatever affection or admiration Catherine might have felt for my mother soured into hatred and envy until she considered Maman her enemy. When she decided to strike against my mother, of course being Catherine, she homed straight in on Maman's most vulnerable spot. Her great love for my father."

Ariane twisted her head to regard Jane. "Have you ever been to the French court?"

No, that had been more to Ned's taste, Jane nearly replied. Her pleasure-loving, ambitious brother had made frequent trips to Paris whenever he could find a valid excuse to obtain a visa.

But thoughts of Ned threatened to unleash a hail of Jane's own unhappy memories, so she merely shook her head and said, "I am like your mother; the glitter of court life has never held any attraction for me."

"You are the wiser and better for it. Likely then you don't know about Queen Catherine's *Escadron Volant.*"

Jane frowned, translating into English. "Her *flying squadron*?"

"Precisely. Beautiful birds of prey, a cadre of seductive young women. Catherine employs them to spy, to seduce and weaken her enemies. She set the most skilled of these creatures, Marguerite de Maitland, to work her wiles upon my father."

Jane cut an uncertain glance toward the man on the bed. "You mean Xavier's mother?"

"So he claims. Marguerite was a dazzling beauty, irresistible by all accounts. Still my father should never have succumbed to her charms, not if he had truly loved Maman.

"He hurt my mother so deeply. She might not have been as devastated if it had been a onetime lapse. But the affair went on and on, Papa absenting himself to Paris more frequently. He nearly bankrupted our family setting that Maitland woman up in her own establishment, showering her with money and jewels.

"Not that my mother cared about that, it was Papa's frequent absences, the betrayal of their love that nigh killed her. Catherine's scheme for revenge might not have succeeded in breaking my mother's spirit, but she certainly broke her heart. She shattered the peace and happiness of our entire family."

Ariane's voice shook with anger. She drew in a deep breath before continuing in a bleaker tone. "I never understood it, Jane. If you could have but known my mother. She was a truly remarkable woman. All who knew her adored her.

"Even if Marguerite was enhanced with all the seductive perfumes and cosmetics Catherine concocted for her sirens, I could not fathom what spell that Maitland witch could have cast to keep such a strong hold on my father, to lure him away from us.

"It appears the great mystery is explained at last." Ariane swallowed, her bitter gaze focusing on Xavier. "There lies Marguerite's magic. The son my mother was never able to give my father. I am only astonished Papa could have kept him secret all these years. I am sure Catherine never knew of Xavier, because if she had, it would have been one more stake to drive into my mother's heart."

Ariane stared at Xavier, her calm features set into hard, angry lines, an alarming expression most unlike the Lady of Faire Isle. Jane suppressed a strange urge to step protectively in front of the sleeping man.

Instead, she rested her hand upon Ariane's arm. "I can understand your resentment, but whatever your father or this Maitland woman did, surely your brother cannot be held to blame."

"Half brother," Ariane insisted. "I daresay he may be guilty of enough sins of his own. I pride myself on my skill in reading eyes, but this Xavier is infernally good at protecting his thoughts even when half out of his mind with pain. Surely not the behavior of an innocent man. He strikes me as rather a hardened and dangerous character."

"Meg said nearly the same thing."

"What!" Ariane exclaimed so sharply that Xavier stirred even in his potion-induced sleep. Lowering her voice, she demanded, "What do you mean? What did Meg say?"

Jane already regretted mentioning the matter, but with Ariane's fierce gaze trained upon her, she had no choice but to explain.

"Meg reacted most strangely to the sight of Captain Xavier. She didn't even want me to help him; just let him be swept back out to sea."

"That is very odd behavior for Meg. She is usually quite tenderhearted unless—" Ariane scowled. "She has not been meddling with that crystal again, has she?"

Jane was loath to bear tales against Meg. Ariane was still weighing her decision over who would succeed her as the next Lady of Faire Isle and Jane had no wish to damage Meg's chances. But neither could Jane bring herself to lie.

"I believe Meg may still have the gazing globe in her possession."

The Lady was not fooled by Jane's hedging. She vented an exasperated sigh. "I wish the girl would leave the cursed crystal alone, though I do understand the temptation all too well. I have experienced the lure of the shadow world myself. But no good can come of such an obsession."

"Can you not command Meg to surrender the crystal or destroy it?"

"I could, but that would ultimately do Meg little good. The choice between light and darkness cannot be forced upon anyone. I can offer her my advice and guidance, but a young woman must learn at some point to employ her own reason, to make her own decisions."

"Oh," was all Jane could think to reply. For most of her life she had been accustomed to being told what to think, what to believe, what to do. She was not sure whether she was disconcerted by Ariane Deauville's revolutionary views or intrigued by them.

"Did Meg give any specific reason for why she shrank from helping this man?" Ariane asked.

"Nothing logical. She merely said that Xavier is dangerous, that he will bring only trouble."

Ariane pursed her lips. "Meg could well be right. Where has the man been keeping himself all these years and why now did he suddenly decide to turn up on my island?"

Jane did not believe that Xavier had decided anything, that he had been no more pleased to wash up on Faire Isle than Ariane was to have him. But since the Lady did not appear in a particularly reasonable mood at the moment, Jane kept these reflections to herself.

As she retrieved her medical chest, Ariane commanded, "Keep an eye on him, Jane. If you notice anything at all amiss with the man, send for me at once."

Jane nodded uneasily, realizing that Ariane was talking

about far more than signs of fever. After Ariane had gone, Jane hovered by the foot of the bed, regarding her charge for a long time.

She had always been so cautious of strangers or admitting anyone new to her acquaintance that her brother had frequently teased her about it.

"Jane even requires the rabbits to furnish a written character before they are allowed to enter the garden," Ned was wont to laugh.

Jane smiled sadly at the memory. Perhaps Ned was right and she had learned to be overcautious. But she had learned at a tender age how easily a woman's trust could be betrayed, especially by a man.

She certainly ought to be ill at ease, keeping watch over a stranger who made both Meg and the wise Lady of Faire Isle so wary. Jane would have been hard-pressed to explain why she wasn't nervous at being left alone with Xavier or the strange, almost proprietary interest she took in the man.

Perhaps it was because she had been the one to mount guard over him and shield him from the incoming tide. She was the one whose hand was bruised from his pain-wracked grip, the only one who appeared to have noted the fear beneath his sarcasm and cursing.

Xavier stirred and shivered in his sleep, and Jane hastened to draw the coverlet higher over his bared chest. Very likely she was a fool, she thought. But as he lay there so pale, and helpless, he did not appear dangerous to her.

Louis Xavier Cheney merely looked lost.

ARIANE PERCHED ON A ROCK, STILL WARMED BY THE AFTERnoon's sun. Her knees drawn up to her chin, she watched her son playing on a nearby sand dune. His chubby legs churned, his curly head thrust forward as he toddled away from his cousins, Gabrielle's two youngest girls.

Lucia and Ninon overtook Leon, each girl capturing a hand. He lifted his legs, swinging between them and squealing with delight. Seraphine hovered nearby, grinning as she kept a watchful eye over the children.

Gabrielle's eldest daughter could be arrogant and intractable at times, but Seraphine had a more tender side and was fiercely protective of those she loved.

They presented an enchanting tableau, Gabby's willowy, fair-haired daughters and Ariane's sturdy little son. Even as she smiled, Ariane's eyes misted as she thought of what it must have cost Gabrielle to send her daughters away, out of war-torn Navarre.

"You'll keep them safe, Ari," Gabrielle had written, the words not a question or a command on Gabrielle's part, just a soul-deep understanding and trust between sisters.

"I will," Ariane had written in return, although she knew such a pledge was unnecessary and perhaps even a little rash.

She had experienced enough of the uncertainties of life to know how disaster could strike in a heartbeat, despite all one's best intentions and vigilance. But for this day in time, her nieces and her son were hale, happy, and safe.

Normally, Ariane would have savored such a golden moment, but Xavier's arrival had cast a shadow over her.

She hugged her knees close to her, wishing it was her husband's strong, reassuring arms she felt closing about her.

Justice Deauville had once been the Comte de Renard, but his marriage to Ariane had cost him, his title stripped away by Catherine's vengeful son when King Henry had mounted an assault against Faire Isle. Justice's estates were the price he had paid for daring to love a woman suspected of being a witch.

Ariane had been more distressed for his loss than Justice was himself. A man of the earth, his tastes and needs were simple, a field to sow, some books to read, a good strong horse, and Ariane to draw close to his heart each night as he fell asleep.

Only with the birth of their son did Justice's ambitions stir, a natural fatherly urge to provide Leon with a secure inheritance. He had begun making journeys to the mainland, seeking opportunities, investing in sea voyages and merchant's caravans. At the moment, he was traveling to the great fair at Tours and Ariane missed him dreadfully.

She twisted the metal band on her finger, the ancient ring whose mystic powers she had never fully understood. But she knew all she had to do was press the ring close to the region of her heart and she would be linked to Justice despite all the miles between them.

One breath, one thought would be all it would take. *"Justice, I need you."* And wherever he was, whatever he was doing, her husband would come racing back home to her.

But exhaust and alarm him for what reason? Merely because a stranger had washed up on the island and reopened wounds Ariane had thought long healed?

Words that her mother had spoken to her so long ago echoed through Ariane's mind.

"All I wanted was the peace of my island, my girls. I knew that that was not enough excitement for your papa. I should have spent more time in Paris with him, kept him from temptation. Louis was never as strong as I, something that I always realized and accepted. It did nothing to diminish my love for him and that is why I was able to forgive him. You need to forgive your father, too, child."

Ariane honestly believed she had done so until the shock of discovering she had a half brother had brought all the old hurt rushing back again.

Ariane sighed, resting her chin on her knees. As if she did not already have enough to deal with, deciding whom to name as her successor as Lady of Faire Isle. *"Ah, you are yet too young to be fretting over such a thing,"* Justice had told her before he had left on his journey. But her brave, strapping husband had ever flinched from facing the prospect of her death.

Ariane was not eager to embrace the thought herself, but she had to be practical. She knew all too well how swiftly illness or a tragic accident could strike down the heartiest person. *Now* when she was at the peak of her strength and mental powers was the perfect time to choose her successor. There was so much training to do, so much knowledge Ariane had to impart and the other daughters of the earth would need time to accustom themselves and accept her choice. She had narrowed her selection to three, their names a constant litany in her mind. Meg, Seraphine, or Carole. Meg, Seraphine, or Carole.

The council was less than a week away, and Ariane still

had no idea what her choice should be. Many would regard it as a trivial thing. The title of Lady of Faire Isle was not an official one, sanctioned by any kingdom or law.

No, only sanctioned by a custom much older and deeper than any present government. The last rite of an ancient order that had been fading for some time.

Ariane had often felt unequal to preserving the ancient role of the Lady of Faire Isle. She had succeeded in reviving the council meetings upon the cliffs for a time only to have the island torn asunder by witch-hunters, Ariane herself driven into exile.

She had tried to delude herself into believing the island had healed. But as she gazed at the women strolling and gossiping in the fading sunlight, she could not help seeing how small this gathering was, how very few there were compared to that long ago day when she had been designated her mother's successor. So many of those wise women gone now. Her mother, even her great friend, Marie Claire.

A tug at her sleeve drew Ariane from these melancholy thoughts.

"Milady. Your sister has arrived."

Ariane stood eagerly. There was no prospect of Gabrielle making the long journey from Navarre at such a dire time. But Ariane had happily anticipated Miribelle's arrival from her farm just outside of Paris. Her joy at seeing her youngest sister was now tempered by the sobering prospect of what she was going to have to tell Miri.

Worldly Gabrielle had always taken a more prosaic view of their father's indiscretion. But Miri had been closest to Papa, all but idolizing the man. Ariane dreaded telling her about Xavier.

Shading her eyes, Ariane watched Miri dismount. The greetings of the other women were respectful, but restrained in a way that pained Ariane to observe.

Miri had committed the greatest sin any daughter of earth could. She had married a witch-hunter. Simon Aristide had renounced his profession and done his best to make amends for the past, but he would always be remembered as the man who had once led the raids against Faire Isle. Miri was no longer regarded as the beloved youngest child of Evangeline. She was now Madame Aristide.

If the lack of warmth saddened Miri, she gave no sign of it. Ariane could not be sure her sister even noticed. A bit fey, Miri ever lived in her own world, more comfortable with creatures who walked on four legs instead of two.

The coldness of the women may have been lost in the joyous greeting Miri received from two Irish wolfhounds, their owner having great difficulty in calling them back.

Spying Ariane, Miri beamed and headed in her direction. Ariane flew to meet her halfway, clasping her in her arms.

"Miri, it has been far too long. Welcome home, my dear."

"It feels like an age since I have been to Faire Isle, longer still since I have been to the far side of the island." Miri trained her gaze wistfully toward the distant cliffs. "Remember how it used to be my favorite part of the year, when we would all make the journey up to the cliffs of Argot to pay homage to the lady giants."

"There is no reason we could not revive the old custom, make it just like the old days."

Miri smiled, but shook her head. "No, we couldn't. Whether we wish it or not, things change. It is the way of life. Faire Isle is no longer my home."

"Miri—"

"It is all right, Ariane. I have no regrets about the path I chose. I am quite content on my little farm on the mainland. I love my husband and he adores me. I have been blessed with a beautiful daughter and now another child on the way."

"Miri! Oh, my dearest, you should not have traveled all this way."

"I am fine. It is early days as yet. No physician or midwife could even detect the babe, not even a healer as skilled as you. But I know he is there." Miri caressed her abdomen. "I can sense him, blooming into life beneath my heart."

"Him?"

"Were you not able to sense that you were carrying a boy long before Leon was born? Speaking of my nephew, is that him?"

Ariane nodded proudly.

"And those must be Gabby's youngest girls. Oh, how they have all grown."

Ariane linked her arm about Miri's waist as they strolled toward the children.

"I am so looking forward to becoming reacquainted with everyone," Miri said. "But first you must tell me all about *him.*"

"Leon. Well, he—"

"No, I mean the stranger you are struggling to find a way to mention."

Ariane froze, peering down at her sister. "I always thought you were better at reading animals' eyes than humans'."

"I still am. But I know you all too well, my protective older sister. And I have been barraged by a full measure of gossip ever since I landed on the island. The speculation has already spread as far as Port Corsair."

Ariane grimaced. Of course. She should have guessed as much.

"Is he really so like Papa?" Miri asked.

"In appearance at least."

"And what is his name?"

"Apparently that Maitland witch presumed to name him Louis Xavier Cheney, but he goes by Captain Xavier. Much more than that, I cannot tell you. He guards his thoughts well, but he all but flung his origins in my face. He is Marguerite de Maitland's bastard."

"And our father's son." An awed expression crept over Miri's face. "So we have a brother, Ariane."

Ariane frowned. This was not at all the reaction she had expected from her sister.

"You do realize what this means, Miri. Father's affair went on longer than any of us ever dreamed, perhaps even Maman. If I were to guess at this Xavier's age, I would wager that he is not much younger than you."

Miri shrugged. "Is the duration of the liaison of that much consequence? It is all in the past now, Ariane. And

Maman forgave Papa before she died. I thought you had, too."

"Forgiving is one thing, but it is not as easy to forget. It will be even more difficult with this Xavier as a living reminder."

"Might he not prove a blessing? As though part of our father had been returned to us."

"He may look like Papa, but there the resemblance ends. Our father was charming, polished, every inch the gentleman. Xavier is rough-hewn and rough-tongued. He swears like—like a sailor."

"Perhaps because that is what he is," Miri replied with a smile. "If he voyaged with Papa to Brazil, think of the stories he can tell us, the questions he can answer about Papa's final days. He is our brother, Ariane. Can we not give him a chance?"

"Half brother," Ariane insisted, although her voice no longer carried the same conviction as before. Miri's generous attitude made her feel a trifle ashamed. "I am not sure that Xavier wants any chances. He did not seem to be more pleased with making my acquaintance than I was his."

"Well, if you had been wrenching my broken arm about and pouring vile draughts down my throat, I would not have been so delighted with you either." Her sister replied so reasonably, Ariane was forced to laugh in spite of herself.

She gave Miri another hug. "Oh, Miri. It is so good to have you here."

Miri beamed up at her, then immediately sobered. "I hope you will think so even though I bring more tidings to make you uneasy. As you know, Simon still has contacts in Paris. He has been attempting to keep an eye on Catherine as you requested."

"Now what is that vile woman up to?"

"Nothing terribly sinister. At least I hope not. There were rumors that last autumn, Catherine was consulting a seer."

"Bah." Ariane gave a contemptuous shrug. "She always had an interest in astrology. Maman never set much store by such things."

"This man may have been more than an astrologer. It is rumored that he was some sort of necromancer as well and he had Catherine completely enthralled."

Ariane's brows arched in surprise at the notion of the ruthless Dark Queen susceptible to anyone's charms, least of all any man's. "She must be losing her wits in her dotage."

"Perhaps, but this mysterious magician has not been seen in many months. He just simply vanished."

"People who get too close to the Dark Queen often do."

"Simon worries that Catherine may have sent this man on some sort of mission."

Ariane tensed, realizing what her sister was implying. "You think Catherine is still searching for Meg and the *Book of Shadows*?"

"I don't know." Miri frowned, looking as troubled as Ariane felt. "The coven of the Silver Rose did threaten Catherine's throne. Unlike our Maman, the Dark Queen does not forgive or forget. Do you think it likely she has ever stopped thinking of Meg?"

"No, but I hoped her other problems with the duc de

Guise would keep her preoccupied. I have assured Meg again and again that she is safe on Faire Isle. I hate to frighten the child."

"There is no need to do so until Simon finds out more about this vanished wizard."

Ariane nodded. The sun dipped lower on the horizon, spreading its golden light across the waves. The summer's day that had begun with such fair promise appeared to be ending the same way. But to Ariane there might as well have been another storm brewing.

Chapter Nine

THE CAVALCADE MADE ITS WAY THROUGH THE STREETS, A contingent of guards leading a horse-drawn litter. Heavy curtains shielded the Dowager Queen from sullen eyes as she was borne from the Hôtel de la Reine to the Louvre. The air was thick with dark mutterings of resentment as Parisians scattered out of the way.

Inside the stifling litter, the hum of angry voices was as distant to Catherine as the drone of bees. Despite her best efforts, her head bobbed, her chin coming to rest upon her chest, her eyes drooping closed. Suddenly she was no longer a fat old woman, her aching bones being jarred by the bumping of the litter. She was gloriously young again.

Catherine tore across the hunting field, her spirited gelding's legs throwing up clods of grass and turf. She leaned for-

ward in the saddle, gripping the reins, feeling the glorious rush of wind through her hair, her heart swelling with pride, the consciousness of being the finest horsewoman in all of France. Surely the eyes of the entire court must be upon her.

Except that they were not. All gazes were trained upon her royal husband Henry cantering beside Diane de Poitiers, the Duchesse de Valentinois. Henry bent toward the dark-haired beauty, exchanging some private jest with his beloved mistress that caused Diane to throw back her head and laugh.

Catherine reined in, shouting, "No, Henry, turn away from her. Look at me!"

Her plea went unheard. She might as well have been invisible. The entire court buzzed about Diane as though she were the true queen of France.

But suddenly the arrogant woman's smile fled. Clutching her throat, Diane tumbled from her horse, sprawling into the dirt where she belonged. Catherine watched with satisfaction as the duchess writhed with spasms, Catherine's poison racing through her veins.

It would not be long now. Nothing and no one could save the haughty duchess. Catherine urged her mount forward, eager to observe the end. But as she drew closer, she saw someone bending over Diane's prostrate form.

Evangeline. Catherine's dearest friend, using her healing magic to revive Catherine's hated rival.

"No!"

But her voice carried no more force than before. A heavy mist crept over the scene, her husband, Diane, the other courtiers vanishing before her eyes.

Catherine found herself afoot, alone in the middle of the field, trembling with grief and rage.

"I did it for you as well. You know that, Catherine." Evangeline's quiet voice echoed from somewhere behind Catherine.

She spun about to glare at her erstwhile friend. "You betrayed me."

"No, I saved you. You already were acquiring a reputation as a witch, an Italian skilled in poisons. If Diane had died, you would have been the first one suspected and I feared not even your position as queen could have saved you from the king's wrath. To say nothing of the damage to your soul. Daughters of the earth were meant—"

"To heal, not to harm. Oh, yes, I have heard it all before from you," Catherine sneered. "You were always so concerned about being the noble Lady of Faire Isle; you forgot what it was like to feel the pain of a mere woman devastated by her husband's infidelity. But I taught you what that was like, didn't I, my dear Evangeline?"

"Yes, you did," Evangeline agreed sadly. "But I forgave you."

"Damn your forgiveness. I never wanted it." Catherine spun away from her, muttering. "What does any of it matter anymore? Henry and his whore are both long dead. So are you."

"As you will be soon."

Catherine shivered and shook her head in fierce denial.

"You must not be so frightened of death, Catherine. It is natural—"

"Don't give me any more of your mystic nonsense

about the cycles of life and returning my bones to our mother earth, my spirit at peace. I don't want your cursed peace."

"Yes, you do, Catherine." Evangeline's hand came to rest gently on her shoulder. "And there is still time for you to find it. Turn away from the darkness and become the queen you always wanted to be."

"And just how am I supposed to do that? I am too old, too worn down. It is too late." Despite her agonized protest, she groped for Evangeline's hand, only to close upon air.

The litter came to an abrupt halt, jarring Catherine awake. She blinked as she regained her surroundings and realized her mouth was hanging agape. She wiped the drool from her chin, disgusted with herself for nodding off in the middle of the day like any pathetic old woman.

But she had not been sleeping well of late, her dreams haunted by the ghosts of her past, sometimes her dead husband and his mistress, sometimes her dead children, sometimes all the bloodied, accusing faces of the Huguenots she'd had massacred that long ago St. Bartholomew's Eve.

But mostly it was Evangeline who stalked her dreams, like some nagging angel, urging Catherine toward peace, the eternal rest she so dreaded. Perhaps it was that more than anything else that disturbed Catherine's slumber, the fear if she closed her eyes, this might be the time she never awakened.

She straightened her ermine collar, composing herself as her retainers came to help her from the litter. Pain lanced through her body as she stepped down, the boning in her bodice creaking in protest, or maybe it was her knees.

The ache in her joints was all but unbearable these days

and she had no longer a drop of Xavier's magic elixir to ease her pain. When she had consumed the last of the potion in January, a great depression of spirits had settled over her. The past winter had been a succession of gray miserable days without the handsome rogue about to charm her with the bold color of his tales. Or the sight of his hard-muscled body swaying to the pulse beat of the drum as Xavier sunk deeper into his mystical trance.

He had been absent from her court for months now, more than enough time to complete his mission by her reckoning. She feared that she had been the one put into a trance, mesmerized into believing she had found a true necromancer at last. Likely he had betrayed her like so many others she had trusted before.

Or perhaps Xavier had tried to abduct Megaera and the present Lady of Faire Isle had proved too much even for a corsair as bold as Xavier. Ariane was not the saint her mother had been. If she had taken Megaera under her protection, Catherine imagined that Ariane could wax quite ruthless in the girl's defense. Ariane had even had the temerity to threaten Catherine once in her own apartments in the Louvre.

The Louvre . . . the white walls of the palace rose up before Catherine, the glazed windows gleaming in the sunlight, flooding her with memories.

As a young woman, she had loved dancing as much as riding. Oh, the fetes, the pageants, the masked balls she had helped plan. But as Catherine crossed the courtyard, these memories were dimmed by others less pleasant.

Her gaze dropped to the paving stones. Nearly sixteen years had passed, the courtyard had been scoured countless times, and still Catherine fancied she could see the bloodstains from that hot August night.

St. Bartholomew's Eve, the night Catherine had woven a dark magic, provoking her mad son, Charles, to order the massacre of the Huguenots gathered in Paris, men, women, and children alike. She was not a cruel woman, Catherine assured herself, only a pragmatic one.

The Huguenots had become such a threat to her power, to the stability of France itself, they needed to be dealt with once and for all. But the violence had gone beyond even what Catherine had intended, the mobs of Paris rampaging out of control for nearly three days, blood spilling and the corpses piling up even in the courtyard of the Louvre itself.

And all for what? Catherine reflected bleakly. The massacre had achieved nothing but the making of martyrs. The new religion continued to spread like the plague, the civil war waging on, draining the royal treasury and swelling the power and popularity of the opportunistic duc de Guise as he championed the Catholic cause.

Catherine swayed slightly on her feet, suddenly feeling so wearied of it all. Her glance flickered wistfully toward the cool green of the gardens and the soft burbling fountains and she longed to lose herself in the winding paths.

She had designed those gardens, along with the new wing of the palace, incorporating much of the dazzling architecture of her Italian homeland. She had done the same for Chenonceau and many other of the royal residences.

So much beauty she had brought to France and she feared she would be remembered for none of it. Only for the bloodstains in this courtyard.

"Turn away from the darkness, Catherine." Evange-

line's voice whispered through her mind. "Become the queen you always wanted to be."

Impossible. Not while she was this weak and worn down, but if she could but recover some of her youthful strength and power . . . Her one hope was laying her hands upon Megaera, wringing from that wretched girl the secrets of the *Book of Shadows.*

"Xavier, don't fail me." Catherine breathed the silent prayer that had sustained her all these months as she followed her escort into the Louvre.

The main salon was crowded as it too often was these days, thronged with disgruntled petitioners and disenchanted courtiers. The king's chair as usual remained empty. The crowd would have swarmed Catherine with their pleas and complaints had not her guards held them at bay.

Steeling herself against each pain-wracked footfall, Catherine trudged up the sweeping stair to the second floor, her breath coming in short gasps. She felt as weighted down by disappointment as by her voluminous black silk skirts.

So her son was still neglecting the affairs of his kingdom, making more enemies he could not afford. Catherine had urged Henry until her voice was hoarse, begging the king to make himself more accessible to his subjects.

Henry had even eschewed the royal custom of dining in public, retreating more and more to his private apartments while his kingdom slipped away into the hands of the duc de Guise.

Henry had always been more headstrong than her other sons, but there had been a time when Catherine could reason with him. Now her voice went as unheard as when she cried out in her dreams. Even those rare times when they still worked together on correspondence, she and Henry sat at separate desks in the council chamber, scarce addressing a word to each other the entire day.

As Catherine approached her son's private apartments, she wondered with dread which version of Henry she would encounter today. The one who liked to paint his face and dress like a woman in violet silk trimmed with red ribbons. Or the one who donned a monk's robes and sang the Miserere, flagellating himself to the point of ecstasy.

When Catherine was admitted to the royal antechamber, she found neither. The king was clad in black velvet, his doublet embroidered with silver death's-heads. Tiny silk skulls adorned his shoes as he paced the room like an edgy wolf.

As she noted the hectic flush on Henry's cheeks, the agitated gestures of his hands, Catherine's heart sank. She felt she almost would have preferred the rouged and perfumed Henry in his violet gown.

"The Dowager Queen, Your Grace."

As Catherine was announced, she winced, forcing her knees into a stiff curtsy. The king came to an abrupt halt, sunlight from the tall latticed windows spilling across his face, revealing every deep carved line.

How old and thin he looked for a man of only seven and thirty years, Catherine thought in dismay, this remaining son who was all that stood between her and oblivion.

A woman who had given birth to four sons should never have had to feel this tug of fear. But her oldest, Francis, had been a sickly youth, the next in line, Charles, both sickly and insane. Neither had held the crown for long. Her youngest, Hercules, had lived but long enough to prove a nuisance, envious of his older brothers, forever scheming and plotting rebellion.

It had been to Henry that Catherine had looked to secure her dynasty and power in France. By far the favorite of her children, Henry was most like her with his sallow Italian looks and ruthless cunning. But years of dissipation had taken their toll.

Concealing her dismay behind a smile, Catherine extended both hands to him. "My son."

"Madam," Henry replied, coldly ignoring her outstretched arms.

Catherine dropped her hands awkwardly back to her side. "I trust I find Your Grace well."

"Well enough for one whose heart was nearly cut to the quick by an assassin's blade."

"Henry!" Catherine's breath left her in a rush of alarm. "You were attacked? You have been harmed?" She closed in on him, running her hands anxiously over the front of his doublet.

Henry impatiently stilled her roving fingers. "Not me, my beloved friend, D'Epernon."

"He is dead?"

"No, he managed to defend himself. The blade only pierced his arm."

"Oh, thank the bon Dieu," Catherine murmured, but she had to lower her gaze to conceal her disappointment. D'Epernon was one of Henry's foppish friends, those painted mignons whose presence at court only further blackened her son's reputation and whose greed was a constant drain upon the royal treasury. D'Epernon's death would have been no great loss in Catherine's eyes. Indeed, she would have accounted it a blessing.

But she managed to summon up a commiserating tone. "Poor D'Epernon. It is most unfortunate. Paris has become such a dangerous place, rogues and cutpurses to be found in every quarter."

"This was not the work of any common thief, but an attack of a skilled assassin."

The man could not have been all that skilled or he would have succeeded, Catherine was tempted to point out dryly, but she could tell from her son's flushed features that Henry was in a dangerous mood.

The king prowled the antechamber, his hands clenched into fists. "I have no doubt who sent this assassin. The insidious hand of the duc de Guise is behind this attack on my dear friend."

"You have proof of that?" Catherine asked.

Henry paused in mid step to glower at her. "No, the villain who attacked mon cher ami escaped, but I will have him hunted down and tortured until he confesses who hired him.

"Not that I require any confession. Who else besides de Guise could be behind such a thing? The bastard is determined to destroy all those I love, to break my spirit, and destroy my sanity. Whittling away at my kingdom, my honor, my reputation."

Henry's voice rose higher with every word. He snatched up a piece of parchment from his desk and thrust it under Catherine's nose.

"Just look at this scurrilous pamphlet they have been circulating in the streets."

Catherine reared back, her vision blurring as she squinted at the paper, but without the special lenses manufactured for her by her Italian glassmakers, she had no hope of deciphering the words on the page.

Henry snatched it back and read aloud in a voice quivering with rage. "A true account of the military exploits of our dread lord King Henry III of France."

He opened the pamphlet and spat out the single word engraved on the next page.

"Rien."

"Nothing," Henry all but roared. "They accuse me of accomplishing nothing, my victories at Moncontour and Poitiers long forgotten while all glory and praise go to de Guise."

"Henry, I have told you so often. Ignore these ridiculous pamphlets. I could shelve an entire library with the nonsense that has been written about me. This is nothing but the work of some foolish—"

"It is the work of that damned de Guise." The king rent the pamphlet in two, flung it down, grinding the pieces beneath his shoe. "He incites the people of Paris to mock me at every turn. Have you heard what they are calling me? The King of the Island of Hermaphrodites."

Then you might be wise to burn your gowns and petticoats, Catherine reflected. Once she would have dared voice the thought aloud, but there was a growing violence in her son that rendered her wary. His eyes glittered in a way that reminded her uneasily of her second son.

Catherine had often had to brew potions to calm Charles and hold his mad fits at bay. But it had been a long time since Catherine had visited her secret workshop. Failing eyesight, unsteady hands, and a faulty memory made it dangerous to attempt to concoct anything.

But it scarce mattered. Henry would not have taken anything brewed by Catherine. Her son had grown increasingly suspicious and mistrustful of everyone, most particularly his mother.

All Catherine could do was attempt to reason with him, but when she rested her hand upon his arm, he shook her off, crying. "I know naught how much more of this torment I can bear. Pain turns to rage when one is wounded too often. Let de Guise not try me too far. I would confer all the riches and titles of my kingdom on whoever would rid me of the villain."

"Oh, hush, my son." Catherine cast a nervous glance at the guards and servitors within earshot. She longed to clap her hand over Henry's mouth, but knew he would never stand such an affront to his dignity.

Instead she managed to catch one of his hands between hers. "Do not say such reckless things lest you be taken seriously. Have you forgotten how Henry II of England set into motion the murder of the archbishop Thomas Becket with one careless remark? All he succeeded in doing was making a martyr of his enemy."

"At least that Henry rid himself of an overmighty subject."

"And nearly got himself excommunicated."

"What do I care for that?" Henry replied sullenly. "I'd forfeit my soul to be rid of de Guise."

"No, what you will forfeit is your kingdom. Touch one hair on de Guise's head and all of Paris will rise in rebellion."

"Then let them." Henry wrenched free of her grasp. "I

would not be having all this trouble with de Guise if you had ever dealt with him as you should have."

Catherine compressed her lips to suppress a bitter retort as she thought of the swollen joints, the blinding headaches, and the exhaustion she had endured, dragging herself to countless negotiations with the duke and his Catholic League while her son sulked and wallowed in his bed.

"I have done my best to mediate with de Guise," she said stiffly.

"Mediate. The mother I remember would have done more than mediate." At least Henry still retained enough sense to lower his voice and lean closer as he whispered. "She would have brewed up something in her secret workroom to take care of Monsieur de Guise. Old age has made a coward of you, Maman."

"No, it has given me wisdom. Destroy the duke and you will bring about our ruin, Henry. You must be patient."

"God's teeth, I am tired of you telling me that. While I bide my time, de Guise will march on Paris one of these days and have me murdered in my bed. I should have him declared a criminal, and march the Swiss Guard into Paris to—"

"Henry." Catherine groaned. "Are you trying to start a revolution? All the presence of the Guard will do is anger the Parisians and provoke de Guise into doing something rash."

"Then let him be provoked."

"The man has grown powerful. He has far more dangerous allies than the people of Paris."

"I am aware of that, madam. The villain has been working with the King of Spain, forming alliances behind my back as though de Guise represented France, not me. Proclaiming himself Defender of the True Faith. That ought to be me."

Henry thumped his chest, angry tears starting to fill his eyes. "I am a good and pious Catholic and yet I am obliged to sign defensive treaties with that heretic queen in England."

"That is merely pragmatic policy, my son. Elizabeth is a good ally, necessary to preserve the balance of power."

Henry shook his head, his shoulders sagging. "I am just so weary of all of it, Maman. Sometimes I fear we are lost whatever I do."

"Don't say that, mon ange." Catherine reached up to cup his face between her hands. "As long as you remain king of France, there is still hope. But we must keep faith, especially with each other."

Henry shied away from her. "Why? When you do nothing but cause me more trouble."

"Me? I have done nothing."

"Not you directly, perhaps. But that pirate of yours has been stirring up mischief."

When Catherine gaped at him, a sly look stole into Henry's eyes. "I still have my spies about, Maman. You didn't think I knew about the tame jungle cat you were wont to entertain at the Hôtel de la Reine? Your precious Alexander?"

"Xavier," Catherine corrected in an unsteady voice. "What—what has he done?"

"According to the Spanish ambassador, he has been interfering with Spanish shipping again. He laid waste to a merchant vessel off the coast of Florida."

"When?"

"Sometime last winter or early this spring."

Catherine was obliged to turn away to conceal the depth of her dismay. So Xavier had never voyaged to Faire Isle as he had pledged to do. He had taken her purse and sailed back to the Spanish Main, no doubt sharing a good laugh with his crew at the foolish old woman he had tricked out of her coin.

She should have expected little better, but the tidings struck her hard. She pressed her hand to her chest as though she had received a blow. She drew in a long breath until dismay wore off, slowly replaced with the ice of anger.

Because she was not some foolish old woman. While she lived and breathed she was still Catherine de Medici, the Dark Queen whose mere name was enough to make grown men tremble.

She faced her son to find Henry taking malicious amusement in her discomfiture. "It is a little late in your life, Maman, for you to be seeking your amusements with a handsome rogue. I shall be sorry to deprive you of your favorite, but I fear I may be obliged to put a price on this Xavier's head."

"Do so," Catherine said grimly. "Arrest the villain and drag him back to Paris. I will deal with him myself."

Chapter Ten

THE MORNING SUN FILTERED THROUGH THE COTTAGE window, warm and gentle against Jane's face as she tiptoed about the room. Stirring the broth that bubbled on the hearth, she took care not to splash her gown. She had dressed with more care than usual this morning, her best black gown a little worn, but still quite serviceable, adorned with a fresh collar and cuffs.

As she bundled her hair into a tidy chignon, Jane nearly caught herself humming an air. The face reflected back to her in the glass by the washbasin was a little pale from lack of sleep. She had snatched no more than a few hours last night.

Yet her eyes were brighter than they had been for a long time, a hint of pink blooming in her cheeks that had not been there before. Perhaps it was owing to the sea air. Or far more likely because she had awakened with a sense of purpose this morning, something important to fill her day, the care of the man sprawled on the bed.

Xavier had scarce stirred since having his arm set yesterday, but Ariane assured Jane it was no cause for alarm, merely the result of exhaustion and Ariane's powerful sleeping draught. The healing slumber would do him good providing he did not take a fever.

Jane crept to the bedside to test his brow for perhaps the hundredth time, relieved to find his skin cool to the touch. She tugged the coverlet higher over his bared chest and then retreated to the window.

Kneeling down, she drew forth her ave beads and commenced her morning meditations. Her prayers often took a sorrowful direction, remembering all those she had lost, her dear old nurse Sarah, her parents, her brother Ned. Today her heart lifted in a hymn of gratitude, thanking God for sparing the life of a man she scarce knew.

She reflected that it was odd she should already feel a sense of kinship with this stranger. Perhaps it was because she knew what it was like to be a castaway flung up on the mystic, oft disconcerting shores of Faire Isle.

"Uhhh!" A groan sounded from the bed behind her.

Jane twisted around to see that her patient had at last started awake. A terrified expression on his face, Xavier clawed at the bedclothes.

Jane scrambled up, sensing the cause for his alarm. She raced to his side, resting her hand on his shoulder.

"No, pray, monsieur. Everything is all right. Your arm is still there. Look."

Jane shoved the coverlet down to his waist so that Xavier could see his right arm splinted between the two slats of wood, the white bandage tied to the wound area.

He stopped thrashing, his breath leaving him in a long rush.

"I changed your dressing myself and there is no sign of infection. Ariane says you are doing well and your arm should mend nicely as long as you remain quiet and give it time . . ." Jane trailed off, uncertain if Xavier was even listening to her.

His gaze darted about the room as though seeking to regain his bearings. He sagged back against the pillow, flinging his left arm over his eyes. He went so still, Jane thought he might have drifted back to sleep.

But when she began to arrange the coverlet modestly back over his chest, he shifted his arm, peering up at her. She rapidly discovered it was one thing to care for a stranger when he was oblivious, quite another when he was awake and subjecting her to such a fixed regard. Her hands fluttered, coming to rest behind her back.

"Good morrow," she stammered.

"Is it?" he asked, his voice a hoarse croak.

She hastened to fetch him something to drink. When he regarded the cup in her hands with deep suspicion, she said, "It is only wine, I promise you."

Raising his head, she coaxed him to take a few sips. He was cautious at first, and then took a long greedy swallow. He spoke more clearly when he demanded, "How long have I been asleep?"

"Since yesterday afternoon."

"Damnation."

"How are you feeling?"

Xavier shifted his shoulders and winced. "Like I was flung from the deck of a ship and dashed up against the rocks."

"Good." She added hastily, "Not that you were washed overboard, but that you remember. Ariane was afraid the blow to your head might addle your wits. Do you recall who I am?"

"Jane . . . the Englishwoman."

"That's right," Jane said, feeling absurdly pleased that he remembered her name. "And you know where you are?"

"Well, Jane, I would reckon that I am tucked up in your bed."

"Not mine. This is Madame Partierre's cottage, her bed."

"What a pity." The wine had revived the man enough that a hint of a wicked smile played about his lips.

Jane stalked away from the bed to place the empty cup on the table in an effort to recover her composure. But before she could do so, he disconcerted her further, by leaning on his left elbow in an effort to sit up.

"Oh, stop. What are you doing?"

Xavier gritted his teeth at the pain the effort must have cost him. "Grateful as I am for Madame Partierre's hospitality, I fear I must—"

He froze, peeking beneath the coverlet. He lifted his head, staring accusingly at Jane.

"Hellfire and damnation, woman. Where are my breeches?"

"I didn't take them." Jane was annoyed to feel the heat rise into her cheeks. "It was Ariane—"

"My *sister* undressed me?"

"No, but she requested Madame Partierre and Madame Bevans to do so. I removed your boots while—"

"While half the island stripped me naked," Xavier cut in, looking more outraged by the moment.

"It is very difficult to undress an inert man, monsieur. Ariane only wished you to be made more comfortable."

"The devil she did. It is far more likely she thought she could keep me captive this way. Obviously my half sister does not know me very well."

"About as well as you know her. The Lady only wishes you to remain quiet, give that arm she labored so hard to save a chance to mend."

"Be sure and thank her for that when next you see her." Xavier struggled to sit upright. "In the meantime, be good enough to fetch my boots and breeches. Also a shirt or jerkin if you can find one. There's a good wench."

"No."

"No?" Xavier paused in his struggles to arch one brow at her.

"You are not going anywhere."

"Loath as I am to quarrel with you, my lady, I beg to differ. If you will not fetch me my clothes, I will find them myself or march out of this cottage stark naked. So you had best prepare to avert your maidenly eyes."

"I have been married and widowed twice, so my eyes are no longer maidenly. You have nothing concealed beneath that coverlet I have not seen before."

"Good, because on the count of ten, I am getting up, Jane."

Jane folded her arms across her bosom and positioned herself in front of the doorway.

"One . . . two . . ."

Jane blinked and gasped, caught unprepared as Xavier tossed the blanket aside and swung his legs over the side of the bed. No doubt he would have been the sort of boy who cheated at nursery games as well.

Despite her boast of having been wed twice, both of her husbands had been modest men and she had never been treated to such a brazen display of masculine flesh. She had to fight the urge to avert her gaze.

Instead she stared hard at Xavier, hoping to shame him into retreat. But the man clearly had no shame, perhaps because he had nothing to be ashamed of.

His calves and thighs were as lean and well-honed as his flat stomach and broad chest. The male member that nestled between his legs was in resting position, but Jane imagined it capable of rising to an impressive length.

He struggled to his feet, only to sway dangerously. He would have fallen flat on his face if Jane had not rushed forward to catch him. She staggered beneath his weight, but managed to thrust him backward.

As he fell onto the bed, he took Jane with him. She landed on top of him with a force that caused Xavier to cry out in pain and curse.

"See what you made me do," Jane said as she struggled to scramble free. "I have likely injured your arm."

"My arm is not what's in danger," Xavier grated.

To her horror and embarrassment, Jane realized she had driven her knee between his thighs in her frantic efforts to untangle herself. Everywhere she placed her hands to brace herself, she encountered warm male flesh.

By the time she clambered off him, she was panting,

her cheeks aflame. Xavier had paled from his efforts, his chest rising and falling with his quick breaths. They might well have just separated from a heated tumble in the sheets, a reflection that did nothing to help Jane feel less flustered.

She brushed back a straggling wisp of hair from her face, then bent to examine Xavier's arm. To her relief, the splint had held.

"You are fortunate you did not break your arm all over again," she scolded. "I trust now you will be more sensible and remain in bed. If you don't I vow I will fetch a rope and tie you down."

Pursing her lips, she dragged the coverlet back over him. Xavier made no movement to resist. But as he shifted his head onto the pillow, he regarded her balefully.

"Do you always make a habit of holding naked men prisoner?"

"No, I make a habit of trying to help."

"Even men who are stupid and ungrateful?"

"Especially them. They are often the ones who need it the most."

They regarded each other steadily for a moment. Xavier's mouth tipped into a reluctant smile.

"I am sorry, Jane, but I am desperate to get out of here." His smile fled as he continued, "I need to find out what happened to my ship, my crew. If the *Miribelle* broke up on the rocks—" He broke off, swallowing.

"I have sailed with some of those men for many years. If aught has happened to them, I am to blame."

"You can hardly hold yourself accountable for a storm."

"No, but if I hadn't indulged . . . if I had had my wits more about me, perhaps I could have . . ." He concluded bleakly, "I was their captain and I failed them."

"I see no reason to despair as yet. There has been no report of any wreck. Surely if your ship had foundered, there would have been some sign of it along the coast."

A flicker of hope appeared in his eyes. "That is true."

"If the *Miribelle* did survive the storm, what would your crew likely do?"

"No doubt they would have given me up for lost. They would probably continue on to make port at St. Malo."

"Ships come and go all the time at Port Corsair on the other side of the island. I am sure Ariane could engage someone to make enquiries on the mainland."

"No, I am already enough beholden to that woman. I will go myself."

He made another effort as if to rise only to sag weakly back against the pillows.

"Truly, I am sure Ariane would not mind. I will ask her for you if you wish."

"It appears once again I have little choice." He issued a defeated sigh, adding grudgingly. "Thank you. I would be most grateful."

"In the meantime, the best thing you can do is rest and build back your strength. I have prepared a most nourishing broth."

She expected him to protest as most men would have done, demanding something more substantial. Her brother certainly would have done so, petulantly demanding a leg of mutton and tankard of ale.

Xavier merely nodded in glum assent. He didn't balk until she perched on the edge of the bed, preparing to feed him.

"No, hand it over. I am not yet reduced to the state of a puling infant."

Jane regarded him doubtfully, but held her tongue, leaving it to Xavier to discover the difficulty himself, of managing a bowl of hot soup with only one good hand.

He scooted into a sitting position, and attempted to balance the bowl on his stomach, while plying the spoon awkwardly with his left hand. When all he succeeded in doing was dribbling broth down his chin and spattering his chest, he surrendered the bowl to her with a disgruntled scowl.

As Jane spooned the broth into his mouth, an uncomfortable silence settled over the room. Xavier's eyes narrowed, studying her face, roving over her figure.

It had been many years since any man had subjected her to such a bold regard. Jane struggled to keep her attention focused on the task of feeding him.

"I liked you better with your hair down," he pronounced at last.

"How fortunate that I do not wear it to please you. I am too old to run about with my hair unbound."

"You cannot be that advanced in years."

"I am nearly two and thirty."

"And disconcertingly honest. I have scarce known a woman be so truthful about her age."

"After a certain point in one's life, the tally of years becomes something of no importance," Jane said, feeding him the last of the broth.

"I agree. I freely admit to being seven and twenty. But don't let that concern you. I have a marked penchant for mature women, especially widows."

He smiled at her and Jane frowned. Was the man attempting to flirt with her? She had never been good at such witty repartee and did not care for it. She decided her best course would be to ignore him.

His dark hair tangled about his lean, weathered face, roughened by several days' growth of beard. Heavy brows jutted over blue-gray eyes that Jane fancied never offered any quarter whether confronting an enemy or staring a woman out of countenance. The only soft part of his visage was his mouth, the generous underlip that both hinted at vulnerability and held the promise of darker pleasures.

She dabbed a linen napkin to his mouth as though afraid he might bite, her touch so tentative, he could not fail to remark upon it.

"So do you find me something quite wild and dangerous, my lady?"

"No," Jane demurred. "Merely a man badly in need of a combing and shave. I could do that for you later if you like."

"No thank you. I don't trust anyone that near my throat with a razor."

Jane's gaze flicked to the white scar on his neck. "But I have had some experience."

"With your husbands? Two of them, I believe you said. So what happened? Did you accidentally slit their throats or simply wear them out?"

"Neither," Jane replied as she rose from the bed to replace the empty bowl on the hearth. She certainly owed Xavier no explanations, but all the same she found herself saying, "Dickon was never in good health. He died of consumption. We were only wed a year. My second husband, Sir William, succumbed to pleurisy."

"I am sorry." Xavier's voice softened a shade. "Did you nurse them as kindly as you are me?"

"Not Dickon. I didn't li—"

"You didn't *like* him?"

Jane bit her tongue. Usually she was far more circumspect. "I didn't know Dickon that well. We were only wed a year and I was quite young, only fifteen."

"And Sir William?"

"I wed him when I was eighteen, far more mature. We were married for ten years."

"Did you love him?"

"He was a great deal older than me. For the most part, I esteemed him—and you ask far too many impertinent questions."

"Pardon, my lady. I hope I have not offended you so that you will refuse to oblige me with another cup of wine. That nourishing broth of yours was a trifle salty."

Jane picked up the wine jug to refill his cup. After rebuking Xavier for his curiosity, she was mortified to discover she could not resist indulging her own.

"What about you? Are you married?"

"Never." Xavier gave a mock shudder. "But I do have the loveliest, most exacting and demanding mistress. You could not begin to imagine how lusty she is."

"I am sure I have no wish to do so—" Jane began primly when Xavier cut in.

"The sea, Jane. I was referring to the sea." His eyes

twinkled, his grin so irrepressible Jane's mouth curled into a reluctant smile.

She settled back on the edge of the bed. He made no attempt to take the cup this time, appearing content to allow her to hold the wine to his lips.

He drained half the cup before speaking again. "So you were wed twice, once to a boy and once to a man in his dotage."

When Jane sighed at his persistence, he said, "Pardon, my lady. But my curiosity is understandable, especially after hearing that you compared my physique to your husbands' and found me wanting."

"I never said that."

"You said I had nothing concealed beneath this sheet that would impress you."

"I said nothing that would *surprise* me."

He studied her through the half mast of his lashes. "If you find me so unremarkable, I just wonder why you kissed me."

Jane started so she nearly spilled the rest of the wine. "I did no such thing."

"Yes, you did. I admit my memory of it is hazy. I thought it was merely a delightful dream. But now I remember quite clearly. When you found me on the beach, you pressed your lips to mine."

Jane flushed. She had hoped he had been too confused to remember that.

"I—I was merely trying to give you the Kiss of Life."

"That's what I said. You kissed me."

"It was not done with any passionate intent. I was trying to revive you by sharing my breath. It is a healing magic I have seen Ariane practice here on Faire Isle."

"That might be what Ariane does. But *you* kissed me."

"I did not. I—"

Her protest was cut off by Xavier seizing her collar and yanking her forward. The wine cup flew from her hand as he hauled her close. His mouth collided with hers in a kiss that was swift, hard, and heated.

"There," he said, releasing her. "That was what you did. Where I hail from, that is called a kiss."

Her face flaming, Jane scrambled from the bed. "Where I hail from, that is called an affront and if you ever try anything like that again, I will—will—"

"Break my other arm?" Xavier offered helpfully.

"Yes!" Jane bent to pick up the remnants of the shattered cup and mop up the wine.

She would have liked to storm out of the cottage, put as much distance between her and this disconcerting man as possible. But she remained to tend to his needs in stony silence. That Xavier did not appear in the least repentant only added to her aggravation.

"It was only a kiss, Jane," he said. "I thought you English were liberal with your embraces. The time I dined with a Portsmouth merchant, his wife kissed all the guests."

Jane compressed her lips, unwilling to admit the truth of his words. As her brother's hostess, she had frequently done the same, bestowing pecks upon all of Ned's friends. But that polite custom was far different from the brash kiss Xavier had stolen from her. None of those other tame embraces had roused feelings in her she had believed long dormant, the wayward side of her nature that had nearly led to her ruin as a girl. She had prayed long, did hours of penance, and believed she had conquered her youthful passions.

She was dismayed that it had only taken one kiss from this man to prove her wrong. Advising Xavier to get some rest, Jane retreated to the far corner of the room. Settling herself on a stool, she took up her mending, hoping he would drift back asleep.

But he remained propped up against the pillows, his good arm resting behind his head as he observed her from across the room.

"So does this mean I am not permitted to ask you any more questions?"

Jane tugged her needle through the fabric so roughly she nearly snapped the thread. "I daresay you will, with or without my permission."

"How did a prim English lady like you end up on this island of witches?"

Although Jane had often asked herself the same question, she bridled at Xavier's words. "They are not witches. They call themselves daughters of the earth and very kind and generous they are. Particularly your sister. Her island has proven a refuge for many people in trouble."

"Like you, Jane? Did you require a refuge? I would wager you did. England is not the most welcoming place for Catholics these days."

Jane looked up from her needlework in surprise. "How did you know I am Catholic?"

"You don't see many of the reformed faith sporting those anymore." Xavier gestured toward an object lying on the floor near the window.

To her horror, Jane realized she had dropped her ave beads earlier when she had been praying. She sprang up and darted across the room to retrieve them. Cupping the strand protectively in her hand, she buried the beads in the pocket of her gown. Here on Faire Isle, it was no longer necessary to hide this relic of her faith, but a lifetime of habit died hard.

"So you lost everything and had to flee England because of your religious beliefs?" Xavier asked.

Jane worried the beads in her pocket, hearing the echoes of the queen's secretary, Sir Francis Walsingham, pronounce her sentence.

"Jane Danvers, all your wealth, estate, and properties are forfeit to the Crown. You will be given a week to settle your affairs and leave these shores, never to return on penalty of death."

At the time, Jane had only been relieved to be released from the Tower and spared her life. It had taken a full year, an endless succession of days in exile for her to appreciate the harshness of her sentence, all that she had lost.

She swallowed, answering Xavier's question at last. "Yes, you are correct. I—I can never go home again."

"I would not say *never,* my lady. Not if the rumors are true."

"What rumors?"

"Of the Spanish invasion."

Jane frowned uneasily. "King Philip has been making that threat for a long time."

"It has gone way beyond mere threat according to what I have learned on my travels."

Despite her resolve to keep her distance from Xavier, Jane drew closer to the bed. "What have you heard?"

"A huge armada has been assembled, the largest flotilla of fighting ships ever seen, perhaps as many as three hundred galleons and flat-bottomed boats as well, to convey horses, arms, and legions of well-trained soldiers to English shores."

"W-when?"

"It could be any day now." Xavier gave an indifferent shrug. "They say the Spanish grandees are already casting lots for their pick of English estates. And of course some of those ships will carry the monks of the Inquisition and all their implements to—er—persuade your erring countrymen to return to the true faith.

"The queen that sent you into exile will have to flee or be tried and burned at the stake. So you see, by this time next year, you could well be back home, rejoicing and setting off fireworks."

"O-hh." Jane backed away from the bed, her mind recoiling in horror from the images Xavier painted with his careless words. "As much as I long to go home, how could you possibly think that I would rejoice— That I could ever want—"

She pressed her hand to her mouth feeling as though she was going to be ill, a sensation akin to panic squeezing the air from her lungs.

She turned and fled from the room, only dimly aware of Xavier calling her name. She burst from the cottage, ignoring the startled looks of the women lingering nearby, hoping for a glimpse of the strange castaway.

Jane raced past them, heading for the beach, her heart thundering in her chest. Half-falling, she clambered atop the highest rock she could manage as though she could somehow span the distance of the channel, find England, and see for herself that her homeland was yet safe.

"An armada . . . the largest flotilla of fighting ships ever seen . . . to convey horses, arms, . . . soldiers to English shores."

Xavier's words pounded in her head like the relentless tramp of heavy Spanish boots as if soldiers already thundered into tiny villages and hamlets, drowning out the cries of terrified women and children. She could not stop herself from envisioning the peaceful lanes awash in blood, smoke blackening the air from cannon fire and thatch-roofed cottages set ablaze.

Or would the smoke hail from a more sinister source, the crackling faggots piled at the feet of a defiant woman with fiery red hair. Elizabeth . . .

Jane shuddered and closed her eyes, trying to block out the disturbing image. There had been a time when she had been so angry with Elizabeth Tudor. The queen was no religious zealot. When she had come to the throne, she had promised moderation, only to yield to the pressures of her council and adopt harsher laws against her Roman Catholic subjects.

But Jane's bitterness against the woman who had signed the order for Jane's exile was softened by other memories, the younger Elizabeth who had been so kind to two orphaned children, even though their father had been steeped in treason.

Jane recalled how tightly she had clutched her brother's

hand, two frightened children clinging to each other as they were ushered into the royal presence.

But by the age of twelve, Jane had already known she could no longer afford to be a child. Although she trembled, she tipped up her head, preparing to confront the woman her Catholic relatives branded as a heretic, a she-devil, and a witch.

Elizabeth Tudor was said to be a vain woman, attiring herself in voluminous costly gowns that kept her subjects farther at bay. But that morning, she had been dressed rather simply for a queen. Jane saw not the painted Jezebel of her father's describing but a tall slender woman with red curly hair and piercing eyes set beneath thin arched brows.

Jane had been instructed in the proper way to curtsy. Instead she had thrust Ned protectively behind her. Determined to know the worst, she had blurted out, "Are you going to imprison us in the Tower and cut off our heads?"

Several of the courtiers present had gasped at her blunt question. The queen's lips twitched, but she replied gravely, "No, Mistress Jane. I have already been obliged to shed the blood of far too many of my subjects."

The queen's voice was far gentler than Jane would have imagined. Ned ventured to peek at Her Majesty from behind Jane's skirts.

"Then what will you do with us?" Jane asked.

"I intend to place you and your brother in the custody of the Earl and Countess of Shrewsbury. They will act as your guardians until your brother comes of age to inherit his estate."

"His—his estate? Then you are not taking our lands away?"

"No, Jane. I do not believe in visiting the sins of the father upon innocent children. All I ask is that you and your brother become my true and loyal subjects. Can you do that?"

Jane gazed at the queen she had been raised to believe the devil incarnate, out to destroy the true faith. But all she saw was a woman whose kindness made Jane long to fling herself at the queen's skirts and burst into tears.

"I—I will try," she faltered.

"Good, because you are the older sister. Your brother will look to you for guidance, but I believe you are up to the task."

The queen crooked her fingers beneath Jane's chin and tipped her head up. "I perceive a great deal of strength in you, child."

Jane blushed, pleased by the queen's compliment but confused as well. "My father always told me that strength is not a becoming trait in a woman. Women are meant to be soft and yielding."

"Only on the outside. Steel sheathed in velvet, that is what a woman must be in order to survive." The queen's smile took on a grimmer cast, her expression weary as she added, "And by God, I know something about survival."

The memory blurred beneath the sparkling waters of the sea. As Jane surfaced back to the present, she touched her fingers to her chin as though she could still feel Elizabeth's gentle touch.

Jane hoped the queen remembered all she had learned of survival because Elizabeth would need all her strength, all her courage in the days ahead. Jane folded her hands together but hesitated, wondering if it was wrong to appeal to God to spare the life of a heretic queen.

Instead she dropped to her knees and sought intercession from a gentler, feminine source. Pleading with the blessed Virgin to have mercy upon her queen and her tiny island homeland, Jane prayed as she had never done before.

Chapter Eleven

XAVIER SHIFTED ON HIS PILLOW, WATCHING AFTERNOON shadows stretch across the floor. He believed he had known what hell was during those months he had spent chained in a Spanish galleon. But he might have preferred being back at the oars to the humiliation of his present captivity. His good arm useless, his body so weak, he was dependent upon a gaggle of females for his simplest need. He could not even take a piss without help.

But he drew the line when Madame Partierre entered the cottage with a jug of water. The old woman all but smacked her lips when she announced her intention of bathing him.

"The devil you are," Xavier said. "Where is Jane? I want Jane."

"Then you should not have distressed her, should you?"

"Where did she go? Is she all right?"

The infuriating old crone refused to answer him. But at least she desisted in her efforts to bathe him. Bearing away his slops, she left Xavier alone to fume and curse his own helplessness.

Madame Bevans, who had looked in upon him earlier, had provided him with a nightshirt belonging to her late husband. The garment was overlarge and would have provided him with ample cover if he rose from his bed and went to search for Jane himself. But he still was unable to take more than a few steps without reeling.

He drummed his fingers against the mattress as he remembered how distraught Jane had looked as she had rushed out. He wondered if he had made her cry. His familiarity with his mother's hysterics had rendered Xavier immune to a woman's tears.

But somehow he imagined Jane would weep more quietly and never where anyone could see. The thought bothered him more than he liked to admit.

He blew out a gusty sigh. His father had always deplored Xavier's lack of finesse with women. Xavier recalled one time in particular when they had made port at a French Huguenot settlement on the coast of Florida. Xavier had wagered one of his shipmates that he could kiss at least twenty girls during his first ten minutes ashore.

He alighted, enthusiastically pouncing on every female he saw, sending one girl shrieking for her maman while another stout wench boxed his ears. But her wrath had been nothing compared to his father, who had hauled Xavier back aboard ship by the scruff of his neck.

"Mon Dieu, Louis! What devil gets into you to behave thus? This is not the action of a gentleman, accosting young ladies, making them the object of a vulgar wager. Women should always be treated with delicate courtesy. They do not like being teased and bedeviled after your ruffian fashion."

"Don't they?" Xavier had asked, observing two of the girls he had "accosted" below on the dock, giggling and waving to him. "Then why do they keep coming back for more?"

His father had scowled over a question he was unable to answer and as punishment had set Xavier to swabbing the deck.

As the afternoon waned, Xavier realized Jane was not coming back and he regretted his treatment of her. Not the kiss. He had enjoyed bringing the heat to her cheeks and it had intrigued him to feel a hint of response in those prim but deliciously soft lips. But he was sorry to have occasioned her such alarm with his report about the Spanish armada.

Callous in matters of religion and feeling no loyalty to any nation himself, it had never occurred to Xavier that Jane would be distressed by the notion of England being invaded. Most people would rejoice at the downfall of the queen who had banished them.

He sensed a generosity of spirit in Jane that Xavier would never have thought possible. He didn't understand it, but he wished Jane would return so he could at least apologize, attempt to make amends.

As time dragged by, his eyelids grew heavier and he

was on the verge of drifting back to sleep when he heard a light footfall in the next room.

"Jane?" he called eagerly, but as he twisted his head, he was disappointed and annoyed to see two small figures poised in the doorway.

A pair of little girls with angelic golden hair and great blue eyes regarded him earnestly, the shorter and younger of the two sucking her thumb and clutching a ragged poppet.

Xavier propped himself up on one elbow. "This is not a menagerie and I am not a bear to be gawked at. Be off with you."

His bark would have been enough to send any of his crew scuttling topside, but the two sprites appeared undaunted.

"If you are not a bear, why do you growl?" the older one challenged, venturing closer.

"I did not say I wasn't a bear, only one that didn't like being stared at. I am in fact a beast and I regularly devour little girls for breakfast."

The smaller one shrank closer to her sister. The older girl crinkled her pert nose and sniffed. "You would never eat us because you are our uncle."

"The devil—I mean the blazes I am. Who filled your head with nonsense such as that?"

"My older sister Seraphine. I am Lucia Remy," the girl jabbed a thumb at her chest, then pointed to the little one. "And this is Ninon."

Xavier frowned. So whoever these sprites were, they were not Ariane's daughters. He supposed that it should have occurred to him that his half sisters must be married by now, even have offspring. But he was uncomfortable enough with the notion of being a brother. The prospect of being claimed as an uncle was downright alarming.

"I don't know what this Seraphine told you," he said. "But she is mistaken."

"Seraphine is never wrong," Lucia informed him loftily. "Actually she said you are a half uncle." Lucia cocked her head to one side, studying him with a mighty frown. "So which half of you is missing?"

"My wits, they have gone a-begging."

His reply surprised a giggle out of Lucia, the sound so infectious, Xavier could not help smiling. He shifted his attention to the younger one, her blue eyes wide above the barrier of her fist.

"What about you, Mistress Ninon? Do you have nothing to say for yourself? Do you even speak?"

"Of course Ninon speaks. When she has something to say."

"What a wise child. Petite Ninon, you do realize that thumb will eventually come off if you keep sucking it that hard."

Ninon plopped her thumb out of her mouth long enough to regard him haughtily. "Imbecile."

Lucia beamed with sisterly pride. "That is Ninon's new word. She learned it from Madame Partierre."

"It is a very useful word and you pronounce it beautifully, mademoiselle."

Ninon's bow-shaped mouth curved into a wide grin that charmed Xavier in spite of himself. He had almost begun to think that being an uncle might not be so alarming when they were interrupted by someone calling.

"Lucia! Ninon!"

An older girl appeared in the doorway. The aforementioned sister, Seraphine? Xavier wondered. But the girl's dark appearance provided too stark a contrast to these two golden fairy children. Her next words dispelled any notion that she was related to them.

"You should not be in here," she told the girls. "Your sister has been very worried, looking everywhere for you. Seraphine is going to be quite cross at you for running off."

"We didn't run anywhere," Lucia said. "We are making the acquaintance of our half an uncle."

The older girl ignored Xavier, her gaze not so much as flickering in his direction. Planting her hands on her hips, she frowned at the little ones.

"You should not have come without permission. Now get along with you."

"But Meg-air-ah—" Ninon wailed.

"Shh!" Lucia gave her little sister a poke in the ribs. "She doesn't like to be called that."

As the dark-haired girl marched his two protesting nieces toward the door, Xavier's brow furrowed.

Megaera? The infamous young sorceress that Queen Catherine had engaged Xavier to find and abduct? The legendary Silver Rose? This thin insignificant chit of a girl? Surely not.

Ignoring his stiffness and aches, Xavier struggled upward in bed, straining for a better glimpse of her as she hustled the two little girls from the room. He expected her to vanish with them.

He was surprised when she returned alone, slowly approaching the bed. Her budding figure hinted at a girl in her early teens, but she looked small for her age, her slender neck appearing too swanlike to support such a mass of dark brown hair. The late afternoon sun painted shadows on a pale face whose features were unremarkable except for her eyes. Xavier had never seen eyes so old and sad in a countenance so young.

"Megaera?" he murmured uncertainly.

"My name is Meg. But *you* may call me Mistress Wolfe."

Her tone was as hostile as her gaze. Xavier might have found it amusing if something about the girl hadn't rendered him uneasy.

"Well, Mistress Wolfe. And what have I done to displease you?"

"Nothing. I do not even know you."

"Then why do you look as though you would like to drive a stake through my heart?"

She forced a rigid smile to her lips. "You are entirely mistaken, monsieur. I bear you no ill will. In fact, I have brought you a gift."

She produced a small vial filled with some clear liquid. Xavier eyed it warily.

"What the devil is that?"

"A healing elixir that I prepared. I have been studying with the Lady of Faire Isle and have learned much from her."

Why did he have this unsettled feeling that whatever was in that vial, it was nothing that Ariane had taught this girl to prepare? He frowned, remembering what Queen Catherine had said about Megaera.

"I have already seen evidence of her power. She knows

how to grow deadly roses, how to fashion a knife with a blade so needle-thin, it can deliver poison direct into a man's veins."

When Meg extended the vial toward him, Xavier made no move to take it.

"No thank you, my dear. I believe I have had my fill of draughts these past few days."

"You would rather continue to lie here helpless?"

"I appear to have little choice, unless you claim that vial of yours contains some magic potion."

"It is not magic. It won't heal your broken bone any faster, but the draught does have invigorating properties. It will restore your strength."

She uncorked the vial and held it out, demanding, "Here. Drink it."

"I think not."

"It's not poison if that's what you're afraid of," she said as though she had read his thoughts. "I'll prove it to you."

She tipped up the vial and took a swallow herself. Wiping her mouth with the back of her hand, she offered the bottle to him, her expression challenging.

Xavier took the vial and sniffed it. The substance had no odor. As he held the bottle, considering, he could well imagine what Pietro would have said to him, the same thing the towering black man had remarked the day Xavier had first ventured to sample the shaman's potion.

"Your reckless curiosity will be the death of you one day, my friend."

Xavier hesitated a moment more, then took a cautious sip of Meg's elixir. It tasted like nothing more than water.

He frowned, wondering if this strange girl was mocking him, having a jest at his expense.

But the next instant an explosion of warmth shot through his veins, unlike anything he had ever experienced even from the most potent of whiskeys.

His senses reeled for a moment, then cleared until he felt more like himself than he had since being cast up on this cursed island.

He moved eagerly to take another swallow, when Meg prevented him. She took the vial and corked it. "You must only take a sip every few hours or the potion can be too strong. It might cause your heart to burst."

"Thank you for the warning. You might have mentioned that a trifle sooner."

"I was watching to see how much you drank. I would not have let you die."

"I am touched, mademoiselle." Xavier leaned back against the pillows. "But as you said before, you do not know me. Why all this concern for my welfare?"

"Because I want you well enough to leave Faire Isle, the sooner the better. You see, I know why you are here, monsieur, and what you are after."

Xavier started in surprise but recovered himself, concealing his alarm behind a bland smile.

"How could you possibly know that, mademoiselle? When I am not even sure myself what the devil I am doing here."

She stared at him. If he had thought the Lady of Faire Isle's gaze powerful, it was nothing as compared to this girl's. Meg's eyes pierced him like a sword, poking and prodding through the thicket of his mind, attempting to drive all of his fugitive thoughts out of hiding.

Although he repelled the assault, he ran his fingers over his brow, half expecting to find blood trickling from a gaping hole in his forehead.

Meg lowered her lashes, muttering, "Perhaps I cannot tell precisely what you are about, but I foresaw your coming."

"What? In your dreams?" Xavier asked derisively.

"No, in my scrying glass. I had a vision of a large fierce black cat stalking through the jungle."

A black cat like the jaguar Xavier transformed into whenever he sank into one of his trances? Once more he struggled to conceal how disconcerted he was by this girl's perception.

He managed to shrug. "What has some black cat got to do with me?"

"I don't know." She glared at him. "I am just certain that there is some connection and—and you had best leave Lady Danvers alone. If you hurt her—"

"Hold, mademoiselle," Xavier snapped, flinging up one hand to silence her. "What has Jane got to do with anything and why do you fear I would hurt her?"

"Because you are a predator, just like that jungle cat. I think you could be careless and cruel and Jane is my most particular friend. So if you harm her, I vow I will—will lay a curse on you and shrivel up your man parts."

She added fiercely, "I could really do that."

"By God, I believe you," Xavier murmured, resisting the urge to protectively cup his balls.

"Good. Just so long as we understand one another." Meg dropped the vial on the bed beside him and flounced out of the room.

Xavier slowly released his breath. Any lingering doubts he had had about Meg Wolfe being Megaera were dispelled.

Perhaps Catherine de Medici was not completely mad in her obsession to find this girl. Megaera was, to say the least, unusual and more than a little disconcerting. Small wonder Catherine was willing to pay a queen's ransom to gain possession of the young sorceress.

Or if not quite a queen's ransom, at least a tidy sum, enough to restore the fortunes of a destitute seaman who was no longer sure he had a ship to call his own.

Xavier grimaced, disgusted with himself, ashamed of the direction in which his thoughts had strayed. He shoved the small vial beneath his pillow, struggling to thrust the tempting possibility out of his head.

Xavier closed his eyes, his last thought as he drifted off to sleep, the sooner he managed to get himself off this be-nighted island, the better. For everyone.

THE MIDNIGHT SKY WAS LIT BY FIRE, THE FLAMES SCORCHING A path through the tiny French settlement. Xavier could feel the heat blistering his skin, sweat trickling into his eyes. He staggered toward the dock where the settlers were scrambling for the safety of the Miribelle, the only escape possible from the oncoming Spanish raiders.

The night was thick with smoke and confusion. Xavier's heart beat harder, reverberating with the terrified cries of those who pushed past him. Only his father appeared calm as he shepherded frantic settlers into the longboats, the chevalier, a heroic beacon amidst all this madness.

Clutching his leg where he had been grazed by a pistol shot, Xavier limped forward. When he saw his father load the last of the boats, he called out, "Monsieur. Wait!"

But his voice, raw with smoke, came out in a hoarse croak. Xavier watched, stunned, as the last boat was launched, the oars pulling for the safety of the Miribelle. *The chevalier never even looked back.*

Xavier's breath escaped him in a mighty sob as he was surrounded by Spanish soldiers. Roughly forced to his knees, his hands were bound behind his back.

"Papa!"

Xavier jerked, nearly coming up off the bed in his frantic efforts to claw his way out of the dream. He opened his eyes wide to discover his cottage prison darkened by night; a pale moon hung outside his window where the sun had once been.

He sank back, dragging his hand over his damp face to rub out the last vestiges of the nightmare. It had been years since he had been troubled by this particular dream and it had never been quite this vivid before. He wondered if it might be a side effect of young Megaera's witch's brew.

He wondered even more uneasily if he had cried out. He had a sinking feeling it might have been the roar of his own voice that had roused him from the dream. His suspicion was confirmed when he heard someone stirring in the next room.

"Merde!" he muttered. He turned his head toward the door. So which one of his gaolers was about to descend upon him now and could he elude their embarrassing and curious concern by feigning sleep?

A figure appeared on the threshold, haloed by the light of the candle she carried. She looked like something out of a dream herself, the mermaid of his visions, her soft gold hair flowing about her shoulders. But a most sensible and modest mermaid, a dark woolen shawl knotted over her white nightgown.

"Jane!" He sat up, mortified by how eager he sounded.

She hastened to the bedside and held the candle up to look at him.

"What is the matter? I heard you call out. Are you in pain?"

He shielded his eyes from the candlelight. "No, I am fine." *Now.*

Frowning as though she did not believe him, she set the taper down on the table. She placed her hand upon his brow. Her fingers felt so cool and soothing, he could not help breathing a contented sigh.

Jane's brow knit in puzzlement. "You do not feel as though you are starting a fever and yet you are damp with sweat."

"Likely because it is a little warm in here," he lied. "Madame Bevans insisted upon closing the window."

Jane went to open it and then returned to retrieve her candle. "There. Do you require anything else?"

"No, only—"

"If you do, I am sleeping on the pallet in the kitchen. You have but to summon me."

She would have retreated as quickly as she had come if he had not managed to get hold of her arm to prevent her. Although she stiffened at his touch, she did not appear as if she were angry with him, only determined to keep her distance. The candle's glow revealed a face that looked pale and tense, shadows beneath her eyes that he feared he had put there with his careless words.

"Jane, I—I am sorry about before," he faltered. He had had to apologize to this woman so many times; he reflected he ought to be better at it.

"It is no great matter, monsieur. As I told you before, I am not some foolish maiden, to keep fretting over a stolen kiss."

"Oh, I am not apologizing for that. I like kissing pretty women, have enjoyed it ever since I was breeched."

He hoped to coax a smile from her. When he didn't succeed, he continued, "But I do regret alarming you with all my talk of the Spanish armada. I never expected to cause you such distress."

"Because I am Catholic?" She lifted her chin proudly. "I am also an Englishwoman and you cannot imagine how difficult that has made my life, torn between loyalty to my country and my faith."

"No, I am afraid I cannot."

"When I was forced into exile, I thought, well at least I would be able hear the mass without fear of being arrested, that I would find some measure of peace. But now you tell me that England is in danger from Spain and the Inquisition—" She faltered, her lashes sweeping down to veil the moisture in her eyes. "I cannot even pray this war to be averted, for my country's safe deliverance, without feeling I am committing some sort of sin and needing to do penance."

Xavier squirmed. He felt he was the last man in the world to advise anyone regarding matters of religion, but he could not bear seeing Jane look so tormented.

"For what an opinion is worth coming from someone who is a bit of a heathen, I don't think God would object to any prayer for peace and safety. And I am sure you have never done anything in your life that would merit penance."

Jane blinked back her tears. "That is because you do not know me very well, monsieur."

"At least I know enough about this Spanish invasion to tell you I don't think England is in any great peril."

"No great peril? From an armada the size that you described and Spain the mightiest nation in the world?" Jane shook her head. "As alarmed as I was by what you told me, I value your honesty, far more than you attempting to soothe me with comforting lies."

"Do you think that I would lie, milady?" Xavier grimaced. "Well, yes, I likely would. I do it all the time, but not in this instance. There are other factors which I would have explained to you if you had not rushed off before.

"Come sit by me and I will tell you." He shifted, patting the empty space on the bed beside him.

When she hesitated, he added, "I promise I will behave like a gentleman."

At least as far as I am able, he was tempted to add as Jane set down the candle and perched on the edge of the bed. But he kept the teasing remark to himself, sensing how little it would take to provoke Jane into flight.

He didn't even attempt to take her hand as he said, "My father tried to teach me many things and I will admit that not much of it took. But there is one lesson I heeded. The chevalier always said that it is not mighty weapons or even superiority of numbers alone that can determine the outcome of battle, but rather the courage and skill of the commanders.

"King Philip has placed his fleet in the hands of the Duke of Medina Sidonia. According to reports, the duke actually got down upon his knees and begged not to be appointed admiral of the armada."

"Is he not a brave man then, this Spanish duke?"

"Oh, quite brave. The duke is a most able commander, but on *land.* He knows little of naval warfare. In fact, I have heard that His Grace cannot set foot on board ship without becoming miserably seasick."

"Truly?" Jane tilted her head to one side, clearly wanting to believe him, but uncertain.

"Upon my honor, that is what I have heard. And this is the man who will be facing such formidable captains as John Hawkins and Francis Drake? Pah, the duke doesn't stand a chance. I sailed with Drake for nearly a year and I never met a more able seaman or a fiercer fighter."

"You sailed with Sir Francis Drake?" Jane breathed.

"Yes, and now you have that awed look on your face ladies always get at the mention of Sir Francis. It is very annoying."

"What is he like?"

"Shorter than me and not half so handsome."

This provoked a smile from her at last. "How did you come to sail with Sir Francis? I thought you were the captain of your own ship."

"Not five years ago, when I first encountered Drake. I—" Xavier hesitated. This was not a part of his past he liked to discuss or dwell upon, but with Jane waiting so expectantly, he had no choice but to continue.

"I was an unwilling guest of the Spanish navy, chained to a bench, manning the oars of the galley that Drake attacked. When the Spanish surrendered, Drake released all the prisoners and even offered some of us employment. I owe him my freedom and my life."

"And you hate being beholden to anyone."

He gave a dry laugh. "You begin to know me well, lady. Yes, I loathe it."

She fell silent for a moment, then asked, "Was it during your imprisonment that you acquired the scars on your back?"

"Aha, so you have been studying my physique."

Jane blushed. "It was impossible not to notice, to surmise that at some point you must have been—been—"

"Whipped like a dog." Xavier shrugged, seeking to make light of it. "I always regarded myself as an entertaining traveling companion, but the Spanish did not seem to appreciate my wit."

"Were you a prisoner for long?"

Three years, eight months, twenty-two days. An ordeal that he had only survived because of the daily diet of anger he had consumed. Hatred for his Spanish captors, bitterness toward his father.

Jane was already regarding him with more sympathy than he found comfortable. Not that he was above taking advantage of it, using her softening toward him as an excuse to capture her hand.

"I scarce remember those days," Xavier lied. "My captivity was all a blur until I was rescued by Drake."

"I remember how Sir Francis was feted when he returned from his voyage around the world. Not that I ever attended any of the suppers or attempted to make his acquaintance." Jane looked a little wistful. "I was warned he is a staunch defender of the new religion and unlikely to welcome the congratulations of a Papist."

"Nonsense. Drake would have been charmed by you. He was ever chivalrous toward the ladies, although he might have made an effort to save your soul. He certainly barraged me enough with his views. The man had his entire crew praying morning and night. Although Drake could certainly break off the psalm singing quickly enough when a plum Spanish vessel hove into sight. Sir Francis is, to his very core, a privateer."

"Is that what you are as well?"

"No, I make no such pretensions. I serve no country, no cause but my own. I am a pirate, Jane, plain and simple."

And a liar as well. Despite all of his assurances to Jane, Xavier would not have wagered a sou on England's odds against the might of Spain. They would have a better chance if France would come to England's aid. Xavier frowned, recalling the portion of the Spanish letter he had decoded.

Spain's hope . . . lies with the duke of Guise. The duke has pledged himself to create a diversion that will prevent the French king from sending military aid to England even should he wish to do so.

A diversion . . . Xavier still didn't have the least notion what that meant. But whatever de Guise and the Spanish were plotting, Xavier doubted it would take much to distract the erratic French king. The English, God help them, would have to be able to stand alone against the power of the Spanish empire.

But Xavier kept such disquieting reflections to himself. The anxiety had been erased from Jane's face, her natural serenity restored. The tense set of her shoulders relaxed, her shawl slipping down.

She was innocently unaware of how her nightgown clung to her bosom, revealing the curve of her breasts. Full and lush, just the way Xavier liked them. Megaera's little potion must have done a great deal to restore his potency because Xavier could feel himself getting hard.

He rubbed his finger in slow, languid circles on Jane's wrist and Xavier was surprised to feel the quiver of her response, her pulse quickening.

His gaze locked with hers and he saw her color rise, her lips part involuntarily. A heightened awareness seemed to rise between them.

He might not possess his half sister's witchlike mind reading skills, but Xavier had an uncanny knack for detecting when a woman was ripe for seduction. Beneath her prim exterior, this lonely widow hungered for a man's embrace. It would not take much, a caress or two, a few heated kisses to ignite the fire Jane fought so hard to suppress.

All he had to do was tighten his grasp on her wrist, draw her closer, coax her into his arms. Instead, Xavier surprised himself. Depositing a light kiss on her fingertips, he bade the lady good night.

THE CANDLE BURNED LOW, SHEDDING A SMALL POOL OF LIGHT where Meg sat on a stool near the hearth, leaving the rest of the cottage in darkness.

That could only be an improvement as far as Meg was concerned. The cottage that she shared with the other girls had long been abandoned by its original occupants. Any tidying, any effort to render the place more comfortable was all owing to Carole, who was far better at housewifery than Seraphine or Meg.

The cottage consisted of one large room with a sleeping loft reached by a ladder. Carole had long since retired up there and was no doubt fast asleep on her pallet, her small son Jean Baptiste snuggled close to her side.

Lucia and Ninon had ceased whispering and were asleep as well. The poor little things had likely drifted off while clutching each other, frightened by the bedtime tales Seraphine had told them.

"True witches, the Fontaine sisters were," Seraphine had cackled, scrunching up her features into a gruesome expression, crooking her long elegant fingers into claws. Lucia and Ninon had hung on her every word, wide-eyed and breathless as Seraphine continued.

"When the witch-hunters invaded Faire Isle, the Fontaine girls fled for their lives. They knew if they were caught, they would be roasted alive. Rather than endure such a fate, they chose to link hands and jump from the cliffs. *Crack!* Splat went their bodies on the rocks, blood and brains scattered everywhere."

"Seraphine," Meg had tried to protest as Lucia and Ninon had squealed, shrinking away from their sister. But Seraphine had ignored her, casting her voice to an even more sinister pitch.

"To this very day, the Fontaine sisters haunt these shores, pouncing upon wayward little girls who don't obey their older sister and go to bed when they are told. Fortunately, one is always safe up in the loft, because ever since their terrible death, the Fontaine specters are afraid of heights."

Lucia and Ninon had all but clambered over each other in their haste to scale the ladder, leaving Seraphine and Meg alone in peace.

It had become their habit to sit up talking far later than they should. Meg perched on the stool while Seraphine combed out Meg's hair, an activity that Seraphine seemed to enjoy although Meg could not understand why.

She could see no beauty in her dark heavy fall of hair compared to Seraphine's silken blond locks. But Meg submitted patiently to her friend's ministrations, making no complaint even when Seraphine struggled with a particularly stubborn knot.

"I don't hear any more rustling from above," Seraphine said. "It sounds as if the urchins are finally asleep."

"And having nightmares no doubt. You should not have told them all those horrid stories, Seraphine. You frightened them out of their wits."

"Not my little sisters." Seraphine chuckled. "It would take more than a paltry ghost tale to scare them. I daresay the little ghouls could tell you a story or two that would curl your hair."

Meg doubted that. She had witnessed enough real horrors wrought by her mother for any fable to have the power to alarm her.

"Besides, if I did frighten Lucia and Ninon, it serves them right. They certainly gave me enough of a scare, disappearing that way." Seraphine gave the knot a final tug and then, to Meg's relief, the comb glided smoothly through her hair.

"Not that I blame my sisters for wanting a peek at Captain Xavier. He is a very handsome rogue."

"Seraphine!" Meg twisted around to direct a shocked look up at her friend. "For shame. The man is your uncle."

"Half uncle." Seraphine shrugged. "The fact that he is related to me does not make me blind to his manly attributes."

She forced Meg's head back around so that she could continue combing. As Seraphine attacked another tangle, Meg winced, then muttered, "I will just be glad when he takes his manly attributes elsewhere. I am sorry, Seraphine. Even if he is your uncle, I cannot like him."

"Pooh! You are just annoyed with him because you could not get into his head and wander through his mind as you do so easily with everyone else." Seraphine bent down to whisper teasingly in her ear. "Or maybe you are simply jealous."

"Jealous? Of what, pray tell?"

"Of the way Captain Xavier has claimed all the attention of your prim Lady Danvers."

"Nonsense," Meg snapped. But she squirmed, fearing there might be a grain of truth in Seraphine's playful accusation. She was a little resentful of Jane spending so much time at Xavier's bedside, especially as the day of the choosing loomed closer. Meg had great need of Jane's calming presence herself.

But to Seraphine, she said, "I am merely concerned for Jane's welfare. There is something about Captain Xavier that I do not trust."

"I do not believe you trust any man besides your father."

"If you had had my experience, you would feel the same."

Seraphine laughed. "Your experience! La! Just listen to the child. Only thirteen and already an expert on the perfidies of men."

"I do not claim to be an expert," Meg said in a small voice. "But I do know what it feels like to be betrayed and have your heart broken."

She feared that her remark would elicit further mockery from Seraphine. But the older girl set aside her comb and hunkered down in front of Meg. The teasing light vanished from Seraphine's eyes to be replaced by one of her rare gentle expressions.

"You are not still pining over Sander Naismith, that boy you told me about? I am glad he got burned up in that fire in London. Otherwise I should have been obliged to kill him for you." Seraphine cupped Meg's cheek. "Sweetheart, he is not worth a single more of your thoughts."

"I know that," Meg tried to smile. "And I have tried to forget him, 'Phine." Her lips trembled and she swallowed hard. "But I thought he was my friend. I loved and trusted him so much. When I was with him, Sander made me feel so extraordinary, like one day I could grow up to be truly beautiful."

"Which you did."

When Meg shook her head, Seraphine leapt up to fetch her sole contribution to the domesticity of the cottage, a small, gilt-trimmed looking glass.

Seraphine thrust it into Meg's hands. "There. Look at that girl. I defy you to tell me she is not lovely."

Meg thought she could have defied Seraphine on that score very easily. But to oblige her friend, Meg studied her own reflection. Her hair pooled about her shoulders, soft and gleaming in the candlelight, but Meg gave Seraphine the credit for that. All that determined brushing.

Meg's papa had once told Meg that her hair was the color of cinnamon, but it suddenly struck Meg that her hair had grown darker this past year, her face leaner, her complexion paler. She looked more and more like . . . like her mother.

Meg shuddered and handed the mirror back to Seraphine. "It would scarce matter if I was beautiful or not. I fear men will only ever want one thing from me."

Seraphine grinned. "The same thing that men want from all of us. A stolen kiss or—" She arched her brows with a wicked look. "Other naughty things which I will explain to you when you are older."

Meg pulled a face at her. "You need not act so superior, Seraphine Remy, just because you are sixteen. I am sure I know as much about what men desire as you do." She paused and added sadly. "At least what men will desire from you. For me, they will only be after the secrets that are locked in my head."

"No, you are wrong, Meggie." Seraphine bent closer and enveloped Meg in a hug. "Someday you will meet someone who won't give a fig that you were ever known as the Silver Rose or possessed a *Book of Shadows.* He will find all the magic he desires in your enchanting face and fall completely in love with you."

"I am sure that will be your future," Meg said as she returned Seraphine's embrace. "For you are truly beautiful."

"Yes, I know it." The complacency of Seraphine's reply made Meg laugh in spite of herself.

"Though it is not at all wise of you to keep telling me so." Seraphine drew away from Meg. "I am already a vain enough creature."

Sinking down on the stool opposite Meg, Seraphine examined her own countenance in the looking glass and heaved a deep sigh of satisfaction. "I think it is a good thing that I am so beautiful because I am nowhere near as clever as you, Meg. My magic is all in my face. However, if you want a truly dazzling beauty, you should see my maman.

"Do you know that she once so completely captivated the King of Navarre that he—"

Seraphine broke off, her features clouding over as they always did at any thought or mention of her home. She turned the mirror facedown in her lap.

"Merde," she muttered. "I wish I had been born a boy."

"Why would you ever wish that?"

Seraphine sprang up, pacing off a few agitated steps. "Because then I would be at home where I belong, fighting alongside my father instead of bundled off to this island. Nothing to do but worry and wait for tidings that never come."

Seraphine dropped down before Meg again. She gripped her hands and pleaded, "Don't you think that you could try—"

When Meg recoiled, she broke off immediately. "I am sorry, Meggie. I swore I would not plague you anymore about using the crystal. I am as bad as that wretched Naismith boy, seeking to exploit your magic."

"Never." Meg patted Seraphine's bowed head. "Oh,

'Phine. If I could control my visions enough to conjure up an image of our fathers, I would."

"I know." Seraphine gave her a lopsided smile. "It is just so hard, this waiting and not knowing. If anything were to happen to my mother and my father. If they were to be killed—"

Her lips thinned, her grip on Meg's hands tightened painfully. "I am afraid I would become so bitter, filled with so much hatred. I would want to destroy the duc de Guise and his entire bloody Catholic league."

Meg fully understood. If any harm were to befall her father or her stepmother, she would feel just the same. But while Seraphine might curse and wish to destroy the duke and his army, Meg possessed the dark knowledge to do it. That more than anything else was what frightened her.

Chapter Twelve

THE PEACE OF THE MORNING WAS INTERRUPTED BY SHRIEKS that carried to Xavier through the cottage window. His first day out of bed and fully clothed, he felt as unsteady as a sailor regaining his shore legs after months at sea.

Alarmed by the sounds of distress, he staggered toward the door, hastening to the rescue. Although he was damned if he knew what he could do to aid anyone, weaponless, his good arm bound up in a sling.

He burst out into the sunlight, blinking as he glanced about him. His jaw fell open in amazement when he homed in on the source of the uproar.

A brawl was in progress on the strand in front of the cottages, the combatants, a pair of elderly females. One was

Madame Partierre, the other obviously an Englishwoman from some of the curses she shrieked.

Xavier's alarm dissolved into amusement as he watched the two old ladies go at each other like a pair of screeching cats, hissing, scratching, and pulling hair. Other women milled about, some uttering cries of dismay, the rest shouting encouragement.

It did not surprise Xavier to see Jane among the peacemakers. She and Meg seized hold of the white-haired English dame, pulling her off. Ariane and young Carole Moreau forced Madame Partierre back. Still shaking with fury, the two old women continued to hurl insults.

"You'll not speak about my Mistress Meg that way, you old hag," the Englishwoman cried.

"Bah," Madame Partierre replied in a tangle of French and English. "I only say what is true, Agatha Butterydoor. Your Meg, she is the *fille* of a witch. It is not *convenable* she should be the next Lady of Faire Isle."

"And you think your friend Mistress Moreau is better? A girl who has had a child out of wedlock! That—that *salope.*"

Agatha Butterydoor clearly spoke little French, but she knew just the right word to inspire Madame Partierre to a fresh spasm of rage.

She attempted to leap at the Butterydoor woman again only to be thrust back by Ariane.

"Damnation! That's enough!"

Xavier would never have imagined the calm Lady of Faire Isle capable of roaring like that or looking so fierce. The other women appeared astonished as well, even the two contentious old ladies were stunned into silence.

Ariane glared at each of them in turn. "Madame Partierre. Mistress Butterydoor, I am surprised at both of you. Is this the sort of example you would set for the younger ladies?"

Ariane's stern gaze swept the crowd. "And the rest of you urging them on. For shame! This is not the way we settle our differences on Faire Isle. You are all behaving as uncivilly and unreasonably as—as *men.*"

Xavier did not know whether he should be more amused or offended, but this last rebuke had the effect of making many of the women present hang their heads.

"There is too much work to be done to engage in this idle mischief. So be about your business, all of you."

The women dispersed, the two combatants limping off in opposite directions, still muttering their complaints but being soothed by their own particular friends. Jane caught sight of Xavier and headed in his direction.

This early in the morning, she had yet to bind up her hair for the day. It flowed loose about her shoulders, the glow on her cheeks and in her eyes as soft as daybreak over the ocean. Her mouth pursed into a moue of disapproval at the sight of him, tempting him to kiss her regardless of who was watching them. He managed to restrain the impulse.

"Captain Xavier, what you are doing up?"

"I had to *rise* sometime, lady," he replied wickedly. "Especially with you so determined to keep me in your bed."

His teasing caused Jane to blush. She cast an anxious glance about her as though fearful someone else might have overheard.

"I meant that after your ordeal, I expected you would

require more rest." Her gaze skated over him, from his boots to the fresh shirt he wore. "I cannot even imagine how you managed to attire yourself."

"I cozened Madame Bevans into aiding me since you were nowhere to be found this morning. But I assumed that I had your approval, since my clothes mysteriously reappeared during the night."

"I was the one who provided the clothes," Margaret Wolfe piped up, insinuating herself between them.

"Meg!" Jane frowned at the girl.

"He is clearly well enough to be up and on his way, Jane. The man cannot be lazing about here forever."

"As always, I am touched by your consideration, mademoiselle."

Meg glared at him. Before she could retort, Ariane hustled toward them.

"Meg, your Mistress Butterydoor is still in an uproar. I need you to calm her down and get some ointment on her scratches. And for the love of heaven, keep her away from Madame Partierre."

Meg looked reluctant to leave Jane in Xavier's company, but she had no choice but to obey. As Meg trudged away, Ariane blew out a breath, still looking rather harried.

"Trouble in paradise, sister?" Xavier asked.

"Nothing that I cannot handle." Ariane glanced over him with a frown. "I am surprised to see you up and about so soon, monsieur."

"All due to Milady Danvers's excellent care." Xavier had decided it was just as well to say nothing of the secret vial Meg had slipped him.

"And of course, I am indebted to you for this." He

wriggled and stretched the fingers of his arm bound up in the sling. "Regrettably I am obliged to beg another favor of you, the loan of a horse."

"A *horse*?"

"Yes, you know. One of those tall creatures with four legs, a mane, and a tail."

While Ariane scowled at him, Jane spoke up anxiously. "Whatever do you need a horse for?"

"I am told it is at least twenty miles across the island to reach Port Corsair and I am unlikely to make it afoot."

"Indeed you are not," Ariane said. "Jane already told me what you require. I dispatched one of my servants yesterday to make the journey. Bette's brother is a fisherman who knows many of the captains who engage in trade between Faire Isle and Brittany. He will find someone reliable to make enquiries after your ship at St. Malo. There have been no reports of any wreck off the coast of the island so very likely your ship did survive the storm."

"That is good news. But you will pardon me if I prefer to make my own enquiries."

"Unfortunately, we don't have many horses on Faire Isle. Only our sturdy island ponies, beasts that can be as stubborn and intractable as you are."

"Then we should get along just fine."

"You would likely end up taking a tumble and breaking your arm again. Besides, I can spare no one to show you the way."

Xavier attempted to smile, concealing his mounting irritation. "It is not that big of an island. I am sure I would stumble across Port Corsair eventually."

"No, the sensible course is for you to remain here

awhile longer. We will all be returning to the other side of the island in a few days."

"I can't imagine why you don't go now. What the devil is the attraction for all you women on this forsaken bit of coast?"

"Nothing that you would understand," Ariane said, cutting off their argument with a dismissive gesture. "Now if you will excuse me, I have more important matters that require my attention."

She strode away before he could get in another word. Fuming, Xavier started after her, only to be intercepted by Jane resting her hand on his arm.

"Please don't importune Ariane further, Captain. I realize she was rather curt, but she does have so much on her mind right now. And it would be more prudent for you to continue to build up your strength before leaving. Why don't you come with me and I will find you something to break your fast. Something a little more palatable than broth."

She smiled up at him in that quiet way of hers. He could feel the warmth of her touch even through the fabric of his sleeve and he wondered if Jane had any notion of the temptation she presented him.

If it had not been for his concern about his ship and crew, he might have been disposed to linger. He had not had a woman in a while and Jane was certainly an alluring prospect with her womanly figure and the hint of passion he sensed beneath that prim exterior. But if Jane did succumb to him, she would spend the rest of her life on her knees doing penance.

And then there was Megaera, the chit presenting a far different kind of temptation. He was intrigued by her, wondered exactly how much dark knowledge the girl did possess. She could make his fortune if he surrendered her to the Dark Queen.

Xavier had not led a blameless life, but thus far he had avoided doing anything so reprehensible that he could not abide the sight of his own reflection. The Lady of Faire Isle could not be as good at reading thoughts as reputed or else his sister would have realized he was doing them all a vast favor by offering to leave.

But with Ariane so stubborn in her refusals, there was nothing he could do about acquiring himself a mount. At least not in broad daylight with so many of these women milling about. All he could do was return Jane's smile and allow her to lead him away.

THE TABLE WAS SET BENEATH THE PINE TREE JUST OUTSIDE THE cottage where Ariane stayed with her family. The spate of fine weather had tempted the women to take most of their meals out-of-doors instead of the cramped confines of the cottage kitchens.

Everyone else had broken their fast much earlier. Jane sat on the bench opposite Xavier. As she watched him make a hearty meal of bread and cheese, she struggled to sort out the tangle of her feelings.

Everything had seemed much simpler yester eve when they had talked long into the night, surrounded by the intimacy of darkness. She had perched beside him on the bed and the man had been nearly naked beneath the covers.

And yet she felt more shy and awkward with him this morning fully clothed in the broad daylight. She rather resented Madame Bevans for helping him to shave and attire himself.

After all, the man was Jane's particular charge. She had only absented herself from the cottage for a brief spell to attend to her own toilette. Xavier might have waited—

Jane checked the thought, castigating herself for being ridiculous. After all, what did it matter who had aided him? She was acting as though she was jealous, which was quite absurd.

Xavier helped himself to another slab of bread, his gaze narrowing as a cart trundled by, its contents concealed beneath a canvas tarp. The roan pony hitched in the traces ambled in the direction of the cliffs.

"So what is this mysterious matter that has Ariane so flustered? If this island was not so clearly beyond the pale of the king's law, I would almost imagine you ladies were engaged in a bit of smuggling."

Jane smiled and shook her head. "Nothing so exciting. That cart only contained firewood for the bonfire atop the cliffs."

Xavier took another swallow of wine and drawled, "What are you women planning to do? Roast me alive? I would imagine young Megaera will be happy to strike the first spark."

"Please don't call her that. She doesn't like it. None of us do." Jane paused. She had noted the tense way Meg had confronted Xavier earlier and well understood the reason for it, but was uncertain how to explain it to him in any way that made sense.

"Meg is really a wonderful girl, warm, generous, but she does get these odd notions in her head." Jane traced a pattern in the tablecloth with her thumbnail and tried to give a dismissive laugh. "For some reason she fears you are like this great predatory cat and I am in danger of being devoured."

"Actually she strikes me as being exceedingly wise for her age. Perhaps you should take more heed of her."

Although Xavier smiled at her over the brim of his wineglass, his eyes simmered with a dangerous heat that sent a shiver through her. It seemed safer to return to the subject of the firewood.

"The bonfire will be lit the night of the gathering atop the cliffs," she said.

"Ah! A witch's Sabbath."

"No! There will be no witchery involved," Jane insisted, although she was not entirely comfortable with the idea of this gathering herself. "As I understand it, the daughters of earth assemble upon the cliffs of Argot once a year to—to hold council. This one will be especially important because Ariane intends to announce who her successor will be.

"I fear that is what the uproar was about this morning. There is a great deal of dissension among the women about who should be named. I am not sure that even Ariane has decided yet."

"Which should make for quite a lively meeting. How intriguing," Xavier murmured with that mischievous glint in his eyes that Jane was coming to recognize.

"Gentlemen are not permitted to attend." She furrowed her brow and then amended. "That is—I am not entirely sure it is forbidden, but I believe it is against their traditions—"

"Don't fret, my dear," he interrupted her with a laugh.

"I have no intention of invading the proceedings. In fact I intend to be—"

He checked himself, lowering his lashes. "Fast asleep by then."

Jane had a feeling that was not what he had intended to say, but her suspicion was diverted as he continued, "So do you mean to attend this council and cast your vote?"

"No one gets to vote, although Ariane certainly welcomes advice. But the decision is ultimately hers. And no," she added quietly. "I won't be going."

"Why not?"

"Because I am not one of them. I don't belong here."

"I imagine that you could if you chose to do so. Perhaps you ought to consider it. It seems a fine place to be if you are a woman. More freedom than you would encounter anywhere, a tiny realm ruled by petticoats and—now who the devil is this?"

Jane was startled by Xavier's abrupt change of tone. He had been lounging over his wine, but he straightened, frowning at something beyond her range of vision.

Jane twisted around to see Ariane bearing down upon them with a petite elfin-looking woman with a braid of moon-gold hair.

"I believe Ariane means to introduce you to Madame Aristide. She is—"

"My father's youngest daughter and favorite child, Miribelle. My ship was named for the woman. I should have rechristened the damned boat." Xavier's acid tone did not bode well. He looked as tense as a man expecting to be ambushed.

Jane could scarce have said why, but she leaped up and

resettled herself protectively on the bench beside him. Ariane did not look any better pleased at the prospect of the introduction than Xavier. She stood poker straight, her face set in tense lines. Only Miribelle was smiling.

"Captain Xavier, may I present to you—" Ariane began.

"Your sister, Miri." Miri rushed around the table and embraced Xavier. He stiffened, looking startled. For a moment Jane feared he would push Miri away.

But he patted her back in an awkward gesture, muttering, "Mind the arm."

She drew back, smoothing her hand over his sling. "S-sorry. I hope I didn't hurt you." Her eyes glistened. "It is just that you do look so very much like Papa. I hope you do not mind my saying that."

"It does me little good to mind," he replied. "Unless you know some magic spell to change my face, I fear it is true."

"You require no magic, Xavier." Miri turned to Ariane. "Our brother is a very handsome man, is he not, Ari?"

Ariane made a noncommittal sound that did little to daunt her younger sister's enthusiasm. Miri beamed as she settled herself beside Ariane on the bench opposite.

A heavy silence ensued, Xavier looking wary, Ariane grim, and Miri expectant.

Jane rose to her feet. "Perhaps I should—"

"No stay, Jane." Xavier seized her wrist, hauling her back down. "There is no reason this tender family reunion need be a private affair. I have been expecting this inquisition ever since I washed ashore. So tell me, my dear sisters, have you brought your rack and thumbscrew?"

Ariane bristled. "Miri and I intend no inquisition, but it is only natural we would have questions."

"We only want to get to know you better," Miri said. "And I am sure there is much you would like to know about us."

"I have already learned quite a bit from Madame Bevans. Ariane is the Lady of Faire Isle, a notorious sorceress. And Miri is Madame Aristide, the witch-hunter's bride."

If Xavier had set out to wound his youngest sister in her most vulnerable place, he had succeeded. Miri flinched and Ariane covered her hand in a protective gesture.

"Madame Bevans is a foolish gossip who does not get her facts straight. I am no more of a sorceress than she is and Simon Aristide long ago abandoned his profession. He is a good husband to Miri and an honorable worthy man."

Miri cast Ariane a grateful smile, her sister's praise of Simon Aristide clearly meaning a great deal to her.

"Now what of you, monsieur?" Ariane leveled her gaze at Xavier. "You have the advantage, because while you knew of us, we never even suspected your existence until three days ago."

"What do you want to know?"

"To start with, where have you been keeping yourself all these years?"

"At sea."

"With our father?" Miri asked.

"No, he's dead."

Both women flinched at the harshness of his tone.

"We are well aware of that. You needn't fling the fact

in our faces every chance—" Ariane began, but Miri intervened.

"We are hoping you will tell us something of Papa's last days. When and how did he die?"

Xavier compressed his lips. Jane thought she understood the reason for his tension. He had spun for her many tales of his adventures on the sea and exploring the jungles of Brazil, talking about Drake, Xavier's own crew, even some of the natives he had encountered.

One figure was significantly absent from his tales, his father. Xavier seldom mentioned the Chevalier Louis Cheney, and for whatever reason he appeared loath to speak of the man. And yet it was natural that Ariane and Miri should hunger for any scrap of information about the father who had been lost to them for so many years.

Xavier took his time replying, reaching to refill his wine cup, making an awkward business of it with his left hand. Jane hastened to help him, grateful for something to do. She felt uncomfortable being here, like someone caught between two opposing armies and not entirely certain whose side she should be on.

Xavier took a long swallow of his wine before finally answering Miri's question. "The chevalier died about two years ago in a Portuguese mission in Brazil. He succumbed after a prolonged bout of the yellow fever."

"Did he suffer much?" Ariane asked.

"I wouldn't know." Xavier shrugged. "I lost track of the man for a while, nearly five years."

Ariane drew in a sharp breath, looking outraged. Xavier sounded as callous as though he had merely mislaid a pair of boots. But Jane was certain that his separation from his father had to have come during those years Xavier was a prisoner of the Spanish and his service aboard Drake's ship.

Why couldn't the man abandon some of his stiff-necked pride and confide in them as he had done with her?

"Perhaps you should tell your sisters why you and your father became separated," Jane suggested.

"I would be happy to—if I thought it was any of their concern." Xavier dove back into his wine cup, lapsing into silence again.

Ariane opened her mouth to make some retort, but managed to contain it by pressing her lips together. It was left to Miri to continue.

"Did—did Papa ever speak of us at all?" she asked in a small voice.

"Incessantly."

"Did he leave any message when he lay dying? Did he say anything at all?"

"Nothing that made any sense. He was delirious by the time I reached him."

Xavier's curt reply dimmed the hope in Miri's eyes. Another heavy silence fell until Ariane took up the questioning.

"And so you sailed here aboard the *Miribelle*?"

"I wasn't sailing *here,* but yes." Xavier took another gulp of wine. "I was aboard the *Miribelle* when I was caught in the storm."

"Our father set sail from Brittany with three carracks. What became of the other two?"

"The *Good Hope* was lost during an attack by Turkish

pirates not long after we first set sail from St. Malo. I believe the *Sea Lion* went down in a storm off the coast of Brazil. I don't know. I was not with the chevalier at the time."

"So of all my father's ships, only the *Miribelle* remains?" Ariane asked.

Xavier set down his cup with a sharp snap. "No, if the *Miribelle* made it to St. Malo, only *my* ship remains. I was the one who risked life and limb to retake the vessel when it had been captured by the Spanish. The *Miribelle* is *mine* now."

Miri spoke up quickly. "I am sure Ariane did not mean to dispute your possession of it."

"Good, because if she is not at the bottom of the sea, that miserable leaky vessel is all I have left." Xavier leveled an accusing stare at his sisters. "It is my understanding that when my mother retired to a convent, she ceded the house in Paris to you ladies."

"Property that was provided for that woman by our father. With money from our family coffers that we could ill afford," Ariane said hotly, but Miri placed her hand on Ariane's arm.

"It hardly matters because the house was eventually confiscated by the Crown, so none of us have it now," Miri reminded her sister. "You never cared about the property in Paris, Ari."

She turned back to Xavier explaining, "The house was used by our other sister Gabrielle for a time. But once Gabby married Remy, she no longer cared about having a dwelling in Paris either."

Miri's expression grew wistful. "What we all most wished for was our father's safe journey home. He promised me before he left that he would return soon and would bring a monkey or some exotic bird from the new world. And he would write down every last one of his adventures to share with me."

Xavier swirled the lees of wine in his cup and admitted grudgingly, "He did leave a parrot and a collection of journals for you."

"Oh!"

"Regrettably I was obliged to eat the bird and I had to use the journals for kindling."

Miri paled, but she rallied, saying, "Well, if you were cold and starving, it is quite understandable. I only hope you remembered to thank the bird for sacrificing his life for you."

Xavier stared at her as though he thought she was mad. Then he emitted a reluctant laugh. "Thank the Sea Beggar? The damned bird would only have cursed me and he is fluent in several languages."

"Is?" Miri challenged, cocking her head to one side.

Xavier met her gaze for a long moment before his lips twitched with a smile. "Yes, I was only jesting. If the *Miribelle* is safe, so are your journals and that infernal parrot."

Miri chuckled and Jane might have relaxed and smiled as well if she had not observed the stony expression on Ariane's face.

"Forgive me if I don't share your sense of humor, Captain," she said. "But our father died over two years ago?"

Xavier's smile fled, the man on his guard again. "Yes, what of it?"

"It strikes me that you have had ample time to sail to Faire Isle and inform us of his passing."

"Maybe I had more *important matters* to occupy my time," Xavier said, flinging Ariane's own words back at her.

Ignoring the taunt, Ariane fired right back. "And maybe you never intended to bring Miri those journals."

"No, I didn't. If it was that important to the chevalier that she have them, he should have entrusted them to someone else upon his deathbed."

"You ignored Papa's dying request?" Ariane gasped, springing to her feet. "Damn you!"

"Ariane, please. I am sure our brother had some good reason."

But this time Ariane ignored Miri's gentle attempts to intervene. Splaying her hands on the table, she leaned toward Xavier, her face flushed, her voice vibrating with anger.

"Do you know how hard it was on me and my sisters? Our father just vanishing that way, the torture of not knowing what had become of him? Those journals would have meant the world to us and you could not even be bothered to make the slightest effort to see them delivered. Papa took you with him. You had our father all those years—"

"I *had* him?" Xavier grated, leaping up as well. Jane reached for him, making her own effort to restore the peace, but Xavier shook her off.

"Do you want to know the only reason the chevalier took me with him on his grand voyage to Brazil?" he sneered.

"It is obvious. Because you were his precious son while we were mere—"

"The precious son he never wanted to claim. When my

mother realized he meant to sail off and we would likely never see him again, something inside my mother finally broke.

"She held a knife to my throat and told the chevalier he would either acknowledge me at last or she was going to kill me and herself.

"Maybe the chevalier didn't believe her because he hesitated." Xavier gave a bitter laugh. "At least that is what I have always wanted to believe was his reason for waiting a fraction too long to answer."

His hand moved to stroke the scar on his throat, the wound Jane had surmised must have come from some vicious opponent or murderous villain. But dear God, his own mother . . . Jane pressed her hand to her mouth as Xavier spilled out the rest of his words in a heated rush.

"Fortunately my mother's hand wasn't steady enough to slice too deep. When my father got the bleeding stopped, he must have reckoned he had better take me with him or have my death on his conscience.

"Even then, I never felt free to call him anything other than what I always had, *monsieur.* And *that,* Madame, is how much I *had* of our father."

Ariane sank back down in her chair. Her face and Miri's reflected Jane's own horror.

"Xavier, I—I—" Ariane faltered, at a loss for words. But it scarcely mattered, for Xavier had already stormed off.

Chapter Thirteen

XAVIER BRACED ONE LEG IN FRONT OF HIM, BALANCING on the edge of the rocks, as close as he could get without tumbling into the waves battering the shore several feet below. Although letting the sea swallow him up seemed like an excellent idea right about now.

He could not believe what an ass he had made of himself. What devil had possessed him to blurt out a memory he found so painful, all but sniveling like some boy scarce breeched? And in front of those women too, his sisters. It was humiliating.

When he heard someone call his name, he gritted his teeth, not feeling up to facing either Ariane or Miri. Glancing back, he was not any better pleased to see Jane picking her way toward him.

He would have liked to roar at her to go back or else just try to ignore her. Neither action was possible. She moved doggedly forward, plucking her gown up out of the way. But the stiff breeze tangled her petticoats about her legs, making her balance precarious.

If he did not intervene, the fool woman was likely to take an unexpected plunge into the cold foaming water. Xavier closed the distance between them in several long strides.

Jane started to slip but he caught her about the waist and hauled her to safety. He used his left arm, but he could feel the wrench, all the way to the muscles on his opposite side. His recently broken arm gave a painful throb.

He shifted his shoulder seeking to adjust the sling, all the while swearing at Jane. "Damnation, woman. What the hell were you thinking to—"

He broke off as she steadied herself and looked up at him. There were tears glistening in her eyes.

"Oh, no!" If he had not been so afraid she would fall, he would have released her and beat a swift retreat.

"Don't you dare," he growled at her. "Just because I was stupid enough to rake up some ancient history and I never would have done if Ariane hadn't provoked me—Damn it, Jane. You are not going to weep over something that happened to me years ago."

"N-no." She sniffed, but her eyes brimmed over.

"Hellfire!" But there was little he could do, not with tears trickling down her face. He had no choice but to draw her closer.

She burrowed her face against his chest, wrapping her arms about his waist. He held her, feeling awkward as the devil. Any other time he was fool enough to rake over his past, he sought relief from the bitter memories by picking a fight in some tavern or at the bottom of a wine cup or by losing himself in a potion-induced trance.

He would never have thought to seek comfort from a woman. But Jane felt good in his arms, soft, warm, the heat of her tears penetrating the fabric of his shirt, like some curiously soothing balm. He relaxed in spite of himself.

Resting his chin atop her head, he murmured into the silky strands of her hair. "Strange, isn't it? Both my father and mother are dead. What is it about one's parents that they always retain such power, that they are capable of reducing one to the level of a child again, even from beyond the grave?"

"I don't know." Jane drew a little away from him, mopping her eyes. He was reluctant to let her go, maintaining a light grip about her waist.

"So how big of a fool did I make of myself back there?" he demanded.

"None. I am sorry that your revelation was born of such pain and anger, but it was a good thing that you were able to be honest with your sisters. They were both much moved, especially Ariane."

"So now the Lady of Faire Isle pities me. Wonderful," Xavier muttered. "Nothing like a little extra salt being rubbed into one's wounds."

"Not pity, but empathy. I believe you were both hurt by your father in different ways." Jane gazed earnestly up at him. "It could be a bridge to a better understanding between you."

"And what makes you think I would welcome that?"

"You should. Your father might have denied you, but with any encouragement from you, I am sure that Miri and Ariane would claim you as a brother."

"I have managed just fine alone all these years." Making sure Jane was steady on her feet, Xavier withdrew the support of his arm.

He returned his gaze to the sea, watching the waves swell and break in their relentless rhythm that was as familiar to him as his own heartbeat. He had had quite enough of this discussion and baring his feelings for one morning. He hoped that Jane might take the hint and leave him, but she persisted in that gentle way of hers.

"Perhaps you don't know what you have missed by not having a family." She paused, adding in a voice so low, he could scarce hear her above the roar of the surf. "All I have left in the world is a cousin living in Paris who finds my kinship little more than an inconvenience."

He frowned, feeling a trifle ashamed as he realized that for all the conversation they had shared these past few days, most of it had been about him. Beyond teasing her about her late husbands, he had never thought to enquire about the rest of her family. He would have presumed she had someone, somewhere. A rather stupid assumption on his part, because if she did, she would hardly be dwelling here on Faire Isle alone.

Turning to face her, he asked, "What became of your parents?"

"They are long dead. I barely remember my mother and I lost my father when I was twelve." Jane wrapped her arms about herself, whether for comfort or warmth, he could not tell. Shifting, he attempted to provide a barrier between her and the wind blowing in from the channel.

"And you were the only child?" he asked.

"No, I had a brother, Edward, much younger than me. He—he was killed shortly before I had to leave England."

"What happened?"

Jane gave a sad smile. "It's rather a long story."

"Since Ariane refuses to lend me a horse, I don't appear to be going anywhere." He brushed back strands of hair that the wind had tangled across her face.

"Tell me," he coaxed.

Jane sighed. "Well I suppose it all began when my brother and I became acquainted with Margaret Wolfe and her father in London. They were the exiles there, hiding from the Dark Queen."

Jane checked herself with a frown. "I don't know how much you know of Meg's tragic and rather incredible history. You may have heard gossip about Meg from Madame Bevans and some of the others, most of it, I fear, distorted and exaggerated. The truth as I understand it is this."

Jane launched into an explanation of how from her birth Meg had been hailed as the Silver Rose, the girl who would grow to be a powerful sorceress and subjugate all men to her rule. The prophecies had been promulgated by Meg's witch of a mother, Cassandra Lascelles. The dreams of a madwoman, that is all they might have been if the coven had not chanced to gain possession of the *Book of Shadows*. A grimoire of such reputed dark power, it was coveted by many, including Catherine de Medici.

Most of these details Xavier already knew, having

learned much from Queen Catherine and the tales that Jambe du Bois had gleaned in Portsmouth.

Xavier had to school his features into an expression of keen interest to avoid giving himself away. It should not have been difficult. He had always been a master of deception, but to his surprise, he was finding it increasingly hard to be less than frank with Jane. Perhaps because the woman was so infernally honest herself.

However, he did not have to feign surprise when she related how she had become entangled in Meg's life.

"I believe my brother's fate was sealed when I was arrested and imprisoned in the Tower of London, accused of being a witch."

Neither being taken to London's infamous Tower or being charged with sorcery were matters to jest about, but Xavier could not restrain an incredulous laugh.

"A witch? *You,* Jane?"

She managed a wan smile. "It seemed quite mad to me as well, but somehow the queen's spymaster, Sir Francis Walsingham, got the notion that I might be the notorious Silver Rose.

"The only way my brother could think of to save me was to find Meg, force her to come forward and confess that she was the one Sir Francis was seeking. But Ned ran afoul of Ambroise Gautier, the assassin sent by the Dark Queen to find the *Book of Shadows.* Ned was—"

Jane's eyes watered and Xavier feared she might weep again. But she blinked back her tears. "Ned was murdered by Gautier. The villain came at him from behind with a knife and—and my brother stood no chance. Meg witnessed the entire thing. She said that Ned looked more startled than anything. His—his death came very quickly. But I think poor Meg still has nightmares about it."

"Poor Meg?" Xavier echoed. "Trouble seems to follow in that girl's wake. Your friendship with her strikes me as being a very costly one."

"My brother's death was not Meg's fault. She never wanted to be this—this Silver Rose or have anything to do with the *Book of Shadows.* Nor was Ned entirely innocent in the affair. He was also trying to lay hands on that book. Ned had an interest in the occult that bordered on obsession."

Jane shivered. "It frightened me. I tried so hard to discourage his alarming pursuit, but to little avail. I should have tried harder. I was his older sister and when our father died, I swore to protect him always."

"You cannot protect someone from their own particular demons, Jane." He stroked his fingers along the ridge of her cheekbone as though he could somehow caress away the shadows that haunted her eyes. "I learned that lesson with my mother when I was very young. There was nothing I could do to alleviate her bouts of hysteria or save her from her dark melancholia."

"Certainly not. You were only a boy."

"And yet I still felt cursed guilty for sailing away with my father, abandoning her. Even more so when I learned what she did after we were gone. Giving up her house, her gowns, her jewels, all the pretty things she loved so much, and walling herself up in that convent.

"I hope it was not merely another of her mad gestures. That she found some measure of peace before she died. Perhaps that is all any of us can hope for."

Jane bit down upon her lip. "That is something I considered myself, taking the veil—"

"No!" Xavier gripped her arm fiercely. "You'll do no such thing." He was as taken aback by his vehemence as she was. He released her, muttering, "Not that it is any of my concern."

"No, it isn't," she agreed, rubbing her arm. "But you needn't worry. My brother Ned often accused me of being a saint, but I am not. Far from it. I fear I am not good or holy enough to embrace such a quiet existence.

"Perhaps because part of me believes there ought to be more to life than merely finding peace, that there is still the hope of discovering great joy and happiness as well. But not if one seeks solitude within a convent or even on the deck of a ship."

She smiled wryly up at him. "So before you make up your mind to live out the rest of your days alone, Captain Xavier, perhaps you should look more closely at the gift your sisters would offer you. It is a very precious one."

IT WAS EARLY EVENING BEFORE XAVIER FOUND AN OPPORTUNE moment to steal into the shed where Ariane stabled her ponies. Most of the women were busy serving up supper or readying the children for bed. Even Jane had been hustled away by Meg, the girl insisting that she needed Jane's help in mending a tear in her petticoat *right now.*

It was but another of Meg's obvious ploys to draw Jane away from him, but Xavier hadn't minded. It had given him the opportunity he needed as well, to explore his possibilities for escape.

As his vision adjusted to the gloom of the shed, he studied the two ponies tied in their stalls. The roan was the one that had been employed to cart firewood up to the cliffs and would not be well rested. From the way he flattened back his ears at the sight of Xavier, he appeared to be an ill-tempered brute as well.

The dapple gray, however, cocked his head and whickered, almost as though inviting Xavier to come closer. The shed was small enough that he easily spotted where the tack was stored. Saddling the pony was going to prove difficult, as was leading it away from the village without being seen.

But Xavier figured he would manage somehow. It was not the thought of either of those challenges that caused him to hesitate, rather the memory of Jane's words.

"You should look more closely at the gift your sisters would offer you. It is a very precious one."

And perhaps it would be for a different kind of man. Xavier had sailed with a wide array of crewmates over the years, from fresh-faced cabin boys to old tars who had been aboard ship so long, they had salt water instead of blood in their veins.

But no matter how well they loved the sea, how eager they became at the prospect of anchoring in their home port. Rushing off to a joyous reunion with wives, children, brothers, sisters, cousins, while Xavier had either remained on deck or gotten quietly drunk in some lonely inn room.

He always told himself he preferred it that way, no ropes to bind him, no anchors to weigh him down. But perhaps it was more owing to all those years he had wasted striving to win his father's approval and recognition. Far better not to yearn after anyone's love than be disappointed.

Xavier took a step closer to the dapple gray only to be arrested by the sound of someone advising him.

"I wouldn't take that one."

Xavier spun around to see Ariane silhouetted in the doorway, drying her hands on her apron.

"Whickers may seem like a charming creature, but I fear he is not to be trusted. He will bite you in the arse as soon as your back is turned."

"Are you talking about the pony or me?" Xavier asked wryly.

"The pony, I hope."

After the scene that had transpired between him and Ariane earlier, he had expected their next meeting to be awkward enough without the added embarrassment of her catching him about to make off with one of her ponies.

He would have expected her to be as discomfited as he was, but there was the glimmer of a smile about her lips as Ariane crept farther into the shed.

"If you are going to steal a pony, don't you think you should have been a bit stealthier about it? You could have waited until later, when we were all asleep. I believe it should be a clear night with a full moon."

He thought of denying her accusation but what was he going to say? That he had had a sudden inexplicable urge to inspect her livestock?

He laughed instead. "I'll take your advice under consideration. I fear I am more skilled at committing thievery upon the high seas than I am on dry land."

"You are a corsair? Why I am not surprised? Well, I guess I am surprised. It is not a trade that I would have ever expected our honorable father to teach you to pursue."

Her face clouded over and she added bitterly, "Of course, I have had to learn to accept many facts about Papa over the years that have astonished and grieved me."

Xavier studied her, wondering what sort of shining notions Ariane and her sisters had entertained about the chevalier. Probably ones very similar to his own when he had been a small boy with his face pressed to the window, waiting day after day, hoping for a visit from that being he regarded as no less than a god. His tall, strong father, the bravest, most noble knight in all of France.

Xavier wondered exactly when his disillusionment had come. The moment his mother had held the blade to his throat and his father had failed to react in time?

Or had it come much later, the day his Spanish captors had clapped the irons on his wrists and he had realized that his noble father had been so heroically rescuing others, he had not even noticed his son was missing.

Xavier had always thought he would take a grim satisfaction in his father's cherished daughters sharing some of his pain and disillusionment. But the sight of Ariane's downcast face prodded him to reassure her.

"Our father was never a corsair. The chevalier would have considered such lawless actions dishonorable, conduct quite unbefitting a gentleman. I took up the piracy all on my own."

Xavier reached out absently to stroke the nose of the dapple gray. He snatched his hand back barely in time to keep his fingers from being snapped.

"Here," Ariane said, fetching an apple from a basket in the corner. "Give him this. Like most men, Whickers has a better disposition after he's been fed."

As the pony greedily lipped the apple from Xavier's outstretched hand, Ariane sidled closer. Unlike the way she had rapped out questions at him earlier, she was more tentative.

"So—did Papa teach you to ride?"

"Yes, mostly I think so he would not have to regard me as a complete disgrace."

"And to swim? Did he teach you that, too?"

Xavier nodded.

"He taught me as well. He even taught Gabby to use a sword, although some of the women here on Faire Isle were shocked. It was considered a strange thing for a nobleman to teach his daughter. Everyone supposed that he only did it because they believed he had no son."

"He didn't, according to him."

"Oh, Xavier." Ariane stepped even closer and for one dreadful moment, he thought she meant to embrace him and weep. It was one thing to endure that from Jane. He was not sure he could handle such an outburst coming from his starchy older sister.

She drew in a deep breath. "I am so sorry for the way I have behaved. Ever since you arrived—"

"No, none of that," he said. "I have had enough emoting for one day. There is only so much a man can take."

But she rushed on, "Please, hear me out. It was just so hard losing Papa that way. I suppose I did feel as though in some way you had stolen him."

"I couldn't have even if I had tried. He never thought of

anything but you, your sisters, and your mother. Her name was the last thing he breathed before he died."

"When Papa left, he took Maman's portrait with him. It was the only likeness of her we had." Ariane regarded him wistfully. "I don't suppose you know what became of the miniature?"

"I buried him with it."

"Oh." Ariane's lashes swept down to veil her disappointment.

"Sorry," Xavier muttered. His voice became gruff as he sought to explain what he still regarded as sentimental foolishness on his part. "I am sure it must be obvious that the chevalier and I did not share the warmest relationship. But his death affected me more deeply than I ever expected. I hated having to bury him in some remote grave in Brazil.

"When he died clutching your mother's portrait, I couldn't bring myself to take it. I thought—well, at least I won't be leaving him out here alone." Xavier's cheeks heated. "A stupid gesture, I know."

"No, it wasn't. I am glad you left the portrait with him. I am sure it was what my mother would have wished." A tremulous smile touched Ariane's lips only to vanish. "But if he loved me and my sisters so much, why did he never come home? Why did he never try to return to Faire Isle?"

"I have no idea."

When he saw that his curt reply pained her, he added, "Ariane, I truly don't know. Any excitement the chevalier had ever felt in exploring Brazil faded quickly and he was too damned honorable to make his fortune in the ruthless way one has to do out there.

"He did become involved in trying to help a group of French Huguenots form a settlement on the coast of Florida. But after the Spanish attacked and destroyed the colony, I would have thought the chevalier would have sailed for home then."

Xavier sighed. "If he had, he might still be alive. The world beyond the line was too rough, too harsh, too wild for such a civilized man. He didn't belong out there."

"And you do?"

"The sea is the only real home I have ever known."

"But surely even a corsair needs a safe harbor to rest his wearied bones once in a while. I—I wish you would always consider Faire Isle to be yours."

Ariane held out her hand to him. Xavier could only stare at those long slender fingers. He was sure Ariane would never make such a generous offer if she knew everything about him, the time he had spent in Paris last fall at the feet of Catherine de Medici. The Dark Queen, the ladies of Faire Isle's greatest enemy.

And yet those days already seemed long behind him. He had no real intention of returning to Paris, did he? But an unwelcome memory surfaced in his mind of his mother, weeping when she had been summoned back to court.

"Just don't go, Maman," he had begged, burrowing his face into Marguerite's silken dress. "Tell the wicked queen no."

"Oh, Louis," his mother had sobbed. "No one says no to Catherine. Once you have taken her coin, you are hers forever."

Perhaps that had been true of his unfortunate mother,

but it did not apply to him. He was quit of the Dark Queen . . . as long as he chose to be.

And Jane was right. It was something precious that Ariane was offering him. He had just not realized until that moment how badly he wanted it.

He reached for Ariane. Grasping her hand within his own, he accepted his sister's offer of friendship, hoping he never gave her cause to regret it.

Chapter Fourteen

THE MOUNTED TROOP CLATTERED THROUGH THE NARROW street heading for the gate that led to the outskirts of Paris. Catherine gazed down from the window of her bedchamber in the Hôtel de la Reine, watching until the horsemen disappeared from view.

"Henry, you damned fool," she muttered, cursing her son. Obviously none of her cautions had made the slightest impression on the king.

Still frothing over the attack on his beloved friend Epernon, Henry had become suspicious and fearful to the brink of obsession. Against all of Catherine's advice, he was ringing Paris with armed men, threatening if de Guise set one foot in the city, the duke would be arrested and branded as a traitor.

The king's proclamations, the cordon of troops, were making the citizens of Paris as edgy as her son. Catherine had heard rumors that some of them had even sent off appeals to de Guise, begging the duke to come and save them from their mad tyrant of a king.

An invitation that Catherine prayed de Guise would ignore. She did not know what Henry would do to the duke if he ever had de Guise at his mercy. She was even more afraid of what the people of Paris might do to her and her son if anything happened to de Guise.

Catherine vented a heavy sigh, so frustrated and bitterly disappointed in Henry. She had always thought that her son had more of the Medici blood in his veins than her other children. Enough to know that the wisest course with an enemy such as de Guise was to smile and take him by the hand, waiting for the opportune moment to strike. Not to provoke a confrontation one could not possibly win.

Catherine had barely survived one revolution during her childhood. She felt entirely too old to deal with another. It had been all she could do to rise from her bed this morning, her joints throbbing with such pain a lesser woman would have wept, her fingers so swollen and crippled by rheumatism she could scarce straighten them.

If she had but one drop left of Xavier's elixir . . . But the mere thought of the man only made her feel worse, sending an angry pulse throbbing in her brow. If she ever got her hands on the rogue again, she'd have him drawn and quartered.

To appease the Spanish ambassador, Henry had sent out commands for Xavier's arrest should he ever weigh anchor in France again. A report had come back that Xavier's ship, the *Miribelle,* had been seen off the coast of Brittany.

The *Miribelle.* Catherine frowned. In all their conversations, she did not believe that Xavier had ever mentioned the name of his carrack. Strange that it should be the same as Evangeline's youngest daughter.

Something niggled at her brain, some remembrance like broken shards of pottery she ought to be able to fit together. She conjured up an image of Xavier's face. The memory flowed like water, freezing until it almost became solid enough to grasp . . .

"Your Majesty?"

The soft voice behind Catherine's shoulder startled her. The memory dissolved as if a strong wind blew through her mind, scattering it to nothing.

Frustrated, she turned upon her young lady-in-waiting. "What is wrong with you, girl? How dare you creep into my presence in this fashion?"

"I am s-sorry, Your Grace." Mademoiselle de Bec shrank back. "I thought you would wish to know. That old woman you sent for is here."

"Woman? What old woman?"

"M-madame Pechard."

"Oh. Yes." Catherine knuckled the throbbing spot on her brow. Lord help her, was she getting to the point that she could not remember anything these days? She attempted to regain some semblance of her usual composure.

"Keep Madame Pechard waiting in the antechamber until I have had the opportunity to finish preparing myself." Even as Catherine gave the command, her lip curled in self-derision. There would have been a time when she would not have been much concerned about presenting a formidable appearance when receiving such a lowly creature as Madame Pechard.

Catherine's eyes alone would have been capable of setting the woman a-tremble. Now she beckoned to Lady Touchet to fetch the bon grace cap that made Catherine look her most severe, the point of the widow's peak resting against her broad forehead.

As Lady Touchet settled the cap upon Catherine's head, she studied her reflection in the mirror. Her eyesight had not faded enough to spare her the sight of the inroads time had made upon her countenance, the heavy jowls, the deep lines that creased her eyes and bracketed her mouth. A permanent cloud seemed to have settled over her once dark and penetrating Medici eyes.

It was so strange, she thought. Sometimes she felt as ancient as though she had lived a century, other days, as though these aged features could not possibly be hers, that somewhere trapped within this decaying hulk of a body was a vital young woman, struggling to reassert her power.

When Mademoiselle de Bec attempted to press upon her a silver crested cane, Catherine waved it aside. She refused to surrender to such a display of weakness, although only she knew how much effort it cost her to keep her pain-wracked shoulders thrust back, her carriage upright.

By heaven and hell, she was still the one they called the Dark Queen. If she could not appear formidable enough to intimidate a sniveling daughter of the earth like Hermoine Pechard, then Catherine might as well be in her grave.

She elected to receive Madame Pechard in the main

salon. None of the chambers in the Hôtel de la Reine could rival the magnificence of the royal palaces of the Louvre, Blois, or Chenonceau. But Catherine had come more and more to prefer the Hôtel de la Reine, her own retreat where she could be more the private woman and less the queen.

The walls of the salon were lined with her most treasured books and portraits of her de Medici ancestors, the heritage that it was unwise to flaunt before French courtiers who had always been scornful and suspicious of her Italian blood.

The Hôtel was built near the site of the Fille Repenties, a convent designed for destitute girls to save them from life on the streets. The irony of that was not lost upon Catherine. During that long ago revolt in Florence, she had been obliged to seek refuge in a convent. She felt as though her life threatened to come full circle.

Catherine gave the command for Hermoine Pechard's admittance. But when the woman was escorted into the chamber, Catherine scowled, fearing that some mistake had been made. Madame Pechard had ever been a scrawny, unprepossessing creature, but she was at least a decade younger than Catherine.

This person with wisps of gray hair straggling about her gaunt face looked far too old to be Hermoine Pechard. But when the woman spoke, Catherine recognized her grating querulous voice.

"Y-your Grace." Hermoine sank down before her, paying obeisance to Catherine's outstretched hand. Catherine winced at her touch. Hermoine's hands were red, dry, and coarse, some of her nails cracked, the cuticles scabbed.

Catherine drew back in revulsion, but she summoned up a pleasant tone. "Rise, my dear Madame Pechard. How good it is to see you again after so—"

The woman interrupted her in a desperate rush. "Please, Your Grace. Why ever you have sent for me, it will do you no good. I have no information that you will find of the slightest use. So no matter how you threaten or torture me—"

"Hermoine! My dear. You have entirely let your imagination run away with you. I seek no information and I certainly mean you no harm."

"No?" the woman quavered. "Then what does Your Grace want?"

"Cannot a woman, even a queen, be concerned and curious as to the fate of an old friend?"

"Friend?" Hermoine sniffed. "You once threatened to have me sewn into a sack and tossed into the Seine."

Catherine's brows rose. Was it possible there was a spark of spirit in this miserable worm? Catherine had always thought that drowning her would have been a kindness and she saw little in Hermoine's wretched appearance to change her mind. Even as Hermoine voiced her accusation, she shook so hard her brittle bones looked likely to snap apart.

Catherine forced a soothing smile to her lips. "You cannot suppose I sought you out to rake over the past, even though you did once spy upon me for the Lady of Faire Isle."

When Hermoine opened her mouth to protest, Catherine cut her off. "All an unfortunate misunderstanding, I am sure. And if you did, I have long since forgiven you, so you need not tremble so. Come, sit down and let me offer you a little refreshment."

Hermoine looked like a prisoner being led to the gallows, but her eyes gleamed when she saw the array of sweetmeats, cheeses, and wine Catherine had ordered displayed at the small table.

Like many of the daughters of the earth, there had been a time when Hermoine Pechard would have been cautious about accepting anything edible from the Dark Queen. But judging from the ragged, much mended condition of Madame Pechard's garb, Catherine suspected that it had been some while since Hermoine had enjoyed such delicacies.

After only a brief hesitation, Hermoine joined Catherine at the table and fell upon the treats. She was missing about half of her teeth and gnawed away like a greedy rat.

Concealing her distaste, Catherine filled and refilled the woman's wine cup. It did not take much to loosen Hermoine's tongue. She had ever been too ready to launch into a list of all her ills and complaints. Catherine's only challenge was to listen until she could steer the conversation in the direction she wished it to go.

". . . and my life has been so hard, Your Grace can scarce imagine," Hermoine said, swallowing a comfit and washing it down with a gulp of wine. "I was actually reduced to begging for a time. Only by the greatest good fortune did I manage to secure a position in the house of a wealthy merchant."

She set down her wine cup and hiccupped. "Good fortune to become a scullery maid! I, who was once the mistress of my own household, the respected wife of a doctor at the university—"

"Yes, yes," Catherine comforted, curbing her impatience, having no desire to hear Hermoine launch into that old lament, how being arrested by Catherine and exposed as a daughter of the earth had cost her everything. The resulting scandal had caused Hermoine's husband to repudiate her, leaving her destitute.

"A scullery maid," Hermoine wailed again. "I used to have such white, beautiful hands and now look at them."

Catherine winced. She was trying not to. "It is a great pity, but I can offer you a special potion that I often concocted for my ladies at court."

Hermoine shrank back shuddering. "No! No more potions for me. My position is a wretched one, but it is all that stands between me and starvation. If my mistress were to ever find out that I used to be a—a—"

"A witch?" Catherine suggested softly.

"No! Never that." Hermoine dropped her voice to a whisper that was still ridiculously loud in the silent chamber. "I was a daughter of the earth. But no more. I—I have done with all of that."

"But is that ever possible for any of us, my dear Hermoine? Once a daughter of the earth always a daughter."

"No, not me." Hermoine swilled more wine and shook her head vigorously. "I have done, I tell you. Just the same as I told that stupid Lavalle woman when she had the impertinence to look me up and see if I wanted to attend the council meeting—"

Hermoine gasped, clapping her hand to her mouth. A

trifle too late, you fool, Catherine thought as she absorbed the first interesting thing that had fallen from Hermoine's lips since the woman had set foot in the salon.

So Louise Lavalle was back in Paris. Pity that Catherine had not known that when she had been trying to track down any daughter of the earth who might be able to give her some recent information regarding Faire Isle.

Louise was clever and more likely to be deeper in Ariane's confidence. Just as Hermoine had once spied upon Catherine, Catherine in turn had bullied the woman into spying on Ariane. A traitoress to everyone, trusted by no one, that was Hermoine.

But Louise would have been slyer, far more difficult to extract information from even if Catherine had been able to corner the wily former courtesan. Hermoine might not be as valuable a resource, but she was certainly a more pliant one.

Catherine refilled Hermoine's wine cup yet again, remarking in a casual tone, "So Ariane has begun to hold her council meetings atop the cliffs of Argot again."

"So Louise says." Hermoine stared morosely into her wine cup.

"And you do not mean to journey with Mademoiselle Lavalle to attend the council?"

"As if I would go anywhere with that trollop. I would lose my situation in a heartbeat if I disappeared for a fortnight. I could not go even if I wanted to—which I don't."

Catherine studied Hermoine. Her eyesight might not be what it had once been, but her hearing was still acute. Was that a note of wistfulness she detected in Hermoine's voice? She suspected that for all of her disavowals of being a daughter of the earth, Hermoine still longed for her connection to that world.

Hermoine's next words confirmed Catherine's impression. The woman's shoulders sagged, her voice mournful as she added, "It is not as if I would be welcome on Faire Isle, not at such a special council meeting, a once in a lifetime event."

She shot Catherine a resentful glance. "Not after the way I was forced to carry tales back to you."

"I don't recall forcing you to do anything, my dear."

"You promised me that if I spied on Ariane, you would help me get my home back, force my husband to return to me."

"Even I cannot work miracles, Hermoine. That is all ancient history." Catherine dismissed the wreckage of Hermoine's pathetic life with a wave of her hand. "So tell me. What is so special about this particular council meeting?"

"S-special? Did I say that?" Hermoine shoved the wine cup away from her, looking as wary and suspicious as if she had been imbibing a truth potion.

"Yes, Hermoine, you did." Catherine had to rein in her mounting irritation. There had once been a time when she could have pinned this puling woman with her gaze and stripped her thoughts as clean as a corbie ripping the flesh from a dead hare. Now all she had was her wits to rely upon.

"You called it a once in a lifetime event. What did you mean—" Catherine broke off as realization struck her.

The choosing. The Lady of Faire Isle was preparing to

name her successor. For a moment, Catherine was flooded with the bitterest envy of Ariane. How simple, how satisfying to be able to choose one's heir rather than relying upon the archaic traditions and Salic laws that bound up the French throne. If Catherine could have designated the next king or better still *queen,* it certainly might have helped to curb the ambitions of men like François de Guise. Her dynasty, her power would not rest upon the barrenness of her daughter-in-law's womb.

She vented a heavy sigh. "So who is Ariane going to choose?"

Hermoine started, then attempted to recover by stammering, "I—I don't know what you mean."

"Yes, you do." Catherine laid her hand upon Hermoine's arm to stop the woman from nervously cramming another comfit into her mouth. "The Lady of Faire Isle is preparing to name her successor. Who will it be?"

"I—I don't know. Neither did Louise. As usual, the woman was only full of malicious gossip, the most pernicious rumors. The Lady of Faire Isle is so wise. She would never make such a dangerous choice—" Hermoine clamped her mouth shut, looking miserable.

Catherine could no longer read eyes, but it was obvious Hermoine did not know that. The woman squirmed, desperately seeking to avoid Catherine's gaze.

A dangerous choice? Surely Hermoine did not mean . . .

Heart thudding, Catherine seized Hermoine's chin. Forcing the woman to look at her, Catherine summoned up her fiercest stare.

"The Lady means to choose Megaera," she hazarded.

"Ariane has been hiding the Silver Rose on her island all these months and now she means to make the girl the next Lady of Faire Isle."

"N-no!"

But Catherine could hear the lie in Hermoine's fearful denial. Releasing the woman, the queen rocked back in her chair. She was stunned. Oh, not that Megaera was actually on Faire Isle. Catherine had surmised that months ago, but it was good to have her suspicions confirmed. But that Ariane would consider appointing the girl her successor—that Catherine would have never imagined.

Hermoine dissolved into incoherent babbling. The Lady of Faire Isle couldn't, she wouldn't, choose that girl. There were other possibilities Louise had said; a niece or one of the other young women of the island.

Catherine scarce heard a word. She had little doubt who Ariane would select. Catherine certainly knew who *she* would have chosen. So now Ariane would have the benefit of all that girl's extraordinary knowledge, all that power, while Catherine watched her kingdom squandered at the hands of her inept son and she dwindled forgotten into her grave.

Fury and resentment swelled inside of Catherine, nearly choking her. If Xavier had but kept his promise and carried out her command, this all could have been prevented. The Silver Rose might even now be within Catherine's grasp.

But there was little to be gained by continuing to fume over Xavier's treachery. The villain had failed her. If she could not rely upon Xavier, Catherine would simply have to find another way. Before it was too late.

Chapter Fifteen

THE SUN SET WITH AGONIZING SLOWNESS ON THE DAY OF the choosing. Or at least so it seemed to Meg, her nerves stretched as taut as a bowstring drawn back to let loose an arrow.

As the golden orb crept lower on the horizon, the cliffs of Argot were already lost in twilight, the monoliths like a ring of tall shadowy giants waiting to pass judgment upon her.

Dressed in her best gown, her unruly mass of brown hair confined to a tight braid, Meg joined the torchlight procession making its way up the rugged path.

All around her, the mood was one of excitement, women gathered in small groups, laughing and chattering. Carole was surrounded by many of the older inhabitants of the island, while Seraphine held court in the midst of an admiring bevy of young girls.

Only Meg walked in silence, left to the mercy of her thoughts. She could have had the company of her loyal old servant, Agatha Butterydoor. But Aggie lagged behind, the steep trek difficult for her. She was aided by her cane and the support of Lady Danvers.

Meg was glad that Jane had yielded to her pleas and agreed to attend the council. But Meg's relief was more for Jane's sake than her own; anything to keep Jane away from Xavier. With the small village virtually empty, only the children and Miribelle Aristide remaining behind to look after them, Xavier would have had Jane all to himself.

Meg noticed that her friend's color heightened whenever the man approached, to say nothing of the soft glow in Jane's eyes. Why was it, Meg wondered, that she was the only one to notice the predatory light in his?

The pernicious man had even managed to cozen Ariane. It was as though he had everyone under some sort of spell, Meg the only one immune to his charm. But Meg had no room left in her head to fret over Xavier tonight, the captain crowded out by more immediate anxieties.

The choosing.

Huffing a little, Meg gazed upward toward the cliff and realized she must be halfway there and it struck her as symbolic of the way her life might go, upward to the heights or down to what depths she feared to know. Sometimes she thought that her entire fate could rest on the Lady of Faire Isle's decision tonight. More often, she despaired, fearing that Ariane's choice would be of no consequence. That her destiny had been charted by her mother from the moment she was conceived. Megaera, the Silver Rose.

Her visions were getting worse. Her sleep disrupted by fragmented dreams, her waking hours haunted by splintered images in her crystal.

The troop of soldiers stood tall and menacing, waiting for the signal to march upon Faire Isle. Meg stumbled forward, her heart beating wildly as she was prodded along by the shadowy figure behind her.

"There is no need for you to invade Faire Isle. This is the girl the Dark Queen is looking for. This is Megaera."

Meg rubbed her temple, fighting to deny the image. The scene in the crystal had been so hazy. She had not been able to see the face of the one behind her, the one betraying her to the queen's soldiers. Even the voice had not been clear. She had thought it rather high-pitched, almost womanish, rather like Alexander Naismith. But that made no sense unless Sander had somehow survived the fire. Unless he was still alive . . .

Meg shuddered at the thought. She nearly jumped out of her shoes when she felt someone's arm slip about her waist. She stumbled and would have fallen, but for Seraphine's steadying hand.

"Whoa. Easy there. This is not the best place for woolgathering. It will be a very poor beginning if the next Lady of Faire Isle had to start her new reign by curing herself of a broken ankle."

Meg responded to her friend's raillery with a pained smile. "Oh, please don't tease me, 'Phine. Not tonight. I am already too nervous."

Seraphine's mischievous grin softened to a gentler expression. "Poor babe. You are taking all of this much too seriously."

"It should be taken seriously," an indignant voice broke in. Meg glanced up to see that Carole had dropped back from her group of friends to join them.

"The choosing of the next Lady of Faire Isle is a momentous occasion."

Seraphine leaned closer to Meg, speaking in a dramatic stage whisper. "Beware, my dear. It is our rival. No doubt she plans to shove both of us off the edge of the cliff to rid herself of the competition."

Even in the gathering dusk, Meg could see the way Carole flushed and scowled. Ignoring Seraphine, she addressed her remarks pointedly to Meg.

"There is no competition as far as I am concerned. I am sure I have no real wish to be chosen. It ought to be you."

"I feel the same way," Meg murmured. "Far better that the next lady should be one of you."

"Oh, please!" Seraphine rolled her eyes. "Are we not all such good little girls, too modest and demure to grab for the only chop on the plate. If we were men, we would be ready to fight each other to the death for the honor."

"But we are not men, thank God." Falling into step on the other side of Meg, Carole regarded Seraphine with a scornful sniff. "Although I daresay dueling with swords would suit you just fine."

"It would indeed. I could take you blindfolded and with one hand tied behind my back."

"That is hardly to the point," Carole snapped. "Since the

Lady of Faire Isle is supposed to be a promoter of peace and harmony."

"No, there would be a point. Quite a sharp one, in fact."

Before Carole could retort, Meg cut in. "Please stop. I am tense enough without you two engaging in another of your quarrels."

"We don't quarrel. We bicker," Seraphine said. "It takes two people of equal wit to make an argument."

Carole sucked in her breath, but for once she did not rise to Seraphine's baiting. "I am sorry, Meg. I would never want to distress you. I just wanted you to know that whatever Ariane has decided, I will be content."

When Seraphine snorted, Carole insisted, "It's true. There was a time when I was all but an outcast on this island. An ignorant, uneducated girl bearing a child out of wedlock. I have already learned so much from Ariane and I now have many kind friends and my beautiful little son. There is nothing more that I want."

"What a load of rubbish. If you truly don't want to be the Lady of Faire Isle, why don't you just find Ariane and tell her so?" Seraphine demanded.

"Because I am afraid there is the smallest chance she might lose her mind and chose *you*."

The path narrowed ahead so they could no longer walk three abreast. Seraphine took Meg's arm and maneuvered her so skillfully, Carole was obliged to fall behind.

Meg was not sorry if it brought their sniping to an end, but she feared Carole's feelings might have been hurt. There was no use remonstrating with Seraphine, who found Carole as prim and irritating as she did Jane. And once

Seraphine took a dislike to anyone, there was no changing her mind.

All Meg could do was cast an apologetic smile over her shoulder as Seraphine hustled her along, leaving Carole farther behind. It was difficult not to feel a twinge of guilt.

She had known Carole far longer than Seraphine. Their friendship dated from the time Carole had been lured into becoming a member of the Silver Rose coven. She and Carole had formed a tight bond despite the difference in their ages, both of them alarmed and repulsed by the coven's plans and activities.

So why had Meg allowed that bond to wane? Perhaps because Carole was an inadvertent but painful reminder of those dark days or perhaps for another reason more shameful. Of the two girls, Seraphine was by far the more intelligent and exciting, a sparkling diamond compared to the dull luster of a pearl.

It was growing dark enough that she and Seraphine had to quicken their steps to catch up to one of the women lighting the pathway with her torch.

Meg nearly had to run to match Seraphine's long strides. As soon as she could catch her breath, she angled a glance up at her friend and asked, "So what about you? Do you wish to be the next Lady of Faire Isle?"

"I don't know."

"You twitted Carole for not being honest. Your answer strikes me as just as evasive."

"Not evasive, just undecided. I am not sure that I wish to spend most of my life confined to this island."

"It is a woman's lot to end up confined somewhere."

"That sounds like something your Lady Danvers would

say. As you well know, we are not mere women, Margaret Elizabeth Wolfe. We are daughters of the earth and are free to roam where we will. At least we should be."

Seraphine's mouth softened with a rare wistful expression. "God, how I miss my home, Meg. Faire Isle is a pretty enough place, but I am used to dwelling beneath the grand shadows of the Pyrenees. And if I did covet the title of Lady of Faire Isle, I fear it would be for a less than noble reason."

"Which is?"

"I enjoy issuing commands, telling people what to do. I think it would be good to be queen of something, even a tiny island."

Although Meg laughed at her friend's appalling frankness, she shook her head. "I don't. I fear the responsibility would be enormous, terrifying."

Seraphine cast a knowing glance at her. "And yet you still would like to be the Lady of Faire Isle."

Meg fretted her lip before confessing what she had scarce been able to admit to anyone, even to herself. "I do want it, 'Phine. I want it so badly it frightens me, although I fear my reason is no more noble than yours."

When Seraphine regarded her questioningly, Meg added in a low sad voice. "If I was the Lady of Faire Isle, perhaps people would finally forget that I was ever the Silver Rose."

THE BONFIRE BLAZED, HOLDING THE DARKNESS AT BAY AT THE top of the cliff. The ring of standing stones loomed like ancient sentinels guarding the small group of women from any intrusion upon their council.

Some sat upon fallen logs, the younger ones upon the ground, feet curled beneath their skirts. They ranged themselves about the Lady of Faire Isle perched upon a flat rock that formed a kind of throne. An uncomfortable one, Ariane thought, shifting her hip. She wondered what those women gazing up at her so respectfully would think if they realized that their revered Lady just longed to have this over with so she could return to her own comfortable home at Belle Haven.

Perhaps it was the task of naming her successor that was making her feel so old tonight. She was hard-pressed to remember the stalwart young woman she had been at the age of twenty, so bold she had even once dared to threaten the Dark Queen.

"I am warning you, Catherine. I mean to revive the council of the daughters of the earth, the guardians against the misuse of the old ways as you have done. Even you cannot fight us all, a silent army of wise women."

She believed she had succeeded in alarming even Catherine, but these days it was but a hollow threat; Ariane's "army" was sadly diminished. Their method of communication in coded messages dispatched by a relay of trained pigeons had long since broken down. So many of the older generation were long gone, her mother, Marie Claire, old Madame Jehan, taking their wisdom with them.

How much Ariane would have given to have had their advice in this, the most difficult and important decision of her life. As her gaze skimmed the crowd, taking in the faces of Carole and Meg, finally coming to rest upon Seraphine, Ariane prayed she had made the right choice.

The conversation in the clearing had faded to a low

hum. An attempt had been made to conduct business as usual. Any woman who had something to say, grievances to air, tidings to report, or any newfound remedies to share was to come forward and seize the staff of office, thus silencing all other tongues.

But such sharing had been desultory, the birch staff now resting against Ariane's rock, unclaimed. There was only one matter on everyone's minds tonight, the choosing, and Ariane supposed the time had come to get on with it.

She stood, taking up the staff of office. An expectant hush fell over the crowd of women. For a moment, Ariane felt tongue-tied, scarce knowing where to start.

Her mother's simple wisdom filled her mind. *The beginning is always the best place, my dear.*

"Once upon a time," she said. "there lived a group of women known as the daughters of the earth."

Ariane saw many faces wreathed in smiles at her words, like children eager to once again hear an old and familiar story.

Clutching the staff, she paced before the small group and continued, "These women were revered for their wisdom, skilled in all the arts of healing and white magic. According to our legends, they lived in a peaceful time when men and women were considered equal and shared in the governing of the various kingdoms.

"But as time passed, the power shifted, men coming to dominate with their warlike ways. Women were gradually denied their rights to govern and to learn."

Seraphine hissed, drawing a spate of giggles from the younger women, looks of reproof from some of the older ones.

Ariane merely smiled and went on. "Many daughters of the earth accepted these changes. Some became angry and took their vengeance by learning the darker arts."

To Ariane's dismay, she saw a few pointed glances cast in Meg's direction. Jane wrapped her arm about the girl's shoulders, but Meg still colored and ducked her head.

"But some women persisted, struggling to keep our ancient ways alive, despite the threat of being accused as witches. They passed on the secrets of the white magic to their daughters for generations. Many of those women came to settle here on Faire Isle."

Ariane sighed. "Alas, during my lifetime, I have seen those brave few become even fewer. Mistrust and suspicion of those ignorant of our ways, and the raids of witch-hunters have helped to decimate our ranks.

"But I fear the chief reason may be something more insidious and difficult to fight. Many daughters of the earth, overwhelmed by daily cares and the current turmoil of the world, are simply finding it easier and safer to surrender, to corset themselves in the roles expected of women.

"I do not envy the next Lady of Faire Isle. I fear she will face far greater challenges than I ever did, to preserve our ancient ways and knowledge."

"But I am sure she will be well prepared by you," Josephine Alain piped up.

"That's right. You have already taught young Carole so much," Madame Bevans said, fondly patting Carole's hand. The broad nature of her hint was not lost upon the other women.

Agatha Butterydoor leaned forward where she sat, to

glare at Madame Bevans. "The Lady has been teaching other girls as well in case you hadn't noticed. My young Mistress Meg already knew a great deal of magic to begin with."

"Yes, but what sort of magic?" someone muttered while Madame Bevans responded, "Traditionally our Lady has always been chosen from the women who inhabit this island."

"That's not true. Ariane's mother Evangeline was half-English, wasn't she?" Jane spoke up and then looked immediately abashed by her own temerity.

Ariane smiled and gave her an encouraging nod, but one of the girls clustered around Seraphine broke in. "But the Lady Evangeline was connected to the island. She was a *niece* of the previous Lady."

The other young women applauded, laughing and nudging Seraphine as though some important point had been scored. But Louise Lavalle was quick to disillusion them. Of all the women present, the aging courtesan was the most neutral.

Knowing Louise, Ariane suspected the woman merely enjoyed deflating the bevy of younger beauties.

"There is no truth in that statement either," she drawled. "Although it pleased the lady Eugenie to claim Evangeline and her daughters as kin and bid them call her aunt, there was no blood connection."

"Well, whoever is chosen," Madame Bevans called out, "it should not be someone with any connection to the dark ways."

"You mean like Carole Moreau?" Aggie retorted. "I believe she was once a member of the Silver Rose coven."

"She was taken by force, tricked and coerced, you old

bat," Madame Bevans shouted back, half-rising. "And let us not forget who actually is the Silver Rose."

"Was! She isn't any longer." Aggie sprang up, brandishing her cane. "And if you think my poor poppet had any more choice than your precious—"

"Peace!" Ariane bellowed, striking her staff of office against the ground. "Madame Bevans, Mistress Butterydoor, you will sit back down and conduct yourselves like civilized women or leave this council."

Madame Bevans sank down immediately, Aggie more slowly, grumbling under her breath.

"I had thought I made myself clear the other day. The daughters of the earth cannot survive if we quarrel among ourselves. The Lady of Faire Isle must be a gifted healer, knowledgeable in the old ways, and harbor a great respect for our mother earth. But even more important, she must be an advocate of peace, eschewing violence of any kind."

Realizing that her voice had risen and she was gripping the staff far too tightly, Ariane forced herself to relax.

"Much as I value all of your opinions, the choice of my successor is mine alone. I have had so many worthy candidates, my decision has been a difficult one. But the young woman I believe best suited to follow me as Lady of Faire Isle is . . ." Ariane fortified herself with a deep breath.

"Margaret Wolfe."

A stunned silence fell over the gathering. Blinking up at Ariane, Meg sat frozen even when Ariane beckoned to her and smiled. Jane bent closer, no doubt whispering encouragement into the girl's ear. She prodded Meg to her feet, urging the girl forward.

Meg stumbled toward Ariane, twisting her hands in the folds of her skirt.

"Margaret Wolfe, do you accept this charge I would lay upon you?" Ariane asked solemnly.

The silence gave way to an angry buzz of murmurs. Meg stole a look at the sea of hostile faces.

"Well, I—I—" she faltered.

"Yes, she does!" Seraphine shouted out. She leapt to her feet and faced the gathering, her hands planted on her hips.

"What is the matter with all of you? Have not most of you grown up here on Faire Isle? Even I know all the stories my mother Gabrielle told me. All about how this island was meant to be a refuge, for women in particular, a haven from the threats of the past. All mistakes are to be forgotten, this is a place to begin anew. Will you deny Margaret Wolfe the same chance many of you have had?"

Snatching the staff of office from Ariane's hands, Seraphine wielded it like a cudgel. "I think Meg will make a perfect Lady of Faire Isle. Anyone who dares say otherwise will have to answer to me."

"And me." Carole rose to her feet, joining Seraphine.

Her niece looked surprised, but then grinned. She edged aside a little to make room for her, the two girls standing shoulder to shoulder, regarding the crowd with such fierceness, Ariane was torn between laughter and tears.

Her heart swelled with pride for both her niece and Carole. Meg looked so overwhelmed, Ariane feared the girl would weep at any moment. Ariane took her gently by the hand, drawing her forward.

"Becoming the Lady of Faire Isle is a daunting prospect, but as you can see, my dear, you have courageous and loyal friends to support you. But the choice is up to you."

"What choice?" Seraphine cried. "Of course Meg wants—"

"Seraphine, Meg must answer for herself. And please kindly return my staff."

Looking slightly abashed, Seraphine returned the rod to her. The entire clearing held its breath, awaiting Meg's response.

Her tears overflowed, streaking down her cheeks, but she looked up at Ariane with a tremulous smile. "Oh, yes, my lady. I accept your charge and I—I promise to try hard to serve you all until my dying day."

Ariane gathered the girl close and hugged her. She reflected that there was no grand ceremony for this occasion, no crown to pass, no ermine robes, no solemn oaths. But perhaps that was just as it should be. The position of Lady of Faire Isle had always been based on a simple concept of trust.

Besides, Seraphine's loud whoops would have shattered the dignity of any more pretentious proceeding. Ariane pressed the staff of office upon Meg. Turning the girl to face the crowd, she rested her hands upon Meg's shoulders.

"My friends, I give you Margaret Wolfe, your future Lady of Faire Isle."

Chapter Sixteen

THE CLEARING WAS EMPTY. ONLY JANE REMAINED, HAVING volunteered to make certain the fire was safely extinguished. She stared into the dying flames as the voices and laughter faded down the path.

For all of her reluctance to attend the council, she was glad that she had. The choosing had turned out better for Meg than Jane could have hoped. The hostility toward the girl seemed to have magically dispersed within this solemn circle of monoliths.

Although many of the women had offered Meg their congratulations with reluctance, Jane had little doubt Meg would win them all over in time. Especially with the help of Carole's gentle persuasion and Seraphine's forceful personality.

Although Seraphine would not have welcomed it, Jane could have hugged the girl when she had sprung so fiercely to Meg's defense. Jane was still not sure the impulsive young woman was the best influence on Meg, but there was no denying that Seraphine had a loyal heart.

Meg had left the clearing, looking much happier than she had in a long time. Jane had been delighted for the girl, but her own sense of elation faded as silence descended over the clearing, broken only by the occasional crackle and hiss of the fire.

Jane poked a stick amongst the glowing embers, the melancholy she had fought all evening stealing over her. She had kept her promise to Meg, remained with the child until the choosing was done. Meg would have little need of her now, and as for Captain Louis Xavier . . . The man was well on the mend, still chafing to discover what had become of his ship and crew. Despite Xavier's newfound accord with his sisters, Jane had little doubt that once they returned to Port Corsair tomorrow, it would not be long before Xavier set sail.

She stirred the embers more vigorously, refusing to examine the heavy feelings engendered by the thought of his departure. She needed to focus on her own prospects, bleak as they were. After all these months, she was left confronting the same abyss as before, the emptiness of her future.

A twig snapped from behind her, the sound giving her a mild start. She had been half-hoping, half-expecting it. She whirled around to see Xavier emerging from the shadows of one of the dolmens where he had been hiding.

He offered her a somewhat sheepish grin. "Sorry, m'dear. I didn't mean to startle you."

"You didn't, not really."

"What! You are not in the least surprised to see me here?"

"Knowing you, I doubted you would be able to resist the temptation to spy upon the proceedings."

"And here I fancied myself so clever and stealthy. Despite all your denials, I fear you must be a witch, Jane. You seem to have a sixth sense where I am concerned."

Jane shook her head, biting her lip to check a laugh. She wondered what Xavier would say if he realized she had not been the only one to sense him lurking in the shadows. She had observed many of the other women nudging each other and stifling giggles. Jane suspected that even Ariane had been aware of his presence, although the Lady had raised no objections.

But Jane kept her reflections to herself. No need to rob her ferocious corsair of all of his illusions regarding his stealth. Except that he was not *her* corsair. Jane was surprised that she even needed to remind herself of that fact.

She replied, "I have no sixth sense although I did know you were there. But I thought that after the council was over, you would steal quietly away before you were discovered."

"Are you pleased that I didn't?"

Jane refused to answer that. She feared that she was far too glad he had remained. It didn't help noting how apt he looked in these stark surroundings.

Jane felt dwarfed, rendered insignificant in the shadows of the dolmens. Xavier appeared as though he belonged here, a bold adventurer from some far-off world, conjured up by the spirits of these mysterious stones. Even his arm bound up in the sling did nothing to dispel the image. Rather it enhanced it, the battered, wounded warrior.

The glow of the dying fire played over his tall figure, the weathered boots, the leather breeches, the swirl of black cloak. He had regained much of his color these past few days, his face no longer pale but shadowed beneath a day's growth of beard and the dark fall of his hair.

As he prowled closer, Jane was reminded again of Meg's strange warning about sleek, dangerous jungle cats. A warning that only seemed to bring a flush to Jane's cheeks, a quickening of her heart that had nothing to do with fear.

She turned back to the fire, but the red-gold embers were a blur, the only thing clear, the tall silhouette at the periphery of her vision as he stepped forward to stand beside her.

Attempting to keep her voice light, she said, "I trust you found observing the council worth the risk you took creeping up here through the dark. You might well have fallen and broken your neck this time."

"The risk is what makes it fun, Jane. I need to teach you all about that sometime. But I confess I was a trifle disappointed. I knew there would not be any sacrifices or burnt offerings. But I had hoped there might be some sort of ceremony involving a goat and naked dancing."

Jane cast him a reproving glance. A mistake. Despite his teasing drawl, there was a dangerously compelling gleam in his eyes. Or was it only a trick of the firelight? She was quick to avert her gaze back to the fire.

"It did, however, get exciting toward the end," he continued with a chuckle. "There was a moment when I thought my niece was going to start hurling daughters of the earth over the side of the cliff."

"Seraphine is nothing if not exciting," Jane remarked dryly.

"And gracious as well, I thought. She did not appear to mind losing the title to young Meg. So now I suppose we must all cry, 'Hail Mademoiselle Wolfe, the future Lady of Faire Isle.' "

Jane frowned. At least Xavier did not tease her by referring to Meg as Megaera as he often did. But Jane caught the edge in his voice and turned to confront him.

"Why do you dislike the poor child so? I would have thought you might have some empathy with her since—since—" Jane faltered.

"Since we both are the offspring of half-crazed mothers?"

"I am sorry. I—I didn't mean—"

"No, it's perfectly true." He shrugged. "Meg and I do have much in common. That is the problem. I comprehend all too well how she wrestles with the darker side of her nature and just how often she is going to lose."

Xavier skated his knuckles down her cheek. "And that m'dear, I am afraid is something you can never understand. You are far too much of an angel."

"Oh, yes indeed. Saint Jane," she snapped, rearing back. The depth of her irritation surprised her as much as it did Xavier. His brow arched upward in astonishment, but she didn't care. She had spent so much of her life being told how good, how virtuous she was. She was suddenly sick of it.

"Jane, I only meant that at Meg's age, I am sure you spent your time dutifully learning to play the virginal or perfecting your embroidering rather than studying sorcery."

"Yes, that is exactly what I did. My guardian, the Countess of Shrewsbury, was an accomplished needlewoman, so I spent hours at my stitching while my brother was whisked off to learn to ride, to hunt, to wield a sword. And it occurred to me that even though he was so much younger, Ned would enjoy a freedom that I as a woman would never know. The freedom to travel, to explore the world, to—to do whatever he wished while the most change I could hope for was marriage. A different home, a different parlor in which to stitch."

Jane compressed her lips together. She had believed the bitter frustrations of her girlhood long forgotten or at least deeply suppressed. But it was like breaking the seal of an old boarded-up well. The flow could not be stopped.

"*I hated it.* So much so that sometimes, I would fling my stitching to the floor and rush from the house to—to—"

"Take a stroll in the gardens?" Xavier asked, an odd smile playing about his lips.

"No!" Jane glared at him. "I would tear off running, away, up into the hills."

Her gaze lit upon the flat stone Ariane had sat upon. Suiting action to her words, Jane hiked up her skirts and rushed toward it, leaping atop the stone.

"And then when I reached the highest summit, I would

tear off my cap and shake my hair free." Jane reached up and wrenched off her net caul, allowing her hair to tumble about her shoulders. "And then I would roar my defiance at the world."

Following her, Xavier gazed up at her. "And what did you roar?"

"Ridiculous things like *It isn't fair* and *I'll be damned if I submit to such a tame existence.*"

"Swearing? You, Jane? How very bold of you." But Xavier's voice held none of his usual mockery. His smile was strangely tender.

"Not so very bold," she said ruefully. "I only did it where there was no one to hear."

"I doubt most young ladies even dare to entertain such rebellious thoughts. So whatever happened to that wild defiant girl shouting from her hilltop?"

What indeed? Jane thought sadly, remembering the small unmarked grave she had left behind in Sussex.

"I suppose the girl discovered how easy it is to fall from such reckless heights."

Suddenly feeling foolish perched above Xavier on the rock, she hiked up her skirts a trifle, preparing to leap down. But he moved to intercept her. He caught her about the waist, even with one arm, lifting her down as easily as though she weighed no more than one of those twigs she had tossed upon the fire.

He set her upon her feet, but made no move to release her. "What if someone was there to catch you if you fell?"

She looked up at him and realized that away from the fire, his eyes were just as dangerous, perhaps even more so when soft with the reflection of night.

He bent closer and she realized he meant to kiss her. She retained just enough sense to lean a little farther away.

"I—I don't think it would be good to depend upon being caught," she said. "I might fall so hard this time I would not be able to recover."

He stopped, his mouth a breath from hers.

"Wise woman," he murmured. He released her and turned to walk away, leaving Jane to wrap her arms about herself, feeling bereft.

For the second time that night, she felt something inside her snap. She was as heartily sick of being wise as she was wearied of being virtuous.

Xavier had not taken that many steps when she charged after him, tugging on his coat to pull him about. He had time to utter one astonished oath before she flung her arms about his neck.

She dragged his mouth down to hers in a kiss that was bruising and clumsy. He stiffened for only a moment before he recovered from his surprise and banded her closer with his arm.

His mouth moved over hers with more assurance than her awkward efforts, teaching, wooing, and coaxing her lips apart. After the initial shock of his tongue invading her mouth, Jane learned quickly, meeting him thrust for thrust.

She buried her fingers in his hair, greedily drinking in the heat, the passion that was Xavier, as though it were some intoxicating brew she had been denied far too long.

It was Xavier who broke off the kiss, gasping for air.

"Hell's fire, woman. I—I—"

"Yes?" Jane quavered, bracing herself for the humiliation of being thrust away from him.

But his lips curled in a piratical grin. "I have wanted you to kiss me that way ever since you made your first attempt that day on the beach."

"I didn't attempt anything. I told you—" Jane began indignantly only to be silenced by his mouth assaulting hers again.

She was not the only one kissing as though she could not get enough. The fierceness of Xavier's hunger thrilled her, increasing her own desire tenfold. No matter how she angled her body, she could not seem to get close enough to him. When his cloak tangled in the way, she tugged at the clasp. Neither of them noticed as it pooled to the ground.

Jane shivered as Xavier caressed the curve of her breast, the touch as frustrating as it was tantalizing. The shawl she had worn tonight lay abandoned where she had been sitting near Meg. She had dressed for comfort, not bothering with a corset. But even her chemise and the light wool of her bodice were far too many layers between her and Xavier's questing fingers.

When he fumbled with the lacings of her gown, he emitted a frustrated growl, starting to remove his injured arm from the sling. Jane stopped him, shamelessly loosening her bodice herself, enough that Xavier was able to thrust his hand inside.

Her sigh matched his as his fingers cupped her breast, warm, rough, teasing her nipple until it crested against his palm. His touch sent such fire through her, all the way to her core.

Her legs trembled and the next she knew, she was lying flat on her back, Xavier's cloak spread beneath her. Jane stared, a little dazed at the panoply of night sky above her. Never had the stars looked so bright or the moon seemed so full, laden with secrets and dark promises.

Why that should be so, Jane could not analyze. She felt as though she had walled off the rational part of her mind, silenced any whispers of conscience, surrendering herself entirely to sensation.

The cool breeze whispering over her exposed breast, the hot moisture of Xavier's mouth as he knelt over her, laving kisses against her skin, the sweet heaviness pooling between her thighs.

In between kisses, he cursed the awkwardness of his sling, threatening to remove his splints. Her eyes narrowed to slits of pleasure, Jane gave her head an admonishing shake.

"You do just fine with one hand."

"That is because you don't know what I can do with two," he replied wickedly.

Tugging at the hem of her gown, he slid his hand beneath her skirts. He trailed his fingers along her leg, pausing to tease the skin behind her knee, going no higher until Jane squirmed in frustration.

She retaliated by going for the buttons of his breeches. Intoxicated by her own boldness, she delved beneath the flap, closing her hand over the hot, hard length of his shaft.

Xavier clutched at her leg, his eyes widening as he emitted an astounded gasp. "Jesu, woman, you've run completely mad."

He made a halfhearted gesture as though to stop her, only to groan as she stroked him.

"And—I am right beside you," he grated.

She helped him to ease his breeches down. But as he shoved her skirts up higher out of the way, it became clear his broken arm presented a problem.

"This might go better if you were the one on top," he murmured ruefully.

"But I have never," she started, only to realize the foolishness of her protest. She gave a shaky laugh. There were a lot of things she had never done before, including surrendering to her passion for a man, making love to him not within the civilized confines of a bed, but beneath the stars, the wind whistling through the stone titans, the sea pounding at the base of the cliffs.

Xavier kissed her again, manfully denying his own desire, trying to slow the pace of their mating to something a trifle more tender, but Jane would have none of it.

Afraid that if she paused to reflect for but a moment, she would flee, retreat to the corner she had been living in all these years. She clambered atop Xavier, easing down, his hard length stretching and filling her as her skirts fanned about them.

He braced his hand upon her hip as he bucked beneath her, guiding her until she caught the rhythm for herself. Her head thrown back, she rode him hard, faster and faster. Every desire, every anger, every grief she had ever suppressed swelled inside of her, finding voice in her broken cry as she climaxed.

Panting, dizzy, she collapsed beside Xavier and to her horror, promptly burst into tears. Xavier lay on his back, his eyes closed, his chest rising and falling as he sought to recover his own breath.

Jane rolled onto her side, trying to stifle her sobs, but it was impossible that Xavier not notice. He raised himself up, peering over her shoulder, trying to see her face.

"Jane?"

She couldn't answer for the tears clogging her throat.

"Oh, hell!" He sighed. "I was afraid this would happen. I just didn't imagine your regret would come so soon."

"N-no! Not re-regret. It is just that I have n-not felt for s-so long. Perhaps n-never. I d-didn't think I could—"

She doubted that he would understand. No man could. But to her surprise, he urged her to face him and gathered her close to him. He cradled her close to his chest, her tears soaked his shirt, but he did not seem to mind.

He rocked her, murmuring, "I know. I know, dearest heart." Strange as it was for this rugged corsair, she believed that he did understand.

Being held so tenderly and comforted by anyone was a sensation as novel to Jane as the passion had been. She savored every one of his rough whispered endearments, the kisses he brushed against the top of her head.

As she regained some control of herself, she was appalled to realize she had not even noticed whether Xavier had reached fulfillment. In her marriage bed with her late husband, William's satisfaction had been of the greatest importance, hers of no account. A wife was merely meant to endure.

She drew back a little, so she could peer at Xavier anxiously, scarce knowing how to frame such an awkward question.

"Er . . . did you . . . were you able to—"

"Oh, yes."

"G-good. I am so glad," she said, provoking a laugh from him.

"Me too." He grinned at her and Jane flushed.

What an idiot he must find her. She had no idea what sort of women he was accustomed to bed, but she doubted any other had treated him to such an awkward display. Pouncing at him like a cat in heat and then dissolving into a puddle of tears.

"You must think me quite insane." She sniffed.

"We both are." He brushed aside the moisture from her cheeks with the pad of his thumb. "I blame it on the moon."

"Or these stones." Jane said, attempting to return his smile. "Miri told me that according to legend they are daughters of the earth, petrified long ago to save them from witch-hunters and to be perpetual guardians of the island. They are supposed to be infused with a special magic."

"Oh, I believe it. I have heard other legends regarding such monoliths. I doubt we are the first couple to succumb to passion beneath their shadows. It is rumored that they have the power to make men potent and women fertile."

Fertile?

The word struck Jane with all the force of a bucket of cold water dashed in her face. She sat up, clutching at the region of her womb.

"Oh, God, oh God. What I have done? How could I be so careless? Not again."

She scrambled to her feet as though by standing she could force Xavier's seed to flow from her womb. She cast a nervous glance up at the omnipresent stones as though they might even now be weaving their fatal magic upon her. Distracted by fears of what might be the consequence of her reckless actions, she plucked at the bodice of her gown to tuck her breasts back inside.

"We—we should be getting back. We will be missed," she stammered.

Xavier stood more slowly. He managed to hike up his breeches, but she was obliged to help him with the buttons, which only rendered the moment more awkward.

He frowned, studying her with narrowed eyes. If the man had not thought she had taken leave of her senses before, now he must be convinced of it.

"What is wrong, Jane? What did you mean, *not again*?"

She was loath to answer him, but she supposed she owed him some sort of explanation. She ducked her head, shamefaced.

"When—when I was fifteen, I was smitten with my guardian's master of the horse. I gave way to my passions and ended up conceiving a child out of wedlock.

"My little girl was stillborn, which was accounted a blessing at the time. But I never conceived again. God's judgment against me, I fear, because of my sin."

Xavier snorted, shocking her by swearing. "God's blood, woman. Even if I was sure I believed in the Almighty, I would think He would have greater affairs to tend besides cursing some poor girl for a slip from grace that was none of her fault. His wrath should have fallen upon this horse master for seducing you. You were but fifteen."

"Old enough to know the difference between right and wrong," Jane said.

Xavier took her by the chin, obliging her to look up at him. "So what we did here tonight—that felt wrong to you?"

"No," she whispered. That was what made her so confused. "But—"

"There is no but," he interrupted her, drawing her close again. "Perhaps we were a trifle reckless. I confess I am accustomed to having congress with women of a more experienced stamp, who know how to protect themselves from any unwanted consequences."

"You mean prostitutes."

"I prefer to call them ladies of enterprise who know how to give a man good value for his coin."

When Jane frowned at him, he chucked her chin and smiled ruefully. "I never laid claims to sainthood, Jane, or even to being a good man. But while I may be an unconscionable rogue, you have nothing to fear on one score. There is one thing I would never do."

"And what is that?"

"I would never abandon my child or his mother."

He meant every word, Jane was staggered to realize. His voice was husky, his expression fierce in its sincerity. She well understood the reason for it. Beneath this man's tough façade, the shadow of the boy denied by his own father lingered.

Yet how many who styled themselves noblemen would have found no fault with the Chevalier Louis Cheney's behavior? Any woman rash enough to give herself outside of wedlock must stand the consequences, the man free to walk away. It was the way of the world.

But clearly not Xavier's way. He kissed her again, her brow and her eyelids before settling on her lips. Jane sighed, longing to tell him how much his assurance meant to her, how much she respected him for it, how much . . .

She loved him.

But that was something she hardly dared acknowledge to herself let alone Xavier, so she held her tongue. Burying her face against his chest, she feared she had already committed enough folly for one night.

Chapter Seventeen

PORT CORSAIR DROWSED IN THE MIDMORNING SUN, THE channel waters as calm as the activities on the dockside. Or lack of them. By this hour, the fishing boats had been launched. Only one small carrack rode at anchor, being loaded in preparation for a trading voyage to the mainland on the next tide.

Xavier wended his way past barrels, crates, and coils of rope as he had done every day since they had returned to this side of the island. He drew in a deep breath, filling his lungs with the tang of salt air as he flexed his fingers protruding from the edge of the sling.

His hand felt stiff and he longed to be rid of the cursed splint. The docked ship filled him with a longing even more familiar, to be at sea again, to feel the waves swelling beneath him.

But the urge was no longer as simple and uncomplicated as it had once been. He had done the one thing he had sworn he would never do, forged a link that would keep him tethered to dry land.

Jane.

He had had leisure enough this past fortnight to regret that wild night among the standing stones. The leisure but not the inclination. All he had to do was think of Jane's soft eyes and generous lips and his body stirred with the urge to repeat their folly all over again.

But he ought to have known better. Jane was nothing like the doxies he usually bedded whenever he made port. Experienced women who knew how to make certain there were no consequences of their liaisons.

This time there damn well might be consequences. Jane was mortified to discuss her womanly functions with him, but when he had pressed her, she admitted that her courses were a week late.

For another woman, that might be nothing to fret about. But according to Jane, she had always been as regular as the flow of the tides. That figured, Xavier thought wryly. That a woman as dutiful and proper as Jane would be punctual in everything. Except the one time that she hadn't been, the time her body had swelled with child.

Well, he had made her no idle promise when he had sworn he would not forsake her. Not after the way his own father had denied and abandoned him. That was a pain he would not wittingly ever inflict upon his own flesh and blood.

If Jane was with child by him, then so be it. He would be obliged to marry her even if he was convinced he would make her the very devil of a husband.

Husband . . . father. The mere words were enough to make him break out in a cold sweat. He would have felt less fear facing all the holy monks of the Spanish Inquisition. But there was time enough to deal with all his qualms about an event that might never happen.

Shielding his eyes from the sun reflecting off the water, Xavier focused on the harbor instead. He scanned the gangplank and the dockside, hoping for the return of the messenger Ariane had dispatched to the mainland to make enquiries after the *Mirabelle.*

Xavier froze when a sight met his eyes, far more welcome than any messenger—a tall dignified man, his ebony skin and powerful physique garnering stares, even from dockworkers accustomed to encountering seafarers from many lands.

The man strode toward the dockside inn, accompanied by a disreputable-looking old sea dog, stumping along on one wooden leg.

Relief surged through Xavier, accompanied by a stronger emotion that thickened his voice as he called out, "Pietro. Jambe!"

The pair stopped beneath the swaying inn sign and turned. Pietro's face lit up, his teeth flashing against his dark skin. Jambe flushed, so excited he lost his balance and would have fallen but for Pietro's steadying arm.

Xavier started forward and they met midway. Pietro seized him in a rib-cracking hug, half-lifting him off his feet. Jambe contented himself with some vigorous backslapping that jarred Xavier's injured arm, but he was too elated to care.

He retaliated with some playful cuffs of his own until he realized they were attracting a good deal of notice. The three of them drew apart, adopting gruffer stances. Jambe attempted to glower at Xavier but was unable to conceal his grin.

"Damn your eyes, lad, but you gave us a fright," he said, the old man blinking away some suspicious moisture from his own eyes. "We had given you up for dead until that boy turned up from Faire Isle asking about the *Miribelle.*"

"I had nearly given up on you as well." Xavier smiled. "But I should have known you two were too ornery to drown. Especially you, old man. But what of the rest of the crew? And what of my lady?"

Pietro and Jambe sobered, exchanging a look that did not bode well.

"We'd best head on inside, Captain," Jambe said, jerking his head in the direction of the inn. "I think you might be wanting some strong drink."

THE PASSING STRANGER SAT AT THE MOUTH OF THE HARBOR, the only male bastion on an island inhabited mostly by women. Of a summer evening the taproom was crowded with fishermen, sailors, and peddlers from the mainland, the drone of masculine voices interspersed with outbursts of raucous laughter.

Much as he had learned to value the friendship of the ladies of Faire Isle, Xavier often frequented the Passing

Stranger for an evening, seeking more than tidings of his lost ship. He found it a relief to be back among his own kind, companions who required little conversation from him beyond a grunt and who were not forever insisting he share his feelings.

Not that his quiet Jane made many demands upon him. No, it was those wistful eyes of hers that did all the asking.

At this hour of the morning, the taproom was empty save for the table Xavier shared with Jambe and Pietro. Phillipe, the inn's current landlord, had served up a bottle of Madeira for Pietro's more refined palate. The innkeeper had presented Jambe with a tankard of ale he had recently purchased from a Portsmouth captain.

England's finest brew, Phillipe had boasted. Piss water had been Jambe's gloomy assessment, but he drank it anyway. Xavier sprawled in his chair, a large glass of whiskey in front of him.

He had rendered his companions a brief and highly expurgated version of his own adventures since the night of the storm. Jambe and Pietro had nodded, making few comments.

Xavier drummed his fingers impatiently on the table. "All right. Now you know what happened to me. So quit stalling. Tell me about my ship."

Jambe sighed and swilled some ale. "Well, it was a bloody miracle we rode out the storm. But the wind shifted, driving us away from Faire Isle back toward the mainland. We ran aground along the Breton coast."

"You know how treacherous those reefs can be, especially near St. Malo," Pietro put in.

"We expected to break up or capsize, but God bless

her, somehow the *Miribelle* remained afloat. We considered ourselves damned fortunate until first light, when our luck ran out."

Jambe took another swallow, pulling a sour face. "We were hit by scavengers, Captain. A pack of Breton fishermen who considered our cargo fair game."

"Some of the men tried to fight them off," Pietro said. "But we were exhausted and there were too damned many of them. The vultures stripped the holds bare."

Jambe slammed his tankard down, quivering with outrage. "One villain even tried to make off with the Sea Beggar, but he escaped and flew back to me first chance he got, the clever lad."

"We did manage to salvage your clothes, charts, and books," Pietro continued. "Father Bernard is keeping your belongings and the Sea Beggar safe at a monastery outside of St. Malo."

Xavier could find little humor in any of this but he managed a grim smile. "Considering the Sea Beggar's vocabulary, that ought to be interesting."

Jambe sniffed. "That wretched priest will probably try to teach my poor Beggar to recite the paternoster."

"Many of the crew believed that it was Father Bernard's paternosters that saved us," Pietro said.

"That and the fact that their devil of a captain was washed overboard."

"Jambe!" Pietro cast him a reproving scowl.

"Well, it's true." Jambe offered Xavier an apologetic grin. "Partly your own fault, Captain. It always amused you to let them think you were some kind of sorcerer. You know what a superstitious lot sailors can be."

The old man drained his tankard and signaled for more ale. "Anyway, the disloyal dogs have all dispersed, seeking out berths on other ships. Me and Pietro are all that's left of the *Miribelle*'s crew."

"And the *Miribelle* herself?"

"I reckon whatever is left of her has broken up on the rocks by now, been dragged out to sea."

Xavier's fingers tightened on his glass. Set against the lives of men he valued, the *Miribelle* was nothing. It was wrong to grieve for a ship and yet he did, pained by the thought of his lady reduced to one of those wrecks that passersby paused to gawk at, eroded by wind and surf until nothing remained but driftwood, perhaps a spar sticking up out of the sand.

The *Miribelle* had served him well over the years. His lady had deserved a far more gallant end. Xavier would have sooner seen her sunk to the bottom of the sea or set fire to her decks himself.

He tossed down his whiskey in one swallow, the fiery liquid doing little to ease the hollow ache inside of him. A heavy silence settled over the table. Pietro sipped his Madeira while Jambe delved into the small leather sack tied to his belt.

"I saved this for you too, Captain. Thought you might be wanting it about now."

Pietro sucked in his breath with a furious hiss of disapproval and Xavier soon realized why. Jambe slid an object across the table to Xavier, the leather flask that contained his shaman's brew.

When Xavier regarded his first mate questioningly, the old man scratched his grizzled beard. "I just thought maybe you might want to conjure up one of those visions of yours. It might help us decide what to do now."

"The captain has no need of that devil's brew to guide his course." Pietro scowled, his hand twitching as though he would seize the flask, but Xavier's fingers closed around it first.

He stared down at the flask, frowning. He had resolved to have nothing more to do with the vine of the spirits, blaming the potion for dulling his wits the night of the storm. If his head had been clear, perhaps events might have transpired differently. And perhaps not.

He experienced the same old temptation he always did when he felt pained or overwhelmed, to lose himself in the splendors of his dream world. Seldom had he had more cause to want to escape. Discounting the time he had been a prisoner of the Spanish, his fortunes had never been at a lower ebb.

Glancing up, he met Pietro's troubled gaze.

"You don't need that stuff, Captain," he repeated.

Xavier tucked the flask inside his doublet. "I am hardly much of a captain with no ship and no crew."

Jambe bristled. "What do we look like? Your maiden aunts?"

"As always, we follow you, Captain," Pietro said.

"Follow me where?" Xavier retorted bitterly. "My prospects appear a trifle dim at the moment."

"Far better than when we thought you were dead," Jambe retorted.

"I am glad my sister's messenger found you and I appreciate your seeking me out but—"

"Your *sister*?" Jambe echoed. He and Pietro exchanged a look.

"Yes, my sister, Ariane, the Lady of Faire Isle." He glared at his men, daring either of them to make something of it.

Pietro's disapproving expression vanished. The flask for the moment forgotten, the Cimmarone smiled at him. "So you have owned your kinship at long last. I think it a fine thing that you made your peace with your sister."

"It's always a fine thing to be on the good side of a witch," Jambe muttered.

"Don't call her that!" Xavier snapped.

"Sorry, but you must have some scheme in mind, Captain. Sister or no sister, why else would you have lingered here on this miserable island so long?" Jambe leaned forward and whispered. "Does it have anything to do with that other witch?"

Xavier stiffened. "Jane is no witch either, damn you!"

"Jane? Who said anything about any wench named Jane?" Jambe demanded, looking bewildered.

"No one." Xavier grimaced, hoping he did not look too self-conscious. He concealed his embarrassment by reaching for more whiskey.

"I was talking about that other chit, the one that the queen wanted you to find. That—that Maria."

"Megaera," Pietro corrected.

"Yes, that's the one. Did you find her?"

"What if I did?" Xavier retorted.

"Then it seems to me we have the solution to our difficulties. Just fetch that girl back to the queen—"

"I'll have no part in abducting an innocent young girl," Pietro said.

Jambe frowned at him. "From what the queen said, this girl is not all that innocent."

No, Meg wasn't. Xavier had felt uneasy ever since Ariane had named the girl as her successor, certain that his sister was only letting herself and her small island realm in for a world of trouble. Especially if Queen Catherine should get wind of the appointment.

Ariane had sworn all those who had attended the council to secrecy until Catherine was in her grave. Considering the queen's age and failing health, that could surely not be long. But Xavier put little faith in the ability of women to hold their tongues.

As Catherine drew nearer to the end of her life, the woman was bound to wax more desperate. Perhaps she would even dispense with her customary subtlety and send a mounted troop to tear the island apart.

Both he and Megaera presented a danger to Faire Isle. Might it not be better for everyone if they were gone, if Xavier fetched Meg to the queen himself? He would do it more gently and perhaps he could convince Catherine that the girl was really of no use to her. She'd release Meg and the girl would finally be free of any further threat from the Dark Queen.

Xavier vented a self-disgusted sigh. Or perhaps he was merely inventing noble excuses to disguise the baser reason behind his temptation—the reward.

He recollected the promise he had made to young Dominique when the boy had lay dying after the attack on the

Spanish vessel. Xavier had sworn to the lad that he would see that the boy's mother and sister were looked after from the proceeds of the sale of the cargo. But it was a pledge he could no longer redeem.

And what of Jane and the possibility of their unborn child? At the moment all he could offer her was a name stained with infamy.

Even if he was entitled to call himself Louis Xavier Cheney instead of the Jaguar, what would it matter? A respectable name in itself could not put a roof over a woman's head or food on her table.

Handing Meg over to the Dark Queen would certainly be the most direct path to recoup his fortunes. Except Jane would never forgive him. She'd likely curse him for it, but she wouldn't have to. He'd damn himself every time he looked in the mirror.

Banishing the ugly temptation from his mind, Xavier shook his head. "No, even if the girl proves to be the most dangerous sorceress this side of hell, I won't use her to fill my coffers."

"But Captain—"

"No!" Xavier repeated more forcefully.

Jambe slumped down in his chair, looking frustrated. "Fine. Then what is our next course of action, Captain?"

"I don't know. I need time to think." Xavier ground his fingertips wearily against his eyelids. "My belongings must be fetched from St. Malo. Most particularly my father's journals and the parrot. They are my sisters' legacy and it is high time I handed them over."

"What? The Sea Beggar? Surrender my clever lad to—

some wench?" Jambe blanched. "Captain, you cannot possibly mean that."

"Jambe, you always knew . . ."

"No!" The old man's lower lip actually trembled. "I won't do it. I—I'd sooner lose my other leg."

Xavier sighed. He attempted to reason with the old salt when Pietro interrupted, a puzzled frown marring his brow.

"But, Captain, why do you not just come away with us now? I am sure none of us would have trouble securing a berth on another ship, some employment to see us through until we decide what to do next. You have made your peace with your sisters. What else could possibly hold you here?

What indeed? Xavier squirmed in his seat. He and Jane had had little opportunity to be alone since that night of passion atop the cliffs. She seemed a little shy around him, often unable to meet his gaze. But when she did, there was a new softness in her eyes that both warmed and panicked him. A woman's heart was far too fragile a thing to be entrusted to his rough hands.

Surely she would be far better off if he sailed out of her life now. But he could not leave her in such straits, not until he was sure he had not planted his seed in her belly.

Xavier stood up abruptly, avoiding Pietro and Jambe's eyes.

"Just return to St. Malo and fetch my belongings from Father Bernard. Then I want you to find young Dominque's family and see how they are faring. Tell them that despite what happened to the *Miribelle*'s cargo, I still intend to redeem the pledge I made to the boy. After that, go to that inn just outside the town, the Cheval Noir. Wait there until you hear from me. I shall join you presently. I still have some unfinished business here."

Xavier strode away before either of them could question him further.

Chapter Eighteen

FAIRE ISLE WAS NOT A TRUE ISLAND. IT WAS CONNECTED TO the mainland by a narrow causeway. But time and tide were slowly eroding the rocky stretch. Only the most intrepid of riders ventured across it now and none dared attempt it during a storm. Both horse and rider were far too likely to end up in the sea.

Sheltered beneath a stand of trees, Xavier gazed in that direction, wistfully, it seemed to Jane. But as she drew nearer, she realized it was not the causeway that claimed his attention, but the sails of a small carrack, growing more distant by the minute as the winds bore it back across the channel toward Brittany.

Xavier's face wore such a look of longing, Jane's footsteps faltered. Word on Faire Isle spread fast and she had already listened to much speculation regarding the two men Xavier had drunk with at the Passing Stranger.

They surely must be members of his crew, coming to bring him word that the *Miribelle* had survived the storm. His ship was waiting for him. His men had returned on that carrack making its way across the channel. Obviously Xavier wished he was with them.

Jane was certain only one thing could have held him back, Xavier's stubborn sense of obligation to her. Much as she respected him for that and was grateful, she took no pleasure in the thought.

Getting oneself with child was a pathetic way to hold on to a man. She wished she could smile and convince him that all was well with her, that her flow had finally come. But she was such a poor liar, he would see through her in a minute.

As the carrack faded farther into the distance, Xavier's expression waxed more despondent. Jane judged it might be best not to intrude upon him at this moment. But before she could retreat, he glanced round and saw her. His countenance lightened.

"Jane." He smiled and extended his hand to her in a way she doubted any woman would have been able to resist.

She approached him shyly. As soon as she came within range, he seized hold of her. They were not that far out of view of some of the cottages near the village green.

Xavier drew her deeper within the shade of the trees before bending closer to steal a kiss. It was chaste compared to the ones they had shared that night atop the cliff, but Jane felt a warm tide of color surge into her cheeks.

"I—I am sorry," she said a little breathlessly. "I don't mean to pry, but I heard that you met with some gentlemen from the mainland today."

Xavier smiled wryly. "I don't think that is a word that I would ever use to describe Jambe and Pietro. But yes, I have finally been contacted by some of my crew."

"Then your ship is safe."

"No." Xavier released her hand and paced a few steps away. He stared out at the channel, an empty look in his eyes.

"The *Miribelle* is gone, wrecked on the reefs near St. Malo."

"Oh, Xavier."

He shrugged. "At least my crew survived. The *Miribelle* was not much of a ship. Timbers rotting, she leaked like a sieve. One could hardly even call her seaworthy anymore, so it is no great loss."

His pose of indifference did not fool Jane. She knew full well how much that ship had meant to him. She had heard it in his voice, seen it in the glow of his eyes when he spun tales of his voyages. The *Miribelle*'s name had rolled caressingly off his tongue, making Jane feel absurdly jealous at times.

She knew Xavier well enough to realize that he would not welcome any outpouring of sympathy. She contented herself with squeezing his hand and murmuring, "I—I am so sorry."

"Thank you, my dear," he said gruffly. As he carried her hand to his lips, she thought he looked grateful for her restraint.

After a moment, she ventured to ask, "What will you do now?"

"That rather depends on you." He searched her face questioningly and she knew what he wanted to hear.

She tried to smile and summon up a lie, but she ended up by miserably shaking her head.

His face fell, but he strove to conceal his disappointment. "Ah well, it is still early days as yet."

"Yes," she agreed. She felt so torn herself. The sensible part of her argued that she would avoid a great deal of trouble if her flow would but start. But another part of her, the part that had buried a stillborn babe and never cradled another in her womb, longed to bear Xavier's child, come what may. Confused by the tangle of her own feelings, she sought to change the subject.

"You were not the only one who received ill tidings from that carrack today."

"Oh?"

"I had a letter from my cousin who lives in Paris."

"The one who cast you off when you became an exile? What the devil does she want?"

Jane winced. Xavier's sentiments, although more blunt, were an uncomfortable echo of what her own had been upon receiving the note. Shamed by her uncharitable attitude, she sought to make excuses for her cousin.

"Abby was fond enough of me when we were girls. I am sure her attitude of late has been formed by her husband."

"Would you have abandoned your only cousin at your husband's command?"

"I hope I would not, but women are obliged to obey their husbands."

"Perhaps I may have cause to remind you of that one day, lady."

She responded to his teasing with a prim frown. "In any case, Abby is in a dreadful state. Her husband, George, has ever been a feckless man, an incorrigible gamester. He ran up so much debt in Paris, he was obliged to flee the city. He abandoned his poor wife. Abby writes that she has fallen quite ill from all the stress. She wants me to come to her."

"I daresay marooned sailors want kegs of rum. That doesn't mean they are going to get them."

When Jane did not respond, Xavier studied her face. "Never tell me you are thinking of going to Paris."

Jane shifted uncomfortably, avoiding his gaze. He seized her chin, forcing her to look up.

"You are! Damnation, Jane."

"She is the last of my family. It would be my duty—"

"Your duty be damned. You are under no obligation to Abigail Benton. That woman threw you off."

Jane regarded him earnestly, trying to will him to understand. "I have never fashioned my behavior after what others do. I must look to my own conscience. If I am not with child, I should go to Abby. It—it would be the right thing to do."

When he scowled at her, clearly exasperated, Jane offered him a wan smile. "I must do something. I cannot remain forever on Faire Isle."

"Why not?"

"I—I don't know. Perhaps because it is too wild and strange, too different from anything I have ever known."

He sighed and traced his fingers gently over the curve of her cheek. "Ah, Jane, you remind me of a little wren caught in a cage. Your door has been left open, but still you won't come out, too afraid to fly free."

"Freedom often comes with too high a price."

"You mean our present predicament. I know you have been often at church. No doubt making confession and doing penance for the night you spent in my arms."

He tried to sound teasing, but she thought he looked a little wounded by the notion.

The church of St. Anne's was little more than a chapel, all that remained of the convent that had once been situated on Faire Isle. Jane had been on her knees there every morning, praying, but even she was not sure what she wanted. To be safe and respectable again or to be blessed with a child regardless of the consequences. Could even God find a way to answer such ambiguous prayers?

"I have been in attendance at St. Anne's," she said. "After being denied my faith for so long, the mass is a most precious gift to me, the one blessing of being forced into exile.

"But I have not made confession. One can hardly ask for forgiveness and do penance when—" She felt her cheeks flame. "When all one wants is to repeat the sin."

It was a dangerous thing to admit to Xavier. Perhaps for once she should have tried harder not to be so honest. His eyes darkened, simmering with heat. He drew her closer and this time the kiss he bestowed upon her was not so chaste.

The man's mouth was sin itself, his tongue hot and thrusting, stirring her to respond with the same madness that had seized her that night atop the cliffs. She fought against it this time, although it took all her will to break free of his embrace.

"And—and what of you?" she asked striving for a normal tone as though the man had not just kissed her senseless. "If there is no babe, I am sure you will be wishing to be at sea again."

Xavier blinked and frowned like a man who had just been snapped back to reality. "Even if you are with child, I shall have to seek employment aboard a ship eventually. I must get our living somehow, and the way of the corsair is all that I know to make our fortune. Not that I seem to be that good at it."

"You—you were not a successful pirate?"

Xavier laughed. "I did well enough, but any wealth I gained has always trickled through my fingers. It has never been about the pursuit of gold for me."

"What then? Revenge against the Spanish?"

"Perhaps in part." Xavier appeared a little sheepish, a tinge of color darkening his cheeks. Intrigued, Jane urged him to go on.

Looking embarrassed, he said, "This will sound foolish, but for me, it is about the adventure. When my father took me to the New World, he was content to confine our voyage only to those places other Europeans had gone before.

"But I always chafed to see what was around the next bend of coastline, across the next expanse of uncharted sea. I wanted to be an explorer the like of your Sir Francis Drake, my course ever fixed upon the far horizon."

Xavier could be so cynical, but his eyes glowed as he spoke, his face almost boyish, softened by such dreams, it made Jane wistful. It had been so long since she had even allowed herself to have any.

If she was the caged wren, Xavier was more like an eagle tethered to the shore and Jane feared she had become the chain.

"Xavier, even if I am with child, there is nothing to hold you here," she said. "You yourself have pointed out to me how women are freer of convention on Faire Isle. Carole Moreau bore a child out of wedlock, yet here she is still esteemed. She appears to be doing just fine."

Xavier's dream-ridden look vanished, his features hardening into stern lines. "Perhaps Carole is, but what of her son? He is not much more than a babe now. But soon he will grow savvy enough to ask about his father. When he realizes he has none to claim him, he will feel the hurt and the shame, I promise you."

Xavier's voice constricted with strong emotion. "I realize I am a poor prospect as a husband and father but at least I can spare our son the pain of being a nameless bastard."

"H-husband?" Jane stammered. "You intend to marry me?"

"Yes, I thought you understood that." He frowned. "Should I have asked you first? Dropped to one knee and begged for the honor of your hand? I did not think you would require any formal or romantic gesture. You have been wed twice before."

Yes, but never to a man that she loved, one of her own

choosing. For a moment her heart lifted with a surge of joy only to plummet as she recalled that none of this would be of Xavier's choice.

She shook her head only to be stopped by Xavier seizing her chin.

"Nay, Jane. Don't shake your head at me. I will not be gainsaid. You do not have to worry. I will not be around much to plague you, although—" He pursed his lips, his brow furrowing. "Perhaps I could become a fisherman or seek a place on one of those ships that trade between England and the Netherlands. That way I would not be gone for years at a time.

"I could return to Faire Isle to visit my sister and satisfy my wife's needs." He cast Jane a wicked look that caused her to blush again. "And I could teach our boy a few things, how to sail, to swim, and to wield a sword."

"Our boy?" Jane demanded. "What if it be a girl?"

Xavier looked daunted for a moment, but then he grinned. "If she would prove to be anything like my spitfire nieces, I would be obliged to teach her how to fight as well."

She laughed in spite of herself, the future that Xavier painted all too tempting if only she could believe he wanted it as well. But she feared he would always regret the loss of his far horizons and grow to resent both her and the child in time.

But when she tried to reason with him, he stopped her mouth with a kiss. "Spare me any more of your logic, my lady. You ought to know by now I am completely ruthless and unprincipled when it comes to gaining my own way. I will march you to church at sword point if need be. You shall not be rid of me so easily."

That was the problem. She didn't want to be. When he drew her closer, she subsided, resting her head against his shoulder with a deep sigh. It seemed pointless to argue about an event that would never happen, a child that might not even exist. Instead of fretting over the future as she too often did, she should simply savor the moment, having Xavier with her. It likely would not be for long.

Xavier brushed his lips against her brow. A man could do far worse than to spend the rest of his days with a good woman like Jane Danvers. Even the prospect of the babe no longer seemed so alarming to him.

He longed to be back striding the deck of a ship, but the call of the open sea was not as simple as it once had been. He would miss Jane with a stronger ache than if he had parted with his right hand.

Was this . . . was this what it felt like to love a woman?

The question itself should have been enough to make him shy away from her. But he only released her when he thought he espied someone coming. He had done his best to spare Jane the embarrassing speculations of the other women of Faire Isle. The one he glimpsed approaching was the last he would have wished to catch him kissing Jane.

Meg. He expected that she was bearing down upon him, to wrest Jane away in a storm of indignation. But Meg didn't seem to have noticed either of them. The girl was too bent upon her own purpose.

With a nervous look over her shoulder, she veered off onto another path, disappearing into the trees. She was obviously up to something she shouldn't be. Xavier had been in enough devilment himself to recognize all the signs.

THE COVE WAS SECLUDED FROM PORT CORSAIR BY THE FOREST of fir trees, a place where Meg could find the solitude she craved. She felt she had not had a quiet moment to think since the excitement of being named the next Lady of Faire Isle.

She took off her stockings and shoes and seated herself on a flat rock near the edge of the shore. She dangled her feet, allowing the waves to lap over them.

The water was cold even at this time of year. Meg shivered, but welcomed the bracing chill with a tired sigh. She had discovered that elation could be as exhausting as despair. Perhaps because her happiness was tempered by the constant fear it might all be snatched away from her in a heartbeat.

The women on Faire Isle had become more receptive to her, although Meg knew that owed more to Carole's influence and Seraphine's persuasions than any of Meg's own merits.

Ariane assured her that she would win them all over in time. Meg only hoped that that was true, but time was not something she was sure that she would have.

She drew her crystal from her pouch, the glass orb sparkling in the sunlight. Meg had not consulted it for weeks. Ariane had changed her destiny that night upon the cliffs, or so Meg desperately wanted to believe. But she needed to be sure, so she had determined to consult her crystal one last time.

Meg drew in a deep breath, peering into her scrying glass, straining hard to focus. She stared until pinpricks of light dazzled her eyes before coalescing into an image. She braced herself, fearing that once more she might see herself being handed over to the Dark Queen's soldiers, her shadowy betrayer lurking behind her.

But the scene that unfolded before her eyes was worse. She saw a sick old woman laid out upon a bed with costly hangings. Meg strained harder, honing her vision until the woman's face came into focus. It was the Dark Queen and she was dying . . .

Meg wanted to shrink away from the malevolent face glaring up at her from the pillows. But Catherine's withered hand clutched at Meg's wrist. The queen's voice was a weak rasp as she accused, "You! You have done this to me."

"No," Meg cried. "You brought this upon yourself. I never wished you any harm. Why could you not leave me alone?"

The hard light in the queen's eyes dimmed to a look of sheer desperation. "Help me. I am so afraid of the darkness, sinking into the grave alone, forgotten. I know you have the power, child. Undo all of this, please."

"I can't," Meg whispered, tears trickling down her cheeks. "It is too late . . . for both of us."

"See anything interesting in there?" The voice drawled close to her ear, snapping Meg's concentration and driving her heart against her ribs.

She whipped around to find Xavier bending over her. The water splashed as she leaped up. She nearly slipped on the slick sand and would have fallen if Xavier had not seized her arm.

Righting herself, Meg wrenched away from him. She panted, glaring at him.

"How—how dare you? What do you think you are doing, spying on me?"

He appeared unfazed by her temper or her righteous indignation. He cocked one brow. "The question ought to be, what are *you* doing?"

Meg moved to hide the crystal, but she realized it was far too late for that. "What—what I do is none of your affair."

Her haughty assertion was ruined when she could not help quavering, "Are you going to tell Ariane?"

"As you say, it is none of my affair. I am not your keeper, thank heaven."

He eased himself down on the bank, bracing himself with his good hand, his movements a trifle awkward with his right arm still in the sling.

Meg wanted to storm away and leave him. But she felt that he had bested her by catching her out with the crystal. She stayed out of sheer defiance to prove that she was not ashamed of what she had been doing or the least intimidated by him.

Flouncing down, she resumed her place on the rock. Toying with her crystal, she observed him resentfully out of the corner of her eye. He had found a piece of broken shell and was examining it as though they were two friends who had gone for a stroll and were spending an idle afternoon together.

"Why are you still here?" Meg demanded.

"Well, this seems a fair spot, quiet, peaceful—"

"Not the cove. I mean here on Faire Island. I gave you that potion to help you regain your strength."

"You did indeed and you have my thanks for that."

"I did not want your thanks. I wanted you gone."

"Alas, it would seem I have not risen in your esteem." He gave a mock sigh. "Have you been seeing any more dire warnings about me in your little crystal? The great jungle cat stalking poor Lady Danvers."

"No, the glass doesn't warn me of things that have already happened."

Xavier's eyes might be impossible to read, but Jane's were not. Meg saw clearly the transformation that had come over her older friend, the hopeful glow in Jane's eyes, all the longings that the quiet lady would never express.

"You have already dug your claws deep into Jane's heart," Meg told him resentfully.

He frowned. Drawing back his arm, he flung the shell far out into the water. "Whether you believe it or not, I do care about Jane. I would never hurt her."

"Not on purpose perhaps." Meg was willing to allow him that much. "But you are one of those dangerous people who draw trouble to you like a lodestar. Just like—"

Meg checked herself, pursing her lips.

"Like you?" he asked.

Meg hated to admit she might have anything in common with him. But she thought of all the people in her life who had come to disaster, her beloved old nurse Mistress Waters, many of the young women who had joined the coven of the Silver Rose, Lady Danvers's unfortunate brother. Meg had come close to being responsible for Jane's death as well, to say nothing of putting her father and stepmother in peril.

No, Meg corrected herself. Megaera, the Silver Rose

was the one who was a danger to her friends. But that was not who she was.

Xavier reached across her in an attempt to pluck the crystal from her grasp. Meg tightened both hands around the scrying glass. Cradling it out of his reach, she glowered at him.

"I only wanted to look at it," he said. "Considering that using that glass only seems to bring you a deal of heartache, I wonder what is your fascination with it?"

"Nothing that you would understand."

"You might be surprised," he said with a strange smile. He drew a flask from inside his doublet. "Do you know what this is?"

Meg eyed it scornfully. "It looks like an ordinary leathern jack, like the kind my stepmother uses to keep her Irish whiskey in. She let me taste it once. It was like swallowing fire and tasted horrible. It made me choke."

"The stuff in my flask would make you do far more than that. The vine of the spirits, the natives of Brazil call it. An Indian shaman taught me to brew it from a certain jungle liana."

"You mean like a potion?" Meg tried to look uninterested, but she was intrigued in spite of herself. "What does it do?"

"It induces a powerful trance, one that will take your mind places you never imagined it could go. You feel as though you are capable of seeing and knowing everything."

"Like when I gaze into my ball and catch glimpses of the future?"

"Not exactly, but it does conjure visions of a sort. It frees you from the bonds of the real world, sets your mind soaring. Of course when I come crashing back to earth, I am usually sick for days."

"Then why meddle with something so dangerous?"

Xavier held up his flask, regarding it with a rueful smile. "Because my dear, just like your scrying glass, the power of it is very seductive."

Meg wanted to deny any comparison between the purity of her crystal and his filthy jungle brew. But his words struck an uncomfortable chord with her. The visions she summoned up in the glass were often alarming. But knowing that she possessed the power to summon those visions was all too alluring.

But she said, "Your potion sounds more dangerous than what I do with my crystal. At least I don't sink into any kind of a trance."

"Perhaps not. But while you are so busy seeking to know what may happen tomorrow, you forget to live today. Your glimpses into the future may be the most dangerous because they deny you your free will, your belief that you can chart your own course. If I were you, I would leave that thing alone."

"You have no right to lecture me." She gestured contemptuously to his flask.

"You are right. I don't." He uncorked the flask. Meg watched him with a mingling of trepidation and fascination, wondering if he meant to perform his magic for her right here and now. To her astonishment, he upended the flask and poured the liquid out into the sand.

"My use of this form of dark magic may well have cost me my ship. That crystal of yours could end up costing you a high price as well."

Meg surprised herself by confiding in him what she had told no one else. "I can't help it, Xavier. I am afraid. I keep seeing *her.*"

His lips tightened. "I assume you mean the Dark Queen."

"Someone is going to betray me to her. I will end up trapped in her palace and—" Meg bit down upon her lip. She had already told him more than she meant to. She didn't add, *I am afraid I am going to do something terrible.*

Xavier looked away from her, a troubled expression darkening his face. Meg would have given anything if she could read the man's eyes. When he turned back to her, his expression was more gentle than she would have imagined him capable of.

He touched her hand. "No, Meg. No one is going to betray you. No matter what that crystal tells you. You will be safe from the Dark Queen. I promise you that."

It was a rash promise. Yet, he spoke so simply, so intently, she found herself believing him.

She looked at her crystal for a long moment, weighing it in her palm. Drawing a breath for courage, she smashed it upon the rocks.

Chapter Nineteen

SIMON ARISTIDE HAD RETURNED TO FAIRE ISLE. ALTHOUGH it had been well over a decade since the witch-hunter had raided the island, women gathered up their children and herded them indoors.

A few dared to linger by their garden gates, staring in stony silence at the man as he clattered by on horseback. The years had threaded silver through his dark hair. He dressed more in the simple breeches and tunic of a peasant farmer than his dark warrior's garb of yore. But there was no mistaking the sinister eye patch and scars that marred the right side of Aristide's face.

Simon nodded, tipping the soft brim of his hat to some of the ladies as he passed. But his efforts to smile were only met with glowers and one elderly dame actually spat at him.

Simon bore her no resentment, after the havoc he had wreaked upon this island during the years of his youthful arrogance and bitterness. He had eschewed his profession as a witch-hunter, but the ladies of Faire Isle would not forget what he had once been or forgive him for it.

Digging his knees into Elle's flanks, Simon urged his horse onward toward Belle Haven where he was at least assured of a welcome from one woman. The daughter of the earth who dared to call him husband.

Elle's pace had lagged ever since they had arrived on Faire Isle. Simon's beloved mare was growing older, no longer possessing the same stamina for long journeying. Elle had ever been skittish about crossing the narrow causeway that stretched between the island and the mainland.

But the mare's ears perked up as they drew near the courtyard of Belle Haven, an ivy-covered stone manor with a single square tower. Exhausted as he was, Simon sat straighter in the saddle himself. His heart lifted, especially when he guided Elle into the stable yard and saw a fairylike woman with flowing moon-gold hair.

Miri crouched down as she held a mastiff puppy in her arms, trying to hold the wriggling creature still so that she could teach her small nephew how to pet him gently. Since Leon gamboled about her skirts, every bit as excited as the puppy, the lesson appeared to be proving quite a challenge.

When she glanced up and saw Simon, her face lit up. Consigning both the puppy and Leon to the care of Seraphine, Miri bolted across the stable yard before Simon could even dismount.

Knowing his Miri and her great love for all four-legged creatures, it would not have surprised Simon if she had greeted his horse first. Although she did caress Elle's forelock, she scarce waited until Simon's boots struck the ground before hurling herself into his arms.

God, how he had missed her. Simon crushed his wife in his arms, then laughed and spun her in a circle before remembering the precious burden she carried inside her.

He placed her reverently back on her feet. He contented himself with a long tender kiss despite the teasing way his impish niece Seraphine whooped and applauded, her hand clapping imitated by little Leon.

Miri pulled a wry face at her niece and nephew. She shooed them off with a wave of her hand before turning back to Simon with a delighted sigh.

"This is quite a surprise, my love. Have you ridden all this way to reclaim your errant wife?"

He tugged playfully at one of her tresses, his gruff tone concealing the way his heart swelled at the sight of her. "You have been gone nearly a month, my lady."

"No? Truly? Has it really been that long?"

"It is obvious that I have been missing you far more than you did me."

Miri crinkled her nose, looking adorably guilty. "I have missed you, Simon, but it has been so wonderful—" When she broke off, he finished for her, "Being home again?"

He well knew all that Miri had given up by marrying him. Of the three Cheney sisters, she had been the one who had most loved Faire Isle.

She cupped his cheek with the palm of her hand. "No,

Simon, home is wherever you are. You should know that. But it has been wonderful being with Ariane again, and spending time with Gabby's girls and little Leon."

She beamed up at him. "And you will never guess what? I have a brother, Captain Louis Xavier Cheney. I am sure you will wonder how that came about. You must come inside and meet him. Seraphine will look after Elle. I am sure she is dying to do so. And while you refresh yourself and wash off the dust of the road, I will explain everything."

Seizing him by the hand, Miri tugged him in the direction of the house. But Simon's elation in seeing her had made him forget the reason for his journey to Belle Haven, the grim tidings that he brought. Miri's evident delight in her newfound brother was only going to make what he had to say that much harder.

As he hung back, Miri sensed his reluctance. Swinging around to face him, she asked, "Simon, what's wrong?"

"You recall that I have been making enquiries, trying to gauge what is going on in Paris. I have learned something recently, something bad."

"About the Dark Queen?" Miri faltered.

"Not just about Catherine." Simon sighed. "It also concerns this new brother of yours . . ."

XAVIER SAT AT THE KITCHEN TABLE, LABORING OVER HIS drawing, the stick of charcoal gripped awkwardly in his right hand. Like many sea captains, he had mastered the art of sketching, the better to record many of the exotic flora and fauna he had encountered in his travels.

But he was hopeless with his left hand and his right was still frustratingly impaired by the splint. It also did not help that he was surrounded by a critical audience, his two young nieces, Lucia and Ninon, hovering on either side of him.

Xavier stole a glance across the room. Jane was preoccupied, instructing one of the younger maids in a method for getting stains out of fine linen. Xavier set down the charcoal and began to loosen the bindings that held his splint in place.

But Lucia sang out, "Milady Jane, look what Uncle Xavier is doing."

"Telltale," Xavier growled.

Jane bore down upon him with a mighty frown. Much to the amusement of his small nieces, she thunked him on the head with a wooden spoon as she scolded. "How many times must you be told? Leave those bandages alone."

"But the blasted thing itches. I surely must be healed enough by now. It has been almost a month."

"Ariane says you must wait at least another week or two."

"By that time my arm will be completely withered from lack of use," Xavier grumbled, but felt immediately ashamed of himself. But for Ariane, he would have no right arm at all.

"Very well," he said. "I shall try to behave myself."

"That, sir, I fear may be quite beyond your power. Perhaps Meg can brew up some kind of potion that will give you more patience."

Meg looked up from the book on healing herbs that she was reading near the hearth. She smiled. "That, I am afraid, would be quite beyond *my* power."

Xavier pulled a fierce face at all of them. He sighed, doing his best to manipulate the charcoal with his fingers protruding beyond the end of the splint.

Jane lingered near the table to watch and as his nieces crowded in even closer, his eyes met Jane's above the two golden heads.

She smiled that particular soft smile that she reserved for him alone and he felt his heart respond. He wondered if she was thinking the same as he. That this is what their life together might be if they were to wed, their own children clustered around them.

The notion did not alarm him as it once had. He was daily growing more accustomed to the idea. Perhaps for the first time in his life, he understood why some of his men had been so eager to debark at their home port after a long voyage. It was because of the warmth and comfort of returning to one's own hearth and family, that sense of belonging somewhere in this vast wide world that he had never had. Until now.

Lucia tugged impatiently at his sleeve, recalling him to his task. As he wielded the charcoal across the parchment, the wings of the creature took form and shape. He eyed his efforts critically. Not as good of a dragon as he could have conjured if he had full use of his right hand, but a creditable enough effort.

Ninon popped her thumb out of her mouth, her eyes wide. She gestured toward his picture with her drool-soaked finger. "You saw that beastie in your jungle?"

"Indeed I did. It nearly toasted me with its fire and had me for breakfast."

"That sounds like another of your stories, Uncle. I do

not believe you ever saw a dragon," Lucia said with a toss of her long blond hair.

"I do." Ninon frowned at her older sister. "You never believe anything."

"That's because Lucia is a perennial skeptic," Xavier said.

"What's a peri animal skeptar?" Lucia demanded.

"Someone who does not even believe they have a nose unless they look in the mirror." Xavier dabbed a smudge of charcoal on his niece's snub nose.

Lucia scrubbed at her face, scowling at him before appealing to Jane. "What do you think, milady? Was that dragon real?"

"I don't know. Perhaps we should ask Meg. I believe she used to have a book on dragons."

"Which I was obliged to abandon when we all left London." Meg closed up her text on herbs and strolled over to study Xavier's drawing.

"It looks like the Ethiopian dragons that were in my book," she said.

"But are dragons real?" Lucia persisted.

"I believe so. Indeed I am convinced *she* exists."

Xavier looked up at Meg's remark. "I am sure you don't have to worry about this particular dragon. She is old and her teeth have been drawn."

Meg smiled, an unspoken understanding passing between them. Perhaps he had done wrong to assure the girl she would be safe from Catherine de Medici. All he could really promise Meg was that she had nothing to fear from him. He would protect Meg if it became necessary and not just because of Jane, but for the girl's own sake.

He could not say that they had become fast friends, but a tentative alliance had formed between them since that afternoon in the cove. Perhaps because they had both renounced their own particular demons when he had poured out his shaman's brew and she had destroyed her crystal. Or perhaps it was something more elemental, a shared understanding of the struggle to overcome the chains and scars of the past.

Meg bent closer over his drawing. "I think your dragon needs a longer tail."

Xavier surrendered the charcoal to her. Ninon wriggled her way onto his lap while Meg put a few deft finishing touches to his picture.

They were all so absorbed that at first none but Xavier noticed the man who stole quietly into the kitchen. Then Lucia squealed out, "Uncle Simon!"

Despite the little girl's customary boldness, she did not barrel toward the man as she was wont to do with Xavier. Xavier could understand why.

There was something intimidating about the man's scarred face, the eye patch that concealed his right eye. The fleeting smile he bestowed upon the little girl was more of a grimace.

So this must be Simon Aristide, the erstwhile witch-hunter who had married his youngest sister. Any doubts Xavier might have had were settled when Miri entered and linked her hand through her husband's arm. She was followed by Ariane.

Something was wrong. Miri's eyes were red and Ariane looked pale. When Seraphine crowded into the room after them, she glared at Xavier as though he had kicked her mastiff puppy. As for Aristide, the man's eyes were like stone.

Xavier eased Ninon off his lap and stood. He had a strong feeling this was not going to prove a continuation of the tender family reunion. When no one offered any introductions, he stepped toward Aristide, extending his left hand.

"I presume you must be my brother-in-law. I am—"

"I know who you are," Aristide said, ignoring Xavier's outstretched hand.

Those few terse words were fraught with ominous meaning. Xavier stiffened, drawing his arm back to his side.

"Seraphine, please take your sisters outside," Ariane said. "Take them to—to see the puppy and play with Leon in the stables."

Both little girls set up wails of protest, but Seraphine dragged them away as though she were rescuing her sisters from the devil himself. A heavy silence ensued.

Meg's brow knit with confusion, but she regarded everyone with a somber calm. Perhaps because the girl had known so much of trouble in her short life, she was always braced for more.

Jane looked far more anxious. Drawing closer to Xavier, she asked, "Ariane, what—what is wrong?"

It was Aristide who spoke up. Ignoring Jane's question, he addressed himself to Xavier. "You are Louis Xavier, the corsair who is known as the Jaguar?"

"A foolish nickname, but yes, I have been called that." Xavier felt Jane's fingers curl about his arm, her touch warm and reassuring. "And yes, I am a pirate. I have never made any secret of that fact."

"But there are other things you have kept secret."

"Such as?"

"Your dealings with the Dark Queen."

Meg gave a tiny gasp, the girl no longer looking so calm at the mention of the queen. Jane frowned at Aristide.

"Whatever are you talking about, monsieur? After the cruel way that witch used his mother, Xavier would want nothing to do with Catherine de Medici."

Aristide's attention shifted to Jane, the stern cast of his countenance softening. "I am sorry to pain you, madame. But since last fall, I have been looking into rumors that the queen acquired a necromancer. I was unable to confirm the identity of that man until recently."

His gaze returned to Xavier. "Do you deny you are that man, monsieur?"

Xavier lifted his brows haughtily. "Do I look like a sorcerer to you?"

"That does not answer my question. *Are* you the man who claimed to be a sorcerer and worked for the Dark Queen?"

"Of course, he is not!" Jane cried.

Xavier was touched by how swiftly she sprang to his defense, but he squirmed inwardly. He felt a surge of red creep up his neck, his gut churning with guilt. He ought to have confessed to Jane about his involvement with the Dark Queen a long time ago, but he was damned if he was going to do it this way before the censorious gaze of some former witch-hunter, even if the man was Miri's husband.

"I am waiting for your answer, monsieur." Even Aristide's tone, cool and demanding, raised Xavier's hackles.

"You may wait until hell freezes over for all I care. Who appointed you my judge? I was told you had abandoned your former profession, but once a witch-hunter, always a witch-hunter, eh?"

Xavier regretted his words when he saw Miri flinch. Flushing, Aristide took a step toward him, but Ariane hastily intervened, positioning herself between them.

"Xavier, please," she said. "No one is passing judgment on you."

"That is not how it feels to me," he said.

Ariane cast him a rueful glance. "I am sorry. I have been telling Simon there must be a simple explanation for all of this. If—if you did ever work for the Dark Queen—"

"He didn't," Jane cried. "Ariane, how can you even think such a thing?" She raised pleading eyes to Xavier. "Xavier, I know how you are when people hammer you with questions and false accusations. But please just set aside your pride and tell Simon he is wrong."

Xavier stared down at her earnest face, those steady honest eyes of hers. Never had he known anyone to have such faith in him. It damn near killed him to disillusion her.

"I am sorry, Jane," he said. "But it is true."

Jane blinked, looking stunned. She attempted to rally, stammering. "N-no. You—you didn't. You could not possibly be in the employ of the Dark Queen."

"I would not exactly say that I was employed by the woman."

Ignoring Simon Aristide's derisive snort, Xavier went on, "I did frequent Catherine's court last autumn. I was seeking funds for my next voyage. I practiced a deception upon her, feigning trances, pretending to be a seer. When I told the queen about how the *Book of Shadows* was destroyed in London, she finally believed in my abilities. She rewarded me with a small sack of coins."

Xavier studied Jane, trying to read her reaction. She looked deeply troubled by his confession. Her fingers tensed on his arm.

"Jane, I never meant—" he began but he was interrupted by Aristide.

"I have heard the royal treasury is strained. Somehow I cannot imagine Catherine parting with a single sou merely to finance a sea voyage."

Xavier glared at Simon. "Your point being?"

"That for a long time now, the queen has only had two obsessions, finding the *Book of Shadows* and destroying Meg. So if Catherine gave you money, what was it really for?"

Xavier's gaze locked defiantly with Aristide's for a moment. Then he vented a bitter sigh. He had confessed to this much. He might as well tell the worst of it.

"The queen paid me to acquire the Silver Rose for her."

"Acquire . . . me?" Meg choked.

Jane's fingers slipped away from his arm, her face draining of color. "But—but you never agreed to do such a thing. Did you?"

Xavier would have given his soul to be able to say he hadn't. "Yes, I agreed. Catherine believes that Meg learned enough from the *Book of Shadows* that the girl could be valuable to her. She no longer wants to destroy Meg."

"So that makes your plan to abduct Meg so much more excusable," Aristide said.

Xavier grated his teeth. "I have no such plan. I took the queen's money, but I never intended to carry out her orders."

"You expect us all to believe that your turning up on Faire Isle was a mere coincidence?" Aristide asked.

"I don't give a damn what you believe," Xavier snapped. There was only one person's opinion that mattered. Jane had moved farther away from him. He reached for her to draw her back to his side.

"I would never hurt Meg. Jane, you do believe me, don't you?"

"I want to, but I—I—" She avoided his hand, burying her fingers in the folds of her skirt.

If only they had been alone, if only he could take her into his arms, Xavier felt sure he could convince her, but Meg stormed in between them.

"You—you lied to me that day in the cove. You told me that I would be safe from Catherine when all along you were plotting to—to—"

"Meg, I swear to you, I was not plotting anything."

"Then where did you get your information about me, about what happened to the *Book of Shadows*?"

Xavier dragged his hand across his face as he explained about his first mate, the strange tale that Jambe had stumbled across, about the ravings of a badly burned prisoner in the Marshalsea.

"It must have been Sander," Meg said, her lower lip quivering. "He survived the fire just as I feared."

"No, Meg." Xavier sought to reassure her. "Whoever that prisoner was, he died in the Marshalsea. Sander Naismith can't betray you anymore."

"He already did and so did you." Tears coursed down Meg's cheeks. "I saw all the portents in my crystal, the menacing jungle cat, the shadow passing over Faire Isle. I sensed from the first you were dangerous, but I was so stupid. I even let you persuade me to destroy my scrying glass so I—I could no longer see what you were up to—"

"It wasn't like that, Meg. If you would but listen to me."

"No! I knew what you were and still I—I trusted you."

With a sob, Meg fled from the room. Xavier watched her go, feeling frustrated and helpless. He turned to Jane.

"Jane, I know this all looks bad, but I never meant to hurt her."

"Perhaps you didn't, but you have." Jane said quietly. Xavier realized she was talking about far more than Meg. The glow that had been on Jane's face these past days had dimmed and it was like watching something precious slip away from him.

"I—I had better go look after Meg," she said.

"Jane!"

When she hurried out of the kitchen, Xavier tried to follow only to have his way blocked by Aristide.

"Leave her alone, monsieur. You have done more than enough damage here."

"Get out of my way!"

Aristide shook his head. "It is you who must go. The queen has put a price on your head. It will only be a matter of time before some soldiers or bounty seekers swarm this island in an effort to collect it."

Xavier swore. Could this disaster possibly get any worse?

Aristide eyed him coldly. "I must insist that you leave this island at once."

"The only one who has the right to bid me leave is Ariane. As far as the world knows, I am dead."

"That cannot last for long, Xavier," Ariane said. "Not after my messenger made those enquiries on the mainland and your crew came here to find you. Rumors spread even from Faire Isle. I fear that I must ask—"

"Ariane, no!" Miri cried. "No matter what he has done, Xavier is still our brother. And I am sure he is sorry."

"Miri, my love," Aristide began gently, but his wife cut him off with a stamp of her foot, tears overflowing down her cheeks.

"No! If Xavier leaves here, he will be in danger of being captured. We—we can hide him. Ariane, please! You cannot ask him to go."

Xavier could see the agony of indecision in Ariane's eyes. There was nothing that he could do to mend the shattered trust or assuage the grief he had caused, but at least he could spare Ariane this struggle.

"Ariane doesn't have to ask me," Xavier told Miri. "Your husband is right. If I remain here, I will be a danger to everyone."

He cast a bleak glance in the direction Jane had vanished. "I must go. It is clear that I have worn out my welcome."

JANE SAGGED DOWN ON THE BENCH IN THE GARDEN, HER EYES dry, her heart heavy as though it were full of the tears she could not shed. Strange that she could not do so. Everyone else was weeping, Meg, Lucia, Ninon, even Seraphine after her own fierce fashion.

Perhaps she remained dry-eyed because her experience was greater than theirs. She knew by now how easily one's world, one's happiness could be shattered. That was why she had been content to live quietly for so many years, never risking her heart.

When Jane had followed Meg upstairs, the girl had barricaded herself in her bedchamber. Jane could hear Meg's sobs but she refused to answer Jane's pleas for admittance. Her hand wearied from knocking, Jane had finally surrendered the attempt.

The girl had been devastated by Xavier's admission of his bargain with the Dark Queen. Jane could still not bring herself to believe it. She knew the man was far from perfect, that he could be ruthless.

But surely he would have never sold off an innocent girl to a woman as evil as Catherine. But Jane could not help recalling that Xavier had never regarded Meg as an innocent. He had called her Megaera, insisted that she had a darker side. He had not approved Ariane's choice of her as the next lady of Faire Isle. If he believed Meg was a witch, perhaps he saw nothing wrong with claiming the reward Catherine offered. There was nothing that Xavier desired more than obtaining a ship, the chance to pursue his far horizons.

And yet this was the same man who had been prepared to abandon all his dreams to stand by Jane if she was with child. Could he possibly have counterfeited all the tenderness he had bestowed upon Jane? The kindness he had shown to Meg of late?

But if he had nothing to hide, why had he kept his connection to Catherine a secret? Jane pressed her hand to her throbbing temple. Logic seemed to dictate Xavier's guilt, but her heart was telling her something far different.

"Jane?"

Her heart constricted at the sound of Xavier calling her name. She leapt to her feet, suppressing the urge to rush into his arms. Xavier drew up short, scowling.

"Jane, where the devil have you been? I have been looking everywhere for you."

"You should not be." She fought to keep the quaver from her voice. "Ariane told me about the price on your head. You must not tarry. You have to get far away from here as fast as possible."

"Did you think I would just rush off without even saying good-bye?"

"I—I don't know. I scarce know what to think." She tensed as Xavier moved closer.

He placed his hands on her shoulders. "I am sorry, Jane. I should have told all of you about Catherine sooner."

"Why—why didn't you?"

"Perhaps because I was afraid that you all would look at me just as everyone is doing now. Like I had turned into some kind of a monster sprouting fangs and horns."

"That is not fair, Xavier. How could you expect all of us not to be alarmed and upset, especially Meg? You know how terrified every woman on this island is of the Dark Queen. She is your sisters' greatest enemy and yet you never saw fit to breathe a word of warning that Catherine was still weaving her plots."

"She can weave all she wants. The queen has little power anymore. She is a sick, twisted old woman. And if she decided to make another attempt on Meg, I suppose I was arrogant enough to believe that as long as I was around, I could protect the girl."

"W-would you?" Jane moistened her lips. She hated asking, but she could not seem to help herself. "So you never really intended to go through with it? You were never going to abduct Meg?"

"If you still have to ask me that, my answer will hardly matter." A muscle in his jaw worked. "No. I admit there was a time when fate first cast me here on the island, that I was tempted. But that was before I really knew Meg or my sisters. Before *you.*"

Jane tipped back her head, intently studying his expression.

"I believe you," she said sadly. "But it still doesn't change anything. You have to go."

He released her and dragged his hand through his hair in a frustrated gesture. "As usual, I have managed to make a proper mess of things. I dare not remain on Faire Isle, but I can't take you with me either."

"You need not worry about me. You have no obligation to—"

"Oh, damnation, woman. Don't start that nonsense again."

"It is true, Xavier. If I am with child, I—I will find some way to cope."

"Or in other words you no longer want any part of

me. A fugitive, a swindler, and a liar is not an attractive prospect as a husband. Your child would be better off as a bastard."

"I never said such a thing." Jane fluttered her hands in a helpless gesture as she struggled to explain. "So much of my life I have suffered from the actions of reckless men. First there was my father risking everything by joining the rebellion against Elizabeth. And then my brother Ned with his mad pursuit of alchemy that led to my being charged with witchcraft.

"You once asked me why I wed a man old enough to be my grandfather. At least William Danvers made me feel safe for a time. That is all I ever wanted."

"And you realize safety is something you can never have with me." His mouth twisted bitterly. "Well, you must congratulate yourself on your narrow escape."

"We both can, because I am sure in time you would have become quite restless and bored with me. You would resent me and any child for costing you your dreams. We—we have been ill-suited from the start."

"I daresay you are right."

A heavy silence fell.

"So what will you do?" Jane asked. "Where will you go?"

"Straight to the devil, I expect. My usual path."

When Jane regarded him with consternation, he gave a hard laugh. "Don't fear for me, my dear. I have always been good at looking out for myself. But what about you?"

"I—I think I must go to Paris to look after my cousin."

Xavier frowned at her. "Damnation, Jane. I realize that your experience with me must have left you a little shaken and bruised. But will you abandon the freedom you have found on Faire Isle to go and be a drudge to that ungrateful wench who has ignored you all these months?"

Jane drew herself up primly. "Abigail is my only kin and she needs me."

She is the only one now who does, Jane reflected, but possessed enough pride to keep from voicing the sad thought aloud.

"I have to go and take care of her. It is the right thing to do."

"It must be a wonderful thing to always be so sure of your path. Things are not always so clear to the rest of us poor mortals."

Jane flinched at his caustic words. She suddenly felt inexpressibly weary.

"There is nothing to hold you here," she whispered. "Please just go. I could not bear to see any harm come to you."

"Thank you for that much." His voice softened as he added, "You take care as well, Jane. My first wish will always be for your health and happiness."

For one moment, she thought he meant to sweep her into his arms and kiss her good-bye. But he only bowed with a formality that was most unlike him before striding away.

As she watched him disappear from view, Jane's eyes blurred. He wished her happiness? How did he imagine that possible when any prospect of such a thing vanished with him?

Sinking back down on the bench, Jane's tears came at last.

Chapter Twenty

THE INN STANK OF MOLD, SWEAT, AND STALE SPIRITS, THE dim candlelight mercifully concealing the layers of grime that had accumulated over the years. Tucked away in a small village along the Breton coast, the Cheval Noir was not the sort of place to attract respectable customers. But for anyone needing a cheap drink and a dank hole in which to escape for a while, the inn was ideal.

Xavier slumped down at one of the corner tables while he waited for Jambe and Pietro to join him. They were out searching for a vessel to bear them all away from France while Xavier busied himself trying to get drunk.

He eyed the half-empty bottle morosely, unable to summon the will to refill his glass. It was poor quality whiskey, especially with the taste of it soured by alternating bouts of self-pity and self-loathing.

Only yesterday, he had been a brother, an uncle, and very close to becoming a husband and father. Now he was nothing, alone again and a fugitive to boot. But he had only himself to blame.

Pietro had tried to warn him. He could not cheat a vengeful woman like Catherine de Medici and expect to remain unscathed.

There had been a time when he would have laughed to hear that someone had put a price on his head. He was after all a corsair and had never lived within the confines of the law. He would have thumbed his nose at the queen and set sail far across the ocean, beyond the line of civilization, and never looked back.

But for the first time, he had weighed anchor in a place that felt akin to home, surrounded by the warmth and the love of family. To his complete amazement, he had *liked* it.

He should have told them all about his connection with Catherine de Medici. But as the days had gone by and he had become enmeshed on the island, it had become harder to blurt out such a confession. That he had not done so made him look guilty. But damn it, did they all have to be so quick to think the worst of him? Although he didn't know what else he should have expected. His father had always been swift to do so.

But nothing had ever cut him as deep as that moment when he had watched Jane shrink away from him. And yet how could he blame her? He had brought her nothing but trouble. He hoped to hell that she was not with child. But even if she was, she was still better off without him. *She* certainly seemed to think so.

She would likely forget him fast enough after she went to wait upon her cousin in Paris, doing her duty, burying herself back in the respectable life she seemed to crave.

And as for himself . . . Xavier attempted to shrug but ended up taking another gulp of whiskey instead in an effort to blot out those last moments with Jane in the garden.

"There is nothing to hold you here," she had said.

Then why did he feel so damned hollow, as though he'd cut out his heart and left it behind on Faire Isle? Before he had met Jane, he had never even thought he had a heart, other than some organ that beat out regular rhythms keeping him alive.

Now all he felt inside his chest was this heavy weight of loss and guilt. Jane had tried to appear so calm, so stoic when she had bid him farewell, but her eyes had told him a different story and Jane's eyes never lied. He knew he had hurt her deeply, just as Meg had predicted that he would.

And Meg—what had his deception done to her? The girl did not trust easily. Xavier understood that because he was just the same. He had promised the girl that she would be safe from the Dark Queen. But hadn't he always been good at weaving lies and making rash promises he was unable to keep? He took another swallow of his whiskey, diving deeper into his glass. As always when he was at his lowest ebb, his father's censorious voice rang loudest in his head.

"I have done my best to teach you the ways of a gentleman. But that glib tongue of yours will be your undoing one day. You have an unholy talent for deception, especially with women, and I have no idea how you came by it."

"Don't you?" Xavier had drawled. "I would have to say I came by it naturally, mon père."

The chevalier had backhanded him so hard, he had fallen off his stool. Xavier rubbed his cheek absently at the memory. It was the only time he could recall his father striking him. The chevalier had raised quite a bruise on his cheek, but Xavier had enjoyed the dubious satisfaction of having pierced through his father's self-righteous façade.

The chevalier had divided himself in twain, pledging devotion to two different women. When he had no longer been able to deal with all the heartbreak he had caused, he had simply fled across the seas.

Xavier's reasons might be different but he was about to do the same thing, just run away. His lip curled in self-derision and he raised his glass in a mock salute.

"Here's to you, Papa," he muttered. "No matter what you claimed, it would appear that I am your son after all."

Xavier started to take another swallow of his whiskey, only to thrust it away from him. He regretted pouring out his shaman's brew. If there had ever been a time when he needed to vanish into his dream world, this was it. It was the only hope he ever had of seeing Jane again, the elusive mermaid of his visions.

All he had was that healing potion Meg had given him. He drew it out, staring glumly at the small vial.

Disillusioned and disappointed in him, Jane would go

to her cousin in Paris, his little wren slamming her cage door shut. Meg would return to living in fear of the old queen, more mistrustful that ever, more tempted to turn to the darker side of magic for answers.

Damn it. He could not just sail away and abandon them. He needed to stop feeling so sorry for himself and find some way to undo the damage he had wrought. But what the devil could he do?

He fingered the vial Meg had given him, holding it up to the candle. Perhaps it was the way the flame reflected against the glass that sparked something in his brain. An idea formed in his mind. A notion so outrageous, so completely mad, it was enough to daunt even him.

Staring at the vial as if mesmerized, he scarce looked up when Jambe and Pietro returned.

Dropping into the seat opposite him, Jambe said, "It is all arranged. We found a small trading vessel making for Portsmouth at first light. The captain said we can work off our passage."

"That sounds fine. You and Pietro go ahead," Xavier murmured. "I have other plans."

"Other plans?" Jambe echoed. "Lad, you may soon have the queen's men scouring the entire coast. What better plan could you have than getting out of France?"

"If the queen has a price on my head and is searching for me, there is only one place for me to go."

"And where would that be?"

"Back to Paris, to the Hôtel de la Reine."

Jambe and Pietro gaped at him.

"You don't look drunk. But it's clear you've had a drop too much." Jambe snatched his whiskey bottle away.

"Have you run mad, Captain?" Pietro exclaimed. "Why would you want to do a fool thing like that?"

Xavier flung back his head and laughed. If his men were worried for his sanity, he was certain he must confirm their worst fears when he grinned.

"Because it's the right thing to do."

JANE FOLDED UP ONE OF HER CHEMISES AND LAID IT CAREFULLY in the bottom of her trunk. When she had been Lady Danvers, wife to a wealthy London merchant, preparing for a journey had been an exhausting ordeal, packing a mountain of clothes and household items, organizing an entire retinue of servants.

Traveling was much simpler when one had more memories than possessions to stow in one's trunk. She followed up the chemise with a petticoat, a shawl, and her handkerchiefs.

One of the squares of linen slipped from the pile and fell, scattering a trail of dried petals across the bedchamber floor. Jane froze, staring down at the remnants of a white rose as she was assailed by a recollection.

Last week . . . had it only been last week, it felt like a lifetime ago, she had been sitting in the garden, virtuously attempting to see to some mending. Xavier had been doing his best to distract her, snatching the net from her hair, playfully tucking the flower behind her ear.

Somehow her stitching had ended up in the rose bed and she had found herself perched upon Xavier's knee, her arms twined round his neck and . . .

Jane bent down to sweep up the petals, doing her best to sweep the memory aside as well. She cradled the withered remnants in her palm. The rose still managed to exude its intoxicating scent and for one weak moment she was tempted to carefully tuck the dried leaves back into the handkerchief.

She marched resolutely to the window and flung them out, dusting her hands. But as the petals were borne away on the summer breeze, she was engulfed by an unbearable wave of sadness.

It would get easier when she was in Paris, she told herself. She would no longer stumble over memories of Xavier everywhere she turned. She would not listen for the rough timbre of his voice, spellbinding her with tales of his travels, all the adventures she would never have. She wouldn't glance up from her book when anyone entered the room, anticipating the sight of his teasing smile, her heart quickening at the prospect of his warm touch, the feel of his lips on hers.

She closed her eyes for a moment, wishing she could somehow be magically transported to Paris, the painful wrench from Faire Isle already accomplished. She had spent last evening paying calls, bidding farewell to friends that she had made on the island.

It had been melancholy saying good-bye to Madame Bevans, to old Agatha Butterydoor, to Carole Moreau, and the little Remy girls. Even Seraphine's eyes had gotten suspiciously moist as she had bestowed upon Jane a fierce hug.

Ariane's face had been filled with sorrow when Jane had spoken of her intention of removing to Paris. But the

Lady had made no attempt to dissuade Jane. As regretful as Ariane was, she appeared to understand why Jane felt obliged to go. Jane was not as sure about Meg. The girl had scarce spoken two words to her since Jane had announced her imminent departure.

When Jane turned from the window to continue her packing, she was brought up short by the sight of Meg standing in the open doorway of her bedchamber.

"Meg, you—you startled me."

"I knocked. You didn't hear me."

"I am sorry. I fear I was preoccupied."

"Simon sent me to ask if your trunk is ready to be carried down and loaded on the cart."

"Almost." Jane snatched up one of her gowns and hastily began to fold it. Meg leaned against the doorjamb, watching her.

"Monsieur Aristide has been so kind, arranging all the details of the journey. He and Miri are returning to their farm outside of Paris. I will accompany them and rest there for a night and the next day Monsieur Aristide will escort me the rest of the way to my cousin." Jane chattered, trying to sound brisk and cheerful in the face of Meg's stony silence.

She studied the girl out of the corner of her eye, wishing she had an inkling of what was going on in Meg's head. Something had hardened in the girl's eyes since the revelations about Xavier. It was as though Meg had constructed an invisible wall about herself that could not be breached.

Jane paused, hugging the folded gown to her chest. She said gently, "I won't be gone forever, Meg. I will come back to Faire Isle as soon as I am able."

"No, you won't. You never really liked it here. At least not until *he* came."

It was the first time Meg had alluded to Xavier since his departure. Jane laid the gown in the trunk. She longed to reach out to Meg, gather the girl into her arms, but the look on Meg's face warned her not even to make the attempt.

"Meg, I—I know that Xavier's confession about being employed by the Dark Queen shocked and hurt you. But I believe him when he said he never meant you any harm."

Meg's only response was an incredulous lift of her brows.

"Only consider. If Xavier had wanted to abduct you, he had plenty of opportunity to do so."

"Maybe he was just biding his time, studying the island. Maybe even now, he has scurried like a lapdog back to his mistress to report to her, to return here with a troop of soldiers."

"Xavier wouldn't do that."

"How do you know that?" the girl demanded scornfully. "You have no ability to read eyes."

"No, I don't." But Jane felt she had come closer to understanding Xavier than anyone. Flawed the man might be, reckless to a fault, but he did have his own code of honor. But she could not expect to convince Meg of that.

Instead she said, "Think about it logically. Xavier cannot return to the queen. She is hunting for him too. He left Faire Isle to prevent her soldiers from coming here, putting us all in danger."

"Oh, for the love of—" Meg broke off, biting her lip. At least Jane had succeeded in provoking some sort of reaction from the girl. Stomping past Jane, Meg took an agitated turn about the bedchamber.

"Xavier never thought about anything but himself. His lies were exposed so he tore off out of here to save his own skin." She rounded on Jane, flinging her hands up in exasperation. "How can you keep defending him? After the way he seduced and abandoned you?"

Jane's cheeks fired. "He—he didn't—"

"Don't tell me that. I can read it all in your eyes, Jane. He broke your heart."

"If Xavier hurt me, it is more my doing than his. He never made me any false promises. He never once said that he loved me."

"Then that's at least one thing the man didn't lie about. How noble," Meg said. "I know you don't want to hear this, Jane. But someone is going to hand me over to the queen's soldiers. I saw it all happen in my crystal. If it is not Xavier, who else could it be?"

"You rely too much upon those visions, Meg."

"Do I? Maybe it is because my crystal was the only thing that I ever could trust."

Meg flounced over to the window, locking her arms across her chest and lapsing back into a brooding silence. Jane ached for her. The girl had always seemed too mature for her years and she appeared to have aged to a frightening degree these past few days.

She felt as though she was abandoning Meg by going to Paris. But she had never been adequate to deal with Meg's visions. Even if she stayed, she knew that Meg would continue to shut her out. There was only one person who could help Meg now.

Approaching the girl, Jane touched her tentatively on the shoulder. "You can always trust Ariane, Meg. She will look after you, keep you safe."

"I don't need anyone to take care of me." Meg managed a taut-lipped smile. "You needn't worry about me, Jane. I can look out for myself."

She looked and sounded so much like Xavier in that moment, Jane was torn between the urge to laugh or cry. She embraced Meg, but the girl remained so stiff and unresponsive, Jane was obliged to give over the attempt.

She returned sorrowfully to her packing. Meg went back to staring out the window to block out the sight, determined not to feel any grief over Jane's departure. She was so angry at Jane for being so blind, loving Xavier, defending him.

But Meg was even angrier at herself for trusting Xavier, giving him the power to hurt and disappoint her. She supposed she ought to be grateful to the man for snapping her out of the dream world she had been living in, imagining that she could bury her past, shake off her dark legacy as the Silver Rose.

He had demonstrated all too clearly that the Dark Queen had not forgotten about her, that somehow the old witch had figured out Meg's secret, that the *Book of Shadows* was still lodged in the recesses of her memory.

If the queen could not have the book, she would never rest until she gained possession of Meg herself. Even though Xavier had failed, Catherine would simply send someone else even more ruthless. The queen was relentless and she would not care who else she hurt and destroyed in the process. Meg and everyone she loved would remain in danger.

There was only one way this could end. The crystal had shown Meg that time and time again. She just hadn't wanted to accept it. There was only one solution, only one way Meg would ever know peace from the threat of the Dark Queen.

And that was only when one of them was dead.

Chapter Twenty-one

THE SUN BEAT DOWN UPON THE STREETS OF PARIS. IT WAS not even noon and Xavier was already sweating beneath the trappings of his disguise, the beard that he had grown to conceal his features, the large soft-brimmed hat and the boot-length cloak.

As he approached the Hôtel de la Reine, he longed to remove his hat long enough to mop his brow, but he did not dare. Not yet.

It was a miracle he had made it this far. The journey to Paris had taken him far longer than he had expected, constantly having to change routes to avoid patrols, any beady-eyed official or miscreant rogue who might be anxious to claim the reward for Xavier's capture.

He had been further daunted by the number of troops

ringing the city itself, keeping careful watch over the city gates. But a conversation he'd overheard between two of the sentries had led Xavier to an embarrassing discovery.

All of these troops had been posted to counter the duc de Guise, should the duke and his army decide to defy the king and try to enter Paris.

Xavier's mouth twisted wryly. It was a bit of a blow to his self-importance to realize that the Jaguar was of little significance compared to a possible invasion. He might have had a good laugh at his own vanity, but the more Xavier saw of the current state of Paris, the less humor he could find in the situation.

If he had thought Paris a city on edge last autumn, he now found the tension here as unbearable as the heat. Everywhere he looked he saw resentful, unsmiling faces. Tempers were short, voices rough, and glances suspicious. Quarrels seemed to break out over nothing, violence ready to erupt if a man breathed the wrong way.

Xavier only hoped that Jane had thought better of her plan to come to Paris. He intended to make enquiries, see if he could find her cousin's residence. It would relieve his mind greatly to discover that Jane had remained on Faire Isle, but knowing the woman's infernal sense of duty, he doubted it. If Jane was here in the city, likely she would not be too pleased to see him. But at least Xavier would be able to ascertain if she was all right.

That is, if he didn't find himself dangling from a rope on a gibbet first.

Xavier slowed his pace as his steps brought him nearer to the Dark Queen's palace. If he had any sense at all, he would change his mind and beat a swift retreat. There were far too many ways in which this mad scheme of his could go awry.

Jambe and Pietro had nearly deafened him on the journey to Paris with their ceaseless efforts to dissuade him. But they had had no more luck than he had, trying to persuade them to turn back. They had remained as stubborn as he. By the time they had passed through the city gates, they had all been hot, weary, and as bad-tempered as the rest of Paris.

Xavier had pushed them so hard on the last leg of the trip, Jambe and Pietro had all but collapsed upon reaching their inn room.

Their exhausted slumber had afforded Xavier the opportunity he needed to slip away. They could swear at him later if they wished. He hoped he would still be around for them to curse, but he was resolved.

The insane risk he was about to take had to be his alone. As he gazed up at the Hôtel de la Reine, his breath caught in his throat. He saw a familiar form silhouetted in one of the windows, the queen in her unrelenting black garb. She seemed to be staring straight at him, her mind reaching out like the delicate legs of a spider, probing his disguise.

He ducked out of sight and then chided himself for being such a fool. He had never succumbed to the legend of the Dark Queen and her extraordinary powers of perception. But he was taking no chances. The element of surprise was all that he had in his favor. If he was seized by her guards before he gained access to her presence, it was all up with him.

Xavier waited until the queen vanished from the window before stepping back into view. He had finally been able to get rid of that damned splint. The bone had healed, but his arm was nowhere near its former strength.

Not that it mattered. If Catherine set her guards upon him, it was not likely he would be able to fight his way to freedom and escape. Everything depended upon his wits, his—what had his father called it? *His unholy talent for deception.*

Since knowing Jane, Xavier felt as though he had lost some of his taste for chicanery, his skills had grown a trifle rusty. His honest mermaid had been a far too wholesome influence on him.

He was going to have to dig deep into the darkest part of his soul to conjure forth his old ability to lie, charm, and deceive as he never had before.

His success, nay, his very life depended upon it. And perhaps Meg's as well.

THE QUEEN LEANED HEAVILY ON HER CANE AS SHE MADE HER way to her salon. When Catherine swayed on her feet, some of her ladies gave an audible gasp, but they had enough sense to keep their distance. Glaring, Catherine dared anyone to try to rush to her aid. She steadied herself, concealing how disconcerted she was by her own weakness.

Seized with an inflammation of the lungs shortly after her conversation with that Pechard woman, it had been weeks since she had been able to get this far from her bed.

Rumors had circulated that Catherine was dying. She had heard that the citizens of Paris had prepared bonfires to be lit as soon as her death was confirmed. She took a deep satisfaction in depriving them of their celebration.

She longed to stand defiantly at her window and show them all that the Dark Queen was not finished yet. But in a city so tense, Catherine was in as much danger from an assassin's pistol as she was from the weakness of her own aging body.

The last time she had glanced out she thought she had seen a rather sinister figure lurking in the street. Garbed in a long cloak, his features obscured beneath the brim of a large hat, he had seemed to stare straight up at her window.

She consoled herself that it had all been a trick of her rheumy eyes. When a cart passed by, the fellow had appeared to have vanished into thin air.

This is what it is to become old, she reflected bitterly, to live in fear of shadows.

Catherine made it as far as the chair by the hearth and all but collapsed into it. Her ladies hovered nearby, whispering amongst themselves. The young had an irritating tendency to do that around the old, the infirm, the dying. As though an advance in years suddenly rendered one deaf, blind, and inane. Catherine had resolved never to tolerate it herself.

Rapping her cane against the floor, she said, "Despite what you all may be hoping, I am not at death's door. If you have anything to say, speak aloud or hold your tongues."

Her attendants fell silent, exchanging uneasy looks. Mademoiselle de Bec approached and sank into a trembling curtsy.

"We were only trying to decide if we should trouble you. There is someone here demanding admittance if it please Your Grace."

"It does not please Her Grace. Do I look in any condition to receive anyone? Unless it is my loving son come to make tender enquiry after his mother's health?"

When de Bec could not meet her eyes, Catherine snorted. "No? I thought not."

"It is not the king." The girl nervously retreated a step. "It is Captain Xavier."

"What!" Catherine was stunned for a moment, then she snarled, "You are either a liar or a fool. I received word but yesterday that Xavier must be dead. He was swept overboard in a storm just before his ship broke up."

"No, it is indeed the captain, Your Grace, or else it is his ghost."

"And a mighty hale and handsome one," one of the other ladies dared venture with a giggle. One black look from Catherine and the girl's smile was erased.

Xavier alive and returned to Paris? Well, if any man was bold enough to cheat death, it would be that arrogant rogue. But cheating *her* was another matter, and then daring to swagger back into her own palace!

Catherine was seized by such a spasm of fury, her pulse throbbed dangerously behind her temple. She took short breaths in order to calm herself.

Her first impulse was to send for her guard, demand to know how Xavier had slipped past them. Then she would have Xavier's neck stretched from the nearest tree in her garden where she could have the satisfaction of watching.

But her curiosity won out. She would like to hear what

excuses the man had to offer before she had his lying tongue cut out.

"Send him in," she commanded as she struggled to her feet. How did he dare return to her without carrying out the orders she had paid him to do? Unless . . . he had.

For a moment Catherine entertained the wild hope that Xavier had fulfilled his mission; that he would come in, dragging Megaera in tow.

The brief flare of hope died when Xavier entered the salon alone, not even accompanied by his large menacing native. Catherine's ire only increased as she noted that he had taken no more pains when appearing before her than he ever had. His boots were muddied, his cloak travel-stained, a beard roughening his chin, his dark hair uncombed and unruly.

And yet he sauntered toward her with an aplomb many a bejeweled and satin-clad duke would have envied. The rogue swept her a gallant bow, looking completely assured of his welcome.

Catherine was torn between fury and admiration for his boldness, a conflict of emotion that could not be good for her heart. She pressed one hand to her bosom to contain its beating.

Xavier dropped to one knee before her. "Your Majesty, I have returned to you at last."

"Then you are either the bravest man I ever knew or a complete fool. Unless you are unaware that there is a price on your head?"

"I am. So I came to turn myself in and claim it."

Catherine was obliged to choke back a laugh in spite of herself and that only rendered her more furious. She would have liked to have brought her cane down upon his head, if she would not have fallen in the process. She nearly did anyway as she leaned forward to box his ears.

"Villain!" The epithet came out as more a cry of pain. Her rheumatic gnarled fingers ached in protest. She feared the blow had hurt her far worse than him.

Xavier did not even flinch. He gave her a look that was all innocence and reproached surprise.

"Majesty, what have I done to deserve such abuse at your hands?"

"What done?" she spluttered. She flexed her throbbing hand, overcome with pain and anger to the point of incoherence. "Took money . . . cheated . . . betrayed."

"Never! I did all that Your Grace required of me."

"Liar." She grated her teeth as she fought to calm herself. She had oft heard tales of Elizabeth Tudor's temper, how the English queen spat at and struck subjects who displeased her.

Catherine had always deplored the woman's want of regal conduct, compared to her own icy dignity. Catherine's anger had ever been more likely to freeze than burn. And so she would do with Xavier, freeze him straight to hell.

Regaining command of herself, she said in clipped accents, "You have been gone nearly a year and I know how you have employed your time. My son has an official complaint from the court of Spain regarding your piratical activities."

"You would believe the Spanish, Your Grace? They cannot tell one Frenchman from another."

"Somehow I doubt anyone who ever crossed your path would be inclined to forget you, monsieur."

When the man smirked, Catherine added icily, "That was not a compliment, Captain."

His smile widened although it took on a slightly sheepish cast. "I admit I did veer a bit off course."

"All the way to the coast of La Florida? That is quite a bit of veering, monsieur."

"I ventured there for your sake, Your Grace. I hoped to discover that Fountain of Youth I told you about."

"Spare me any more of your fairy tales."

"It was not so great a chimera as the one you had me pursue. On my return journey, I went to Faire Isle as you asked and found Megaera."

"Then where is she?" Catherine asked impatiently.

"I deemed it would be a waste of time to return to Your Grace with such a worthless creature."

"You *deemed*? Who asked you to judge? All I required was that you—"

"But as your emissary, I had the opportunity to observe the girl closely," Xavier said, daring to interrupt her tirade. "She is but a thin, insignificant creature. Her true name is Margaret Wolfe and the reports you have had of her were all misleading. Meg's mother may have been a great sorceress, but the girl's reputation is all founded upon Cassandra Lascelles's mad hopes for her daughter. Margaret Wolfe scarce has the wit to brew the simplest posset."

"And yet I have heard that the Lady of Faire Isle means to designate Megaera as her successor."

"Another false report. She did not choose Mademoiselle Wolfe."

When Catherine scowled down at him in disbelief, he insisted, "I was there. I managed to spy upon the council atop the cliffs. The Lady chose her own niece, Seraphine Remy."

"Remy?"

"She is the eldest daughter of Gabrielle and Nicolas Remy."

Catherine compressed her lips, not wanting to believe a word of this. And yet . . .

"I remember Gabrielle well," she murmured. "Of all the Cheney sisters, I thought she showed the most promise until she was foolish enough to fall in love. She was a great beauty, with a subtle mind. Intelligent, daring, and worldly-wise."

"Her daughter is much the same. Set next to Seraphine Remy, Margaret Wolfe seems even more insignificant. A peasant in the shadow of a princess."

"Humph!" Catherine tapped her cane against the floor, unable to believe she was even listening to such tales. But she was troubled by her own recollections of the one glimpse she had ever had of Megaera. The infamous Silver Rose had indeed been a scrawny frightened child. The mother, Cassandra, with her mass of dark hair and eerie empty eyes had seemed the dangerous one.

While she pondered this, Xavier stood, wincing a little as he straightened from his stiff posture kneeling at her feet.

"I did not give you leave to rise."

"But I must if I am to present you with the gift that I have brought from halfway around the world."

"What would that be?"

"Your Grace did not ask me about the success of my other venture."

Catherine sniffed. "You mean your search for your mythical fountain."

"A myth no longer. I found it." Delving beneath his cloak, he produced a small vial of some clear liquid.

Catherine glowered at him. "Do you think to play me for a fool a second time, monsieur?"

"No more than I did last autumn. How would I dare? This is indeed a sampling of waters from the Fountain of Youth."

"If you do not propose to deceive me, then I fear you deceive yourself."

"Not so, Your Grace. I was badly injured in the engagement with the Spanish ship, my right arm all but crushed. I would have died or lost my good arm except for this magic elixir."

Catherine arched her brows skeptically, but she took the vial from him. Uncorking it, she sniffed at the contents. "It seems nothing but mere water."

"Yes, mere water, the essence of life itself. Take one sip and you'll see."

"Bah!"

She would have dashed the vial to the ground had he not seized her hand to prevent her.

"Your Grace, I beg you. You trusted me once before with your health and life. You must admit that my other potion did you much good. This one is ten times more powerful."

She scowled at where his fingers encircled her wrist, the man having the temerity to touch her unbidden. She, Catherine, daughter of the powerful de Medicis, Dowager Queen of France. And yet his hand felt warm and strong against the fragile skin of her wrist. Her pulse gave a most foolish flutter.

"Release me."

He did so reluctantly. Catherine stared at the vial in her hand. Xavier had no need to remind her of the restorative brew he had once shared with her. She had thought wistfully more than once of that potion when her joints had throbbed and her bones ached this past long dreary winter.

Drained by her recent illness, she suddenly felt exhausted and completely dispirited. If what the man told her about Megaera was true, then she really had run out of options.

What more did she have to lose? Bringing the vial to her lips, she ventured a small sip.

Running the drops of moisture over her tongue, she swallowed and then upbraided Xavier. "It *is* nothing but water, you rogue. I vow I will have your head for this chicanery—"

She broke off with a gasp. A mere sip of the liquid sent a fire coursing through her veins. For a moment, she feared the man had been reckless enough to poison her before her entire court of ladies.

But the warmth was more like a purging flame, burning away all weakness, all pain. She felt stronger than she had in weeks, perhaps even in months.

She regarded with wonder the vial she grasped in her trembling hands and would have drained the entire contents in one gulp if Xavier had not stopped her.

"Nay, have a care, Your Grace. No one's constitution is able to bear consuming too much of this healing water at once. You must use it but sparingly."

Catherine regarded the vial longingly, but she was persuaded to replace the cork.

"This one small vial is all that is left of what I was able to draw from the spring before I was driven off by the Spanish. But if I had a small fleet of ships and enough men, I would be able to bring you back barrels of the stuff."

Catherine said nothing. Fingering the vial, she regarded him thoughtfully. No doubt this was a most powerful elixir. But did she truly believe Xavier's tale of how he had come by it?

The potion had done much to clear her head and her vision. Perhaps a little more would even restore the greatest ability she had ever possessed as a daughter of the earth. The gift to read a man's eyes, to strip his soul bare of every secret he possessed, all with the mere power of her gaze.

Settling back into her chair, she smiled and beckoned Xavier closer.

"Come. Tell me more," she purred.

Chapter Twenty-two

THE SUNLIGHT POURED ACROSS JANE'S BED, PRODDING HER awake whether she wished it or not. Her eyes fluttered open and she felt disoriented. She had been dreaming she was back on Faire Isle, the dream so vivid she could have almost wept when she awakened to discover that she was in Paris. Even after a week in her cousin's rented house, the gilt-trimmed walls of her bedchamber still felt strange to Jane after the peaceful simplicity of the room she had known at Belle Haven.

She sat up, her night shift sticking to her sweat-soaked skin. It promised to be another hot day. She rubbed the sleep from her eyes, feeling resentful of the merciless sunlight streaming through her window.

It had aroused her from a good dream for once, not any of the nightmares that had plagued her ever since leaving the island. She dreamed she had pulled back the blanket, proudly displaying the face of her newborn son. All the ladies had crowded around her bed, Ariane, Seraphine, and Meg all cooing over the babe. Xavier had hovered protectively over Jane and the infant, smiling tenderly.

"If you don't want the boy to grow up to become a pirate, we had better name him—"

But that was where she had awakened. Now she would never know what Xavier had been about to suggest. Jane winked back tears at the unbearable sense of loss that swept through her.

She thought she would have preferred one of her nightmares to such an entrancing dream. It only served as a cruel reminder that there was no Xavier . . . and no babe either.

Her flow had finally come during the journey to Paris. She knew she ought to have been glad, but despite the hardships she would have faced as an unwed mother, she realized how desperately she had wanted that child. Now it was as though her last link to Xavier was gone.

Their time together had taken on the quality of a dream. A knock on her bedchamber door brought her back to her present bleak reality.

The little housemaid Violette poked her head in the door to call, "Madame Danvers? Are you awake? Your cousin is asking for you."

Already? Jane stifled a groan.

Violette looked apologetic. "I am sorry to disturb you,

my lady, but Madame Benton, she says she has such a dreadful headache, she is like to die—"

"I understand," Jane interrupted wearily. "Tell her I will be right there."

Violette bobbed a curtsy and disappeared, leaving Jane to stagger out of bed. Jane washed and dressed as quickly as she could. She hastened down to the kitchen to break her fast and prepare a cooling compress for Abigail's brow.

Only one week beneath her cousin's roof, and Jane felt drained. She did not know what was more wearying, ministering to her cousin's incessant demands or trying to deal with the creditors besieging the house.

The scavengers had already stripped away Abigail's jewels, the silverplate, the tapestries, and much of the furniture. She and Abigail were fortunate to still have beds to rest upon, although the bed hangings were long gone.

Most of the servants had decamped as well, only one of the footmen, Gerard, remained and the kitchen maid, Violette.

Jane's footsteps made a lonely echo on the marble tiled floors as she went to her cousin's bedchamber. Abigail set up a plaintive wail as soon as Jane slipped into the room.

"Oh, Jane, where have you been? It has taken you forever and my head feels fit to burst."

Abigail sat up in bed, her face as pinched and peevish as a querulous child, her dark brown hair in stark contrast to the delicate white lawn of her nightgown.

Summoning up all her patience, Jane tiptoed over to her cousin. "You will be better presently, Abby. But you must lie quiet."

She eased Abigail back down onto the pillows, placing the damp cloth steeped in lavender water over her eyes.

Her cousin groaned. "Oh, I will never be well. You must send for Dr. Marchand. I need to be bled again."

Jane shuddered. After her time spent among the learned women of Faire Isle, she had come to regard the practice of bleeding as barbaric, as Ariane did.

"That is the last thing you need. Dr. Marchand refuses to wait upon you again until his reckoning is paid. I think you would be much better off if you would allow me to crack the windows open and let in some fresh air."

"Fresh air?" Abigail shifted the compress to her brow so that she could peer reproachfully at Jane. "Are you trying to kill me? I do not know where you came by such strange notions."

"From the Lady of Faire Isle. She knows far more about healing than your Dr. Marchand."

"Have—have you truly become a witch yourself then, Jane?"

"No. If I was, my dear cousin, I might be tempted to transform you into a more agreeable companion, like a kitten."

When Abigail gasped and shrank from her, Jane patted her hand. "I am only teasing you, Abby."

"You never used to make such shocking jests." Abigail drew her hand away. "Someone on that island has been a most wicked influence on you."

Yes, someone had, Jane reflected. An image rose to her mind of Xavier's devilish smile and eyes that could be so teasing one minute, so warm the next.

The vision was so strong it brought a bittersweet ache to her heart. She suppressed the remembrance as she tucked the coverlet more snugly about her cousin.

Abigail pouted up at her. "And what do you mean, I am not agreeable? I am sure I cannot help being cross. I am so dreadfully ill, Jane."

"Yes, my dear, but you might be better if you would be sensible and take some nourishment, get out of bed. If you could but exert yourself a little—"

"Exert myself? You would not suggest such a thing if you knew all that I suffered being wed to such a scoundrel as George Benton. But I could not expect you to understand. You were fortunate enough to have been married off to two respectable, worthy men."

"And yet here I am, quite as destitute as you."

"But that was your own fault, getting tangled up in treason plots and witchcraft," Abigail retorted, but the next instant, she winced, groping for Jane's hand.

"I am sorry, Jane. I did not mean that. I am being disagreeable. But it is just too much, being abandoned by George, having those awful men take away all my pretty things, my tapestries, my jewels, even my best gowns. I am so miserable, I just want to die." Tears flowed down Abigail's cheeks.

"Oh, hush, my dear." Groping for her own handkerchief, Jane dried her cousin's eyes.

Abigail sniffed. "I am so grateful to have you here with me. You cannot know how much I have missed you."

No, she couldn't, since Abby had scarce written a word to her during the entire time of her exile. But Jane patted her hand and thanked her for the sentiment.

"Remember the night before your first wedding?" Abigail asked. "How I sneaked out of bed and into your room? How much fun we had, staying up until dawn, gossiping and giggling."

That was not exactly the way Jane recollected it. She had been heartsore, grieving over the babe she had so recently lost, frightened about her future prospects as wife to a boy as sullen as Richard Arkwright.

But Abigail had been a welcome distraction. She had been such a sunny-natured little girl. It was sad to see so little trace of that bright, mischievous imp in the woman lying listlessly in this bed.

"Strange, isn't it?" Abigail said. "How different our lives turn out from the way we expect. It is good we have no knowledge of the trials and disappointments that lie ahead or we would never have the courage to face them."

Jane nodded in agreement, but she was astounded when Abigail added, "My life would have been so much more content if I would have been permitted to marry your brother."

"Ned?"

Abigail smiled and sighed. "I realize I was a little older than he was, but nothing to signify. He was so handsome and so charming. I am sure I would have been happy as his wife. I was desperately fond of him."

Jane had loved her brother, but not enough to forget his faults as Abigail appeared to have done. With his penchant for gaming, combined with his reckless pursuit of alchemy, Ned would have made Abby a far worse husband than George.

But Jane said nothing, holding Abigail's hand and allowing her to mourn for her lost love. Perhaps because it was easier for Jane than thinking about her own.

When Abigail drifted off to sleep, Jane almost regretted it. As wearying as Abigail's fretfulness and demands for attention could be, at least it kept Jane's own unhappy thoughts at bay.

But as silence settled over the room, those thoughts crowded in upon her. She wandered over to one of the chamber's tall windows. The room felt so close she longed to open the casement, but knew that it would only distress Abigail.

Jane rested her head against the pane of glass, staring down into the garden below without really seeing it. Instead, she closed her eyes and pictured a ship, with the wind billowing its sails, skimming over the ocean, a dark-haired man striding across the decks. Where was Xavier now? Long gone from these shores, she was certain. The days that had elapsed since his departure from Faire Isle were more than enough time for him to be somewhere out in the vast reaches of the Atlantic, far away from her.

Except that he wasn't.

A hail of pebbles rained against the window, startling her into opening her eyes. A cloaked figure stood below her in the garden, gazing upward. Xavier.

Jane's mouth fell open and she blinked, certain that the longings of her heart must have seized control of her mind. She had to be imagining this.

But Xavier swept her a bow after that insouciant fashion that was uniquely his. He beckoned to her to come down to him.

Jane sucked in a deep breath. As distraught as she had been over the way she and Xavier had parted, at least she had drawn some comfort from the thought he would be safe, far from Catherine de Medici's grasp. Was the man completely mad to have risked coming to Paris?

Stealing a nervous glance at her cousin, Jane assured herself that Abigail was still asleep. She raced from the bedchamber down the stairs and through the kitchens. The household's remaining maidservant had nodded off, Violette's cheek pillowed against the table. The poor girl was no doubt as worn down by Abigail's fretful demands as Jane was.

Jane slipped past her and out the kitchen door. The garden was little more than a small park, enclosed by a wrought iron fence, a series of trees and bushes shielding the expanse of lawn from the street beyond. The place looked peaceful, a shady arbor tucked beneath the late morning sun. And completely deserted.

"Xavier?" she whispered, moving uncertainly toward the stone bench in the center of the garden.

He seemed to spring at her out of nowhere. Jane was so startled, she nearly cried out, but his hand clamped down on her mouth.

His mere touch, the feel of his calloused palm against her lips was almost enough to undo her. His right hand, she noted. His sling was gone, his arm healed.

How could she have ever imagined him to be an illusion? There was nothing of the dream hero about this man, smelling of sweat, his clothes travel-stained, his jaw beard-roughened. He looked every inch the disreputable pirate he proclaimed himself to be. So solid, so warm, so real, she had to resist the urge to fling her arms about his neck and weep for joy.

Prying his hand from her mouth, she squirmed away from him. Too overcome to speak, she could only regard him reproachfully.

"Sorry," he muttered. "I was only trying to prevent you from crying out."

"What are you doing here?" she interrupted, finding her voice at last. "Are you quite insane?"

"Well, yes, but I am sure you always knew that. That at least is one thing I never concealed from you."

"What—how—" Her mind reeled. She scarce knew what to say. It seemed so impossible that he should be here, that they should even be having this conversation.

"How—how did you know where to find me?" she finally managed to get out.

"I admit it took me a day or two. But eventually all I had to do was follow the line of disgruntled merchants beating a path to your cousin's door." He frowned at her. "Blast you, woman! Why couldn't you have listened to me and stayed on Faire Isle. And yet . . ." His tone softened. "Damn my selfish eyes, but I am glad to see you again."

He attempted to take her hand, but Jane whipped them both behind her back, out of his reach. "Well, I am not glad to see you. I hoped you were long gone, halfway around the world by now."

"Have you truly come to hate me that much?"

"Hate you?" Jane choked. "If you could have any idea of

the sleepless nights I have had, the nightmares w-worrying what might happen to you if you were caught. In London, they—they stake pirates to the banks of the Thames, leaving them to the mercy of the tides and—and the crabs."

"You need have no fear of that. The crabs would never have me. I am far too tough."

"Damn you! This is nothing to jest about." Tears stung her eyes and she slammed her fists against his chest, all the worry, the heartache, the frustrated longings of the past fortnight boiling over.

She staggered away from him, groaning. "Oh, what have you done to me? I never used to swear or strike anyone."

"Feels good, doesn't it?"

"Yes," she admitted, but she refused to be drawn in by his smile. She sank down upon the garden bench. "Why are you here?" she demanded again.

"I needed to see you, make sure you were all right, after the way I was obliged to leave you on Faire Isle, not knowing . . ." His gaze roved speculatively over her figure.

"I am not with child, Xavier, if that is what you are still afraid of. My courses came not long after I left the island."

"Oh."

Jane was surprised to see something akin to disappointment flicker across his face. But the expression was gone so quickly she thought she must have imagined it.

"Well—that is a huge relief," he said. "All for the best."

"For the best," Jane agreed hollowly.

"Even if you are not with child, I still think it was foolhardy for you to make the journey to Paris."

"Foolhardy? *Me?*" Jane all but choked on her indignation. "I am not the one sauntering about Paris, in danger of being arrested at any moment."

"Neither am I." A defensive look came over his face as he said, "I have been to see Queen Catherine and made my peace with her."

"You what?" Jane gasped.

Xavier scowled, misinterpreting her horror. "Don't look at me like that Jane. I didn't do it by betraying Meg."

"I—I never thought—"

"Didn't you?" He arched one brow. "Far from betraying the girl, I believe I have persuaded the queen that Meg would be of little use to her schemes."

"But—but how?"

"By practicing my own brand of magic. Unlike you, my dear, I am a very gifted liar." Xavier's lips twitched, his expression a trifle smug as he related his recent audience with Catherine.

Another woman might have applauded his daring or admired his cunning. But Jane could only stare at him with mounting trepidation, especially when he added, "She wants me to call upon her again and perform another of my trances."

He shrugged. "I figure all I have to do is predict a long and glorious future for her if she forgets about the Silver Rose and places all her faith in the riches of La Florida—"

"You mustn't," Jane cried, leaping up and clutching hold of his arm. "Xavier, please, I beg you. You must not go near her again."

Xavier rolled his eyes. "I know all of you women from Faire Isle have this fear of the Dark Queen, even my wise sister, Ariane. But whatever Catherine once was, she is now just a sick old woman. I might feel ashamed of taking such advantage of her if she wasn't such a scheming witch."

"That's just it! She is a witch and—and dangerous. You must not risk your life any further, not even for the sake of pursuing your far horizons."

"My far horizons," he murmured, an odd expression darkening his eyes. "Yes, why else would I hazard my neck? Considering the way Catherine toyed with the lives of my mother and father, all the misery she wrought, I think she owes me a ship, don't you?"

Jane shook her head, pleading with him to be sensible, but he did not even appear to be listening to her. He crooked his fingers beneath her chin, examining her face.

"You look far too pale and exhausted. This cousin of yours is draining the life from you."

"I am fine," Jane said, pushing his hand away.

"No, you aren't. This city does not agree with you. You said that all you wanted was to find someplace safe, but believe me when I tell you, Paris is not that place."

"Not for you, perhaps," she retorted.

"Jane, you have to go back to Faire Isle. If you would but heed what I have to say—"

"No, why should I when you ignore all of my warnings?" Jane tipped her chin to a defiant angle. "My cousin needs me. I have no intention of leaving Paris."

"Neither do I." Xavier regarded her with a mingling of ruefulness and frustration. "Which brings us to a complete impasse, my dear."

Xavier raised her hand lightly to his lips and bid her a

rather disgruntled farewell. Jane returned to the house, her mind in complete turmoil.

Neither of them noticed the shadowy figure watching from just beyond the gate.

The costly cut of her riding habit concealed beneath a plain cloak, Catherine peered into the garden. This morning, she had risked another swallow of Xavier's miraculous elixir. Although her heart had raced alarmingly, she had felt strong, so much better. Enough to indulge herself in a pastime she had been obliged to abandon years ago.

She had oft amused herself by riding out in disguise, to gauge the mood of the populace, garnering information she could not come by immured in her palace.

When the groom had fetched her horse, she had had difficulty mounting, no longer the lithe young princess who had impressed even the jaded French court with her equestrian skills.

It had taken two attendants to heft the bulk of her weight into the sidesaddle, and her joints had groaned in protest when she had curled her leg into the awkward position ladies were forced to adopt when riding.

But she had forgotten all of that in her joy in being back in the saddle again. She would have loved to urge the mare into a canter but the crowded streets of Paris would not allow that. Besides, for her own safety, she must draw as little attention to herself as possible.

So she had contented herself with plodding along between the two grooms who accompanied her, her striking features obscured beneath a dark veil.

She had ridden past the inn where she knew Xavier was staying. She had formed no clear intention of spying upon the man, but when she had observed Xavier setting out upon some errand, the opportunity had been too good to lose.

When he had clambered over the fence into this garden, curiosity and suspicion had overwhelmed her. Her guards had been startled by her command to halt. When she had insisted upon dismounting, they cast an uneasy look around and she knew they would have dissuaded her if they had dared.

Commanding them to await her in a nearby alley, she had drawn near the secluded garden and peered cautiously between the bars of the fence.

Now she almost regretted the decision. When she had set out riding from the Hôtel de la Reine, she had felt giddy, almost young again.

But as she had watched the two lovers through the webbing of her veil, her gloved fingers gripped the iron rails of the fence. *Lovers.* Despite the tension between the pair, Catherine had no doubt that was what they were. This Jane person could not disguise her looks of longing, nor could Xavier suppress a certain tenderness in his voice. Although Catherine could not imagine what attraction this prim, pale Englishwoman could possess for him.

Against her will, the years crept over Catherine again. Remembrance flooded back in a cruel rush of those long ago days when she would lie upon the floor of her bedchamber. Her eye pressed to the hole she had bored, she peered into the apartment below watching her husband make love to his mistress, the elegant Diane.

Mon Dieu, Henry, Catherine had longed to cry out in her agony. Diane de Poitiers was nearly old enough to be his mother. How could Henry prefer this woman to his young adoring wife? Watching them together had proved a most exquisite torment to Catherine and yet she had been unable to help herself.

She had lowered herself by such behavior, just as she was doing now, spying upon Xavier. And this time not for a king, the husband she had so blindly adored, but for a trickster, a miserable scum of a corsair.

She sucked in a sharp breath between her teeth, wondering why Xavier's treachery should pain her so. She had never fully trusted the man. But she was dismayed to realize that she had wanted to. It would have been a comfort for once to have one ally she could reply upon.

She could not decide which was worse, overhearing him refer to her as a sick old woman or that other betrayal that ran far deeper than she could have imagined.

He had spoken of Ariane as his sister. Brother to Catherine's great enemy, the Lady of Faire Isle. How was that even possible? Evangeline and her beloved chevalier had never had any son.

As yet as she observed Xavier raise his lady's hand to his lips in a courtly gesture, the memory that had long eluded Catherine crystallized in her mind.

Beneath Xavier's rough-hewn appearance, she discerned at last what had long nagged at her: the corsair's uncanny resemblance to the Chevalier Louis Cheney.

And if Xavier was the chevalier's by-blow, his mother could only have been Marguerite de Maitland. One of Catherine's own women, a member of her Flying Squadron, familiar with Catherine's inflexible rule. None of her courtesans were permitted to bear a child, to mar their usefulness to her with the encumbrance of a babe. Yet somehow Marguerite had managed to do so and concealed Xavier's existence, taking her secret to the grave.

Not only had Catherine allowed the bastard son to make a fool of her, but she had permitted herself to be deceived by the half-mad mother as well. At a time when Catherine had prided herself on being at the height of her powers.

Catherine's hands trembled, but she checked her rage. At least Xavier had done her one good. That elixir, wherever he had acquired it from, had given her more command over her emotions.

Her anger coursed through her in its familiar form, a river of ice through her veins. She would have her vengeance, but nothing so crude as a knife to Xavier's heart or a rope knotted round his neck. She would bide her time until she found a way to humiliate him as he had done her, crush him so completely he would consider death a blessing.

Chapter Twenty-three

DARK CLOUDS ROILED ACROSS THE SKY, THREATENING TO unleash a barrage of rain at any moment. But Jane found it an improvement over the previous day of heat and unrelenting sunshine.

The gray skies seemed better suited to her own mood and that of her companion at the kitchen table. She had succeeded in coaxing Abigail to dress and join her belowstairs, although Jane was now sorry that she had.

As they broke their fast together, Abigail did nothing but lament the loss of her fine plates and being obliged to eat from a wooden trencher.

"And the bread is stale," she grumbled. "There is no butter and I so long for some fresh grapes."

"There were none to be had, madame," Violette said from her fireplace corner where she was busy darning hose. "The crops have all been very bad again this year."

"You might have found some if you had looked harder."

"I am sure Violette did the best she could. You can survive without grapes," Jane said, her tone more acid than she intended.

Abigail nibbled at her bread and frowned at Jane. "You certainly have been in an ill humor these past few days. I have no idea why. I am the one who aches so that I am fortunate to snatch more than three or four hours sleep a night."

That was four more than she had had, Jane thought. But she suppressed the retort. When Abby was in one of her peevish moods, she had no interest in anyone's misery but her own. If Jane had complained of sleeplessness, she might have to explain the reason for it and she had no wish to do so.

She believed she had begun to reach some sort of center of calm, of resignation, when Xavier had erupted back into her life two days ago and completely overset her again.

Why he had done so, she was still uncertain. She supposed that his unique code of honor had demanded that he make certain she was not carrying his child.

Jane had been relieved to discover that he was no longer a fugitive, but the mere sight of him had reopened all her longings, all the heartache she had sought to suppress.

Since she could not deter him from his course with regard to the Dark Queen, Jane would as soon not know what he was up to. She was no longer troubled by any wistful dreams or alarming nightmares. That was because she could scarce sleep at all for tossing and turning, worrying about Xavier.

It was far more than the man deserved, she had fumed as she punched her pillow, wishing she could have pummeled some sense into him. He had managed to get the price lifted from his head, so why must he risk his life by continuing to dupe the queen with his feigned magic?

Did acquiring another ship really mean that much to him? Apparently it did, far more than she had ever meant to him, Jane reflected bitterly. Otherwise he might see how afraid she was and pay more heed to her advice.

"Jane!"

Her cousin's voice cut into Jane's unhappy musings. She straightened in her chair and focused her attention back on Abigail.

"Have you been listening to a word I've said?" Abigail demanded.

"Yes, you said you do not like—" Jane racked her mind for something that Abigail had yet to complain about. "The weather?"

"As it so happens, I do hate all this rain. It does nothing but storm in Paris."

"This is the first day the sun has not shone since I arrived," Jane attempted to point out, but Abigail had already continued on.

"What I said was how much I have come to loathe Paris. But I have had a letter from the Margates. At least some of my old friends have not forgotten me. They have asked me to come and stay with them in Calais. I am sure I could get them to invite you as well."

"How good of you," Jane murmured, but her dry tone was completely lost on Abigail.

"It would be perfect if we could but find a way to get there. Calais would be a convenient place to embark for England if the invasion succeeds."

Jane stiffened. "I beg your pardon?"

"The invasion of the armada. Do you hear nothing of what goes on in the world on that witch island? If the rumors are true and the Spanish succeed in overthrowing Elizabeth . . ."

Abigail faltered before Jane's icy stare. Apparently even her cousin was not so obtuse that she failed to notice the tension that had come over Jane.

"You would rejoice, would you not, Jane? You do want to go home."

"I have no desire to see—" Jane began sharply, only to break off. Realizing that her cousin was staring at her, Jane amended, "That is, I see no sense in making plans for something that may never happen."

"But—"

Jane stood up abruptly. If Abigail went on rejoicing at the prospect of England falling prey to the Spanish, Jane knew she would become angry and they would quarrel. And when quarreling with Abby over matters of politics or religion, one might as well shout at the kitchen cat.

"I believe I shall go out for a while, tend to the marketing. We have need of more bread and perhaps I shall find you some grapes."

"Dear God, Jane, have you forgotten you are a lady? To go wandering about the stalls bartering for food like a common maidservant—that is Violette's task."

"Violette is already doing the work of ten servants and that footman of yours is of little use."

"Scrubbing floors and washing linen is beneath a footman. It is Gerard's task to—to run errands and to fetch things."

"And to look fine in his livery," Jane said. "The man is a lazy lout, Abby. I suspect you hired him mostly because he has strong calves and fills out his trunk hose so well."

Abigail's cheeks reddened. "That may have been a consideration. A footman should reflect credit upon one's household."

Jane smiled wryly and went to fetch the market basket.

"It is going to rain. You'll get soaked and catch your death," Abigail called.

"I am not as delicate as you, Abby. I shall make haste and return before the storm breaks."

"But what if I need you for something? My head—"

"You will be fine. I will be back directly." Jane snatched up the basket and darted out the kitchen door before Abigail could raise any further objections.

She only slowed her steps when she reached the gate, half-fearing to be pounced on by more of the Bentons' creditors. But perhaps the tradesmen had finally given up. The past two mornings Jane had been left in peace.

Mindful of the sky threatening overhead, Jane set off at a brisk pace. As she wended her way through the streets, Jane could not help recollecting how much her poor brother had adored Paris.

Ned had waxed almost lyrical over the city's exuberance, gaiety, and excitement. Glancing about her, Jane saw little sign of that Paris. The city struck her as being as sullen and dismal as the clouds gathering overhead.

The constant civil war, too many seasons of bad crops, and blighted livestock had taken their toll. There appeared to be far more beggars thronging the streets than there were housewives and servants patronizing the open stalls.

The wares offered by the greengrocer, the baker, the wine merchant, and the butcher were scant and overpriced. Jane paused by the poulterer's, wondering if she could afford one of the scrawny hens on display.

The woman in charge of the stall was a hard-faced creature. When she quoted her price, Jane flinched. The woman watched unsmiling as Jane dug through her purse and pored over her meager amount of coin.

She had learned many valuable things about managing a large household when she had become the wife of Sir William Danvers, but bartering in the marketplace was not one of them.

"That—that seems terribly expensive," she said.

"I cannot give my birds away, madame," the woman huffed. "Do you want the hen or don't you?"

"No, I—I am sorry, I—?"

"Yes, she does," a voice cut in.

Jane whirled about, startled to find Xavier standing behind her. Small wonder he was able to convince the queen he was a necromancer. The man possessed the uncanny ability to spring out of nowhere.

Too confounded to say anything, Jane watched agog as Xavier swept past her. In a few moments, not only had he persuaded the vendor to cut her price in half, but he had charmed a smile out of the woman.

Only when Xavier prepared to hand over his own coin, did Jane snap to her senses.

"No," she said. "I can't allow—that is, I don't want the hen."

Cheeks firing with embarrassment, she turned and walked rapidly away. She did not get very far when Xavier overtook her. Seizing hold of her basket, he plunked the hen inside.

"Stop," she cried. "What do you think you are doing?"

"Keeping you from starving?"

"I—I am not. My cousin and I are doing well enough."

"So well that you have milliners and tailors and boot-makers hovering outside your door, ready to snatch the last crust of bread from your table."

"As a matter of fact, no we don't. Only this morning—" Jane broke off, regarding Xavier with sudden suspicion.

"How do you know which tradesmen have been dunning us?"

"A logical surmise."

But Jane was not fooled by his air of studied nonchalance. She regarded him with a mingling of dismay and mortification. "It was you. You have been paying them off. That is why they stopped hounding us." She was struck by another realization. His arrival in the marketplace could have been no coincidence.

"You have been watching the house, following me."

Xavier blustered, starting to deny it only to shrug and give over the attempt. "Someone has to look out for you if you persist in staying in this damned city."

"But you have no obligation to me." She looked around and lowered her voice as she added. "I am not carrying your child. You owe me nothing."

"And you would as soon not be indebted to me either." He heaved a vexed sigh. "You aren't. As ever, I have my own selfish motives. I would like to be restored to my sister's good graces. If you write and tell Ariane how generous I have been, perhaps she will no longer despise me."

"I don't believe that she does, nor Miri neither. But I also don't think Ariane would approve of money that you acquired—" Jane bit down upon her lip, unable to give voice to the suspicion that troubled her.

But Xavier appeared to understand her reluctance all too well.

"It is not money I obtained from the Dark Queen if that is what you are afraid of. I can occasionally earn money through honest means."

"I am sorry," Jane faltered.

"I acquired it by—"

"You don't have to explain, Xavier."

"Yes, I do." A hint of color stained his cheeks as he went on. "I am rather good at sketching out maps of the voyages I have taken and I have been able to sell a few to men who also hunger for a glimpse of a far-off horizon. It seems even in a city as desperate as Paris, there are a few other foolish dreamers like me."

"If your maps are anything like your drawings, I am sure they are wonderful."

"Yes, occasionally if I am not sure of the route, I even invent an island or two. I could name one after you, Jane."

"Oh, no," she protested, horrified. "You must not."

The taut set of Xavier's mouth widened into his familiar grin. "I was only teasing you, my dear. I make my charts as accurate as possible. We would not want to send some poor fool sailing off the end of the world, would we?"

"No," Jane agreed, reluctantly smiling back at him. The tender amusement in his eyes, the warm curve of his lips wreaked havoc with her emotions. Xavier would be the first to deny it, but the man was capable of great kindness. She was sure that his continuing to look after her betokened no more than that. She could not allow herself to be charmed into losing her heart again.

When several fat droplets of water struck her cheek, she glanced up and said, "It is beginning to rain. I must be getting back to my cousin's."

"You'll never make it," Xavier said, seizing her hand. "You had best come with me."

"But where are we going?" Jane asked, stumbling in her efforts to keep up with his long strides.

"Back to the inn where I am staying."

"W-hat?" Jane hung back, her heart racing with a mixture of alarm and anticipation.

"Only to have a glass of wine in the taproom." Xavier angled a wicked look down at her. "What else did you think I meant?"

THE RAIN BEAT AGAINST THE WINDOWS OF THE ROYALE François, but the interior of the taproom was snug and dry. The tavern was thronged with Parisians seeking refuge from the downpour, the conversation heated as it had been most of the summer, condemning the king for his extravagant follies that had brought the kingdom to the brink of ruin.

Fear ran strong that another massacre was in the offing, but this time the target would not be Huguenots, but the king's rebellious Catholic subjects. And where was the duc de Guise? Never had Parisians been in greater need of their great hero, the champion of the true faith. Complaints and speculation ran rife through the tavern, but were conducted in low terse voices, as though His Majesty's spies lurked everywhere.

The only ones who appeared oblivious to the tension were the odd quartet seated near the taproom's front window. The lady appeared far too prim and proper to be seen abroad with such disreputable-looking companions.

Jane perched on the edge of her chair, feeling slightly bemused. Since her banishment from her life in England, she had been in all manner of situations she could never have predicted. Becoming the confidante of a girl who had been hailed as a notorious witch, attending a council of daughters of the earth, making love to a man at midnight within a circle of mysterious standing stones.

But never in her wildest flights of fancy had Jane imagined herself doing anything like this, the proper Lady Danvers frequenting a tavern, drinking with pirates.

There had been something challenging about the way Xavier had introduced her to his two shipmates. His stern gaze seemed to warn his two men to be on their best behavior, a warning that was unnecessary.

Jane had never met two men more courteous, even

amongst all the nobility of London. Especially the one called Pietro. She had heard tell of the savages who inhabited the New World but she had never been this close to one before.

Despite his alarming size, there was nothing of the savage about Pietro. He had a voice like velvet and the eyes of a sage, gentle and wise.

As for Jambe du Bois, his piratical appearance was greatly diminished when he doffed his cap, revealing a balding pate.

"Pleased to make your acquaintance, your ladyship," the little man addressed her in her own tongue. "After one sight of your lovely face, I can see why our captain was in no hurry to leave Faire Isle."

He raised her hand to his lips and proceeded to salute it with great enthusiasm until Xavier intervened.

"That will do, you old dog," Xavier said, rescuing her hand. His fingers lingered over hers before releasing her.

"You did not get too wet, did you, my lady?" Jambe asked. "We could shift to a spot nearer the fire."

Jane shook her head, assuring him she was fine. "It was a happy chance that your inn was situated so close to the district where I reside."

"Oh, that was no chance. When the captain learned where you were living, he insisted upon us moving from—ooof." Jambe broke off, apparently upon receiving a sharp jab in the ribs from Xavier. His threatening scowl caused the old man to subside.

Jane mulled over what Jambe had blurted out. So Xavier had changed residence from one inn to another. To be closer to her? Jane tried not to reflect too much upon that.

She twisted her hands in the folds of her skirt, feeling a trifle shy. She had no idea how one went about conversing with pirates.

She turned to Jambe. "So you are an Englishman, Master . . ." She floundered, unsure how to address a man who went by such a strange sobriquet. "Master Leg?"

The old man grinned. "Actually the name is Arthur Inchcombe, milady, formerly of London."

"Inchcombe?" Jambe du Bois's true name stirred her memory. Owing to her late husband's connection to the wine trade, Jane had become familiar with many of the prominent guilds and artisans of London.

"You are not by any chance kin to the glaziers who had their workshop in Cheapside?"

Jambe beamed, puffing out his chest with pride. "Indeed I am, milady, although I never had any talent for the trade myself. But my great-grandfather was a most skilled artisan and helped fit the stained glass for many of the city churches. My father always said it broke the old man's heart when the reformists smashed much of his beautiful work, calling it idolatry."

"So your family is Catholic?" Jane asked softly.

"We were until the old King Henry outlawed it. Then we were members of the king's church, but we almost had to become Protestors under his son. Then came Bloody Mary and back we went to the Popish ways again. Now under Elizabeth, we follow old Henry's ways again, taking care to stay away from the Puritans because good Queen Bess don't like them any more than she does Papists."

"Mind your tongue, Jambe," Xavier warned. "Lady Danvers is a Catholic, although she certainly has paid a heavy price for remaining true to her faith."

When Jambe regarded her questioningly Jane explained, "I have been exiled from England, partly because I sought to smuggle a priest into my house to say the mass."

That was a part of her history she had never even confided to Xavier. He twisted in his chair to scowl at her. "What in heaven's name were you thinking, Jane? To risk everything, your home, your life for such a trifle."

"I suppose it was *heaven* I was thinking of," she replied with a sad smile. "The rituals of our faith were not trifling to me or the members of my household.

"Of course, I had no idea the priest that I found was involved in a plot to assassinate the queen. That I would never condone. But even though it nearly cost me everything, including my life, I do not regret defying English law to secure the comforts of our religion for my people. Because—"

"I know." Xavier vented a long-suffering sigh. "Because it was the right thing to do."

Jane smiled ruefully. To her surprise, it was Pietro who appeared to be the most understanding. He nodded in quiet approval while Jambe scratched his head.

"Beg pardon, your ladyship. Perhaps these matters of faith be more clear to one of your birth and education. But it gets fair confusing for the more common people like me. Sometimes it seems safest to be a heathen like friend Pietro here."

"Unless the Spanish Inquisition ever lays hold of you," Xavier drawled.

"Damned devils." Jambe clapped his hand to his mouth. "Sorry, milady."

"You must forgive my friend," Pietro said. "While we were in St. Malo, we heard tidings of the Spanish that angered Jambe greatly."

"What tidings?"

Xavier leaned forward and fixed Jambe with a warning glare. "I don't think her ladyship needs to hear any idle reports you chanced to pick up."

"Yes, I do," Jane cried. "Please."

Jambe cast an uncertain glance from her back to his captain. Xavier scowled, but then he shrugged and leaned back. Taking that for assent, Jambe said, "It is considered fair certain the armada will set sail this month. If France does nothing to intervene, those Spanish dogs could be swarming up our coast."

Jane felt herself pale, her grip tightening on the edge of the table. Jambe's eyes glistened fiercely as he added, "If that happens, Captain, I am going home.

"I don't know how much use an old man with one leg will be against all those Spanish swords and muskets, but I'll give every last drop of my blood afore I ever see Philip of Spain on the throne at Whitehall instead of our grand old Bess."

Pietro placed his large hand on the little man's shoulder. "I am with you, my friend. I am pleased to fight the Spanish anytime, anywhere." He turned to Xavier. "That would be the best course for all of us, Captain, to seek out Sir Francis Drake. He said if we ever required employment, he would be pleased to take us on again."

"Aye," Jambe put in eagerly. "And you know Sir Francis. Even in the midst of a bloody war, Drake will manage to take a few prizes. We could come away with our pockets well lined with gold."

"Bah, is that all you ever think about?" Pietro asked. "My people, the Cimmarones, used to raid the Spanish mule teams and take their gold all the time. We buried it in the hills never to be found, just to annoy the Spanish."

"Don't speak of it, lad," Jambe groaned. "It makes me ill just to think of such waste. All that lovely gold."

"Gold is of no importance. Now iron, that is a useful metal. With iron you can make fine weapons and cooking pots."

"Humph. If you have enough gold, you can buy all the weapons and pots that you want."

The two fell into an amiable bickering that might have amused Jane under other circumstances. But talk of the armada filled her with anxiety. She looked to Xavier for reassurance, but found none in the grim cast of his countenance.

Xavier sipped his wine and frowned. "I have no wish to distress you, my dear. But I fear England's best hope for victory lies with the French. From what I have heard, King Henry and his mignons already have a great admiration for Drake and his exploits. One of those painted fops actually wears a miniature portrait of Sir Francis. That could well inspire the king to come to Elizabeth's aid. It is not impossible."

"But not damn likely." Jambe snorted. "Especially since the real power in this country seems to be that duc de Guise and his Catholic league."

"Jambe speaks true, Captain," Pietro said. "Didn't that letter you deciphered say that de Guise has made some sort of devil's bargain with the Spanish?"

"Letter?" Jane asked, glancing questioningly toward Xavier. He explained about the missive he had intercepted when he had captured the Spanish ship last spring.

"It was in code but the message implied that the Spanish king has paid de Guise to prevent the French from allying with the English by causing some sort of diversion."

"What kind of diversion?" Jane asked anxiously.

"I have no idea. I am not even sure that I translated the letter correctly." Xavier shrugged. "In any case, the duke never received the letter, so he has done nothing."

"But surely by this time the Spanish will have found some other way to contact the duke," Pietro said.

"Likely they have." Xavier took a sip of wine. "As I told the pair of you before, I have no objections to seeking a place with Drake. But I must conclude my business with Queen Catherine this afternoon."

Jane sucked in a deep breath. If talk of the armada made her fearful, Xavier's intention to seek another audience with Catherine had the power to tighten her stomach into a hard knot.

"Captain, I know you want to protect that young girl by convincing the queen to leave her alone, but have you not already accomplished that?" Pietro demanded.

"No, I need to be sure."

"But this game of yours has always been too dangerous."

"Ah, but this time, I intend to win."

Xavier cut off any further argument by getting to his

feet. "The rain appears to have stopped. My Lady Danvers must get back to her cousin's and I have a rendezvous with a queen."

He tossed some coins to Jambe to settle the reckoning and then extended his hand to Jane to escort her from the inn.

Jane rose slowly, gathering up her basket. Xavier had left her with the impression that his purpose in charming the queen was to secure himself another ship. But clearly once again Jane had misjudged him and Xavier in his pride had allowed her to do so.

As they emerged from the inn, Jane pressed his arm. "Xavier, please, may I have a word alone with you?"

"That sounds ominous. What have I done now?" he jested. He led her away to a quieter corner of the yard, out of the path of a troop of mounted traveling merchants. Smiling down at her, he tripped over a stray board that had fallen from a stack of haphazardly piled lumber.

Smothering an oath, he caught himself, clutching at a barrel and dislodging the lid. As Xavier was replacing it, an angry voice shouted out, "You there! What do you think you are doing?"

Xavier glanced around, his brows lifting in haughty surprise. "Nothing that need concern you."

The man that had shouted strode toward them. One of the inn's ostlers, he had an unpleasant countenance, his complexion the hue of raw meat. He bore down upon them in such a menacing fashion that Xavier stepped in front of Jane.

"Get away from there!" the man roared. "We will tolerate no spies here."

"Spying? Upon what?" Xavier asked, looking nonplussed.

The ostler flushed, his chest heaving with indignation. "Upon the establishment of an honest Catholic citizen, that's what you Huguenots do, isn't it?"

"Do I look to you like the sort of man who sings psalms? This is my only religion." Xavier shifted his cloak, his hand coming to rest upon the hilt of his sword.

The gesture filled Jane with more apprehension than their antagonist. Not yielding an inch, the ostler doubled his hands into fists.

"Maybe you aren't a Protestor, but I'd wager your lady there is. She's English, I heard her accent."

"You have no business remarking upon my lady at all."

Jane's heart raced with alarm that this incident could escalate out of control owing to sheer masculine pride and belligerence.

Slipping from behind Xavier, she addressed the angry ostler in her most reasonable and earnest tone. "Pray, sir, you have nothing to fear from me. I am English, but I am a Catholic exile and I have no interest in spying upon anyone. Whatever we have done to alarm or offend you, it was most unwitting."

Gazing down at Jane, the ostler's face softened, his hard expression waxing a trifle sheepish. "Pardon. My mistake," he muttered. "These are tense days here in Paris, my lady. It is not a good time to be prying into what does not belong to you."

"We have no interest in your damn barrels," Xavier snapped.

Jane tugged on Xavier's arm, managing to draw him

away. She did not feel easy until she saw the ostler disappear inside the stable.

But now Xavier was the one who was frowning with suspicion. "What the devil was that all about?"

"I daresay that man was hiding something of an illegal nature in his barrel," Jane conjectured. "Perhaps from the king's revenue officers."

"That barrel held nothing but rocks, Jane." Xavier's brow furrowed. "It is strange, but now that I think upon it, I have noticed such refuse heaped up near the other inn where we stayed. Stray boards, barrels, crates, piles of rubble almost as though people were preparing."

"Preparing for what?"

"I don't know." Xavier shook his head. "It would make more sense if they were gathering up weapons. There should not be anything alarming about a few barrels and old boards, and yet it renders me damned uneasy."

He seized Jane's hands in a firm grip. "I want you out of this city. Go back to Faire Isle and take your wretched cousin with you."

"Abby would never consent to go to Faire Isle."

"Then knock her over the head. It is too dangerous for you to remain here."

"How can you talk to me of danger when you insist upon going back to that witch?"

"If Catherine is a witch, then this city is a seething cauldron. Paris seemed bad enough to me when I was here last autumn and that was before the king banned the duc de Guise from coming to the city. The duke is practically a patron saint to the people of Paris. If he should defy the king's order, you could find yourself in the middle of a revolution."

"I don't care anything about dukes or revolutions," Jane said. She laid her hand alongside his cheek. "All I care about is you. I beg you, Xavier. Don't return to the queen. I am sorry if I ever doubted you. Your bluster about hoping to acquire a ship was all nonsense. You are doing this because of Meg, aren't you?"

Xavier's pursed his lips as though he was seeking a way to deny it. Finally he sighed. "The girl trusted me and I disappointed her as well as my sisters. And you. Maybe I would like to prove to you all that I am not such a worthless rogue."

"You have nothing to prove to anyone."

"Perhaps I need to prove something to myself. For most of my life I have been motivated by pure self-interest. I have always had a gift for chicanery and deception. This time I can put my talents to good use and convince the queen to leave Meg in peace forever. Just one more trance is all it will take."

He caught her hand and pressed a kiss against her palm, cajoling her with his eyes. "I have always been a scoundrel. Let me play the hero for once, Jane. I swear I won't make a habit of it."

Xavier untied his purse from his belt. "If anything should go wrong, I want you to take this and use it to leave Paris."

Jane backed away, shaking her head vehemently. "N-no, it would be like saying you won't come back."

"Then take it just to keep it safe for me," Xavier insisted, forcing it into her hands. "I swear I will come to claim it in a few hours."

He brushed a kiss upon her cheek. "Although it wouldn't hurt if you said a prayer for me. I haven't had much trade with the Almighty for years. But I am sure he would listen if the prayer came from you."

Jane nodded, her throat too thick with tears to speak. What a fool she had been to think she could guard her heart from this man. She had not been able to stop loving him and never would. She ought to find the courage to tell him so.

But Xavier was already striding away, entrusting her to Jambe and Pietro, bidding them to see her safely back to her cousin's.

Jane would far rather the two men accompanied Xavier, but it was clear he had resolved to go alone. Jane stood on tiptoe, straining for a last glimpse of Xavier. Almost as though—Jane could scarce acknowledge the fear—almost as though she would never see him again.

As he disappeared from view, she could not still the dark shiver of apprehension that coursed through her.

Jambe patted her shoulder. "There, now, my lady. The captain will be all right. I think the man is a bit of a magician. I never saw him land in any scrape he could not get out of."

"Indeed," Jane rallied, attempting to smile. "I should not let him worry or tease me so. He—he is a very wicked man."

"Or at least he tries hard to be," Pietro added softly.

Chapter Twenty-four

XAVIER KNELT IN THE CENTER OF THE PENTAGRAM drawn on the salon floor. He would have preferred feigning his trance up in the astrological tower, alone with Catherine as he had done before.

His performance did not seem as effective to him in the sunlit salon. But the queen had declared that she was not well enough to mount the tower stairs. She had sagged down in her chair, the woman appearing as though she scarcely possessed the stamina to hold her head upright.

Her advancing years appeared to be telling upon her to a marked degree. Her life did not look as though it could be of much longer duration.

Xavier knew this would be his last audience. All he

needed to accomplish was to see that she forgot Meg for all time.

Xavier closed his eyes and extended his arms. Without Pietro to play the drum, Xavier was forced to focus on the rhythm of his own heart. To fake his trance, he recalled the sensations of what it had been like to fall into a real one. What it had been like when his magic elixir had seized hold of his mind. He pictured the bursts of colors behind his eyes, the sensation of soaring, his body transforming itself.

He chanted softly, feeling the power surge through him. He became the jaguar, sleek, swift, and cunning. Flinging back his head, he emitted a low growl. He fixed his gaze in a glazed expression as though he no longer saw the room, but peered into some hidden realm.

In truth he was fully aware of Catherine. The queen's head bobbed forward, her chin all but resting on her chest. For one outraged moment, Xavier felt that she had fallen asleep, during what was surely the best performance of his life.

"You may ask your questions now," he intoned.

When no response came from her, he had to repeat his command a little louder. Catherine's head snapped up. She dragged her hand across her face as though willing herself to be more alert.

She said, "Tell me my future. What does the next year hold for me?"

"I see wealth and prosperity, a new zest for life as your ships sail the ocean to harvest for you all the riches and mystery of the New World."

"And who do you see leading this expedition?"

For a moment, Xavier experienced the old temptation, to use his influence over Catherine to advance his own interests. But he had already come too close once to selling his soul to this woman.

"That part of the vision is not clear to me," he said.

"Indeed?" the queen murmured. "And what does the future hold for my young enemy, Megaera?"

Xavier furrowed his brow as though lost in deep consideration. He closed his eyes. "She—she will perish of pneumonia. All memory of her will fade, her legend forgotten."

Xavier was a little startled. Where had that prediction come from? In his mind, it was not Meg that he saw vanishing into the grave, but Catherine.

Silence descended after this prophecy as Xavier awaited the queen's next question. She asked, "What is your greatest fear?"

The question surprised Xavier into opening his eyes. He was further startled to find the queen standing over him. Far from appearing weak, her eyes blazed into his.

"What is your greatest fear?" she repeated.

Xavier felt her gaze pierce his mind like a burning brand. Before he could prevent it, the old images flashed through his mind, being abandoned by his father, taken prisoner by the Spanish, the endless days chained to the oars of the galley.

He closed off the memories, steeling his expression, struggling not to betray himself.

"I don't understand the question," he said.

Catherine cocked her head to one side, regarding him with a smile. "How strange. That is what your mother always used to say when seeking to evade my questions. It never worked for her either."

"My mother?"

"Marguerite de Maitland."

Xavier stared at her, the breath in his lungs seeming to freeze before her chilling expression. How could she possibly know or have guessed? That didn't seem to matter. It was clear to him the game was up.

He was no longer the jaguar or the powerful necromancer, merely a man making a fool of himself kneeling half-naked before a haughty queen. No doubt that was what Catherine had intended.

He refused to allow her the satisfaction of seeing how chagrined or alarmed he was. Rising to his feet, he gathered up his discarded shirt and shrugged back into it.

"I gave you no leave to end your performance, monsieur."

"There seems little point in continuing. It is clear that your performance was far better than mine."

"What? No protestations of innocence?" the queen mocked him. "No seeking to deny who you are?"

"I never waste my breath in useless denials." He donned his jerkin with a nonchalance that masked his tension. His gaze darted around the room, seeking opportunity of escape. At some point during his trance, two burly guards had slipped into the room and were blocking the doorway. Xavier suspected that more waited just outside the door.

He had no weapon. He had had to surrender his sword before being admitted to the queen's presence. He glanced speculatively at the window, but Catherine appeared to divine his thoughts.

"It would be a long drop to the ground, Captain. Despite the fact that you are called the Jaguar, I doubt that you would land on your feet."

Her lips thinned into a smile. "I trust you have at least enjoyed your efforts to play me for a fool."

"Yes, I have," he admitted.

Catherine looked irritated. Perhaps she had thought to have him groveling for mercy by now. She beckoned to her guards to seize hold of him. Xavier tried to resist, but it was futile. His hands were bound swiftly in front of him, but he continued to regard the queen with defiance.

"It is a pity," she purred. "You are a magnificent specimen of a man, ruthless, cunning. Who would have ever thought foolish little Marguerite and the noble but weak Chevalier Louis Cheney capable of getting such a son?"

The queen traced her fingers along his throat and over the curve of his scar. "Your mother died in the convent that adjoins this palace. Did you know that? I believe that she still pined for her chevalier until her very last breath. Her heart was broken when he never came back to her. But if he had, he would have returned to his wife. That is usually what men do in the end."

"Truly? I had heard that your husband spent his last hours calling for his mistress."

Catherine turned bright red and slapped him with the full force she could muster. Although his head snapped to one side and his cheek stung, Xavier still cast her a taunting smile.

She stormed away from him, drawing in deep breaths until she regained control. "Enough of this banter. I have one final question for you." She produced the nearly empty vial. "Where did you really get this?"

"I don't know, but sharing it with you was obviously a great mistake."

"Obviously it was. I have never come across a recipe for any elixir so powerful, not in any grimoire I have ever owned. *Where did you get it?*"

"From the Seine. Very likely it contains traces of the blood of all those Huguenots you slaughtered long ago."

The queen emitted a furious hiss. Xavier braced himself for another blow, but her eyes probed his, seeking to batter his mind instead. Xavier was prepared for her this time. He closed off his thoughts, blocking all her efforts.

Catherine held up the vial. "I know the origin of this brew. It could only have come from the *Book of Shadows,* and the one who concocted this elixir is Megaera, the girl you claimed was nothing but a witless dolt."

"If you are so certain of that, why are you asking me?"

"Because I want to hear you admit it."

Xavier compressed his lips. He had betrayed Meg once. He refused to do it again.

Catherine stared at him for a long moment and then laughed. "Very well. Go ahead and play at being noble if you wish, Captain. It is a very unconvincing performance coming from you. I will be able to question Megaera myself soon enough. I know she is on Faire Isle."

"For such a small island, it is a rather difficult place to search," Xavier drawled. "Ariane will make sure that you never find Meg."

"I am long past worrying about keeping the peace with the Lady of Faire Isle. Ariane won't be able to protect anyone if she is dead. I will send an army to slaughter every daughter of the earth on that cursed island if I have to in order to obtain the Silver Rose."

"Oh, do you have such forces at your disposal? I thought you needed every available soldier merely to keep the duc de Guise from your door," Xavier taunted. But it was growing harder to maintain his calm, to conceal how much Catherine's threat alarmed him.

"Actually I have always deplored using brute force." Her lips curved in a sly smile. "You are not the only one who knows about Megaera and where her favorite haunts on Faire Isle might be. Perhaps I should question that prim English friend of yours. Now what was her name? Ah, yes, *Jane.*"

The mere mention of Jane's name was enough to crack Xavier's cool façade. "Lady Danvers has no part in any of this. Torture me, hang, draw, and quarter me if it amuses you, but leave Jane alone."

Catherine's smile broadened. "I have no intention of killing you, Xavier, because I know your greatest fear now. I'll keep you chained in my darkest dungeon for the rest of your life. Perhaps after I have finished making use of your Lady Jane, you can have her. Your prison will become her coffin and you can end your days watching the rats gnaw on her bones."

Xavier growled as he lurched upward with a strength born of fear and rage. But there was no breaking free of his captors' grip.

Catherine watched his struggles for a moment, then waved him off with an expression of bored indifference.

"Get him out of here. Take him to cool his heels in the Bastille for now."

Xavier cursed her roundly as the guards dragged him from the room. He continued to try to fight them until the largest drove his fist into Xavier's stomach. He gasped in pain, the blow winding him.

He ceased his struggles as he fought for air.

"Think," he adjured himself. Lashing out blindly was going to gain him nothing but a mass of bruises. He had been in worse situations than this. He needed to calm down and assess his situation.

But it was nigh impossible with one panicked thought going through his head. Jane. That witch meant to go after Jane, who was likely even now somewhere on her knees, earnestly praying for his safe return.

Xavier hoped that someone up there was listening to her because it was going to take a miracle to get them out of this. Flanked by four guards, he was hustled out into the stable yard where a horse was being hitched to the traces of a cart.

Xavier balked, trying to dig his heels in, knowing that once he was incarcerated in the Bastille, he would have no chance of escape.

His guards merely cuffed him about the head, propelling him forward. He slipped and crashed to his knees.

His ears rang from the blow he had been dealt along with his guard's curses. He became dimly aware of other sounds, upraised voices coming from the direction of the street beyond.

He lifted his head and saw some sort of commotion taking place, people running, a word, a name being shouted over and over again.

"De Guise! De Guise!"

He could make out the approach of mounted horsemen, one slightly in the lead, a tall dark man.

One of the guards bent down to drag Xavier to his feet, but the man froze, staring in consternation. His other captors were likewise distracted by the approaching rider and Xavier saw his chance.

He reared back, driving his head against the face of the nearest guard. He heard the gratifying crunch of bone as the man's nose broke. His own head throbbed, but Xavier ignored the pain. Ramming his shoulder into another guard, he tipped the man off balance.

Xavier tore off running. He was handicapped by his bound hands, but the guards were at a disadvantage as well. The Dark Queen wanted him alive, so they could not discharge any weapons.

Xavier surged forward, weaving in and out of the crowd that was gathering in the street, growing larger by the moment. He didn't pause, didn't think, didn't even risk looking back as he hurled onward.

Only when he had gone down several streets and darted down an alley, did he dare to stop and catch his breath. He leaned up against a brick wall, panting, listening for sounds of approaching feet and hearing nothing.

Either he had eluded the guards in the crowd or they had been presented with a more urgent mission, protecting the Hôtel de la Reine from de Guise's oncoming forces.

Xavier could scarce believe his luck—or was it a genuine miracle? Whatever it was, he didn't deserve it after his recklessness, his arrogance in believing he could hoodwink the Dark Queen. He feared he had only made matters worse for Meg and the women of Faire Isle.

But he would have time enough to curse his own stupidity later. Right now he needed to get this blasted rope off his hands and go find Jane.

CATHERINE SAT AT HER DESK, QUILL POISED IN HER HAND AS she paused to savor her triumph over Xavier. She had finally succeeded in breaking the arrogant rogue. Now she needed to issue a writ for the arrest of Lady Danvers and, more important, lay her plans for the capture of Megaera.

Years ago her son had sent a small army of witch-hunters to invade the Faire Isle. They had done quite a bit of damage, burning houses and destroying property, but most of the daughters of the earth, most notably Ariane and her sisters, had escaped.

Those women simply knew the island too well, too many places to hide, especially on the rockier, wilder side. Catherine would have Xavier and the Danvers woman as hostages. Would they provide enough leverage to negotiate a trade for the Silver Rose? Or would the threat of another invasion be enough to make someone on the island betray the girl?

Catherine would need to have a sizable force to make that threat seem real, and as Xavier had so impertinently pointed out, she did not have such a troop at her disposal at the moment.

While Catherine pondered these difficulties, she was interrupted by one of her guards bursting into the salon. The man's nose was swelling, blood spattered over his face and tunic.

Catherine started to rebuke the man for coming before

her in such a state when beneath the bruises and swelling, she recognized Captain Arnaud, the man she had charged with conveying Xavier to the Bastille.

Tensing with an unwelcome suspicion, Catherine rose to her feet. "What means this, Captain? Never tell me you let that villain escape," she said in an ominous tone.

"S-sorry, Your Grace. Couldn't help it. De Guise." Arnaud's voice was so thick Catherine could scarce understand him. The man could not possibly have said—

"De Guise? What has the duc de Guise got to do with any of this?"

"He—he's here."

"What!" Catherine gasped. "You insolent fool. You—you lie."

"No, Your Grace. But go to the window and you will see for yourself."

Her heart thudding with dread, she stumbled across the room. From her window, she could see the crowds gathering in the street, forcing their way into her own courtyard despite the efforts of her guards to hold them back.

The cry went up, "De Guise! De Guise! *Vive* de Guise!"

The crowd parted for a tall, arrogant figure who bowed left and right, grasping outstretched hands. Women sobbed and flung themselves at the man's feet, kissing the hem of his cloak as though he were the Lord himself come amongst them.

Xavier and his escape faded to insignificance. Catherine clutched her hand to her throat as she watched her greatest nightmare coming true. De Guise. Here in Paris. Could that wretch's timing possibly be any worse?

The thought caused a bubble of nigh hysterical laughter to rise in Catherine's throat. Would there ever have been a good time for her most dreaded enemy's arrival?

She took a deep breath, forcing air into her lungs. This was no time to give way to fear or panic. There was only one way she was going to survive, the same way she always had, by sheer nerve and wits.

By the time the duc de Guise strode into her salon, Catherine was able to greet him with some semblance of dignity. The duke advanced upon her with a purposeful stride. Handsome and vigorous, the scar on François de Guise's cheek only enhanced his reputation as France's premiere general, the hero of countless battles. The war god Ares and the beautiful Apollo combined. He was all that her son should have been and wasn't, Catherine reflected bitterly.

That thought only made her hate the duke more, but she concealed her enmity behind an icy façade.

"Your Majesty." De Guise swept her a courtly bow and dropped to one knee before her. At least the man still chose to counterfeit that much respect.

Catherine managed to extend her hand without trembling as she bid him rise. As the duke saluted her fingertips with a perfunctory kiss, she addressed him sternly, "What treason is this, monsieur?"

The duke's brows shot upward in pained surprise, or at least the semblance of it. "No treason, Your Grace. Why would you even speak such a word to me?"

"Because you know that my son, the king, has forbidden you to come to Paris with your army."

"And I have not done so. I have come quietly with but a handful of my own personal retinue."

So that was how the duke had been able to slip through the gates of Paris without sparking off a confrontation with the king's troops.

Catherine pursed her lips, not fooled by the duke's innocent protestation. Yes, he had come with only a handful of retainers, because the arrogant man realized that he needed no more. His army lay out in the streets, his half-mad followers that could become out of control at any minute. The mob that ecstatically shouted the duke's name beneath her windows was far more dangerous than any trained troops.

"Why would you come here at all?" Catherine demanded. "You could not possibly have any other purpose than to wrest the crown from your lawful king."

"No, Your Grace, I swear, that is not true." The duke dramatically splayed his hand over the region of his heart. "Someone has been filling the king's head with lies about me. I am his most loyal subject. I have only come to Paris in sheer desperation to defend myself and to be restored to my king's good grace."

Catherine honed her gaze, seeking to bore into his eyes. The potion had helped restore much of her old ability. She had broken through Xavier's defenses, but only because she had taken him by surprise.

The duke was too much on his guard, too well prepared for her probing. She could catch only a glimmer of the duke's thoughts, enough to reassure her.

He had not come to Paris with any intentions of dethroning her son. At least not yet. But then what the devil was the man after? He had some deeper motive beyond what he stated. Would that she had some idea of what it was. She had ever disliked groping her way through the dark.

The duke backed away, sweeping another bow. "I have only come here to assure Your Grace of my good intentions. And now I intend to set out for the palace to wait upon my king."

Catherine's heart leaped with alarm. At the moment de Guise might not have any malicious intentions toward the king, but Catherine could not answer for Henry or vouch for her son's uncertain temper.

If de Guise was foolish or arrogant enough to stride into the Louvre with only a handful of men, Catherine dreaded what the outcome might be. As terrified as she was of braving the mobs in the streets, she had only one recourse.

"Very well," she said. "If you go to the king, I insist upon accompanying you."

Chapter Twenty-five

JANE HAD PROMISED THAT SHE WOULD REMAIN SAFELY AT THE house until Xavier's return. But after an hour of pacing and worrying, she could endure it no longer.

She turned to the solace that had sustained her through the worst times of her life. She sought out the nearest church and stole inside to pray. The nave was cool, dark, and peaceful after the afternoon heat and the clatter of the streets. The air was redolent with the comforting aroma of incense that seemed to have seeped into the very walls, conveying blessings upon decades of sinners seeking redemption.

Jane lit a candle and knelt down before the side altar that honored a statue of the Blessed Virgin.

"Holy Mother, please intercede for Louis Xavier. I am

sure you must know he is a good man at heart. He—he may not always choose the most honest way to go about things, but his intentions are pure and oh, please, protect him from the queen and send him safely back to me. If you do, I promise—"

But Jane had no chance to complete her vow. She heard the sound of boots thundering down the aisle toward her. She glanced around, at first overjoyed to see Xavier rushing toward her, but then alarmed by his aspect.

His hair was sweat-soaked and disheveled, his forehead bruised—and was that dried blood on his shirt? She blessed herself hastily and rose to her feet.

Xavier stumbled toward her. "Jane, there you are. Jambe told me this is where he thought you went. I should have guessed as much, but this is no time to be at your prayers. Come on."

He seized hold of her hand and began hurrying her back down the aisle.

"But what is the matter? What's wrong?" She frowned at the object she saw attached to his hand. "Is that a rope tied around your wrist?"

"Yes, I managed to free myself, but I couldn't get the blasted thing entirely off. The queen's guard ties a wicked knot."

"The queen's guard?" she cried. Remembering she was still in church, she lowered her voice to a hushed whisper. "You were arrested?"

He nodded grimly. "It all went wrong, just as you feared. You can clout my ears and damn me for a fool later. But right now Catherine might be the least of our worries."

She couldn't imagine what he was talking about until

he shoved open the church door and hauled her outside just as the church bell started to toll. Jane blinked in the bright sunlight. After the cool and quiet of the nave, the commotion taking place in the streets assaulted her senses in a great wave of heat and noise. The clamor of the bells, the pounding of running feet, the excited shouts.

Jane gazed about her, bewildered by the sudden flux of people pouring out of shops and houses, like a gush of water from a broken cistern. Jane had never seen such a swell of humanity. There had to be hundreds and hundreds of Parisians amassing in the street, their faces lit with an almost frenzied ecstasy.

"On second thought," Xavier muttered, "this might be a very good time to pray."

"What is it? What's happening?" she asked.

"The duc de Guise. He's come to Paris and I fear there is going to be hell to pay."

Xavier tried to lead her down the street, but they had not gone far from the church when they were caught up in the stampede. Jane fought down a sensation of panic as the crowd surged around them. Jostled on all sides, Jane was nearly torn from Xavier's grasp.

Xavier seized her about the waist and guided her to a place of relative safety in the doorway of a barber's establishment. The roar that went up all but deafened her. "De Guise. De Guise."

In the distance Jane made out the approach of a tall, dark-haired man mounted upon a white horse. He doffed his feathered cap, acknowledging the shouts of the crowds.

She was just able to make out a litter as well, bearing a grim-faced woman garbed all in black. Jane stood on tiptoe so she could make herself heard above the crowd, speaking into Xavier's ear.

"Is that the queen?"

Xavier nodded.

The litter lurched alongside the duke's horse almost as though the queen was his captive. Although the crowd jeered and taunted Catherine from all sides, the queen stared ahead of her with a look of stony indifference.

"By God," Xavier said. "No matter what else you might say about that old devil, she does not want for courage."

"Is she de Guise's prisoner?" Jane asked. "The sheer size of this crowd is alarming, but everyone seems to be rejoicing."

"For the moment. But I'll wager the king will not greet the duke with cheers. If His Majesty sends for the Swiss Guard, this will take an ugly turn very fast."

As the duke and his entourage lumbered by, Xavier turned to Jane. "Pietro and Jambe will be waiting for us back at the inn. We have to get out of the city before someone decides to close the gates."

"Xavier, I can't leave. Not without Abigail."

He swore. "Jane, the woman would likely abandon you in a trice."

"No, she wouldn't. And even if that were true, it makes no difference what she would do. I cannot behave that way."

"All right, all right," Xavier groaned. "Let's go fetch her. But we have got to hurry."

She drew in a deep breath as they left the safety of the shop doorway. With everyone bent upon following after the duke, it was like trying to swim upstream. But Xavier led the way with Jane clinging to him as they plunged into the crowd, fighting for every inch.

⁂

"LONG LIVE THE DUC DE GUISE!"

The shouts hammered at Catherine as she braced herself against the sway of her litter, her progress through the city impeded by the mobs of the duke's followers. The fragile wooden barrier of her litter and the goodwill of the nobleman who rode at her side were all that stood between Catherine and the crowd.

As much as they all adored de Guise, the Parisians despised her. Being thrust into their midst was like being dangerously close to the jaws of a hungry beast, leashed at the moment. De Guise had but to relax his hold on the tether for Catherine to be devoured.

The crowd's suppressed hatred felt like a palpable thing, threatening to cut off her air. Catherine stifled a gasp as she tried to keep her features cold and impassive so that none might guess the depth of her terror.

Her mind threatened to spiral her back into her past when she had quaked before another threatening mob.

"Give us the girl. We will hang her from the city walls."

Catherine gritted her teeth, fighting to keep herself in the present and shake off the echoes of her worst childhood memory. She could not afford to let them reduce her to the state of a quivering little girl.

Her life and that of her son depended entirely upon her ability to keep calm. She knew she would never be able to rely upon Henry to keep his wits during this crisis.

Catherine drew in a deep breath, forcing herself to relax even as her ears were assaulted by the roar of the crowd, the perpetual shouts pounding in her head until she thought her skull would split.

"De Guise! God bless de Guise!"

The duke kept a firm hand on the reins of his horse as he acknowledged the shouts with nods of his head, his face wreathed in smiles. No doubt the man fancied himself quite the conquering hero, completely invincible.

Catherine silently cursed the man's insufferable pride and blind ambition. He believed that all he had to do was stride into the palace and the king would be cowed.

But Catherine knew her son far better than that. Weak and vacillating Henry might be, and often lacking in courage. But the duke had no idea what Henry might be capable of if he fell into one of his mad rages, something that Catherine must prevent at all costs until she found a way to gain the upper hand in this situation.

The journey to the Louvre normally would have been a short one. By the time they arrived in the courtyard, Catherine felt as though she had been jostled and barraged for days on end.

When she was helped down from her litter, she already felt exhausted by the strain of subduing her terror. She would have welcomed a brief respite, but she was given none.

De Guise in his impatience charged ahead of her up the stairs that led to the king's private apartments, ignoring Catherine's pleas to wait for her. She had no choice but to hurry after him. But even during her best days, she could never have kept pace with the duke's long strides.

Catherine paused midway up the stairs, wheezing for breath, her legs weak beneath her, threatening to give way. She groped for her vial of elixir. So few precious drops left. She took a small sip, waiting for the familiar rush of warmth and renewed strength. Her heart raced to a degree that was almost painful.

But she forced herself onward. She staggered into the king's antechamber, pausing once more to catch her breath and assess the situation. What she saw filled her with apprehension.

Henry had retreated to the far end of the room like some desperate cornered animal even though he was surrounded by his private guard, an edgy group of men. They were little better than mercenaries. For a mere handful of coin thrown down, any one of these men would have no qualms about cutting down de Guise.

Why did de Guise have to be such a fool, Catherine thought, torn between fear and contempt. The duke's head was stuffed full of aristocratic notions of honor and the protection he felt accorded him by virtue of his noble blood. The idiot seemed to have no notion of his own danger.

As Catherine entered, the duke was arguing his case. Fearfully, she studied the king's face. Henry's color was high, his expression hard and impassive. But Catherine knew that stillness in her son all too well, the calm that presaged a storm.

"I have not come here to threaten Your Majesty. I am ever your loyal subject," the duke declared. "My only wish is to make peace, to dispel the falsehoods that all of my enemies have been pouring into your ears."

"I care not for your wishes, monsieur, only your defiance. You chose to come to Paris, knowing that I have expressly forbidden you to do so. How dare you flout my commands."

Henry turned away from de Guise. Catherine caught the look exchanged between her son and the head of his guard. The commander reached for the hilt of his sword.

Desperately, Catherine rushed forward. "Your Grace, I beg you. Do not be displeased with the duke. Monsieur de Guise only dared come to Paris because—because I invited him to do so."

The words she blurted out seemed to ring through the chamber with the force of a pistol shot. Even de Guise regarded her with astonishment. There was a moment of thunderstruck silence before the king rounded upon her, his eyes blazing.

Catherine retreated as the king advanced upon her. For a heartbeat, she was actually afraid of her own son.

"You invited de Guise?" the king raged. "So you have turned traitor to me as well."

"Henry! You know better than that. I have always striven to serve your best interests."

"Your own, you mean."

"Are they not one and the same?" Catherine moistened her lips and declared loudly for de Guise's benefit. "I have been much grieved over the discord between you and the good duke. There can be no prosperity for France while this quarrel continues. You must allow me to put forward a proposal for peace."

Catherine risked drawing closer to the king so that she could mutter in his ear. "For the love of God, Henry! I realize the duke's behavior is an outrageous affront to your authority. But pause to reflect before you do something we will both regret. Have you not seen what is happening outside your very gates?"

Somehow she managed to drag Henry to the window, all the while directing a placating look at de Guise. The duke's expression was so insolent and confident, Catherine would have liked to run the man through herself.

But she forced herself to focus on Henry. As he stared out the window, the king went white as he took in the growing crowds outside the Louvre.

Catherine addressed him in a low terse voice. "I know you want to arrest de Guise—"

"Arrest him? I want him dead."

"Think, Henry! If the duke does not leave here, unharmed, what do you imagine will happen to us?"

Her son's lips thinned in an ugly line. "I don't care. We are already undone. If I give way to this man one more time, I will no longer be king."

"You will no longer be *alive* if you don't. That mob you see at the gate is but a fraction of the people pouring into the streets to support the duke. There are hundreds more, nay, very likely thousands."

"Then I will send for my Swiss Guard, move my troops into the city, and slaughter them all."

Catherine closed her eyes briefly, praying for patience. "If you do that, you will spark a confrontation for certain. You will have open warfare, the streets stained with blood, a massacre to rival the one of St. Bartholomew's Eve."

"Paris has become a nest of traitors. It needs another cleansing, starting with de Guise." The king regarded her contemptuously. "You never used to be so squeamish, Maman. It was you and your scheming that incited that massacre to rid us of our Huguenot enemies."

"And look how that turned out. The violence spun out of all control, the mobs rampaging for days. Is that what you want, my son, to be hailed as a second Nero?" Catherine hunched her shoulders. "Then fine. Destroy de Guise. Destroy Paris and destroy us as well."

The king fretted his lip, a flicker of uncertainty in his eyes. "And what would you have me do, Maman?"

"Be patient awhile longer, negotiate with the duke." When Henry sucked in his breath with a furious hiss, Catherine captured her son's hand.

"I have been steadily regaining my strength and laying plans that will restore our power."

"What plans?"

"I will reveal them to you when they are closer to fruition. For now, you must trust me."

Henry scowled at her. Whether it was the sight of the mob outside his gates or anything she had said, Catherine thought she saw the light of reason return to his eyes.

Thrusting her hands away from him, the king returned to greet the duke after Henry's usual sullen fashion. Catherine released a tremulous breath of relief. Somehow she had once more averted disaster.

But for how long?

She was unable to breathe easy until Henry's brief meeting with de Guise was over. It resolved nothing just as Catherine had expected. But at least the duke would be leaving here alive. Catherine accompanied him, bracing herself to once more face the hostile crowds.

Henry brooded in silence until he was certain his mother had gone. Then he summoned his guard and issued commands.

"Send word to my commanders. I want my troops moved into the city at once. I will have order in my own streets. And once this rabble is driven back into their homes, I shall be able to deal with Monsieur de Guise."

THE CHURCH WAS BUT A SHORT WALK FROM HER COUSIN'S, BUT by the time they reached Abigail's courtyard, Jane felt shaken and exhausted.

She hurried ahead of Xavier, leading the way into the house. The first sight that met her eyes was Violette huddled at the foot of the stairs, looking terrified.

The girl leaped up at the sight of Jane. She nearly knocked Jane over as she hurled herself against her, wrapping her arms about Jane's waist.

"Oh, Madame Danvers. It is the end of the world. Everyone said this was going to happen. The king has plotted with the Huguenots to take back Paris from the Catholics. They will come to murder us all."

"Nonsense," Jane said bracingly, patting the girl's back.

"It isn't nonsense." Tears streamed down Violette's cheeks. "I remember the horrible sound of those bells from when I was a little girl. It was the same signal that started the St. Bartholomew's Massacre."

"The bells are only ringing to welcome the duc de Guise back to Paris."

But this information did little to comfort Violette. "T-the duke was ordered to stay away from Paris. The king will be so angry. He will bring up his troops and the duke will summon his. There will be war in the streets, killing, pillaging."

The girl trembled. "We will probably be ravished and—and our tongues cut out and our breasts hacked off."

Jane stared at the girl. Who would have ever imagined meek little Violette to be possessed of such a lurid imagination?

"Calm yourself, Violette. Nothing like that is going to happen. Captain Xavier is going to get us all to safety."

Violette peered around Jane at Xavier, but even Jane had to admit that in his disheveled state, Xavier looked more like a marauder than a rescuer.

Violette shuddered and Jane had to all but peel the girl off of her. "Where is your mistress? Is she upstairs?"

The question produced a fresh spate of sobs from Violette. "Madame B-benton is gone. She left at the first hint of trouble."

Jane frowned, incredulous. "What do you mean she left? She is out there in those streets alone?"

Violette shook her head. "No, Gerard is with her. He—he procured a horse and they are headed for Calais."

"And Abby did not even trouble to leave a note for me?" Jane asked.

"She said to tell you that she could not wait, but that you should follow as best you are able."

"As best as I—Damnation," Jane swore, leaving Violette gaping at her in astonishment. Jane knew her cousin for a flighty, inconsiderate woman, but this passed all bounds even for Abigail.

"Let me understand this correctly," Xavier said, stepping forward. "This Gerard. He is your cousin's husband and he returned for her?"

"No," Jane said, her face stinging with mortification. It was she who had convinced Xavier to come back for Abigail.

"He is the footman." She could scarce look Xavier in the eye, fearing he would be furious.

But to her astonishment, Xavier let out a roar of laughter. "Your cousin ran off with the footman? That's marvelous. I hope he at least was a handsome one."

"He was, monsieur. Very," Violette confirmed with a sniff, setting Xavier off into fresh peals.

To her astonishment, Jane found herself joining him. Perhaps it was the strain of these last hours, finding release, but they both laughed until they were on the verge of tears.

It was Xavier who stopped first, abruptly. Even his smile faded as he listened intently.

Checking her own mirth, Jane said, "What—"

But Xavier motioned her to silence. Her breath stilled as she heard it too. Jane had never been near a battlefield in her life, but even she recognized it—the distant sound of gunfire.

Ordering her to remain where she was, Xavier charged out of the house. But Jane ignored his command and raced after him.

They did not have to go far to discover the source of the sounds. At the end of the street, a contingent of the king's troops was under attack from a mob of angry Parisians armed with rocks, clubs, anything they could find.

Despite their weapons, the guard was badly outnumbered and with no place to retreat. The end of the street had been barricaded with barrels, boards, and heaped-up rubble.

Pistol shots blazed, swords flared. One overwhelmed soldier tried to scramble over the barricade, only to be dragged back down. The mob surged around the terrified young man, beating him with clubs.

Jane cried out in horror, but there was nothing to be done. Thrusting her behind him, Xavier marshaled their retreat back to the house.

JANE LIT THE CANDLES IN HER BEDCHAMBER AS NIGHT FELL, bringing some measure of peace to a day rife with fear and tension.

Jambe and Pietro had managed to get through and join them at the house. The tidings they brought were grim. Barricades had been erected at various points all through the city, effectively containing the king's troops. The Swiss Guard had been obliged to retreat, leaving the Parisians in control of the city.

Gazing out her window, Jane could see fires blazing in the distance, hear the occasional sound of gunshots, but it seemed to come from farther off. Hostilities appeared to have ceased for the moment, but there was no telling what the morning might bring.

Xavier and his men had barricaded the doors and windows of the house and were taking turns mounting guard. Violette had spent most of the day hiding in the pantry. Jane surmised the girl had fallen asleep in there.

She knew she ought to try to get some rest herself. She was exhausted, but she could not even close her eyes. A light knock sounded on the door and Xavier appeared, bearing a tray of bread, cheese, and wine.

Jane thanked him, but shook her head. "I have no appetite."

"You must try to eat something, Jane. You have hardly taken a morsel all day. At least try some of the wine."

To please him, she took a sip. She ran her hand self-consciously through the ends of her hair that was half tumbling out of its chignon.

"I must look a terrible fright."

"You always look beautiful to me," he murmured.

She managed a wan smile. "Yes, but we both know what a gifted liar you are."

"Not about everything," he chuckled, tucking a stray wisp of hair behind her ear.

Her gaze locked with his. "Please tell me the truth, Xavier. What do you think is going to happen tomorrow?"

"I have no idea," he admitted. "The duke and the king appear to be at an impasse, but they must come to terms eventually. We just have to wait it out. I am sure we will come through this unscathed."

"If we do, it will be no thanks to me." Jane paced away from him, rubbing her arms. "It is my fault we are trapped here. I was the one who insisted we return for Abby. You may feel quite free to tell me 'I told you so.' "

"It would be far more fitting if you hurled those words at me. Pietro, Jambe, and you all warned me about practicing my tricks on Catherine de Medici. But I was so damned sure of myself, I wouldn't listen. I completely underestimated the woman."

He sighed. "If de Guise had not arrived when he did, we would both be prisoners of the Dark Queen and she would be preparing to launch an attack on Meg and Faire Isle as well."

The candlelight reflected in his eyes, dark with self-reproach. "I was unbelievably stupid, reckless, and foolhardy."

"But incredibly brave. You didn't take such a risk for personal gain. You were trying to put things right for Meg and everyone on Faire Isle."

"Yes, but—" He was silent for a moment. "I don't think I did it for Meg or even my sisters.

"I did it to impress you, Jane," he said, his voice as intense as his eyes. "When you learned the truth that day on Faire Isle, I could not bear the disappointment I saw on your face. I had grown too accustomed to that soft light that would steal into your eyes whenever you looked at me." He swallowed. "Even though I know I do not deserve your approbation, I crave it like the air that I breathe."

Jane gazed wonderingly up at him. "But why? Why would my opinion matter so much to you?"

"Because I love you, you little fool."

Jane blinked. She had never expected to hear him say such a thing, but how like Xavier to fling the words at her in such blunt fashion in the middle of a revolution.

She started to laugh, but her emotions overflowed in a gush of tears instead. He wiped her cheeks with his knuckles.

"There, there, my dear, I think I would weep myself to learn that I was to be burdened with the heart of such a scoundrel. Never mind. You may still tell me to go to the devil."

But Jane hurled herself at him instead, burying her face against his chest. He cradled her close, kissing the top of her head.

"Oh, Jane," he murmured against her hair. "I tried to stay away from you, knowing you would be the better for it. All you ever wanted to be was safe, respectable."

"No," she said. "I realize I want so much more than that. I—I want to feel bursting with life when I awake each morning. I want days filled with wonder, excitement, and surprise. I want *you.*"

"I am glad to hear that because I am just too damned selfish to leave you again."

She sniffed, managing to smile through her tears. She shifted her head to look up at him. "Then I hope you will always continue to be so selfish."

"You may count upon it, my lady. I am a villain through and through."

He proceeded to prove it by kissing her in a ruthless way no respectable man ever would, his tongue breaching her lips, plundering her mouth until she was breathless.

It was only now when she was back in his arms, that she acknowledged the pain of these past weeks, how she had felt bruised and bleeding inside as though a part of her had gone missing.

Swept up in his embrace, she was whole again, as if after being lost, she was back where she belonged. The threat of the Dark Queen, the possibility of revolution—all for the moment was forgotten.

Kissing and caressing, they tumbled feverishly into bed, impatiently thrusting clothing aside, making love as though it were both for the first and very last time.

Chapter Twenty-six

CATHERINE KEPT CLEAR OF THE WINDOWS FOR FEAR OF ANY stray pistol shot or even an intentional one. The conflict between Paris and the king had resumed with the break of day. Catherine wondered if there would be anything left of the city after many more days of this, but she felt too wearied to even curse her son.

Henry had always been weak and given to vacillation. When the man did decide to take action, why must it always be the wrong one?

She had warned him not to bring the Swiss Guard into Paris, although for a brief moment it had seemed Henry might gain the upper hand.

But the citizenry of Paris had been strangely well prepared for the king's maneuver, hemming the royal troops in with their crude barricades.

There was only one man now who could bring this madness to a halt. But the duc de Guise sat at the conference table, calmly cleaning his nails, waiting for her to comment on his list of demands.

They were ridiculous of course. Catherine glanced down at the paper in her hands. De Guise was to be appointed lieutenant general of France. The king's cousin and nearest male relative, the Huguenot King of Navarre, was to be excluded from the succession.

Worse still, Henry was to dismiss all his favorites from holding office and his private guard was to be disbanded.

Catherine was fully prepared to set her seal to the agreement. Her motto had always been to promise anything that bought one another day to scheme and retaliate. But she knew Henry would never be that reasonable. He would sooner die and take her down in the process.

Catherine perused the document, hedging for time, when a messenger rushed into the room.

One of the duke's men, he bowed to de Guise, barely acknowledging Catherine's presence.

"My lord. The king—" The man panted too hard to get out the rest of his words.

Catherine's heart stopped, fearing the worst, that in his rage and grief over the situation, Henry might have done something desperate, like fall upon his sword.

What the messenger finally blurted out was nearly as bad. "The—the king is gone. He has fled, escaped from Paris."

Catherine reeled in shock, the duke's demands fluttering from her hands. She had always thought her son weak and erratic, but even she had never believed Henry was such a coward that he would abandon his throne, his city, his friends. Worse still, that he would abandon his mother, leave her to the mercy of their greatest enemy.

As de Guise rose to his feet, Catherine braced herself for the duke's fury. No doubt he would think Catherine was behind this, that her negotiations with him had all been a pretense to allow the king to escape.

But all de Guise said was, "I had best ride out and do what I can to placate the populace. I fear the Parisians will see this as a further sign of the king's treachery and not take his defection well."

As the duke bowed and left her, Catherine watched him go, torn between amazement and suspicion. The duke and his supporters had Paris well barricaded, completely under their control.

How could Henry have managed to escape unless . . . unless de Guise had allowed him to do so? The duke had never had any intention of allowing this rebellion to surge out of control, to go so far as to completely depose the king.

Then what had been the purpose behind all this madness? Catherine could not fathom it, but she did not waste much effort trying.

All she knew was that her son's cowardice appeared to have furnished her with what she desperately needed. The king's troops were now hers to command. She would have more than enough men to march against Faire Isle and to take care of her other problem. Xavier. The Jaguar would not escape her this time.

XAVIER STIRRED AWAKE AT THE SOUND OF PIETRO KNOCKING at the bedchamber door. He gently shifted Jane out of his arms. She was so exhausted, he was loath to wake her until absolutely necessary. He hastened to dress before joining Pietro in the hall beyond.

The tall native looked exhausted. Xavier buckled on his sword preparing to relieve Pietro of his turn at guard. They headed down the stairs so their voices would not carry and disturb Jane.

"Any sign of trouble last night? Did anyone attempt to approach the house?" Xavier demanded.

"No, Captain, I would have roused you. All was quiet after midnight. We heard some gunfire early this morning and then—"

"And then?" Xavier prompted when Pietro hesitated.

"And then nothing. Jambe ventured out into the street for a look." Pietro's brow furrowed with an expression of unease and puzzlement. "It is the strangest turn of events I could have ever imagined. You had best come see for yourself, Captain."

Xavier joined his two men in stealing through the garden. As they neared the scene of yesterday's battle, Xavier braced himself, scarce knowing what sort of aftermath of violence and carnage to expect.

The sight that met his eyes caused Xavier to slowly expel his breath in amazement. It was almost as though the turmoil of yesterday had never happened. The last of the barricade was being removed, rubble carted away.

Some of the merchants were even opening their shops, Parisians going about their business, returning to their normal tasks of the day.

"What the devil?" Xavier murmured. He became aware that he had awakened Jane after all. She had dressed and followed him from the house. As she approached, Xavier draped his arm about her shoulders and drew her closer.

She gazed about her looking as bewildered as Xavier and his men.

"Is—is it over?" she asked.

"Damned if I know." Xavier saw a mounted rider passing by. The man's livery marked him as one of the duke's men.

"You there!" Xavier called out. "What's happened? Has the conflict been resolved?"

The horseman reined in long enough to grin down at Xavier. "What conflict? There was never much of a battle as far as I am concerned. The cowardly king has turned tail and fled the city."

"Fled? So de Guise has claimed the throne?"

The duke's man looked affronted. "No, my noble master is no traitor to the crown. He has been riding out over the city all morning, calming the people and urging them to return to their homes. This was all nothing but an unfortunate misunderstanding."

The man rode off, leaving Xavier gaping after him. A misunderstanding? Jane looked confused, Pietro thoughtful, and Jambe angry.

"So there is not going to be any revolution?" The old

man sounded almost disappointed. He tore off his cap and flung it down upon the street. "Then what was the point of getting a man all lathered up and alarmed, scaring the wits out of all of us for nothing?"

"Not for nothing. The duke's arrival did provide the diversion Xavier needed to escape," Jane reminded Jambe with a smile.

"Yes," Xavier began when the realization struck him with all the force of a cudgel.

"The diversion," he muttered, and let loose a long string of curses. When the others stared at him, Xavier explained impatiently, "Don't you understand? All those barricades that went up so swiftly and were so well placed. This so-called uprising was cleverly planned. This was it, the diversion that the duke promised the king of Spain. With Henry on the run, driven from Paris, there is no way he could ever send any aid to England."

Jane paled. "So then you think that the armada—"

"Has already set sail for England, yes. I am sorry, my love."

Jambe reached down to retrieve his cap with fingers that trembled. "I have to leave, Captain. I have to get home."

Xavier nodded. "You go, Jambe, and take Pietro with you."

Pietro scowled. "But what of you, Captain?"

"I have to look after my lady. We must get back to Faire Isle and take warning to Ariane. One of the unfortunate consequences of this uprising being over is that the Dark Queen will now be free to carry out her plans."

There was no time for long farewells or sentimental good-byes. Jane bestowed hugs on both of his men. Xavier contented himself with hearty handclasps and gruff wishes for their safe journey.

Back at the house, he sent Jane to gather up a few belongings and to make arrangements for Violette. It seemed that the girl had a friend who could help her to other employment, but Jane insisted upon furnishing the maid with a letter of character.

As Xavier ranged about the hall, waiting, his mind flooded with remembrance of all the passionate and tender embraces he and Jane had shared last night. Once more they had made love in the heat and madness of the moment. But this time Xavier swore he would give her no cause to regret it.

Considering that his machinations with Catherine had only worsened the situation, Xavier was unsure of his welcome back on Faire Isle. But if Ariane could be persuaded to forgive him, perhaps he and Jane could be married on the island—

Xavier's thoughts were disrupted when the door to the house crashed open. Lost in his musings, he was slow to react. Several men swarmed in, led by a familiar figure, the guard whose nose Xavier had broken.

He eyed Xavier with a vengeful gleam. "So Monsieur le Jaguar, the queen feared you might have been wily enough to slip out of Paris, but it appears you were not so clever."

Xavier swore and started to draw his sword. He only had it halfway out of his scabbard before the men fell upon him. He lashed out, leveling one of them with a blow to the jaw.

Out of the corner of his eye, he saw Jane appear on the stairs. "Run, Jane," he bellowed.

To his horror, she charged down the stairs instead, wielding a poker in an effort to come to his aid. Xavier felt the butt of a musket strike against his temple.

He reeled from the blow, dropping to his knees, black webs dancing before his eyes. He felt the warm gush of blood down his cheek as he fell to the floor.

"Jane," he rasped.

The last thing he saw before he lost consciousness was the poker being wrestled out of her hand.

THE HÔTEL DE LA REINE WAS IN A FLURRY OF ACTIVITY, servants bustling in preparation for the queen's departure. The king had taken refuge at Blois Castle and a meeting of the Estates General had been summoned, another attempt to make peace between His Majesty and the duc de Guise.

Catherine expected little from it. Her son's cowardly actions had left him completely impotent. He would have to accede to every one of the duke's demands if he wanted to keep his crown.

Her only source of satisfaction was the report that Catherine had received from Captain Arnaud. The man had managed to redeem himself by capturing Xavier and the Englishwoman.

Catherine had issued commands that both of them should be transported to the castle at Blois. She had no time to confront or question her captives, no time to lay any careful plans, no time to do anything but dispatch troops to Faire Isle.

She examined her precious vial, which was now empty. She could already feel the strength she had acquired from Megaera's powerful elixir beginning to fade.

Her time was ebbing along with it. This was her last and final gambit. She must capture the Silver Rose or die.

Chapter Twenty-seven

THE HOUSE OF BELLE HAVEN WAS SILENT AT SUCH A LATE hour. Meg had the melancholy sensation that she was the only one awake in the entire world. Never had she felt so alone.

Her devoted servant Agatha Butterydoor snored softly on her pallet next to Meg's bed. Keeping a careful eye on the old woman, Meg bent down and retrieved the modest bundle of belongings she had stowed beneath her bed earlier that day.

She paused to gaze down at Aggie, fearing she was about to break the elderly woman's heart by disappearing in this fashion. But she could not even risk planting a farewell kiss on Aggie's withered cheek.

Meg tiptoed from the room, an ache in her chest. She

had known so much happiness here at Belle Haven. It had indeed proved a haven, a rare thing in Meg's brief life. When she left here tonight, she would never see this house again.

Rumors had flocked to Faire Isle like a bevy of dark-winged ravens. Travelers to the island, merchants, sailors, had carried warnings of a troop of soldiers that had been seen on the march, cutting a swath through Brittany.

The reports had stirred up alarm and panic on Faire Isle that had never been far from the surface since Xavier's treachery had been exposed. The women on the island, especially those who remembered the witch raids of a decade ago, trembled in terror of a fresh assault.

Ariane as ever remained a beacon of calm. Meg was one of the few who realized how worried the Lady of Faire Isle was. Ariane had spent many hours in late-night consultations with her husband since his return to the island.

Justice Deauville went about quietly seeking to strengthen the island's defenses, recruiting men to help patrol the island. No matter what he did, Meg knew it wasn't going to be enough.

Everywhere Meg went, she saw fear and resentment in the eyes that turned her way. Meg could not blame them. She had been named the next Lady of Faire Isle. Her sacred task should be to protect the women of this island, not bring destruction upon them.

There was only one way she could avoid that, by taking a fearsome action that would leave her unfit to be the Lady of Faire Isle forever. But Meg could not think too much about what lay ahead of her or she would lose her courage entirely.

As she made her way through the silent house, she could not resist peeking into one room. Moonlight spilled across the bed where Seraphine lay cuddled next to her two younger sisters. The older girl's arm was flung across them in a protective gesture, even in her sleep.

Meg's throat worked and she had to swallow hard. One of the most difficult parts of this was not being able to say good-bye to Seraphine. But her friend would never understand what Meg had to do and would have tried to prevent her.

"Forgive me, 'Phine," she whispered.

She studied the three golden heads nestled against the pillows, all looking so innocent and lost deep in their dreams. Had she ever looked that way? Meg wondered sadly.

If she had, it was so long ago, she couldn't remember. She felt as though from the moment of her birth, her mother had leaned over her cradle like some malignant fairy, marking Meg for darkness.

Meg closed the door and went quietly on her way, slipping out of the house. It was a full moon and the golden orb served as a lantern as she wended down the road leading away from Belle Haven.

At times she was obliged to abandon the road and crouch down in the underbrush to avoid the vigilance of Justice Deauville's patrol.

But she made it to Port Corsair undetected. The moon had risen higher in the sky by the time she stole past the conifer trees and hastened down the path to the cove that had been her private refuge.

She thought that she saw something glitter against the

rocks, a shard of glass perhaps, all that remained of the crystal she had smashed.

She still resented Xavier for tricking her into destroying it, but she no longer needed the scrying glass. Its prophecies were etched into her mind.

Meg paused, groping through her pack for the other forbidden object she kept hidden away all these months. She drew it carefully out into the moonlight. The witch blade looked like a stiletto with a needle-sharp tip. The hilt was hollow and it could be pushed, sending a lethal poison through the thin blade. A silver flower was engraved upon the hilt.

Another legacy from the *Book of Shadows*, one that Meg's mother had put to fearsome use. Meg shuddered at the feel of the weapon in her hand. She tucked it gingerly in the hidden pocket she had fashioned for her cloak.

Then she set herself to wait. She did not have to do so long before she heard the splash of an oar. She saw the small boat approaching, bobbing on the waves as it neared the cove. The dinghy was occupied by a single youth, the young fisher lad Meg was bribing to take her off the island.

The boy looked nervous as he waded ashore to help her into the boat. No doubt he feared the displeasure of the Lady of Faire Isle, should Ariane ever discover his part in Meg's flight.

But his fear was not enough to overcome his greed, Meg thought cynically. If you offered enough coin, you could motivate a man to do anything. Only consider Xavier.

Or perhaps like almost everyone else on Faire Isle, this boy merely wanted Meg gone. He said nothing as he settled Meg into the dinghy. The trip across the narrow channel of water between Faire Isle and the mainland was accomplished in silence. That suited Meg just fine. She drew her cloak tighter around her, withdrawing beneath the hood.

One of the questions that her mother had constantly posed snaked through Meg's mind.

"What is the greatest mistake any woman can make, Megaera?" Cassandra Lascelles was wont to demand of her daughter.

"Trusting a man," Meg would solemnly reply, knowing that was the answer her mother expected from her. Any other would earn her a sharp rebuke or a cuff to the ears.

Meg had not believed it then as she did now, since she had been betrayed. First by Sander Naismith and now Xavier. She saw clearly that she had never been able to trust or rely upon any man save her father. And even Martin le Loup was far away, fighting for someone else's cause when Meg needed him most.

But it didn't matter, Meg assured herself fiercely, winking back tears. Papa could not have helped her. No one could. Her fate had been revealed to her by her crystal ages ago and there was no longer any point in resisting.

When they reached the opposite shore, Meg rummaged through her pack and produced a handful of coin. The boy muttered something that sounded like merci. He clambered back into his boat and manned the oars as though he could not get away from her fast enough.

Meg shivered, feeling a little lost, abandoned in the unfamiliar terrain. Then she squared her shoulders and trudged toward the only light she saw in the distance, far up the beach.

As she neared the small fishing village, she found it increasingly hard to breathe as her surroundings took on an aura of familiarity—the dark slated roofs of the cottages, the narrow lane, the light emanating from a modest tavern on the green. She had seen it all before in her vision.

She heard whickers and the occasional stamp of a hoof from the horses tied up in the yard. Meg drew close enough to peer into the inn window. The tables of the taproom were thronged with a contingent of the queen's soldiers just as she expected.

She shrank away, trembling, feeling her resolve waver. It was always at this point in her vision that her faceless betrayer stole up behind her, prodding her inside. She glanced fearfully about her, but there was no one. All she saw was her own pale reflection in the window.

Steeling herself, Meg approached the inn door and crept inside. No one noticed her amidst the clamor of masculine voices and rough laughter.

One complaining voice rose higher than the rest. It belonged to a plump young man with bewhiskered cheeks. "Well, I say we had best wait for the rest of the troop to catch up with us before assaulting the island."

"What, are you afraid of a pack of women, Alphonse?" one of his drinking companions taunted.

"Not women, *witches.*"

"Aw, are you scared some Circe will turn you into more of a pig than you are already?"

The young man flushed and appealed to an older gray-haired man lounging in his chair. "Bear me out, Captain. Are there not too few of us to comb that entire island? How are we supposed to find one girl?"

The captain shrugged. "By torturing the first woman we

get our hands on. I doubt it will take much. All wenches have loose tongues."

His comment produced a spate of ribald retorts and more laughter.

Meg gulped, but the ugly threat was the spur she needed.

"There is no need to torture anyone," she spoke up in a quavering voice.

All conversation abruptly ceased, a myriad of hard and curious eyes turning in her direction.

Her heart thudded and her hand shook as she pulled back her hood.

"I am the girl you were sent to find. I am the Silver Rose."

BLOIS CASTLE PERCHED ON THE HEADLAND DOMINATING THE small town of the same name and a stretch of the river Loire. The royal castle was a jumble of architecture of the centuries, the medieval towers giving way to the more elegant designs of the new wing.

The main gallery had played host to a brilliant gathering, the ladies of France dazzling in their gowns, the gentlemen almost as resplendent. Everyone had looked on while the king of France had received his enemy, the duc de Guise. Although pale and sullen, Henry had tried to give the semblance of still being king as he had pardoned de Guise for his part in the Day of the Barricades. But everyone present had known that the duke required no pardon.

He was in every sense now the master of France.

As Meg was escorted through the palace by a tall sentry, the gallery where the king had suffered his final humiliation stood empty, the throne vacant.

Meg regarded it through indifferent eyes. The wearying journey that had finally brought her to this point was as much of a blur as her surroundings.

Considering that within moments she was about to encounter the figure of her nightmares, she was astonished by her own calm. Something strange had happened to her after she had plucked up the courage to surrender herself to the queen's soldiers. She was numbed by a curious sense of resignation.

She wondered if this was how prisoners felt when they reached that final moment, mounting the steps to their own execution. There was no longer anything to fear when all resistance was futile, all one's choices stripped away.

After traversing a succession of halls, Meg was led into an antechamber. She blinked at the sunlight pouring through the windows, brilliant against the multicolored tiles of the fireplace.

Set against all the array of color, the queen was a shadow in her black gown. She lay stretched out on a day bed, her face almost as gray as the hair swept back from her face. She looked ill and she applied her handkerchief to her mouth, her shoulders shaking with a ragged cough.

The sentry turned Meg over to one of the queen's ladies. The young woman leaned down to whisper in Meg's ear to stand up straight and not stir or make a sound until the queen had finished her visit with the king.

That man positioned near the queen's daybed was the

king? Meg thought in astonishment. Despite being sumptuously clad, he did not look very regal with his stooped shoulders, gaunt face, and sunken eyes.

The king bowed over Queen Catherine's hand, but even though he enquired after her health, his expression was one of complete indifference. He looked distracted, as though his mind was elsewhere.

"So Maman, how are you faring?"

"Much better, I believe," the queen said, suppressing another cough.

The king's mouth twisted petulantly. "Would that I could say the same, but I still have de Guise here swaggering about the palace as though he owns the place. I have set the seal on the treaty that gave him everything. What more does the man want of me?"

"Treaties are worth no more than the ink and parchment they are written upon. Be patient, Henry. Our time is coming."

"That is what you keep telling me and I grow weary of hearing it. I have been more than patient, heeding your advice and biding my time." An angry look darkened his saturnine features, but he forced his lips into a smile.

"But I know that you were right, Maman. I would have been ill-advised to harm the duke in Paris. As you say, a wise man keeps his enemies close and waits for the opportune moment to strike."

His reply clearly pleased his mother. He bent to kiss her cheek and turned to leave. Meg followed the example of the queen's ladies and sank into a deep curtsy.

As the king drew closer, Meg risked a glance up at his face. His eyes had that murky look of one whose mind is no longer in a state of balance. It was often difficult to read mad eyes, but the king's were calm in their cunning as Meg peered into them. Henry might have managed to fool his mother, but to Meg, the king's murderous intentions were clear. She shivered as he swept past her.

An elderly man attired in the robes of a physician bent over Catherine, taking her pulse and frowning. The young lady who had admitted Meg into the room crept forward to whisper something in the queen's ear.

Catherine's eyes turned in the direction where Meg hovered just inside the door. A surge of energy seemed to return to Catherine. She sat up higher and Meg felt like a mouse that had attracted the attention of a large, hungry cat.

"You may leave me now, Dr. Caberini," the queen commanded, never taking her eyes off Meg.

"But Majesty," the doctor protested. "You are quite ill. You are feverish and I fear the pneumonia may be settling into your lungs."

"Leave me," the queen snapped. "I have no further need of your services."

As the physician bowed and retreated, the queen lifted her hand in a gesture toward Meg, indicating she should approach.

Meg felt some of her calm desert her. She remained frozen until the young lady-in-waiting rustled over to urge Meg forward. She whispered more hurried instructions into Meg's ear.

Meg had never possessed Seraphine's grace. She sank into a wooden curtsy. She had been told to stay down until bidden to rise, to keep her eyes lowered. But Meg could not refrain from looking up. She feared to have the Dark Queen's eyes fix her with all the mesmerizing force of a basilisk.

But the queen's eyes seemed a trifle cloudy. They narrowed as though straining to see her better.

"Come closer, Margaret Wolfe." The irony of the way the queen pronounced her name was not lost upon Meg.

She moved forward slowly, nervously folding her hands in front of her. The queen coughed into her handkerchief, her eyes watering. She blinked several times and then cocked her head, studying Meg.

"I admit my eyes are a little tired today, mademoiselle, but I believe you have changed a great deal since I saw you three years ago. You are no longer quite such a frightened little girl."

"And you are not nearly as terrifying," Meg blurted out before she could stop herself.

She braced for the queen's anger, but Catherine only smiled. "Am I not? We shall see about that. I admire impertinence to a degree, but it is not becoming in one so young. I advise you to have a care, my dear."

Meg tipped up her chin in a show of bravado. "Why? You—you probably intend to have me killed anyway."

The queen clucked her tongue. "Is that why you look so grim, child? You fear that I brought you all this way to have your head? I assure you that I mean you no harm."

"You did once. You sent an assassin to London to kill me."

"A mistake on my part and you have my sincere apology. That was before I understood what an extraordinary girl you are. Now I hold you in the highest esteem."

"I cannot imagine why that would be, Your Grace."

"Because—" the queen dropped her voice lower. "As far as I know, you are the only one who has ever managed to translate and read the *Book of Shadows*."

"The book is gone," Meg insisted.

"Is it?" Catherine smiled. "I don't think so. I believe you learned a great deal from it."

Meg swallowed. "That was my mother's doing. She insisted that I learn how to read the book."

"And you were such an adroit student, fashioning those nasty witch blades, conjuring up poisons and those deadly white silver roses. What a brilliant girl you are, Megaera."

"Th-that is not my name and I no longer do any of those things. I have forgotten everything I culled from the book," Meg said, even though she realized from the way Catherine was smiling that her denial was futile.

Catherine produced a small glass vial. "Then wherever did you learn to brew the powerful elixir that you gave to your friend, Xavier?"

Meg flushed. "That man was no friend of mine."

"Truly? He certainly behaved as if he were. Risking his own neck in an effort to convince me that you were nothing, that the potion in this vial was water he had obtained from some magic fountain." Catherine's lips twisted. "I must confess the man can be very glib and convincing, but not quite convincing enough."

Meg listened, her eyes widening. So Xavier had gone back to Paris to see the queen. Not to betray her as she had feared, but to deflect the queen's interest away from her.

"He really did that for me?" she said. "I don't believe it."

"You may ask him yourself if you like. I was obliged to punish him for his treachery."

"Wh-what did you do to him?" Meg asked, struggling to conceal her dismay.

"Nothing so terrible yet, merely locked him up in the dungeon. Captain Xavier is not fond of imprisonment, owing to an unfortunate experience aboard a Spanish galley. He may well be on the way to losing his mind." The queen shrugged. "But since he is no friend of yours, you need not distress yourself over his fate. Or that of the Englishwoman."

"What Englishwoman?" Meg asked, her stomach knotting with another layer of dread.

"Oh, did I fail to mention that when Xavier attempted to escape, Lady Danvers was foolish enough to come to his aid? I was obliged to detain her."

"Jane?" Meg cried. "Oh, what have you done to her, you evil witch? Did you hurt her?"

"There is no need to resort to unkind insults, child. Lady Danvers is quite well. See for yourself." The queen gestured to a point behind Meg.

Meg whirled around to see that Jane had been escorted by two guards into the antechamber. Jane looked paler and thinner than Meg remembered, but she appeared unharmed.

Meg had resolved to present such a brave front to the Dark Queen, icy and controlled. But the sight of Jane was her undoing. She stumbled across the room into Jane's outstretched arms.

Jane held her so tight, cradling Meg in her arms, burying her face in Meg's hair.

"Oh, Meggie," was all she could say.

Meg wished she could remain locked in the safety of Jane's embrace forever. Her tears wet the front of Jane's gown.

"How touching," the queen drawled.

Jane raised her head to glare at the queen. "Why did you have to bring Meg here? Why can't you leave her alone? She is only a young girl."

"Oh, Megaera may be many things, but a mere girl is not one of them. Is that not so, my dear?"

"Yes." Meg stiffened her spine, drawing away from Jane. She furiously mopped at her eyes before turning back to face the queen.

"I am sure now you understand how matters stand," the queen said. "Lady Danvers's continued well-being is entirely in your hands."

"Do not lay that burden upon her," Jane began, but it was Meg who cut her off.

"It is all right, Jane," she said tersely. Any reluctance, any remaining doubts Meg had about carrying out the purpose that had brought her here were at an end. She could feel her heart hardening.

"What do you want from me?" Meg demanded.

The queen held up her empty vial. "More of this potion to begin with. After that we will see . . ."

Chapter Twenty-eight

THE DARKNESS OF XAVIER'S CELL WAS UNRELENTING WHEN night fell. The sheer weight of the black chasm that engulfed him seemed to press against his eyes. His body was a mass of aches and bruises, his wrists and ankles raw from his futile efforts to free himself from the manacles that bound his hands and feet.

The room in which he was confined was small and dank, outfitted with little more than a thin pallet and the chamber pot, nothing that could serve him as a weapon. The only window was a narrow aperture set far above his head.

Xavier could remember little of the journey that had brought him to this place. He had nightmarish recollections of slipping in and out of consciousness as he had been jolted along in a cart over rough roads.

At some point, someone had attended to his wound. Xavier believed it might have been Queen Catherine's own physician. The witch was clearly determined to keep him alive, if for no other reason than the pleasure of tormenting him to the brink of madness.

He feared he was halfway there. His days and nights were a blur. He had no notion how much time had passed, how long he had been the queen's prisoner. Worse still, he had no inkling of what had happened to Jane.

He cursed, threatened, and in the end had begged his guards for information. But they brought him food and carted away his slops in stony silence, obviously under strict orders not to speak one word to him.

He was tormented by recollections of the threats Catherine had made against Jane. The fear that these images aroused was so great, he had to force them from his mind in order to keep his sanity.

The only thing that prevented him from slipping over the edge was his ability to slow his breathing, to ease himself into a self-induced trance. In his mind, he assumed the form of the jaguar. He was back in his tropical paradise, near the cool stream with his mermaid bathing his brow.

Her caress felt so gentle, so real, Xavier opened his eyes. After being in total darkness, even the soft glow of the candle felt painful. His eyes gradually adjusted, focusing on Jane's face.

When he realized she was not an illusion or a fever-induced dream, his heart constricted painfully.

"God damn it, no," he rasped, tossing his head weakly from side to side, unable to stop the flow of tears from his eyes.

"It is all right, Xavier. I am here," Jane said, trying to wipe his tears away.

"No!" he groaned. "Don't want you here. I prayed you 'scaped. Why didn't . . . run? Why did you t-try to—"

"Hush, my love," she soothed. She continued to bathe his face and forced him to take a sip of some wine.

It was a potent vintage, heavy and sweet. Xavier was unprepared for the rush of warmth it sent through him, seeming to radiate along every vein, every nerve. Even his head felt a little clearer.

The candle set in its iron holder rested upon the floor next to Jane. The burning wick cast a soft flickering glow over her features, but the illumination was not enough for him to see her as well as he wished. His gaze roved desperately over her.

He took another swallow of the wine and it cleared his throat. He was better able to articulate his words.

"You are not harmed? That witch has not hurt you?"

Jane smiled sadly. "No. I am close watched but other than that I have been well treated. I don't believe the queen considers me of any significance other than a pawn to persuade Meg to do her bidding."

"Meg?" Xavier's breath hitched in his chest. "The queen has Meg too?"

He moaned. The situation seemed so hopeless.

"Tell me everything that has happened," he said.

Jane related as much as she knew of Meg's capture and arrival at the castle.

"The queen is so desperate for Meg's cooperation, she has made many concessions. It was Meg who persuaded Catherine to allow me to visit. The queen has accorded Meg a certain measure of freedom and given her a still-room to work in. She badly wants more of Meg's elixir."

"Meg must not brew it for her. It only makes Catherine stronger."

"Meg knows that. She has been stalling for time, but I don't know how much longer Catherine will give her. Meg has succeeded in making more of the elixir. She put a few drops in this wine."

That explained the potency of the wine. Xavier managed a wan smile. "Considering how the girl feels about me, I am surprised she didn't try to slip something else in the cup."

"Meg knows the truth about you, Xavier."

"What? You mean about how my blundering only resulted in the Dark Queen being more determined to capture her?"

Jane stroked the hair back from his brow. "No, she knows how you risked your life in an effort to protect her."

"Damned little good that it did." The irons on his wrist clanked, but at least they allowed him enough movement to gather Jane's hand in his. "Jane, I don't know how much more time we will be granted together, so you must listen to me.

"Meg is remarkable, so clever. I suspect that elixir is only one part of what she learned from that *Book of Shadows*. She can use her knowledge, figure out something that will help the two of you escape. I know it must sound mad, trusting your fate to a girl—"

"Meg is not a girl anymore," Jane interrupted him, her expression somber. "She has changed into someone I scarce recognize and it frightens me. It is as though she is actually becoming Megaera."

"Megaera may be the one needed to defeat the Dark Queen. Have her conjure up whatever dark spell, whatever is necessary. If you find any opportunity for escape, you have to take it."

"I won't leave you," Jane said quietly.

"Damn it, woman," Xavier said, in his agitation struggling to rise. "There is no hope for me, can't you see that? Catherine believes that she read my greatest fear, being shackled and held prisoner in some dank hold. But she understands so little of love, she doesn't know, could not comprehend."

Xavier regarded her with a mingling of love and desperation. "My greatest fear is anything happening to you, Jane."

"And what do you think mine is? Losing you."

Xavier swore again and tossed his head, racking his mind for anything that he could say to convince her. But Jane captured his face between her hands.

"Damn you, Louis Xavier Cheney," she said fiercely. "You listen to me. I—will—never—abandon—you."

He stared deep into her eyes blazing with so much love for him it filled him with such joy, such despair, such frustration at his own helplessness, he felt his eyes well up all over again.

Jane wrapped her arms about him, cradling him close, tears spilling down her own cheeks. She whispered in his ear, "We survived a near revolution. We will get through this somehow together, you, me, and Meg. I know we will."

She was glad that her face was buried against his neck and he could not see her eyes. If she and Xavier did find a way out of this, it would not be because of Meg.

Some darkness indeed seemed to have taken possession of the girl. Meg showed very little interest in escape.

THE STILLROOM THAT CATHERINE HAD PROVIDED FOR MEG was set in the older part of the castle, far away from the main flow of the household.

The queen had stocked it well with every manner of herb, mortar and pestle, vials and cauldrons. The chamber was strangely little different from Ariane's workroom.

But Meg was certain that the concoction steaming in her cauldron was nothing that had ever been brewed by any Lady of Faire Isle. As Meg worked, she was aware that a guard hovered just outside the door.

She knew that Catherine's servants were supposed to be keeping close watch and reporting everything she did, every ingredient she used. But they were lax in their duties for a reason that astonished Meg when she realized it.

They were all more afraid of her than Catherine. Her reputation as the Silver Rose had spread and was talked of in hushed whispers. For once Meg did little to try to disprove her legend. The fear of the servants worked to her advantage. Although she was disturbed when even her burly guard shrank away from her, it also gave her a heady taste of power.

As she carefully added another ingredient to her cauldron and the liquid bubbled violently, she saw the guard inch even farther from the doorway.

Meg smiled until she caught sight of her own reflection in the looking glass mounted on the wall. When had the set of her mouth turned that hard, almost cruel? She reached up to touch her hair. It seemed so much darker in the dim lighting of this room, illuminated only by candles. Her face looked thinner, her cheekbones more pronounced, her skin so pale. She was starting to resemble her mother to an alarming degree.

Not that it mattered what she looked like anymore, Meg told herself. The queen's patience was wearing thin. The vision in her crystal must be fulfilled very soon. Meg approached her guard and demanded he fetch her some more water from the well.

He should have found a servant to do it, but Meg insisted her need was urgent.

"You can wait until someone else can be summoned. The queen's elixir will be ruined and I shall have to begin all over again. If you want to explain to Her Majesty how that happened—"

The guard clearly didn't. He raced off to fill her request. Meg knew she did not have much time. She bent down and felt beneath the bench, where she had hidden her witch blade.

She untwisted the hilt and carefully filled the hollow with some of the liquid from her cauldron. Cassandra Lascelles had preferred to employ a poison that was slow-acting, allowing her victim to suffer in agony for several days.

This poison was far more merciful than her mother's had ever been, Meg comforted herself. Death would be swift and sure. For a moment, Meg quailed from her own thoughts. Could she really go through with this?

"Of course you can, Megaera." Her mother's voice whispered through her mind. *"This is your destiny. You were born for this."*

She wrapped up the witch blade carefully and slipped it back into its place of concealment. She would have to see that the rest of the poison was disposed of and the cauldron well-scrubbed. Meg had no desire to see any innocent person inadvertently come to harm.

She glanced down and noticed that her palms were sweating. Meg wiped them in the folds of her apron. She had much to do before tomorrow.

Tomorrow . . . that was the day she had decided upon when she must be prepared to meet her fate.

Meg emerged from the older part of the castle an hour later, her lumbering guard trailing after her. Her thoughts far away, she collided with a tall dark-haired man.

Meg reared back, mumbling her apologies. "I am so sorry," she began, but her voice trailed off when she realized she was looking into the handsome face of the duc de Guise.

As she sank into a nervous curtsy, the powerful nobleman merely looked amused. "The fault was entirely mine, mademoiselle."

Meg sought for some response, but what else could one say when confronted by a dead man? She had read the king's murderous intent too clearly the day she had first arrived at the castle.

Meg realized she was staring, holding the duke's gaze far too long. Looking a trifle discomfited by her, His Grace strode past.

Meg was tempted to rush after him, try to warn the man, but she knew he would never heed the word of some insignificant young girl.

Perhaps she could find some other way to put the duke on his guard. But she had enough worries of her own. There was one more thing she needed to do before tomorrow. She had to see Xavier.

XAVIER SAT UP ON HIS PALLET, BRACING HIS BACK AGAINST THE wall. The sips of Meg's potion had helped to restore some of his strength, but he almost thought he had been better off when he was half-delirious.

He had nothing to do but watch the progress of the spider weaving a cobweb in the corner of his cell while he stewed over his own helplessness and worried what might be happening to Jane and Meg.

He had managed to chip a small piece of mortar out of the wall. The next time his silent guard entered, Xavier had determined to bounce the chunk off the man's head if he refused to tell Xavier anything.

The rock was too small to do any harm, but at least it would allow Xavier to vent some of his frustration, even if the guard retaliated and beat him senseless.

Xavier tensed, his fingers curling around the shard of stone when he heard the key grate in the lock. But rather than the dour lump that was his guard, it was Meg who entered the cell.

The rock fell unnoticed from his hand as Xavier stared up at her. Meg returned his regard with equal gravity as the cell door was shut behind her.

They studied each other for a long moment, then Meg said in her usual blunt fashion, "You look worse than you did after the day you washed up on the island."

Xavier laughed. "Thank you. You look—" But he was hard-pressed to say exactly how Meg looked. He understood why Jane was so worried about the girl. In the dim light of his cell, Meg appeared almost wraithlike, as though she were in danger of disappearing right before his eyes.

"Are you all right?" he asked.

Her lips drew back in a taut smile. "That's a strange question coming from you."

He flushed. "Meg, I don't know what I can say to convince you, but I do care about you. I never meant to betray—"

"I know that. I only meant it was strange you should be worrying about me. You should be more concerned for yourself."

"Unfortunately, that has been my first concern for far too many years."

She ventured closer, entwining her fingers together. "It doesn't sound as though that is how you behaved in Paris. I know about your scheme to protect me from the Dark Queen."

"Pretty stupid, wasn't it?"

"Yes." Her lips curved in a smile that was more like Meg, wistful with just a hint of mischief in it. "But I do thank you for trying."

"It might have worked, if your potion wasn't so blasted

good. It restored her strength." Xavier shook his head ruefully. "I had no idea the woman was so powerful. Those eyes of hers . . . the sheer force of them, she can strip you clean."

"The Dark Queen is dangerous. She always will be until the day . . . she dies." Something about the way Meg pronounced those last two words, the glazed look that came into her eyes, rendered Xavier uneasy.

The girl appeared to give herself a brisk shake. "The guard will not allow me much more time, so please listen to me."

She glanced over her shoulder as though fearful of being heard. She came even closer, hunkering down beside Xavier and lowering her voice.

"I have been racking my brain for a way for you and Jane to escape. I am going to slip Jane another potion I have brewed. When she drops it in the corridor, it will break and issue a mist that will render the guard temporarily unconscious. Then Jane can get the key, but you and Jane must take great care to keep your faces covered and not breathe any of the mist.

"There is bound to be a great deal of confusion tomorrow. Hopefully that will afford you and Jane the opportunity to steal away from the castle. It is not a great plan, but it is the best I can come up with."

Xavier frowned. "Why will there be confusion tomorrow? And why does this plan include only me and Jane? What about you?"

She ducked her head, not answering him. Then she said in a small voice, "Because I don't think I will be able to go anywhere after—"

"After what? What do you think is going to happen? What are you planning to do?"

He managed to get her to look up at him. He studied the expression on her face, a mixture of despair and resolve. His breath caught as he suddenly understood what Meg had in mind because it was the same sort of dark temptation he would have felt himself.

"Meg, you can't."

Her lower lip trembled. "I have to. The Dark Queen will always be a threat to anyone I care about. She will hurt anyone that she has to, all to get at the secrets in my head.

"Do you realize what I might tell her if she held an ax over your head or Jane's? Or anyone I love. What wouldn't I say to stop her, what dark knowledge wouldn't I share, that never should be shared?"

The torment in Meg's young eyes was enough to break his heart.

"She's an old woman, Meg. She cannot last that much longer."

"Long enough to hurt you or Jane if I don't give her what she wants. I have known for a long time it would come to this. I have seen myself destroying the Dark Queen over and over again in my crystal."

"Forgot that damned crystal, Meg. You have a choice."

"No, I don't."

"But if you are caught—"

"I will be. I won't make any attempt to conceal my crime. Dark deeds must be answered for. That is something my mother or the queen have never understood."

"You will be tried, executed."

"I know." She regarded him sadly. "And then the *Book of Shadows* will die with me."

"Meg, this is not the answer—" he began desperately as he heard the guard returning. But from the look in her eyes, he could see that Meg had already slipped away from him.

She brushed a kiss against his cheek. "Good-bye, Xavier."

Chapter Twenty-nine

THE HOUR WAS YET SO EARLY THAT THE SUN HAD NOT arisen. A chilling rain battered the windows of the council chamber where the duc de Guise had gathered with some of the other council members for an early morning meeting with the king.

He shivered, and drawing a light cloak about his shoulders, he moved nearer the fire. But the bleakness of the day didn't bother him, his own prospects were shining so bright.

Word had reached him that the armada had failed. He could no longer rely on Spain for an ally, but that suited him well. He had never cared for being Philip's pensioner. After all, he was the head of the noblest house in all of France, and now he was king in everything but name.

"Your Grace?"

The duke glanced around. One of the king's new secretaries—the duke had not troubled himself to remember the man's name—bowed to him. He was not a very prepossessing fellow. In fact, he appeared exceedingly pale and nervous about even addressing the duc de Guise.

"The king would—would like a word with you in his private chambers before the council meeting."

The duke arched his brows in haughty surprise. But he supposed that he could be magnanimous. Everyone knew who was the master here now.

Excusing himself to the rest of the council, he followed the young secretary, leaving his own escort behind. No one was permitted to be accompanied by retainers into the king's private chambers.

De Guise had been warned many times against attending the king in private. Someone had slipped a note in his napkin at supper last evening, telling him his life was in danger. He did not know why he should think of her now but he recalled the strange young girl he had encountered in the corridor who had stared at him so intently. His footsteps faltered for a moment but he had never been a coward like the king of France. He dismissed the warning from his mind, as he had done all the others.

Besides, the king would not dare to harm him now.

De Guise trailed the secretary down a narrow corridor that led to the king's private chamber. The corridor was lined with guards who respectfully touched the brim of their black velvet caps as the duke passed.

The secretary had already disappeared. He heard the slam as the door to the corrider was shut. He became aware of the guards leaving their posts, falling into position behind him.

Reaching out, the duke parted the curtain that led to the next room. He saw eight more guards awaiting him, their daggers drawn.

He hesitated in disbelief at the trap he saw closing around him. He reached for his sword, but it was entangled in his cloak. The first man rushed him and the duke swung, punching him in the face. He managed to fell two more before he felt the blade pierce his side.

He cried out, but leveled another of his assailants to the ground. But they fell upon him, the blades stabbing him again and again.

He reeled from the shock of the assault as much as the pain. He forced his way down the corridor, although he nearly slipped on his blood. He managed to make it all the way to the king's bedchamber, reaching the end of the king's bed, before the last blade was driven through his shoulders.

He sagged to his knees, realizing he was going to die. His lips were numb as he tried to form the words of a prayer. "My God. Misericord."

The duke shuddered and lay still. Only then did Henry of France creep out from his hiding place. He scarce dared release his breath as he came forward.

Half-dazed himself by what he had done, the king stared down at his fallen enemy and murmured, "I never realized he was so tall."

THE LIGHT OF MORNING SPILLED THROUGH THE WINDOWS AS Meg was escorted into the queen's chamber. The queen was still tucked up in her bed, a robe draped around her shoulders. She appeared worse than she had yesterday, her cough more pronounced.

The doctors hovered around her bed, looking grave, her ladies, somber and silent. Everyone appeared surprised when Meg entered, but Catherine must have given her commands because no one stopped Meg as she approached the bed.

Meg groped toward the concealed pocket in her gown that hid the witch blade. Her heart banged so hard, she feared that even the Dark Queen must hear it.

Catherine dismissed her doctors and beckoned Meg closer. Catherine's raspy voice demanded. "Have you finished the potion? Have you brought me what I require?"

Meg nodded.

"Give it to me then."

Meg handed over the vial. Catherine's fingers trembled as she worked the cork loose. In a moment she would take a sip and realize there was nothing in that vial but water. Meg had been afraid to put anything more lethal in the vial lest Catherine force someone else to taste it first.

Meg's hand inched into her hidden pocket. If she was going to act, she must summon the courage to do it now. She started to withdraw the witch blade. But at that moment, the king burst into the chamber, startling everyone.

He had a hectic flush in his cheeks, a manic light in his

eyes. He rushed toward the bed, gripping the newel post. He announced exultantly, "Maman, I have done it."

Catherine froze, the vial still clutched in her hand. "Done what?"

The king smiled. "The duc de Guise is dead. I have had him killed."

Catherine let out a strangled gasp. "Henry!"

But the king silenced her with an imperious wave of his hand. "No, madame. I never want to speak of that man again. I am no longer a prisoner or a slave. I am the king of France at last."

He bowed and strode out as quickly as he had come. He never heard his mother's bitter response. "No, you foolish boy. You have lost everything."

The vial slipped from her fingers, falling and shattering on the floor. Catherine gave a sharp gasp and clutched at her throat.

Meg was forgotten as her ladies rushed to her side and the doctors were summoned. She was forced back to the outer chamber. A surge of weakness overtook her and she was trembling. She sank down on the window seat, thinking of what she had almost done. But for that one moment of hesitation on her part, if the king had not come in when he had, she would have acted out the scene in her scrying glass.

Xavier had been right. Her belief in the crystal had robbed her of her will, her ability to make her own choices. Recovering herself, Meg prepared to steal from the antechamber, scarce knowing where she was going to go or what she was going to do next.

She was surprised and uneasy to find herself summoned back to the queen. Again Catherine beckoned her close. No one else in the room could hear the low words she directed at Meg.

"You . . . you did this to me," she said.

"No, I didn't." Meg's response was not frenzied as it had been in her vision. She was quite calm as she stated, "You brought this all upon yourself."

Catherine stared at her with a fixed regard. Her eyes had cleared with that strange insight many people acquired just before dying.

"You knew," the queen whispered. "Somehow you saw what Henry was going to do, yet you did nothing to prevent him from bringing down this disaster upon us."

"I tried," Meg said sadly. "Not for your sake but for his."

"I am crushed in the ruins of our house." Catherine swallowed and then asked, "Am I dying?"

Meg stared deep into the queen's eyes. "Yes."

The queen's face convulsed. "Dear God, I am so afraid of the darkness, the emptiness, being forgotten. Can you do nothing to help me?"

Meg shook her head, any hatred or fear that she had felt for this woman gone. All that was left was pity.

"No," she replied. "That is no longer in my power."

The queen's lips thinned in a strange smile. "You would never have helped me anyway. My soldiers never had to capture you, did they? You surrendered. You came here on purpose to kill me."

Meg made no reply, but her silence was confirmation enough.

The queen issued another weak laugh that dissolved into another horrible coughing spasm.

"You truly are something, little girl. Only thirteen years old and already capable of plotting to murder a queen. I regret I will not be around to see what you will become. Who would have ever thought it? You are not Ariane's successor. You are mine."

⁂

THE DARK QUEEN WAS DEAD. BUT THE TIDINGS CAUSED scarcely a ripple in a palace that was in the throes of a panic. Soldiers, guards, servants all rushed to and fro in an effort to fortify Blois Castle, fearing reprisals from the duke's followers and the Catholic League against the king.

Meg wandered unnoticed amidst all the chaos. Her great enemy was gone. She should have felt more of a sense of peace or at least some relief at this moment. But Catherine's parting words echoed in her head.

"*You are not Ariane's successor. You are mine.*"

She shook her head to clear it, trying to forget the queen's words. As she wandered into the courtyard, she saw Jane and Xavier.

Her plan was working. They were escaping unnoticed in the confusion. As Meg hurried toward them, she saw the relief on Jane's face, the troubled question in Xavier's eyes.

"I—I didn't," Meg said. "It wasn't me." She burst into tears.

She felt Jane's arms go around her, Xavier stroking her hair.

"It is all over, sweetheart," he said. "Now let's get out of here, back to Faire Isle. It is time we all went home."

THE KING GAZED OUT THE WINDOW, STARING AT THE SUN sparkling on the river Loire far below. He was aware of all the uproar in his palace, all the panicked preparations, but he felt untouched by it.

Someone clamored outside his antechamber, begging for an audience with the king. Henry assumed it was another messenger bringing more bad tidings from Paris. The word had spread quickly, the citizens were rioting in agonies of grief for their beloved duke. The king's arms had been torn down and thrown into the Seine, statues of him smashed. He had even heard that the royal apartments of the Louvre had been looted and everywhere in the city, people were crying for his blood.

He could not imagine what worse news there could be to report. Instead it was his secretary who entered, coming for instructions about his mother's funeral.

"According to the queen's will, she wishes to be buried in the Valois tomb at Saint Denis."

The king gave a mirthless laugh. "If I brought her anywhere near Paris, the mobs would rip her body to shreds."

He frowned, thinking. "No, it is best that my mother be buried under cover of darkness. She should be interred in the Saint Sauveur churchyard in an unmarked grave."

"An unmarked grave, Your Grace? The Dowager Queen?"

Henry turned to glare at him. "You heard me. See to it."

Looking slightly stunned, the secretary departed. The king turned back to the window. De Guise was dead and his formidable mother as well. Both of them had cast long shadows over his reign.

"From now on we must be king," Henry murmured. "For we have been a slave for too long."

Epilogue

As DAYLIGHT FADED, ARIANE PLACED A SINGLE CANDLE upon the altar rock. Here amongst the ancient standing stones seemed the most fitting place for her to pay private tribute to a fallen enemy.

Many women on the island wanted to celebrate the death of the Dark Queen, Ariane's own niece amongst them. Seraphine was only too eager to burn Catherine in effigy. But Ariane had firmly put a stop to all such plans.

It was wrong to take such savage satisfaction in anyone's death, even Catherine's. Had not the Dark Queen herself provided a tragic example of what could befall a daughter of the earth when she gave way to thoughts of bitterness, hatred, and vengeance?

Ariane had more reason than most to rejoice at Catherine's death, after all the harm and discord that the queen had wrought in Ariane's own life. But she felt nothing but a pang of sadness and regret.

No one could fault Catherine for her courage and intelligence. She would have had so much to offer the world if she had remained a true daughter of the earth. As Ariane lit her candle, she mourned for all the misused and wasted gifts of such an extraordinary woman.

Closing her eyes, Ariane murmured, "Wherever your soul has flown, Catherine, may you finally be at peace."

She maintained another few moments of respectful silence until she heard the footfall behind her. Turning about, she saw Meg hovering just inside the ring of stones.

The girl's return to Faire Isle had been greeted with an outpouring of relief and affection. With Catherine a threat no longer, the women of the island had been happy to welcome Meg back into their midst.

This time, it was Meg who held back. Not precisely rebuffing all the offers of friendship, so much as avoiding everyone, even Seraphine.

Ariane sensed that the girl had something heavy weighing upon her heart. But Ariane had not pressed the girl, knowing that when she felt ready, Meg would unburden herself.

Smiling gently, she beckoned Meg to join her by the altar rock. The girl approached slowly, appearing so small in the shadows of the great monoliths, her face haunted with a mingling of resignation and despair.

How was it possible for anyone to at once look so young and so old? Ariane ached to scoop the child up into her arms. But after all that had transpired within the last month, Meg truly was a child no longer. Ariane accorded her the dignity of distance that Meg seemed to require.

Meg stood in front of Ariane, folding her hands together like a penitent facing her confessor.

"I am sorry to disturb you at such a moment—"

"You aren't," Ariane assured her.

Meg summoned up a wan smile, but the effort to maintain it appeared too much for the girl. Her expression dimmed. "I have been waiting to speak to you alone ever since I returned. I never seemed to find the right moment or the courage. But perhaps this is the fitting time and place."

Meg's gaze traversed their surroundings. "After all, this is where you named me as your successor and I took the staff of office into my hands."

Her gaze came to rest upon the candle that Ariane had placed upon the altar. Meg took a deep breath.

"I can't do it, Ariane. I can never be the Lady of Faire Isle."

Ariane had been half-expecting this. She did not react with the shock or outrage that Meg had clearly been anticipating.

As though fearing Ariane had not understood her, Meg rushed on, "I am not fit to lead the daughters of the earth. I have done something so terrible—"

Meg's lips trembled and she was unable to go on.

"Something that happened when you were captured and taken to Blois Castle?" Ariane probed gently.

"I was never captured, Ariane. I went there on purpose to—to kill the Dark Queen."

"And did you?" Ariane asked, although she read enough in Meg's troubled eyes that she already knew the answer.

"No. The queen died of an inflammation of the lungs or it might have been the shock and despair that killed her after she learned what her son had done to the duc de Guise."

Meg swallowed. "But it could just as easily have been me that killed her. I wanted to. I actually stood at Catherine's bedside, preparing to use my witch blade. I had watched the scene played out in my crystal so many times. The moment had come to strike. If I had not hesitated—"

"But that is just it, Meg," Ariane said. "You did *hesitate*. When the moment actually came, no matter what your crystal showed you, you chose to do the right thing."

"But I am afraid I am just like the Dark Queen or my mother, seeking to make excuses for the evil I do. No matter what I do, the *Book of Shadows* will always be in my head, tempting me to use its dark power whenever I feel threatened or in trouble."

Tears shimmering in her eyes, Meg peered at Ariane. "You are so good, Ariane. You cannot possibly understand."

"Yes, I can, my dear. Far better than you can imagine. Do you realize that I once had the *Book of Shadows* in my possession?"

"N-no."

"Oh, I was not as good at translating the text as you. But I managed enough to be able to work a rather lethal bit of magic. My sister Gabrielle was being held hostage by a witch-hunter. I tried to produce a diversion by setting off a small explosion. Instead, I succeeded in burning down an entire inn and harming a good many innocent bystanders."

Meg regarded her, wide-eyed. "You did?"

"So you see, you are not the only one who has ever

been lured by the dark ways. Strength is not acquired through never being tempted. Each time you stumble, every mistake that you make and what you learn from it, that is what will give you the wisdom you need to be the Lady of Faire Isle."

Ariane smiled ruefully. "I myself am still struggling, still learning. It is a lifetime process."

She placed her hands on the girl's slender shoulders. "Please don't give up on yourself, Meg. I assure you that I have not. But I can choose another successor. If that is what you really want?"

Meg looked up at Ariane, her tears spilling down her cheeks.

"No." She said and flung herself into Ariane's arms. A gentle wind blew through the clearing. As Ariane held Meg close, she watched as the Dark Queen's candle flickered and went out.

JANE STOOD AT THE EDGE OF THE ROCKY SHORE, GAZING OUT across the channel toward England, but no longer with the fear and desperation she had once known.

Xavier slipped his arm protectively about her waist to steady her upon the rocks. "So Jane, your England is safe. They managed to defeat the armada without the aid of the French."

"Perhaps because England had the aid of a more powerful ally," Jane murmured.

The channel was so calm today. It was difficult to imagine the fierceness of the storm that had been the destruction of the Spanish fleet.

"I daresay they will be finding traces of wrecked galleons along the Irish coast for years to come," Xavier said. "I have heard that many of the Spanish sailors who managed to struggle to shore were beaten to death by wild Irish clans."

Xavier added after a moment. "Poor devils."

Jane gazed up at him in surprise. "But I thought you hated the Spanish."

Xavier shrugged. "I guess the rank and file were merely seamen like Jambe, Pietro, or myself. Not overly concerned with kings, religion, or politics. The poor bastards sailed for the love of the sea. They were just looking for a little adventure and hoping perhaps to make their fortune upon the way."

"Jambe has certainly made his. He earned his share of the prize money by sailing with Drake."

"That he did." Xavier grimaced. "To say nothing of the fact that he also got that blasted bird of his back. Miri returned the Sea Beggar to him. Apparently, the parrot told her that he did not wish to seem ungrateful, but the Beggar prefers Jambe's company to hers."

"The parrot can talk that well?" Jane asked in astonishment.

"Apparently he can—to Miri." Xavier laughed. His expression sobered as he added. "My sister had something to give me as well. She—she has been reading through the journals our father kept for her. She discovered the reason the chevalier never returned to France."

"Oh?" Jane asked anxiously. She could not tell from Xavier's expression if that was good or bad.

"It seems that the chevalier was rather distraught after

the Spanish raid on the French settlement. If Miri should ever receive his journals, he wanted her to know how much he loved her and her sisters, but he could never come back until he found his—his son."

"Oh, Xavier!"

"Yes, well, that was it. Just that one mention of me, just those two words. *My son.*" His mouth twisted ruefully. "But somehow, it is enough."

Jane could only imagine how much that revelation meant to Xavier. His eyes had misted, but he was clearly embarrassed and behaving so gruffly about it, Jane allowed him to change the subject back to Jambe.

"The old pirate is in fine fettle. Not only does he have his bird and his gold, but he will be able to boast forever that he was one of the men who stood with Drake against the mighty Spanish armada."

Jane thought she detected a note of wistfulness in Xavier's voice. "Do you regret that you did not leave Paris to sail with Drake instead of remaining to defend Meg against the Dark Queen?"

Xavier shook his head. "I only regret that I was fool enough to let myself be trapped by that witch. I should have protected you better."

"I am stronger than you think, Xavier."

"I never underestimated your strength or courage, Jane. Like most of these women on Faire Isle, I sometimes doubt if you have need of me or any man," he joked, but there was no mistaking the wistfulness in his eyes this time. "I hear that you have received another letter."

"Yes."

"From that miserable cousin of yours, I suppose?"

"No, strangely enough this one came from an old friend that I had nearly forgotten. During the attack of the armada, Philip expected the English Catholics to turn against their queen. But very few of them did. This has left Elizabeth disposed to be generous toward her Catholic subjects, even the exiled ones. Her Majesty has offered me a pardon."

"I see." Xavier's hand fell away from her waist. "And of course, you wish to accept it and return home."

"Once that is all I would have desired. I was devastated to be branded as a traitor and witch. I am neither. But I have come to realize three things. One, that I am a daughter of the earth after all. Two, that I don't belong in England anymore."

"And the third thing, Jane?"

She draped her arms about his neck. "That my home is wherever you are."

It touched her heart to see how moved Xavier was by her words, and how much, despite all his bravado and bluster, this man needed her reassurance.

"You know I don't have much to offer you. But Ariane's husband might be willing to invest in a small ship. I appear to have intrigued him with all my tales of the New World."

Xavier drew her closer, teasing as he always did to cover his deeper emotions. "So Jane, would you be willing to set sail with me and become a pirate?"

She smiled up at him. "Of all the prospects I considered for my future, I confess that is one I never thought of."

"Why not? Your time on Faire Isle must have taught you that women are capable of anything. Have you never heard of Grace O'Malley, the Irish pirate queen?"

"Yes, but *she* was bred to the sea from her earliest years. I have a tendency to become unwell when the waves get too rough and I fear that every time you managed to steal another ship's cargo, I would be begging you to return it."

"My beautiful conscience," Xavier said, his eyes gleaming with tender amusement as he kissed her.

She drew back, regarding him seriously. "Whatever the future holds, Xavier, I never want to be the one who denies you your dreams, who holds you back from all those wondrous new lands and uncharted seas you dreamed of sailing."

"Foolish woman, you still don't understand, do you?" he said huskily as he kissed her again.

"I have already found my far horizons in your eyes."

About the Author

Susan Carroll is an award-winning romance novelist. Some of her most recent titles include, *The Huntress, The Silver Rose, The Courtesan*, and *The Dark Queen.* She lives in Rock Island, Illinois.